Locked & Loaded

Julian Papadia

Contents

Copyrights	VIII
1. Prologue	1
2. Chapter 1	7
3. Chapter 2	15
4. Chapter 3	20
5. Chapter 4	26
6. Chapter 5	35
7. Chapter 6	42
8. Chapter 7	46
9. Chapter 8	51
10. Chapter 9	56
11. Chapter 10	58
12. Chapter 11	61
13. Chapter 12	66
14. Chapter 13	70
15. Chapter 14	76
16. Chapter 15	79
17. Chapter 16	82
18. Chapter 17	84
19. Chapter 18	89
20. Chapter 19	95

21.	Chapter 20	99
22.	Chapter 21	105
23.	Chapter 22	111
24.	Chapter 23	114
25.	Chapter 24	118
26.	Chapter 25	121
27.	Chapter 26	125
28.	Chapter 27	131
29.	Chapter 28	134
30.	Chapter 29	137
31.	Chapter 30	142
32.	Chapter 31	153
33.	Chapter 32	159
34.	Chapter 33	160
35.	Chapter 34	164
36.	Chapter 35	167
37.	Chapter 36	172
38.	Chapter 37	178
39.	Chapter 38	182
40.	Chapter 39	186
41.	Chapter 40	189
42.	Chapter 41	191
43.	Chapter 42	194
44.	Chapter 43	201
45.	Chapter 44	206
46.	Chapter 45	210
47.	Chapter 46	213
48.	Chapter 47	217

49.	Chapter 48	219
50.	Chapter 49	223
51.	Chapter 50	227
52.	Chapter 51	228
53.	Chapter 52	230
54.	Chapter 53	233
55.	Chapter 54	235
56.	Chapter 55	237
57.	Chapter 56	240
58.	Chapter 57	242
59.	Chapter 58	245
60.	Chapter 59	247
61.	Chapter 60	250
62.	Chapter 61	253
63.	Chapter 62	257
64.	Chapter 63	260
65.	Chapter 64	263
66.	Chapter 65	265
67.	Chapter 66	269
68.	Chapter 67	275
69.	Chapter 68	284
70.	Chapter 69	288
71.	Chapter 70	290
72.	Chapter 71	306
73.	Chapter 72	308
74.	Chapter 73	310
75.	Chapter 74	313
76.	Chapter 75	316

77.	Chapter 76	320
78.	Chapter 77	322
79.	Chapter 78	328
80.	Chapter 79	331
81.	Chapter 80	333
82.	Chapter 81	335
83.	Chapter 82	337
84.	Chapter 83	340
85.	Chapter 84	343
86.	Chapter 85	345
87.	Chapter 86	349
88.	Chapter 87	351
89.	Chapter 88	353
90.	Chapter 89	357
91.	Chapter 90	360
92.	Chapter 91	363
93.	Chapter 92	365
94.	Chapter 93	373
95.	Chapter 94	375
96.	Chapter 95	379
97.	Chapter 96	381
98.	Chapter 97	385
99.	Chapter 98	387
100.	Chapter 99	389
101.	Chapter 100	393
102.	Chapter 101	395
103.	Chapter 102	397
104.	Chapter 103	400

105.	Chapter 104	403
106.	Chapter 105	406
107.	Chapter 106	410
108.	Chapter 107	412
109.	Epilogue	415
Also by Julian Papadia		441

Copyright © 2024 by Julian Papadia

All rights reserved.

No part of this publication may be reproduced, distributed, or transmitted in any form or by any means, including photocopying, recording, or other electronic or mechanical methods, without the prior written permission of the publisher, except as permitted by U.S. copyright law. For permission requests, contact [include publisher/author contact info].

The story, all names, characters, and incidents portrayed in this production are fictitious. No identification with actual persons (living or deceased), places, buildings, and products is intended or should be inferred.

Book Cover by A G P

1st edition 2024

Prologue
Bill

January 17th, 2023

"Of course, your latest plans for this year include the first run of mass produced hydrogen cars," smiled the well-seasoned talk show host, Freddie Glazer. His bronzed forehead shone as brightly as his teeth beneath the studio lights. "How does it feel to be making history?"

Sir Bill Lovecroft leaned back in his chair and paused for dramatic effect. Smoothing down his red, silk tie with his manicured hand, he cast his eyes up towards the audience and flashed a dazzling yet grandfatherly smile.

"Well," he began, drawing out the word. "The hydrogen car has been an idea close to my heart for decades. You know it's been a dream simmering at the back of my mind since I was a boy. Since the moment I began tinkering with my father's cars, I was fascinated by the concept of emissions, and in turn what effect these has on our surroundings."

"Yes, I read that in your autobiography," grinned Glazer, reaching his golden hand down to the coffee table between them to pick up the hardback book. "Made for terrific reading. You've had such a colourful life. And a successful one too."

"I just worked hard," smiled Bill, turning once again to the audience.

They were all enraptured by his grin, all of them hanging on his every word, but they had been before he'd even spoken. His presence alone commanded their attention, and as he looked over the faces of all the people in the front row, he felt their adoration. Absorbing it into his bones. Sure, he worked hard for his success, for the money and of course for the good causes his businesses supported, but he'd be lying if he said he didn't also do it for this feeling. This sensation that he was at the centre of the universe and everyone orbited his ego like satellites around a god.

He leaned back further in his seat. Despite the cameras and the audience, he was more relaxed than ever and felt at home beneath the bright lights and the thick make-up.

"Worked hard?" laughed Glazer. "You must have slogged away like a carthorse over the course of your life with everything you've accomplished. Your too numerous to mention business endeavours, your environmental work, your rapid climb to the top of the Forbes rich list."

"Ooh, I'm not quite at the top just yet. Currently sitting at number three."

"Number one for the United Kingdom, though. You became Britain's richest man this year."

Bill smiled coyly to himself in an attempt to appear modest in front of the cameras, but inside he was thinking, *You're fucking right I'm Britain's richest man. I have everything I've ever wanted and I still want more.*

Inside, the cogs of his shark-like brain turned as he thought ten steps ahead of Glazer, anticipating what he was going to ask next. But to the audience, sat in his Harris Tweed suit, Church brogues and crisp, white shirt, he looked like everyone's ideal grandpa. The type kids dreamed about tucking them into bed at night. He had the personality, charm and ability to soothe those around him like the narrator of a nature documentary. And he had the uncanny ability to make everyone around him feel safe, if not a little in awe of him.

"Britain's richest man," repeated Glazer. "Yet it's rumoured that you give large quantities away in anonymous donations, is that true?" "Oh..." Bill smiled like a schoolboy caught out in a lie. "I couldn't possibly tell."

"Such modesty."

"I don't like to brag about such things."

"Is it true you gave a hundred thousand pounds to the environmental group, Power to the Planet?"

Bill parted his lips to answer, but something stopped the words from getting out. It was a feeling that crept up from the pit of his stomach up the back of his neck. A peculiar sensation that there was a change in the energy of the room. Bill wasn't a superstitious man, and he wasn't the sort of man to fall to the whims of his feelings or invisible energies, but the sensation was undeniable.

He looked through the centre of the cameramen out into the audience. Through the bright lights he could barely see to the top of the room where the booth sat to control the lights, but he could sense movement up there. He tried to ignore it and answer Glazer's question, but he couldn't quite shake the feeling something was wrong.

Then he saw them.

The multiple figures emerging through the glare of the lights behind the top row of the audience. There were six of them in total, and although their faces were shrouded in shadows, he sensed their expressions were hostile.

"What.. What's happening?" Glazer panicked, turning to his producers as he saw the figures.

Bill and Glazer watched, confused as the figures moved towards the centre staircase and picked up pace, jogging down to them. Only now could Bill see their caps and high-vis jackets.

"What's going on?" yelled Glazer, outraged as he jumped out his seat. "What are the police doing here?"

A stocky man with a grey buzz cut appeared from Bill's left side with the show's producer beside him. He looked apologetically at Bill, then over to Glazer, signalling him with his eyes for him to get off the stage. But Glazer remained frozen to the spot in shock. In twenty years of hosting his own talk show, he'd never so much as had an episode cancelled let alone have the police storm the stage.

"What are you doing?" he cried, as the man with the buzz cut moved in closer to Bill flanked by four uniformed officers.

"Sir Bill Lovecroft," he announced. "My name is Detective Jones. I am arresting you on suspicion of tax evasion."

"What? Is this some kind of joke?"

Bill laughed to hide his shock, and simply chuckled in Jones' face.

"This can't be happening," said Glazer, clutching his chest as though he was on the verge of a heart attack. "This is a live broadcast. The whole nation will see this!"

"You do not have to say anything," continued Jones. "But it may harm your defence if you do not mention when questioned something you later rely on in court."

Two of the officers moved in closer, one of them with cuffs in their hands. Bill instinctively flinched and backed away, but they moved in closer. The nearest one placed a heavy hand on his shoulder and spun him around.

Bill looked at the camera, in his eyes you could see the confusion and shock had already given way to creativity and clear thinking. The producer was shouting to cut off the transmission, but no one from the control room answered his request. For Bill that was a positive sign he could use to his advantage. He had all the attention in the room, and therefore the power. "Genius is nothing more than intuition and speed of execution," he used to repeat in his early days. He drew on those words now.

With his hand he signalled the producer, who only had one thing on his mind. This spectacle was going to skyrocket the ratings and therefore his career. Bill raised his eyebrows at him inquisitively, and he responded with a single nod as if to say, *The show's all yours. Do your worst.*

Bill knew he still had his microphone on, so with a loud voice he declared, "Whatever happens today, know I am innocent."

The officers and Detective Jones scoffed in his face.

Bill continued.

"The police here might not believe me, but you the public do. I *trust* that you do. And I trust that one of you will help me. Will come through for me. I'm going to make a promise now."

"Urgh, come on," moaned one of the officers, grabbing at Bill's wrists.

Bill ignored him and continued staring into the cameras.

"I'm making a promise," he said. "A promise to the public. This is a scandal. This is nothing but pure injustice! Someone has to help me. And whoever does. Whoever saves me from this absolute crime against my human rights. Know that I will be indebted to you. I will give you half of everything."

The officer with the cuffs looked up at Bill as though he'd lost his mind. Behind him, Jones continued to read Bill his rights.

"Half of everything," he repeated. "Fifty percent of my wealth."

A collective gasp sounded around the room. No one quite believed what they'd heard.

"Half!" called out Bill. "Of everything!"

"Anything you do say may be given in evidence," finished Jones, nodding authoritatively to the officers. "Now you will be taken to the nearest police station."

"This is absurd."

Jones and the officers appeared expressionless, but as Bill was roughly pushed from the stage, the cameras tracking the spectacle, he was sure he noticed a look of pure glee hidden in the darkness of Jones' eyes.

Fuck you, he thought. *Bringing down a man like me because you've got a badge. Bet you'll go home to your tiny, grim, mould riddled flat and lie in bed knowing arresting me is the closest you'll come to touching class.*

"You will regret this," Bill whispered to Jones, his usually calm face finally turning crimson as he looked back up to the crowd. "You're making a terrible mistake," he cried theatrically. "I've never broken the law in my life." This last sentence was more for the audience than for the officers.

Still, the officers pushed him through the group of cameramen who were following him through the studio as the audience stared slack-jawed and stunned behind them.

"You'll not get away with this!" shouted Bill. "You can't. I've done nothing wrong!"

"Yeah, yeah," replied Jones with a roll of his eyes. "Everyone says they're innocent when the cuffs go on."

Bill, enraged by the look on Jones' face, dug his heels in and turned over his shoulder to the nearest camera with his eyes ablaze. He opened his mouth to make one last plea, but Jones interrupted.

"You've had your fun. Time to get you in the cells."

"If you think for one second I'm spending the night in a police cell."

"You got any other ideas?"

"I'm calling my lawyer. He'll have me out within the hour."

"I doubt that," laughed Jones.

Now away from the cameras, the officers tightened their grip on Bill and pushed him roughly down the long corridor passed the dressing rooms and towards the car park. As they reached the main exit at the end of the hallway, Bill became aware of someone watching more intently than everyone else. In a red suit the same colour as his cheeks and with icy eyes, the statuesque figure of chief prosecutor, Elizabeth Hawkins greeted Jones and the officers with a curt nod and a polite smile. Her eyes met Bill's as he passed her, the two of them transfixed for a moment pulled together by each other's gaze.

"Didn't know you'd be here," said Jones, his voice cutting through the moment.

"I wouldn't miss this for the world," she replied, her eyes still focussed on Bill's.

"You're not really supposed to be here," said Jones, lowering his voice, but she ignored him and stepped back to clear the way for the officers to push Bill through the door.

"Good luck, Bill," she said with a sardonic smile. "There'll be no champagne where you're going."

His eyes burned into hers in response.

"Who's this bitch?" he snarled.

She laughed and slapped Jones on the back.

"Have fun," she said.

Chapter 1

Fitz

January 17th, 2023

Fitz wondered if he was getting old or whether the music playing from the old speakers really was as bad as he thought it was. He sat in the corner of his former local pub and watched an old man mumble under his breath as he lost yet another fiver on the fruit machine. He used to lose pockets full of change himself on the same machine, but that was years ago. He knew better now, or at least he tried to think he did. He'd long given up on gambling, given up the cigarettes too. He'd even given up pints. Something he never would have imagined himself doing. But six years in Wandsworth had changed him. Made him crave the things he never realised the value of and forget the things he used to crave.

He'd spent every night in there wishing he could play the silly make-believe games his daughter, Sarah loved that he used to think were annoying. He would have done anything to have a tea party with her as she sat in her princess costume. Fuck the pints and the adrenaline buzz and the money. Anything just to sit on the couch and watch Beauty and the Beast for the hundredth time as she swung her legs and sang along to every song at full volume.

He sat now sipping his drink with his eyes glazed over thinking about her. She'd be ten now, and he wondered what she'd look like or whether she'd even remember him.

"Jesus what you looking so fucking glum for?" pierced a voice through the music.

Fitz looked up and at first didn't recognise the figure in front of him with the bald head, the beer gut and the acne. Then he did a double take as he recognised the eyes. "Christ,

John!" he burst, leaping from his seat to hug his old friend. "Didn't have a clue who you were there. Man, you look different."

John pulled him into a bear hug and sat down across from him.

"Ordered you a Guinness," said Fitz. "You still drink those, don't you?"

"About ten a night," laughed John, slapping his beer belly. "Not that it's obvious."

He grabbed the glass and sunk his top lip into the foam before taking a long drink and slamming it back down on the table with a satisfied sigh.

John wiped the back of his hand along his mouth, then squinted down to the table at Fitz' drink.

"Mate, is that an orange juice you're drinking?"

"Yeah, I'm on the wagon."

"Since when?"

"Since I got out."

"You're kidding me."

"Nope. I've gone straight. Ditched the fags too."

"Shut the fuck up. Why?"

"Because I wanna be clean."

John cocked his head to the side as though offended at hearing this, his eyes narrowing at Fitz.

"That's too bad," he said, taking another gulp of Guinness. "Because I wanted to offer you a job."

"Really?"

Fitz raised his eyebrows. He knew already that he wasn't interested in any job John would have to offer him, but he was nonetheless curious and wanted to hear more.

"Yeah, the safety deposit joint on Marsh Street," said John. "You wouldn't wanna be part of the team, would ya?"

Fitz looked from his left to the right to make sure no one was in ear shot, then leaned in closer to John.

"Safety deposit boxes, seriously?" he asked John. "When?"

"Next Friday at eleven. That's when the main security guard takes his tea break. Leaves two newbies at the door. We need a driver. The position's yours if you want it. We'll be splitting it three ways."

"I'm not interested."

Again, John looked offended, took one last gulp of his Guinness until his glass was empty then crossed his meaty arms over his huge stomach.

"Not interested, eh? Thought you'd be in dire need of cash what with you just getting outta the slammer."

"Like I said, I wanna be clean. Besides, I'm a little fucking upset to be honest with you."

John laughed and slid down in his seat as the Guinness relaxed him.

"You, upset? Since when did you go soft?"

"Look, I just think it's a cheap shot, alright? Robbing safety deposit boxes for Christ's sake. It's a little..."

"What?"

There were numerous words floating around Fitz' head.

Amateur? Beneath him?

But he didn't want to make the situation any more tense so he went with, "Boring," and left it at that.

John rolled his eyes at him and scoffed, "Boring? Are you having a laugh? How exactly is it boring? You never know what's gonna be in those boxes? It's like that TV show, Storage Hunters."

"It's not a bloody advent calendar," laughed Fitz. "Besides, if you don't know what you're getting in each box then you don't know who you're robbing either. It could be someone's granny for all you know."

John sighed and rolled his eyes again.

"Urgh, there you go with all the moral stuff," he moaned.

"What's that supposed to mean?"

"It means you always were the one to hold a guilty conscience. You're just about the most moral, upstanding crook I've ever known. Shoulda guessed you thought you'd be too good for this."

"I'm just saying I have standards."

"Oh, yeah. Of course. Always liked to think of yourself as the Robin Hood type. Only robbing people who were bastards."

"That's right," smiled Fitz.

It was something he had been proud of. Sure, he had robbed his fair share of people in his life, but he believed he was doing the right thing. Like the time Gavin Jenkins, Conservative MP and vocal advocate for fox hunting was caught on camera beating his wife. He'd got away with it, and his case was never brought to trial.

The whole story had sickened Fitz. And as he lay in bed thinking about him going home to his wife every night, he concocted a plan to get his own revenge. He'd bid his time, waiting until Jenkins was on holiday in the Bahamas before breaking into his home and stealing twenty thousand pounds in cash from the safe in his study along with an original Picasso sketch that hung behind his desk. The feeling of justice and pride swelled up within Fitz when he handed eighteen thousand of the cash to a women's shelter in Jenkins' constituency, keeping a measly two grand for himself to tide him over and pay his bills until his next job. The sketch was left at the door of the nearest charity shop.

He regretted nothing about that job. Or the next one, or the next. He was proud of his work and felt he was making a difference in the world and making a little cash for himself in the process. Where was the harm done?

Men like John laughed at him, called him a mug to his face and sometimes things a lot worse behind his back. They couldn't understand why he had to be so moral all the time, or why his jobs had to be so meticulously planned out and executed with precision. They were all about using brute force tactics, and he was all about the planning and the consequences.

It was a huge reason why, although Fitz kept a large circle of friends who worked in the same business as him, he never quite gelled with them at a deeper level, and always felt their beliefs were at odds with his.

"You still think of yourself as a Renaissance Man, don't you?" mocked John.

"Renaissance Man?"

"That's what everyone calls you now. Well, since you got banged up anyway."

"They do?"

Fitz didn't know what to think about that name. On the surface it sounded complimentary, but he knew it wasn't.

"Yeah, you know after-"

John cut his own words off. He knew he had gone far enough already.

"After what, John?"

"Nothing."

"No, tell me. After what, John? Fucking say it."

John at least had the decency to look embarrassed and bowed his head.

"After, you know... The whole thing with the Caravaggio painting."

Fitz knew it was coming, but he didn't want to hear it.

"I'll see you later," he said, rising from his seat. "This was a mistake."

"No, Fitz wait. Sit down."

John's arm shot out and lightly landed on Fitz' elbow. Fitz stared down at it as though he was deciding what to do. Then he looked around the pub. It was filling up with dinner time punters and the last thing he wanted to do was make a scene. He looked into John's face and saw a softness creep into his eyes, a look of regret.

"Sorry, mate," he said to Fitz. "I didn't mean to be a prick bringing all that up."

"It's okay. It's just... It's been a long while but... It doesn't get any easier."

"I can't imagine it ever would. Listen, you're an old pal. I know you've had it rough. Stay and have another drink on me. Even if it is another orange juice. For old time's sake."

Fitz lowered himself back down into his seat and gave a solemn nod.

"Sure. Just one."

John gave him an apologetic, tight-lipped smile and got up to go the bar. Fitz watched him walk away and looked around at all the people now filling up the nearby tables.

He'd been out of Wandsworth for three months, but he still couldn't get used to life on the outside. Things had changed considerably over the last six years. Fashion had changed, music had changed and technology looked as though it had moved at the speed of light. He found himself still using an old brick of a mobile phone when everyone around him had sleek smart phones.

After a few minutes, John returned with the drinks and some crisps which he dropped into the centre of the table. The two were silent for a moment as John sipped his second Guinness. An old Motown classic started playing over the speakers and Fitz was pleased to recognise it. He found himself tapping his foot beneath the table.

"I'm really sorry about what happened," John blurted out. "Was a crying shame. We're all still pretty upset about it all. I mean, I wasn't there. Wasn't in your team that day but... What happened to Danielle..."

Fitz shot him a look to silence him and John's mouth shut instantly. Fitz stared at him for a little longer then said, "I'm sorry too."

"It's not your fault."

"Then why does it feel like it is?"

"There was nothing you could have done to save her."

"How do you know that?"

John didn't know how to answer and let his mouth drop open like a fish. He only closed it when he took another gulp of his drink and started fidgeting nervously with a bag of crisps.

"So, you seen Sarah?" he asked, picking out a cheese Quaver and crunching on it.

Fitz shook his head.

"Can't get near her, can I?"

"Father-in-law still being a dick?"

"Well, he's got every right to be, hasn't he? He got legal custody of her after Danielle died and I was in jail. As far as the law's concerned I ain't got any right to see her."

"But you're her father."

"You don't need to tell me that."

"You must miss her."

"More than anything."

"Must miss Danielle."

Fitz felt his muscles tense up at the mention of her. There wasn't a single hour of every day when he didn't think about her. When he didn't think about the last moments he spent with her. When he didn't think about the beautiful, perfect daughter he created with her that he now wasn't allowed to be anywhere near.

"Must be weird," John suddenly said. "Having your daughter live with Britain's richest man while you're piss poor and just out of prison. Does he not even have the decency to throw you a few quid."

"I wouldn't take it from him."

"Why not? I would."

"Yeah, and you'd rob a granny if you could. Look, all I care about is that Sarah is safe, and as much as me and Bill never got along, I know he can give her a good life with all his money."

"Wouldn't you want her back with you?"

"Sure I would. More than anything. I will do, someday."

"Would be pretty tough, though," said John, pouring the crumbs at the bottom of his crisp packet into his open mouth. "Imagine how good his lawyers would be with all his money. How could you fight against that for custody?"

It was a question Fitz had contemplated many times before. He was torn. On one hand he wanted nothing more than his family back, or at least what was left of it. But he knew fighting for it and coming up against Bill was an impossibility. Then he was faced with another gnawing thought that always left a dark feeling sinking into the pit of his stomach. What if Sarah was better off without him?

He could give her a loving home, he knew that, but Bill could pay for her to have the best education, the best home life, the best nannies and tutors and holidays and whatever else she wanted. She could grow up to be beautiful, educated and respectable like her mother was. Or God forbid grow up to be the spoiled princess Danielle's sister, Cecilia was. *Christ*, thought Fitz. *Anything but that.*

As he stared into his orange juice, the word respectable kept swimming around his head. Danielle epitomised the term. Or at least she did until she met him.

"You okay?" asked John, his voice penetrating his day dream.

"Yeah... Look I'm gonna make a move. Catch you around, yeah?"

"Yeah, sure thing Fitz. And if you change your mind about the job, you'll get in touch, won't ya?"

"Will do."

Fitz clapped a hand on John's broad shoulder in farewell then snaked his way through the busy tables towards the exit. The sun was dipping as he walked outside and the temperature was dropping. The streets were packed with people either going home after a long day at work, or heading out. He wanted to do neither.

***

Fitz arrived home in a foul mood. He didn't know what had annoyed him the most, John's assumption that he would take some tiny, amateur job or the fact he just had to bring up Danielle.

He thought of her face as he pushed the key in the door. This should have been a home he shared with her. He always found himself doing something and suddenly thinking of how she would have done it. He wondered what colour she would have painted the bedroom or what couches she would have bought. How he would have loved to have a touch of her personality in his home. At the moment, it looked more like the home of some first year student with minimal Ikea furniture lying sparse across the cream floors.

As soon as he stepped into the hallway, he hung up his coat and kicked off his boots before entering his bedroom and searching the drawers for his running gear. He pulled it on quickly before stepping into his new trainers, zipping his keys into his pocket and pushing in his ear buds. He was in and out in less than a minute, and didn't even do his usual stretching routine before he started jogging out his building and up the main road.

All he was interested in was burning off stress. He picked up the pace and ran faster, then a little faster, weaving his way around all the evening commuters and groups of guys out on their stag dos.

Time blurred as he moved and the world around him disappeared. All that mattered to him right then was the burning in his chest and thighs and the sweat that dripped down his back. He didn't know how far he had run. All he did know was that after some time it felt as though his calves were going to snap and he had to slow to a halt or risk being crippled.

He drew to a stop next to a greasy spoon cafe. The kind where you could smell the fat frying before you even walked in the front door. It was busy inside with bright fluorescent lights bouncing of the runny egg yolks on the customers' plates. As Fitz caught his breath, he noticed them all looking up at the small TV on the wall above the cake counter. He wondered what they were all fascinated by, but then noticed the face on the screen and the police officers closing in around it.

"What the…"

Propelled by curiosity, he found himself entering the cafe as though magnetically pulled towards the counter.

"What's going on?" he asked, his eyes fixed on the screen.

The waitress behind the counter sipped on her coffee and pointed her cup at the TV.

"Sir Bill Lovecroft's been arrested live on tele. Can you believe it? The old man's a national treasure. Just look how the police are treating him. If they think I'm paying for my TV licence after this then…"

He tuned her words out as he stared at the screen. Bill's face was growing bright red beneath the spotlights as he spoke.

"Turn it up!" called out a customer and the woman behind the counter reached for the remote.

"Half! Of Everything!" Bill's voice filled the room.

For a long minute, Fitz stared at the TV as the surprised chatter grew around him.

"Crazy, ain't it?" said the woman behind the counter, setting down her coffee. "Reckon the old man will go to jail?"

"I hope not," said Fitz.

I hope not for Sarah's sake.

Chapter 2

Hawkins

January 18th, 2023

Elizabeth Hawkins sat in front of the mirror applying her lucky shade of red Chanel lipstick. It was the same one she had worn every single day for the past twenty years and it never let her down. She had applied it so many times she barely needed to look in the mirror to feel the contours of her lips.

Her eyes darted between the mirror and the TV at the end of her bed. A cheery breakfast show was playing, and she noticed in the bottom right hand corner of the screen it was already showing the time reaching nine o'clock. Not that she was in a hurry. She had two hours until her first appointment of the day. It was one of the perks of being semi-retired. She could take as long as she wanted to do almost anything she wanted, and she didn't miss the busy rat race that was her previous life. She could choose how she worked and how she played.

After blotting her lips with a tissue and sealing in the colour with some powder, she leaned back in her seat and turned her face from one side to the other to check her make-up was flawless. Then she reached for her coffee and took a slow sip, closing her eyes as the caffeine hit her. It was always her favourite part of the day. At least it was now she didn't have to wake up at the crack of dawn and rush into the office. Now she could linger in every moment, watch the sun rise across her bedroom as she sat in her silk pyjamas, meditate if she wanted to and watch the cheesy morning shows she had missed out on for so long.

She was only half paying attention to the television as the talking heads yapped about celebrity gossip. Her gaze was focussed out the window across the Pimlico skyline. It was going to be a beautiful day and she was already thinking ahead to the afternoon. She had a lunch meeting, but that shouldn't last too long, then a coffee with an old friend. After that, the day was hers. She smiled softly to herself as she wondered what to do with her evening.

Of course the previous night had been a blip on her usually leisurely schedule, but it had been worth it. She couldn't get the look of Bill's face out her head. The anger in his icy eyes, the way his already thin lips pulled themselves tight with rage, the way he was trying to appear so calm but was clearly shaking inside the cuffs.

Tax evasion, she thought. It was hardly armed robbery or murder. In some ways it was the gentleman's crime. Something that was only traceable on paper. But it was enough to get Old Bill sent away.

She smiled to herself as she took another sip of her coffee. *Bless him,* she thought, if only condescendingly. He knew what he was doing. But as she sat and felt the warmth of the morning sun burn through her window and across her legs, she couldn't help but feel a twinge of guilt.

It was a feeling that surprised her. She didn't arrive at being one of the most respected and feared prosecutors in the country by feeling guilty every time someone was put behind bars, but this felt different. This was, dare she think it, personal?

Her mood darkened slightly as she finished her coffee, but not because she was worried about Bill. He was a grown man with an iron will and a formidable character. He could handle himself. *No, fuck him,* she thought. *I'm more worried about that little girl. How old would she be now? Ten? Old enough to know what's happening.*

Hawkins cast her mind back to when she was ten years old. She remembered the year clearly because it was the same year her father had died and her world fell apart. She was no longer a tiny infant, but not old enough to have the blossoming confidence of a teenager. She had just felt so lost as though her life had suddenly become rudderless.

Would that be what little Sarah would be feeling now? Lost? Afraid? She had already lost her mother and her father may as well be dead too, and now Bill wouldn't be around to care for her.

Don't beat yourself up about it, she told herself. *You know what you're doing and Sarah will be all right. You're going to make sure of that later.*

She tried to hold onto this thought as she moved to get dressed, peeling off her pyjamas and feeling the strong sunlight on her naked body. As she picked out her clothes from the walk-in wardrobe, she heard her phone ring from her night stand, but she ignored it.

That was another luxury she had nowadays. She didn't have to answer to anyone at every waking minute of the day.

Her fingers searched her shelves for something colourful. God knew she needed some vibrancy in her day to lighten her mood. As she picked out a light pink blouse she heard her phone was still ringing. Again, she ignored it, but when it started to ring for the third time, she rolled her eyes, grabbed the blouse and moved to grab her phone.

She saw the name, Richard on the screen and rolled her eyes again. Hadn't she told him explicitly not to bother her today?

"Hello, Dickie," she huffed.

"Please stop calling me that. You know I hate it."

"That's why I call you it."

He couldn't help but laugh even though he didn't want to, but she always had this effect on him. It was like whenever he heard her voice he morphed into a schoolboy.

"So, Lizzie," he began. "Old Bill."

"What about him?"

"Don't act like you don't know. That televised shit storm last night. I know you've got something to do with it."

"Now how would you know that?"

He didn't answer for a second, knowing she was toying with him.

"Can we cut the shit?" he said. "I'm calling you professionally."

"Are you now?"

"Listen. I don't know what you're planning, but I've had it up to here this morning. The press are going batshit crazy. Everyone wants to ask the MET's commissioner why Britain's most loved old man is in custody."

"Because he didn't pay his taxes," smiled Hawkins. "It's pretty simple to understand."

"No, Lizzie. You're never easy to understand."

"Me?"

"Yeah, you. I don't know what game you're playing, but I sure as shit know you don't give a crap about if someone pays their taxes or not. Especially when that someone is the father-in-law of a certain you-know-who."

She dropped her smile. Richard's voice was grating against her nerves. Since when did he get to grill her like this? He was all sweetness and smiles when he was taking her out for secret dinners and rolling around in her bed behind his wife's back. But now he wanted to talk professionally?

The anger swelled up inside her, but she spoke calmly.

"Don't question me," she told him. "It's my job to try and put people away when they break the law. It's your job too, remember?"

"Speaking of putting people away. I suppose you've timed this all perfectly as the most infamous person you put away is out now."

She looked down at her feet as she thought of Fitz. There it was again. The guilt for little Sarah.

"Yeah, of course I know he got released."

"Been keeping tabs on him?"

"No…"

Richard lowered his voice. He may have been angry with her, but he could sense the sadness in her voice. Their relationship, not that they ever used that word, had begun the summer Fitz was sent to Wandsworth. He had known how much the case had affected her. Not just because of the spotlight it put her under, but because the whole thing was so convoluted, so dangerous and twisted. And although he knew she was a tough woman, he had to admit he was worried about her. How could she expect to put away gangsters and not be on the receiving end of some form of retribution?

"Lizzie…"

"Yeah."

"I know what you're thinking."

"How would you know that?"

"Because it's the same thing you always think when we talk about Fitz. You get all weird and maternal when you think about his daughter."

"What have I told you about saying the M-word."

"I'm just saying, I know you always had a soft spot for Sarah after what happened to her mother."

"It's not her fault her dad's a criminal that dragged her mum into the gutter. I mean, shit, how did those two even meet?"

"Same way all people do," replied Richard, remembering all the facts of Fitz' case. "Met in a swanky club. He saw an angel and she saw a bit of rough that would piss off her daddy."

"And they had to bring a child into the world."

"A child that was well cared for and spoiled rotten under Sir Bill's care before you got him arrested last night. Do I have to remind you of that?"

She didn't reply. Instead she narrowed her eyes and felt the impending pulse of a migraine.

"Fuck off, Dickie. You don't have to guilt trip me. Oh, and dinner's off tomorrow."

She hung up and tossed her phone onto the bed before pulling on her blouse and a skirt she had hanging over a nearby chair.

"Urgh," she moaned to herself as she searched her night stand for some painkillers.

Behind her, the sun disappeared from the window as the sky clouded over. Her day was ruined.

Chapter 3

Bill

January 18th, 2023

Detective Jones sat across from Bill in his crumpled high street suit with his tie loosened around his neck. It wasn't even noon yet, but having been working all night trying to secure evidence against Bill, it had already been a long day.

Beside him, Detective Kane stifled a yawn and took a big gulp of coffee. The tension in the room was evident. Everyone was staring at each other wondering who was going to make the first move. Kane looked to Jones and decided he was in no fit state to do the talking so took the lead and switched on the recorder.

"The time is now eleven-forty-five. I am DCI Kane and in the room is DCI Jones, Sir Bill Lovecroft and his legal counsel."

"May I interject," butted in Bill's lawyer, Lucien.

Kane glowered at him. He disliked the man the moment he walked in the room in his Savile Row suit. He had the same expression, sharp face and cunning demeanour as a starving fox waiting to pounce in a bin for scraps.

"My client has been here for fifteen hours and much of that has been spent terrified out his wits by the constant noise and-"

"Now, now Lucien. I haven't exactly been terrified," interrupted Bill.

Lucien shot him a look to silence him.

"Please, let me speak. As I was saying. He's been here fifteen hours. May I remind you, detectives that he's entitled to eight hours uninterrupted rest, and that you're only allowed to hold him for twenty-four hours without officially charging him."

Kane sighed and leaned back in his seat. He knew full well how long he was allowed to keep Bill and that he needed to officially charge him or let him go. He also knew Bill hated every second of being cooped up in the interview room without his usual luxuries. Bill's anxious sweat and stale aftershave permeated the air, and his unease was something Kane took great delight in.

Let him stew a little while longer, he thought. *Let the rich bastard have a bad day for once.*

"We'd just like to ask your client a few questions," he said, addressing Lucien.

"How many more questions can you ask me?" seethed Bill through a clenched jaw. "You've been asking so many bloody questions, most of them irrelevant."

"Please, just a couple more. Let's start with the financial records for your bank account in Jersey, shall we?"

"If we must," replied Bill, crossing his arms.

He was desperate for some real food and his stomach rumbled. When he'd woken up from his broken sleep at dawn he'd been offered nothing but tea made with instant granules and cheap, watery milk along with two slices of toast. He'd rejected it all and instead sipped on some bottled water Lucien brought him.

Now he was starving, overheated in the cramped, sweltering interview room and in desperate need of some fresh air and better company.

"Okay," began Kane. "Can you tell me when it was opened?"

"You know when it was opened. You have the records."

"Just answer the question please."

"No comment."

"Okay, what about the bank account in the Cayman Islands?"

"No comment."

"The money you've got tied up in a company called Entro Investments?"

Bill said nothing and just kept his eyes focused directly into Kane's as though goading him into asking another question.

"Mr Lovecroft?"

Bill kept glaring.

"Can you please tell me when you began a professional relationship with Entro Investments?"

"No comment."

"And your donations to the Power to the Planet group?"

"What about them?"

"Can you elaborate on why your most sizeable charitable donations are to them?"

Bill cringed inwardly as he heard the name, but didn't let his poker face slide.

"No comment," he repeated.

Kane pinched the bridge of his nose and let out a long, frustrated breath. Then he looked over at Lucien who was sitting still with blank, beady eyes. The only part of him showing emotion being the corners of his mouth that were curled up ever so slightly into a smirk.

Smug prick, thought Kane.

He looked back to Bill who's eyes were still penetrating his, then over at Jones who looked ready to fall asleep.

"Okay, I think we're done here for now," sighed Kane, standing up and screeching his chair back.

"That's it?" asked Lucien.

"Let us know when your client is going to cooperate."

Kane nodded towards the door and Jones got the hint. The two of them walked out, slamming the door behind them leaving Bill and Lucien alone.

"This is bullshit," exploded Bill, finally letting his guard drop.

"Relax," Lucien told him, leaning in close to his ear. "They'll be watching. We've got this all under control. I promise."

"Really? Then why am I still in this shithole?"

Lucien didn't know how to respond and turned his attention to shuffling some papers inside his briefcase.

"You're supposed to be getting me out of here," said Bill.

"I will, in time, but I'll be honest. Things aren't looking too terrific for you."

"What the bloody hell does that mean? I thought you said we had everything under control."

Lucien tried his hardest to not let his aloof expression drop.

"Okay, Bill listen. I can get you a deal. But they've got you by the bollocks. I mean, shit, they know about Entro and they're asking questions about Power to the Planet. They've done their homework, followed the paper trail for every single one of your pennies. They've got you."

Bill's eyes flashed with anger. Beneath the table, his hands curled themselves into fists.

"Do not tell me you just said that," he raged.

"I'm sorry, but if I may speak freely I have to tell you that your accountant isn't as skilled as your lawyer."

"You're saying you're better than my accountant..."

"I'm saying they got you into this mess. I have to get you out."

"You're not making any sense, you fuckwit. Have they got me or are you going to get me out of this?"

This was the moment Lucien was dreading, but he knew sooner or later he was going to have to say the words he knew Bill would never want to hear.

"You're going to have to plead guilty," he told him. "I'm sorry, Bill. It's just the way it is."

Bill was too stunned to answer and just stared at him as though he was waiting for the punchline to a joke.

"You're... taking the piss."

"I'm sorry, Bill. I wish I was. The solid truth is that..."

Lucien paused for a second as he collected the right words.

"The truth is that they really have got you, but we can make this work in our favour."

"You better not be-"

"Please, Bill. Plead guilty and I can cut you a decent deal."

"That seriously can't be our best option."

"Regretfully I have to say it is. It'll be easier to nip this in the bud now than create more of a media circus."

"Not fond of a media circus?"

"You know I'm not," sighed Lucien, thinking back to The Glazer Show. "What you did last night. Christ, Bill. What a clusterfuck."

Bill chuckled to himself.

"There's nothing wrong with what I did last night."

"You offered half of all your cash to whoever gets you out of this. Do you know how guilty that makes you look?"

"Don't be ridiculous, Lucien. I thoroughly doubt I looked guilty. People love me in this country. I'm England's bloody grandpa and the offer of my cash is going to make every one of my metaphorical grandchildren feel a need to do the right thing."

Lucien looked doubtful and drew his lips into a tight, sceptical line.

"You know I'm right," continued Bill. "I'm the victim in all this. People will always cheer for the victim, especially if it's likely to make them a billionaire."

"Well, victim or not the media are only interested in one thing, the promise of cash."

Lucien rummaged through his briefcase and pulled out the morning's papers before fanning them out across the table. Bill was instantly faced with the image of himself being carted off Glazer's stage with his face contorted in outrage. One tabloid ran with the headline – BUST OUT BILL FOR BILLIONS. While another newspaper went for a more subdued headline – SIR BILL LOVECROFT OFFER OF ASSETS IN EXCHANGE FOR FREEDOM.

Bill smiled to himself as he saw them, but Lucien didn't know what he was so happy about.

"It's a nightmare," he told Bill. "The story's spreading like wildfire on social media. There's a hashtag already, #freebillforbillions. As of this morning it was used almost half a million times."

Bill's smile broadened, even if Lucien wasn't seeing the funny side.

"It's a PR disaster," moaned Lucien.

"You and me appear to have differing opinions of what a disaster is."

"I'm just saying the media coverage is more focussed on your cash than your credibility. They need to be on your side, not encouraging people to make a crude cash grab for your freedom."

Bill rolled his eyes, shuffled the papers together and tossed them into Lucien's briefcase.

"Enough," he said. "You're my lawyer, not my media consultant. Just deal with what's in front of us right now."

"Okay, well right now I'm suggesting you plead guilty. You know it's the right thing to do. We've got carnage in the media today, but if we deal with this swiftly it'll all be over with and people will move onto the next scandal. A long, drawn out trial will make that almost impossible. Not to mention if you get found guilty by a jury you're more likely to get a lengthier sentence."

Bill was starting to realise Lucien was right, at least about the sentence. He always was. He'd been the head of his legal team for over a decade and never put a foot wrong before.

"What's likely to happen to me if I plead guilty?" he asked. "What will I get? A fine or something?"

"I can push for that. You may get a custodial sentence."

"No. I can't have that."

"In which I'll argue the case for you to be sent to an open prison. Somewhere nice in the country where Sarah can live nearby and you can visit her every day. It'll be like a little holiday camp, but with worse food."

"So basically Butlins."

Lucien smiled broadly for the first time since he arrived at the station.

"Like Butlins. Who knows, they might give you community service and be done with it."

Bill thought that sounded terrible but not as bad as it could be.

The door opened with a creak and in stepped Kane and Jones, both with fresh coffees and a new look of determination.

"So," said Kane, blustering through the small room and taking his seat. "Had time to think, have you?"

"I have," said Bill. "I'll cooperate."

Kane raised his eyebrow at Jones.

"You will?"

"Yes, let's just get this over with. I'm guilty, okay. I have nothing else to say on the matter. My counsel here will speak on my behalf from now on."

Kane smiled wryly to himself as he sipped on his coffee.

"Very well," he said. "Glad to hear you've come to your senses."

Chapter 4

Lucien

January 18th, 2023

Lucien didn't say goodbye to DCI Kane as he led him out through the reception to the station's exit. All he did was shoot him a sneer before departing without a word. Kane watched him leave, walking down the station steps towards the car park with a freakishly erect posture. He couldn't take his eyes off the lawyer. Everything about his mannerisms were aloof to the point of looking bizarre, and he couldn't quite understand where he got his inflated ego.

He watched him walk across the car park to his blacked out Mercedes, his nose turned up at the world and his briefcase held in his slender fingers. Kane had shaken his hand when he'd arrived and thought it felt like a wet fish.

Lucien was aware of Kane's watchful gaze as he climbed into his car, but it only amused him. The hatred was mutual.

"Arrogant bastard," Lucien said to himself as he turned the key in the ignition and pulled out his parking space.

He watched Kane in the rear view mirror, his stocky frame standing stoutly on the station steps.

"What the bloody hell's he looking at?"

Lucien despised how Kane watched him, judged him, made him feel as though he was doing something wrong by just doing his job. As he drove away from the station, he reasoned to himself that the gnarly old detective was probably just jealous. How many hours did he spend busting his balls for a salary that Lucien made in an average month?

"Urgh, I need a drink," said Lucien as he pulled to a stop at a red light and rubbed his eyes.

He heard a honk behind him and when he next looked up he saw the light had turned green. He'd grown exhausted over the course of the morning. Bill, although being his most profitable client, was also his most demanding.

As he glided his car through Mayfair, turning the corner into Carlos Place, his favourite hotel and bar, The Connaught appeared on his right. He'd always had a penchant for the Cubist movement, although he'd never told his friends explicitly about his love for the fine arts. It was a secret passion of his. He'd even thought to himself that at some point he would have liked to have taken up a life drawing class if his confidence allowed him. His ego may have been large in the court room, but it withered away to nothing when he had to do anything creative.

To him, an artist's world was pure anarchy, a place where laws written in black and white were largely meaningless, and therefore so was his own world full of legal jargon.

The valet smiled as he parked in front of The Connaught. It was the same young man who had parked his car the previous week and he'd obviously remembered Lucien fondly. No doubt because of the large tip he'd left him.

"Thanks," said Lucien with an insincere smile as he stepped out and threw the keys at the valet.

Entering The Connaught, he ignored the doormen and moved his way through the plush surroundings to his usual table at the back of the room. It was the most discrete table in the place, but one in which you could see every angle from the corner; a perfect place for people watching.

The second Lucien began lowering himself into his seat, a waiter appeared. It was one thing Lucien didn't like about the bar. Sometimes it felt as though there were more staff than customers.

Like the Apple store, he thought as he made himself comfortable.

"Would you like to see a menu, Sir?"

"No, I'm just in for a drink. Saffron Smoke, please."

"Of course."

The waiter departed leaving Lucien alone with his thoughts and the sound of lounge jazz playing over the speakers. He didn't know if he should love it or hate it. Jazz was as mysterious to him as art was. He just couldn't understand it.

Looking around the bar, he saw the place was unusually quiet, but he put that down to the gloomy weather. However, he did notice that two tables down from him, a beautiful blonde in a tight, black dress was drinking alone. He wondered if she was with someone who had perhaps stepped into the bathroom, but then he noticed the single glass on her table. He also noticed her obviously expensive blow dry, perfect manicure and thick make-up. It looked like she was all dressed up for a night on her own. Then it dawned on him.

She's looking for customers.

Sensing she was being stared at, she turned to face him, her glossy, red lips parting into an attractive smile. He couldn't decipher her real age beneath her make-up, but he didn't care. She was blonde and trim and that was all that mattered.

He was so lost in her appearance that he didn't notice the waiter return with his drink, then slip away wordlessly back to the bar.

"Hey," the woman mouthed at him. "You looking for company?"

It didn't take long for Lucien to give his answer. He was already reaching into his wallet as he gestured for her to take the seat across from him. He waited for her to rush over to him, but she rose from her seat with a deliberate slowness that surprised him. She was in no rush for anyone, and he admired that. Respected it even.

As she stood up he could now see her body in all its glory. Slim to the point of being athletic with long legs he instantly imagined being wrapped around his waist.

"Hello," she smiled as she approached.

Her desire to shake his hand formally surprised him, and his need for her grew. She oozed an intoxicating mix of detached professionalism and sensuality. His perfect woman.

"You're gorgeous," he blurted out, annoyed at himself for sounding so desperate. "What's your name?"

"Melissa."

"Where are you from, Melissa?"

"Napoli."

"I did wonder what your accent was. Been in London long?"

"Three months."

With another act of deliberate slowness, she lowered herself down into the seat across from him making sure to take her time so his eyes fell on every inch of her body. As she sat, she leaned forward, her large breasts pressing against the table the moment Lucien's cock pressed against the inside of his pants.

"How much?" he asked, not wanting to waste any more time.

"Five hundred an hour. I can stay all night if you need."

Lucien nodded in agreement and opened his wallet.

I'll charge it to Bill, he laughed inwardly. *Call it a business expense. Lord knows I need it after running around like a blue arsed fly for him all morning.*

He looked up to Melissa who was sipping daintily on her Martini, rolling the glass over her sticky lips.

"So, Melissa..." he said. "Tell me about Naples."

***

Hours passed without Lucien noticing the time. Not just because it was Bill's money he was spending, but because he was genuinely enjoying Melissa's company.

He looked at the clock and saw it approach six. They'd shared drinks that turned to lunch that turned to more drinks and they were both now moving through the threshold from playfully tipsy to full blown drunk.

Lucien felt as though he'd loosened up for the first time in a long while, and was now sitting low in his seat with his eyes fixed on Melissa's cleavage. She had only grown more desirable in his eyes as the afternoon wore on. Her curves and smile becoming more exaggerated with each drink he had.

She was in the middle of talking about a holiday she'd taken to Crete when he decided he didn't want to hear her talk any more.

"Let's go upstairs," he declared, interrupting her.

She paused for a second, sipped the last of her drink and replied, "I thought you were never going to suggest it."

Lucien paid the bill quickly and took Melissa's hand. It was warm and soft and squeezed his fingers with a promise of what was to come. At the reception, he booked a room on the top floor, sloppily taking the key card off the desk before staggering into the nearby elevator.

The second the doors closed and he had Melissa in the cramped, mirrored space, he made his move and pulled her close to him, kissing her and smearing her lip gloss.

She giggled and pulled away flirtatiously, and it only made him want her more. As the doors dinged open on the top floor, Melissa took the keys from his drunken hands, made a note of the bedroom number and led the way.

What Lucien didn't know was that she was sober on account of her ordering non-alcoholic cocktails after her first Martini. She always tried to stay as close to sober on the job. She needed to keep her wits about her.

Lucien latched onto her as she led him to the room, slipped the key card in the door and took him inside. Now in the privacy of the room, he didn't bother with pleasantries or more talking. He simply moved over to the bed, pulled down his trousers and underwear and lay back with an entitled sneer.

"You know what to do," he said.

She stood in front of him and looked down at his body. Slowly, with her gaze meeting his, she pulled her tight dress from her taught body and stood in front of him in her Agent Provocateur underwear. His eyes widened at the sight of her and his body reacted by drawing all his blood below his waist.

"Take it all off," he ordered, and she obliged.

Snapping the straps of her bra, she revealed her breasts to him before bending down to lower her panties to her ankles. She kicked them off gracefully before moving onto the bed, straddling Lucien as she reached into her purse for a condom.

He was so ready and desperate for her his eyes were wide like a wolf's.

He's not going to last long, she thought to herself. *He's almost frothing at the mouth.*

She was right. The second she lowered herself onto him, he was almost finished and the entire encounter lasted less than a minute.

When it ended, she rolled off him and lay on her back staring at the ceiling. Beside her, Lucien gasped for air and closed his eyes as he saw stars.

"You're incredible," he slurred. "The best."

She smiled to herself knowing that she was.

Thinking the night was over, she moved to pull her clothes back on, but as she leaned over the bed, she felt Lucien's hand curl around her wrist.

"Will you stay the night with me?" he asked.

"You want to go again?"

"Not yet I... I..."

He wasn't sure what he wanted, just that he didn't want her to go.

"Just lie with me, will you?" he said.

"It'll cost you."

"Yes, yes. I know. Just lie with me."

Melissa forced a smile and drew herself closer, laying her head on his chest. She hoped he wasn't one of those guys who liked to cuddle all night. Somehow she always found those the hardest to deal with. Sex made sense to her. It could be intense but it was also fast. Cuddling and kissing required more emotional labour, and it was usually something she wanted to do with men who weren't paying.

"I'm so… so drunk," laughed Lucien, his eyes going blurry as he watched the patterns of the chandelier across the ceiling. "And you're so… so beautiful."

He turned to face her. Cupped her jaw in his skinny fingers and kissed her cheek.

"I've had a wonderful night," he said. "I'd like to see you again."

"I'd like to see you again too."

"You know, I feel like I've known you forever."

"I feel the same way," she lied.

"You do? I just… I feel as though we've connected. It's not often I meet a woman I can talk to for so long and feel so comfortable with. You're very special."

She smiled and draped her arm over his waist.

"Do you need some water?" she asked him. "Or a coffee perhaps?"

"A coffee," he smiled.

She kissed his forehead with little more than a feather's touch and stood up. At the end of the room, a small table sat beneath the television with a kettle, a coffee machine and some china cups. After filling up the coffee machine, she flicked it on and the room was filled with the scent of Arabica beans.

Lucien watched her naked body as she moved, and he let himself fall into a daydream. He imagined she was his wife and woke up to this sight every day.

A wife, he thought. *I could never quite figure out how to hold onto one of those.*

"So, are you in London for business?" she asked as she set out the coffee cups.

He was struck by the suddenness of her small talk, and he realised that over the course of the evening they had discussed nothing of himself at any personal level. He had charmed her with stories of his travels and some of his previous high profile clients, but nothing more.

"No," he replied. "I live here."

"A lawyer in London. You must be a very smart man."

She looked over her shoulder and flashed him a smile. Not realising she was flattering him as part of her job, he felt his heart bounce at the compliment.

"I suppose I am rather smart," he said. "If I may toot my own horn."

"I suppose I could toot it for you," she giggled as she poured his coffee.

He laughed at her corny innuendo and felt himself relax even more. It had been a long time since he felt so at ease in someone's company, and he had the strangest urge to talk to her about all sorts of things that he couldn't tell anyone else. Maybe it was because he was drunk, the anonymity of the encounter, or the fact that she was just so outrageously beautiful, but he found the longer he stared into her eyes, the looser his tongue became.

She brought both their coffees to bed and sat beside him.

"Would you like to get under the covers?" he asked her.

"Sure."

Taking off the last of his clothes, he climbed beneath the duvet and she shifted up beside him. As they sipped coffee together, looking around at the luxurious room, Lucien felt as though they were a regular couple.

"Tell me more about yourself," he said.

"What would you like to know?"

"I don't know. Erm... What's your favourite colour?"

"Ooh, yellow because it reminds me of the sun. But I like blue too. Reminds me of the sea."

"What's your favourite movie?"

"I think Breakfast at Tiffany's."

"TV show?"

"Hmmm?"

"What's your favourite TV show?"

"Oooh, I don't watch much TV but I do like talk shows. There is one I have become most fond of since I moved to England. The Glazer Show. Have you heard of it?"

Lucien's chest tightened. He'd heard enough about it.

"Yes," he sighed.

"You have? It's very good, isn't it? I hope there's a chance I could meet Freddie Glazer while I'm in London."

"Oh, I think I could maybe arrange that for you."

"Really?" she beamed.

"Absolutely. As a matter of fact we share a mutual friend and I see him around quite socially."

"Mutual friend? Someone close?"

"Have you heard of Sir Bill Lovecroft?"

Lucien knew this was the time he should stop talking or change the subject, but for some reason, he continued.

"Yes, I saw the episode where he was being arrested."

"Then you might be surprised to know he is one of my clients."

"He is!"

"Yep, that's right. I've been representing him for years. Not that he acts like it. I'm his bloody skivvy half the time. He treats me like a slave that comes in to mop up his problems."

"You don't like him?"

"It's not that I don't *like* him. It's just that…"

"He doesn't make you feel valued," suggested Melissa, moving in closer.

Now realising his clients were more high profile than she'd previously thought, she felt herself warm to the idea of seeing Lucien again and meeting Freddie Glazer. She wondered who else she could meet if she hung around Lucien long enough.

"You're totally right, Melissa," said Lucien, placing his coffee cup on the night stand with a clunk. "He doesn't value me at all. And after everything I've done for him. The arrogant dick."

"So are you going to drop him as a client?"

"Am I fuck? He's the biggest paying client I have. Even if he is an arsehole."

"But you can't have him treat you like garbage," she said, leaning against his shoulder and stroking his chest. "You deserve better."

He felt a spark go off inside him as she said this. It was something he'd thought plenty of times before but had never had someone else confirm.

"This will be the last time the bastard gets to walk all over me," he said, leaning into the warmth of her body. "I'm taking all I can get. Every last penny and he can go fuck himself."

Melissa didn't know what he meant, but sensed there was something deeper to his statement. Then she remembered what Bill had said on television. How he had promised half his assets to whoever could get him out of trouble, and in that moment she realised the person most likely to do that was surely Lucien.

A string of thoughts moved through her head.

This man beside me could end up a billionaire?

And he clearly likes me, could we have more than this encounter?

Could I be a billionaire too?

She leaned in closer to him, kissed his cheek and ran her hand down the center of his chest towards his stomach. Against the palm of her hand she felt his heartbeat quicken.

As she looked down between his legs, she saw the bed sheets rise.

"You're right, darling," she said, kissing his neck. "Take him for every penny. You deserve better. You deserve the world."

He felt his breath quicken as she slid her hand down beneath the bed sheets, but just as she was about to curl her fingers around him, her phone beeped from inside her purse, cutting through the moment.

"I'm sorry, darling. I must check this."

"Do you? No..." moaned Lucien.

"I'll be back in just a second. You wait here for me."

She climbed out of bed and walked slowly to her purse making sure to accentuate each movement of her hips. The longer his eyes were on her body, the less they were on what she was doing with her phone.

"Stay there," she said playfully, pointing at him. "Be a good boy."

"I'm your loyal servant," joked Lucien in response. "I'll do anything you say."

Grabbing her phone, she backed into the bathroom and closed the door. Looking at her screen, she saw a message with the four words she'd been expecting.

You got him yet?

With a smile, she typed back.

Detective Kane. I got him.

Less than ten seconds later, a reply pinged back.

Good girl. You've never let me down yet.

Chapter 5

Fitz

December 9th, 2017

His footsteps echoed across the wooden floor of The National Gallery. He took in a deep inhale of the air around him and breathed in the smell of antiquity. The smell of museums, art galleries and libraries had always soothed him. It felt as though he was inhaling history.

Ahead of him, he saw single spotlights illuminate the priceless paintings that lined the crimson walls of room thirty-two. He paused as he reached a Rembrandt, and gazed up to take in the sight. It was a painting he'd seen in books and documentaries dozens of times, but up close it was more breathtaking that he imagined it could be.

Behind him, he heard the footsteps of his team, but he paid them no attention.

"Fitz?" he heard Danielle's voice whisper. "There's no time to hang around."

He felt her hand on his arm and snapped out his daydream. Turning to her, he saw her pale blue eyes through the darkness of her ski mask. She looked beautiful. Even now dressed head to toe in baggy, black clothes with nothing visible but her eyes she was still the most beautiful woman he'd ever seen. Even lovelier than the women depicted in the oil paintings around him.

Lovely...

It was a word he'd frequently used to describe her, and it was a word that always seemed plain and uninteresting to him until he found the right reason to use it. Danielle was loveliness personified. Nothing but sweetness and sunshine with a look in her eyes that always made him feel as though nothing could go wrong.

He even felt this way now as his team moved through The National Gallery with their faces shrouded and their gloved hands itching for the Caravaggio painting hanging at the end of the room.

"We need to move now," she urged him, nudging him along. "Come on."

He followed her down the length of the room. It felt so much larger now, so much longer as though it had morphed and elongated from what it was when he had reconnoitred it during the day. A strand of Danielle's blonde hair was poking out from under her ski mask, catching the light of the nearest spotlight. She paused as she reached the end of the room and looked up. He followed her gaze up to the painting that hung above them. The Caravaggio looked so much larger than it usually did.

Looking over at the rest of his team consisting of four friends he'd known most of his life, he gave them an affirmative nod and moved in closer.

They all knew what to do. They'd rehearsed it a hundred times. Cut the painting from the frame, roll it and go. Fitz' calculations estimated they would lose a width of around three inches around the border, but he could live with that.

It was large enough to need three people to carry it at speed and another three to act as lookouts. As the team leader, Fitz insisted he would be the one to cut the painting free. He dipped his hand into his pocket and pulled out the Stanley blade. It felt like such a crude implement in which to take such a beautiful, sacred piece of art.

He looked up at the painting, the blade held tight in his hand.

"What are you waiting for?" Danielle hissed at him.

The truth was that he didn't know what he was waiting for. He was just so busy staring up at the painting in sheer awe he felt as though he was on the cusp of having a religious revelation. But the moment didn't last long and he felt himself come to his senses.

Holding the blade tighter, he moved towards the painting and pressed the tip of the blade to the thick, cracked oil paint.

You're really doing this.

His heart beat so fast he could hear his pulse in his ears, could feel his tongue turn dry like sandpaper.

Then the noise started.

Instant and deafening, it reverberated around the entire room with such ferocity he had to hold his hands to his head to stop his skull hurting. Lights flashed all around the team, making them disorientated.

No, No!

The alarms were supposed to be disabled.

His first thought was to grab Danielle's hand and run. His team were already on the move, running so fast their shoes were skidding on the polished floor. His second thought was to dump the blade. If the cops caught him with the thing they'd insist he was carrying a weapon and he couldn't risk it.

Danielle wasn't as fast as Fitz but she was trying her hardest to keep up as they ran around the corner, blustering through the heavy double doors and down the corridor towards the fire escape; their planned escape route.

Christ it wasn't supposed to happen like this!

Fitz' stomach sank as they reached the fire door. As they pushed their way out through the green door onto the long, metal staircase that wound its way down to the ground, he saw the van waiting for the team with the getaway driver, Harry in front, the engine running and the side door open. Harry's head popped out the window and looked up. Even through his balaclava Fitz could tell what the look in his eyes meant.

Where's the painting?

But right that second Fitz stopped caring about it. All he wanted was to get Danielle to safety. Grabbing her roughly, he pulled her across the landing of the staircase.

"Run!" he yelled over the siren.

The second her foot touched the top step of the staircase, another noise joined the alarm. Police sirens. They sounded as though they were coming from every direction. Soon, the getaway van was covered in flickering blue lights.

"Shit!"

Fitz grabbed Danielle again. Tried to pull her back into the building even though he knew security were now on the prowl. He just couldn't bear the thought of her being dragged and cuffed by some meathead cop and bundled into the back of a van.

A bang sounded from somewhere nearby. The noise of a door slamming perhaps or a leftover firework from bonfire season.

Danielle opened her mouth to speak, but instead of words, a burst of noise flew out of her gaping lips. At first, Fitz thought he was hearing another siren, then soon realised he was hearing her voice as she screamed in agony. He saw a flash of red burst out from her chest as though in slow motion, like an explosion of crimson hibiscus petals. But his brain didn't process it was blood until he felt the heat of the viscous liquid hit his cheek.

"Danielle!"

He lunged forward to grab her and her body fell limp against him, the two of them crumpling to the floor. Pulling off her ski mask, he saw her face clearly as it paled and turned grey.

"It's okay. I'll get help!" he cried, placing a hand on her chest.

She didn't say a word in response, and as he looked down at her, he saw her grow incapable of speaking. The spark that usually lay in her eyes dimmed in front of him until it dwindled away to nothing. The remaining colour drained from her face and her eyelids flickered shut.

"Danielle? Danielle!"

He shook her shoulders hard, desperate to wake her. All around him, the sirens grew louder as the screech of tires sounded from all sides of the building. Flashing blue lights danced on Danielle's dead face, the blood running from her body appearing purple on the steel stairs. It felt as though his life was being sucked out of him. He couldn't breathe, could barely see. All he could do was grip onto her body and continue to shake her.

"Danielle wake up!"

He looked around for someone to help, but he couldn't spot his team anywhere. But through the darkness he could feel the heat of someone's gaze. He turned to look through the railings and saw a dark figure beside the getaway van. Desperately, he tried to see the face, but couldn't make out the features clearly. Despite there being no eyes visible, he was aware of them staring at him intently. Suddenly, something caught the corner of Fitz' eye. His gaze moved rapidly to something metallic at the figure's side. Realising it was a gun, Fitz noticed a trail of smoke drift up from the barrel.

He felt the urge to leap over the railings and pounce on the figure, but before he could move, he felt the staircase juddering beneath the weight of a dozen officers bounding up the steps.

It had all come to an end.

Everything was over.

***

January 18th, 2023

Fitz was shocked upright in bed as though he had been hit by a bolt of lightning. Sweat dripped down his face and as he placed his hand on the bed sheets, he felt they were soaking wet.

"Shit…"

He could barely breathe and the air was stuck in his throat. Reaching a trembling hand out towards the bedside table for a glass of water, he swallowed hard and felt his dry throat ache. With his other hand, he placed his fingers against his sweat covered chest and felt his heart beat faster than it ever had before.

"Oh God," he breathed, gulping down the water and slamming the glass down.

For a long moment, he stared into space trying to get his bearings as his heart rate slowed. It was the same dream he'd had every night for six years. The same one he'd had every single night in Wandsworth as he relived the moment he watched Danielle die over and over again. It was always the same. His brain just couldn't escape the confines of his guilt or the memory of that night, and so it became stuck on replay the second he fell asleep.

Yet somehow, this night the dream felt more vivid than usual, as though he was really there. He could smell the fear, could feel the heat of Danielle's blood. He was sure he could even feel the rough texture of the metal staircase against his knee caps.

"No… No it was just a dream. I'm here in bed."

But there was also a bittersweet realisation that came from knowing he was in bed. If he was really at home and not reliving that night then he wasn't with Danielle. And even though the recurring dream tormented him night after night, he felt a peculiar sense of comfort from it because it meant that in his sleeping state he was reunited with her, if only for a short, tragic time.

As his breathing returned to normal, he climbed out of bed, took his empty glass and walked into the kitchen to fill it up. He watched in a daze as the water flowed out the tap. He still felt as though the dream was clinging to the back of his mind. He couldn't stop thinking about the faceless figure and that ribbon of smoke drifting up from their hand. It was so vivid in his mind he could almost smell the gun powder.

"Who are you?" he said into his kitchen. "I'm gonna find you eventually."

It was a promise he'd made to himself a hundred times, but was never sure he could fulfil no matter how much he wanted to.

If only I could have seen a face.

Since his release he'd walked down the streets looking into the face of every man thinking, *Was it you that fired the gun? Was it you that fucking killed her?*

It was the sound of the sink almost overflowing that brought him back into the moment. He took a long drink and clenched his eyes shut in a futile attempt at blocking out the fading images of his dream.

As he walked back through the living room, he paused in front of the small fireplace and watched as a sliver of moonlight snuck through the blinds and landed on the silver photo frame that sat pride of place.

Flicking on the light, he walked over and picked it up, noticing his own fingerprints on the glass from the countless times he'd spent holding it. From beneath the glass, his favourite photograph stared back at him. It was the image of Danielle and Sarah, both of them with the same shade of blue eyes and blonde hair. He'd taken the picture himself when the three of them had taken a trip to Brighton beach just two weeks before the job at The National Gallery.

He couldn't remember the amount of times he had woken up in the middle of the night and picked up the picture just to imagine what he would do to rewind time and be back in that moment.

If only I hadn't taken you on that job.
If only I hadn't done that job at all.
If only you were still here.

He drew the picture closer, kissed the glass then returned it to the fireplace. Tears began to burn his eyes as he stepped away from it. It was the closest thing he had to Danielle, the only reminder he had once had the most beautiful and meaningful thing in the world, a family.

His eyes focused on Sarah's face. She appeared to be nothing more than a baby, but now she would be approaching her teenage years. It had been so long since he'd seen her, but he knew he'd recognise her. She was always Danielle's double.

The sadness had been welling up in him since he woke up as though his stomach was filling up with black tar, but now it felt like it was reaching the point of being unbearable. It was so intense and dark it felt as though he was in physical pain and he felt the need to place a hand to his chest to hold the ache deep inside him.

He desperately needed something to make it stop hurting. Just something to make him forget, if only for a few hours. His eyes moved to the kitchen doorway from where he could see the cupboard in which he kept the one bottle of single malt whiskey he had been saving. It wasn't a special occasion he was saving it for, but rather his own sanity. He kept it as a test. If he could last a night without opening it, then he could get through anything.

But right now, he felt as though he couldn't get through the next two minutes. The whiskey beckoned to him with the seductive promise of plunging him into an abyss. All it would take was a few more steps and it would be in his hands like an old lover ready to take away his problems.

He lurched towards the kitchen, ready to grab it, then glanced back at the photograph and stopped himself.

No, he thought. *I can't do it.*

He knew the second he started to drown his grief in booze it was a slippery slope to ending up like the hundreds of people he'd seen in Wandsworth whose lives had been consumed by bad decisions. He knew the moment he fell into the velvety bliss of a drunken stupor he would never be able to get out of it.

With a deep breath, he picked up the picture once again and looked deep into Danielle's eyes.

"I'm going straight," he told her. "For you… I'll sort myself out. I'll get Sarah back."

Chapter 6

Danielle

June 2nd, 2002

"Daddy? Why do you like this painting so much?"

It wasn't the first time Danielle had asked Bill that question. She'd often find him standing at the bottom of the spiral staircase where the grand hall of their home stretched out its marble floor, gazing up at the painting with a glazed look in his eyes. She was too young to know what a trance was, but she was aware that when her father loitered in front of the painting, he appeared to forget the world around him, and that included her.

"Daddy?"

"Oh, hello, sweetheart. How long have you been standing there?"

Something flickered in his eyes as he stepped away from the painting as though he was awakening.

"I've been watching you," said Danielle.

The tone in her voice made Bill uneasy. She sounded so mature when she spoke and curiosity appeared to always bring out a side of her personality that was too adult for a five-year-old.

"You didn't answer my question," she said. "Why do you like that painting so much?"

He flicked his eyes up to it and smiled fondly.

"Because you see that little cherub there?" he said, pointing up to the right hand corner.

The painting was too large for Danielle to see in its entirety and she found herself reaching up on tip toes to see the cherub he spoke of. Seeing her struggle to see, Bill bent down and picked her up, cradling her carefully as he lifted her. When her eyes fell on the cherub, she immediately thought it was the cutest thing she'd ever seen with cream coloured pudgy cheeks and pink lips the same colour as the sweets her grandparents gave her. She had the strongest urge to reach up her tiny hand and touch the painting, but before she could, Bill grabbed it and cradled it inside his fingers.

"No, sweetheart. You can't touch it. It's very valuable and fragile."

She looked closer and could now see that some of the paint on the cherub's face had cracked.

"Why do you like this cherub?" she asked. "Is it because it's an angel?"

She'd heard of angels before although she didn't fully understand them. When the family's cocker spaniel, Bernie had died a few months previously, Bill had explained to her that he was in Heaven and had turned into an angel. As he explained, he'd conjured up images in her mind of the dog running through the clouds chasing tennis balls with wings sprouting out his ginger back. It was a thought that made her giggle, even if she was sad she wouldn't see him again.

"Yes, cherubs are a kind of angel," explained Bill. "But that's not why I like it. I like it so much because it looks like you."

She screwed up her face, confused, staring intently into the cherub's face.

"No, it doesn't!" she squealed. "That cherub is a boy."

Bill laughed and gently placed her back down on the ground.

"It's the face," he said "The look in his eyes. Adorable and perfect. Just like you. You know not many people know about this painting. It was painted a long time ago by a very famous man."

He knelt down in front of her and took her little hands in his.

"This man was named Caravaggio and he was one of the greatest artists that ever lived. But this painting? Well, it's a secret."

"It is?"

Danielle loved secrets. Especially the ones Bill often told her. He'd once explained how there was a fairy that lived in the woods at the bottom of their garden, but she mustn't tell a soul about it, because if she did, the fairy would cease to exist.

"Why is the painting a secret, Daddy?"

"Because it's very special. Just like you are."

"Why is it special?"

"Because it was painted as a gift for a very important lady many years ago. Almost five hundred years ago to be precise."

"Five hundred years ago!"

Danielle couldn't comprehend how long ago that was.

"Yes, a very special gift," continued Bill. "A secret gift to a secret lover. There are many clever people who know everything about art who don't even know about this painting."

"So how do you know about it, Daddy? You're not an artist."

Bill chuckled as he kissed her on the forehead.

"That's true. I'm no artist, but I have a lot of very important friends and that means I get to know about a lot of secret things. Such as this painting. I bought it because of that cherub, you know. Because the first moment I lay eyes on it I thought of you. Because you're my angel."

Danielle still couldn't figure out what he meant. She looked nothing like that little cherub with its wings and the flute held up before its pursed lips.

"One day you'll understand," said Bill. "When you have children of your own. It'll make you see beauty in all kinds of places. And nothing will be more beautiful than your own child."

He kissed her again and she wrapped her arms around his neck.

"It'll be yours some day," he told her. "There will come a time when you will be old enough to appreciate it. When you have a daughter of your own perhaps."

She looked up at it with its cracked paint shining beneath a single sun beam that flooded through the stained glass window at the top of the staircase. The painting was of no interest to her, but she liked the way her father loved both it and her, and she loved that it was special, a secret created by a clever man many years ago. It felt to her like a relic from a fairytale, and so she nodded and said, "Can I have it on the wall of my bedroom one day?"

"Of course you can, sweetheart."

Her eyes moved back up to it, studying its surface.

"But I think it could be better," she said.

"You do?" laughed Bill. "How could it possibly be better?"

"If there was a pony in it."

Bill laughed louder and picked her up again.

"But you have a real pony," he said, carrying her away from the painting. "Butternut is outside right now. How about you go see him."

Before she got a chance to answer, her nanny, Sylvia appeared in the hall and smiled politely to Bill.

"That sounds lovely," she said, having only caught the tale end of the conversation. "How about we go feed Butternut some carrots."

At the mention of Butternut, Danielle instantly forgot about the painting and set her heart on brushing his golden mane.

"Butternut!" she squealed, reaching her hands out to Sylvia. "Can we feed him sugar cubes too?"

Chapter 7

Bill

August 7th, 2023

Bill stepped out his chauffeur driven Bentley onto the pavement only to be assaulted by the bright lights of the waiting photographers. They all loomed in at him barely giving him enough room to breathe.

"Bloody hell," he said to himself. "Lucien?"

"Right here."

Lucien tried his hardest to keep close as they both jostled their way through the crowd, but he was disorientated by the constant flashing of the cameras and the barrage of questions from the reporters.

"Sir Bill? What are you hoping for today?"

"Bill, you plead guilty. Does that mean you really did defraud the government?"

"Sir? Are you still committed to giving half of your wealth away to whoever gets you out of this?" "Please!" interjected Lucien. "Let the man through."

"It's okay," said Bill, raising a hand to the reporter who'd asked the last question. "I'll answer this. In short yes, I'm still committed to the promise I made eight months ago, but hopefully it won't come down to anything so drastic."

"Does that mean you think you'll be walking out this court a free man?" chimed in another reporter.

"Oh, we can only hope," said Bill with a reassuring smile.

More reporters leaned in to fire their questions, but he didn't have the time or patience to answer them. He felt like a rugby player pushing through a scrum as he forced his way through the hordes of people. When he reached the entrance to the court house, he was already exhausted, but he refused to let his strong, controlled demeanour drop. He simply put on his best grandfatherly smile and pressed on inside the building.

The court room was packed out with reporters looking to catch a glimpse of Bill as he got sentenced. He'd rehearsed the scenario so many times in his head he felt as though he had nothing to worry about. Lucien had done a good job of making sure he hadn't been on remand for the last eight months.

Lucien looked at his client beside him and smiled to himself as he thought about the cash he had earned from this job alone. Enough to buy a nice house somewhere in the Dordogne region of France, or perhaps The Algarve.

"You look happy today," noted Bill, his voice rising over the bustling sounds of the court room.

"I'm feeling good about this."

"Me too. Community service. I can do that. Or at the very worst a few months in an open prison. It's not ideal..."

"No, of course not."

"But I can manage it."

"I'll try to negotiate that you'll be comfortable wherever you are. Make sure you're protected from the other prisoners."

"That would be appreciated."

Bill smiled to himself knowing that it was all going to be okay. He even managed to look over his shoulders and give some of the reporters a friendly wave.

It'll be over with soon enough and if luck's on my side I'll be out in time for lunch at The Ritz.

His positive mood, however, wavered when he felt the laser pointed gaze of Hawkins from across the court room. Slowly, he swivelled his head to meet her gaze.

"What's she looking so bloody happy about?" he said to Lucien out the corner of his mouth. "Why's she looking at us like that?"

"Relax, it's all mind games with her. Always has been."

Bill knew this more than anyone.

"How does it feel having her here?" asked Lucien. "What kind of stupid question is that?"

"I just mean that she put away your son-in-law and now she's trying to put you away too."

Bill didn't answer, just kept staring into Hawkins' face. She had the uncanny ability to never get her nerves rattled, and she looked as comfortable staring him down in court as she would be lounging on the beach. Slowly, she curled up the corners of her mouth and smiled at him. Bill couldn't take her eyes off her scarlet lips as she parted them to speak.

But before she could, the atmosphere in the room changed, falling silent as Judge Taylor appeared. With low, bushy grey brows, dark eyes and red, ruddy cheeks, he had the expression of an exhausted beagle who was still eager for the hunt.

He took his seat, adjusted his wig and gown and looked down to Bill. Some preliminary administrative steps began, but Bill paid little notice. He felt as though he wasn't really there, as though the whole scene around him was nothing but an inconvenience.

Lucien spoke to the judge but he didn't quite catch the exact words he said. He was too busy thinking about where he could take his next holiday. Florida maybe. It was always a destination he thought of as being a bit too touristy and cheap for him, but Sarah had been nagging him to take her there for the last couple years and he felt she deserved a nice treat.

He wondered what she was up to now with her nanny. No doubt playing without a care in the world just the way he wanted her to be. He had ensure that she'd remained oblivious to his case. She'd had enough stress in her own life and there was no sense in her worrying about losing her grandpa either.

Bill was nudged out of his thoughts by Lucien digging his elbow into his arm.

"What's Hawkins doing?"

Both men looked over as Hawkins shuffled some documents on the table in front of her, glanced over her shoulder at them then proceeded to step towards the judge. She spoke in hushed tones as she pointed her long nails at the documents. A moment later, the judge frowned and gestured for Lucien to step forward and join them.

Bill, perplexed, sensed that something was wrong and leaned forward to hear better, but all he could make out was the low murmuring of Lucien as he argued with the judge and Hawkins. He could see the expression on his face darken and his hands angrily grab at the documents in Hawkins' hand.

"You can't do this now!" Lucien bellowed. "Your Honour, you can't allow this."

There was more low murmuring and Bill looked over his shoulder. People were starting to suspect something was wrong, and Bill's stomach lurched.

"What's going on?" he said to himself, watching the scene unfold in front of him.

At last, when he felt as though their argument would never end, Lucien stepped away from the bench and stormed back to his place beside Bill.

"Shit," he raged.

"What's up?"

"Hawkins is a sly bitch is what's up. She managed to pull up some banking records about Power to the Planet."

"What records?" Bill demanded to know.

Lucien clenched his eyes shut for a second as though he was physically pained by the revelation then looked down at his files.

"The ones that show how you took funds from the government furlough scheme, funnelled them away from your business into Power to the Planet before funnelling half of the amount back out to your account in the Caymans."

Bill felt a short, sharp pain stab into his chest. He tried to suck in a deep breath but felt as though his rib cage was being strangled by a rubber band.

"No... Lucien, no! She can't just turn up with this shit now. Not today. You should have at least known about this!"

The both looked over to Hawkins who was back sitting comfortably at her table like the cat that got the cream.

"This can't be happening. I'll appeal this. I have to."

"Shhh..." hissed Lucien. "He's about to sentence you now."

"No, this can't be happening. This is bullshit and totally illegal."

Bill felt as though he was tumbling into a bad dream.

This wasn't supposed to go like this!

"Mr Lovecroft," boomed Judge Taylor's voice.

Bill looked up and saw him staring menacingly into his face. The look startled him. He had, after all, shared mutual friends with the old judge and expected a friendly face, not this glowering droopy expression.

"In light of recent developments and newly received evidence, I am sentencing you to..."

Hawkins can't do this...

Judge Taylor paused and Bill felt his stomach drop in anticipation and his breath catch ever so slightly in his chest.

"Twelve years with immediate effect with time being served in HMP Belmarsh where..."

Judge Taylor's voice faded away as Bill grew dizzy. He had to grip the table in front of him to stop himself collapsing. Suddenly, he had the simultaneous urges to both vomit and run away. Looking across at Lucien for reassurance, he saw the man he had trusted couldn't even look him in the face.

"Lucien?"

He looked down into his briefcase, his cheeks burning an even deeper shade of red. Bill became overcome with rage with the sudden urge to strangle him.

"You piece of shit. You said you'd-"

His sentence was cut short by the sensation of cuffs being clicked around his wrists. He felt a tugging sensation which he tried to resist.

"Come on, Old Bill," said the guard. "Don't make this difficult on yourself."

He had no choice but to let himself be pushed unceremoniously from the court room as the reporters all gawped. At least he was grateful there were no cameras present.

As he reached the door, he looked over his shoulder and saw Lucien staring after him apologetically, and only now did the sadness hit Bill like a tidal wave.

Twelve years. Sarah would be in her twenties when he got out. Almost the same age Danielle was when she died.

In twelve years he could be dead. He was already an old man and would be nearing eighty by the time he was released.

"No!" he declared to the guards as they lead him through the court house to a waiting van. "There's been a terrible mistake!"

"Come on, Old Boy. Stop panicking."

"No. No!"

The guards laughed at him as they gripped him tighter.

"It's only Belmarsh," one of them said. "Not a bloody war zone."

"Yeah, you're more likely to die in Belmarsh," the other guard chuckled.

A dark sense of dread fell on Bill, but as he was pushed roughly into the back of the van, he held onto one thought.

Half of everything to whoever can get me out of this.

I meant it then.

I mean it more now.

Chapter 8

Hawkins

August 8th, 2023

Lying in the bath, she breathed in the scent of the bergamot and black pepper candle she had burning at her feet. The water was so hot it was almost scalding, but it was doing nothing to soothe her tense muscles.

She couldn't stop thinking of the day before when she had stood less than ten feet away from Bill as he was sentenced, and he hadn't even had the courtesy to glance at her.

The selfish sod was so wrapped up in himself he didn't even notice me.

Not that she would have expected a friendly smile from him anyway. She was there to do a job and she'd done it bloody well.

"Twelve years," she smiled to herself as she reached for her glass of wine. "The look on his face."

She laughed as she drank, remembering the way he looked ready to have a heart attack as he heard the judge's sentence. A man couldn't have been more pale.

Placing down her glass, she lay back and watched the steam rise to the ceiling. Closing her eyes, she focussed on her breathing. She never was as good at meditating as she wished she was, but right then she needed to try more than ever to relax.

But the second she placed her attention on the rise and fall of her stomach, the doorbell rang. Ignoring it, she kept her eyes closed and once again brought her focus back to her breathing.

And once again the doorbell rang, this time with added urgency.

"Oh, for fuck's sake."

Blowing out the candle, she rose reluctantly from the bath and grabbed a large towel. As she reached the top of the stairs on the second floor of her town house, the doorbell rang for a third time.

"I'm bloody coming."

As she reached the bottom of the stairs and walked down the hallway, she could see the silhouette of her visitor in the frosted glass of her front door. Despite their features being obscured, she guessed who it was immediately by their posture.

"Dickie..." she said, opening the door as water dripped onto the hallway carpet.

"Out of your clothes already? I'm not even in the front door yet."

She sighed and tightened the towel around her.

"Are you here for business or pleasure?"

"Actually I'm here to see how you are."

She raised a sceptical eyebrow.

"Don't look at me like that. I'm allowed to care about you, you know."

She took a step back and let him inside. He kissed her gently as he entered then slipped off his shoes and coat, leaving them at the front door.

"Wine?" she offered.

"That would be nice."

He wandered into the living room and made himself at home. Sitting down on the grey, Bo Concept couch, he looked up at the tasteful decor and wondered why Hawkins hadn't followed her true calling of working in interior design. She certainly had a flare for it.

"It's nothing fancy," she said, entering the room with two clean glasses. "Just an average red."

"Sounds great."

After filling up the glasses, she disappeared out the room momentarily, returning a few seconds later in a long, flannel dressing gown and slippers in place of her towel.

Richard felt his mood dip as he saw her cover herself up. Sure, he had dropped in to check on her, but he'd be lying if he hadn't hoped for something more. His eyes fell to the soft curve of her slender neck and the slope of her collar bones.

"I know you hate it when I talk like this," he began, taking a sip of his wine. "But I worry about you."

She laughed and threw her head back.

"Why would you say that?"

"Because…"

He paused for a second as he tried to arrange his thoughts.

"Because you're alone."

"Alone, yes. Lonely, no. Besides, why would that worry you?"

He took another, longer sip of wine and pursed his lips.

"I just don't like the idea of you being alone. You know, being in this big house. Being single."

"Ah, single. The magic word."

"What's that supposed to mean?"

She smirked at him and swirled the wine around her glass, watching as it left a thin, burgundy veil draping from the rim.

"You're not worried about me. You're just worried I'll meet someone else."

She was right, and he knew it, but he said nothing. After all, he had no right to speak about her love life. His own was in the gutter.

"Ever think about coming back to work full-time?" he suddenly blurted out to change the subject.

She looked at him for a moment as though she was sure he had lost his mind.

"Come back to work full-time? Really?"

"You were the best."

"I still am."

"So why not stay top dog?"

She smiled to herself.

"Because I don't need to. I have it easy, Dickie. I do the occasional legal consulting work when I have to and charge what I like. And in the mean time I can take on cases like Lovecroft's for my own amusement when I'm not enjoying myself. Which reminds me, I have a holiday booked for Venice next week. You went with your wife last year, didn't you?"

He lowered his head at the mention of her. He never felt comfortable when she entered the conversation between him and Hawkins. She was an elephant in the room he wanted to remain firmly in the corner.

"I still think you should come back," he said. "Pick up where you left off. You must miss it, right?"

Her smile dropped and she stared down into her wine.

"Sometimes I think I do," she said. "But I don't think I can give up the freedom I have now. Don't exactly miss the long hours, the sleepless nights, the stress of it all. No, I'm happier now."

He searched her eyes for the truth. Was she really happier now? Or was she just telling herself that?

"So…" he said, taking the last gulp of his wine before placing down his empty glass. He wasn't quite sure what to say next and hoped she would pick up the conversation. She was always good at filling in the gaps, of taking the lead around people when she needed to. But right now he noticed she was remaining ominously quiet. He watched as she sipped her wine with darkness in her eyes.

"You look troubled," he noted.

"Just thinking."

"About what?"

She shook her head as though trying to free her brain from her thoughts.

"Doesn't matter."

"By the look on your face it looks like it matters a whole lot."

She sighed and closed her eyes for a second and wished she was back upstairs in her hot bath. She wondered if it was still warm.

"Can't stop thinking about the little girl, Sarah. Her mother…"

"Don't…"

"Don't what? Bring her up?"

"It's like picking at an old wound."

"Sometimes old wounds need to be picked."

Richard suddenly felt the wine wasn't sitting so well inside him. He wanted to stand up and seek the fresh air of outdoors.

"Not this one," he said, aiming for the hallway. "Anyway, I'm glad you're okay. Just… call me if you need to."

Hawkins watched as he let himself out and waited until she heard the click of the front door before she rose from the couch. Walking over to the window, she watched as Richard walked down the street without looking back at her house. Usually, he'd give her a last wave through the window, but right now he looked like a man laden with a thousand heavy thoughts.

Danielle Lovecroft... she thought to herself. *And now little Sarah.* She'd always prided herself on being hard-hearted, she had to be in her job, but even she couldn't fight her conscience or sadness when it came to Danielle. She knew too much, and so did Richard.

Chapter 9

Danielle

March 10th, 2013

The drunken teenage boy staggered down the stairs narrowly missing the stained glass window as he gulped from the champagne bottle.

"Hey! Hey Cecilia!"

From the bottom of the staircase, Danielle's sister giggled and threw her arms up, jokingly acting as though she was going to catch the boy.

"Cecilia, let me slide down this bannister," he yelled.

"Do it, Lucas!"

He threw the empty champagne bottle onto the floor and took a running jump onto the bannister, straddling it with his long, skinny legs clad in his sixth form uniform and began sliding. Except he didn't realise just how slippery his trousers were or how waxed and polished the bannister was. His body gained speed as it slid down the spiral bannister and he let out a yelp as he moved faster.

Amelia watched in horror as he slid at such a speed she was worried his trousers would catch fire. His drunken body went limp as he reached the bottom of the staircase and she lunged forward to catch him. But it was too late. His body, having gained momentum, took on a life of its own as it flew off the end of the bannister. He tried in vain to catch his balance, but too drunk to stand and dizzy from the ride down the stairs, he crashed into Cecilia, the two of them falling backwards against the wall before slumping to the floor.

"Cecilia!" came a scream from the front door.

The two teenagers looked up from the floor to see Danielle storming into the hall with her school books in her arms.

"What are you doing?" she cried. "The painting!"

Only now did Cecilia and Lucas realise their shenanigans had resulted in them crashing into the Caravaggio which was now swinging from its wall fixture. Danielle ran up to inspect the damage.

"What have you done!" she screamed.

She looked down to her sister and her boyfriend, smelled the alcohol coming from them. The light shone off something on the staircase and she looked up to see the empty bottle of champagne lying on its side.

"Did you skive school to drink again, Cecilia?"

"Shut up. Why have you got to be such a goody two shoes all the time?"

"Your fun almost wrecked my painting," yelled Danielle, pointing at it.

"You mean Daddy's painting. And we so did not almost wreck it. There's just a tiny scratch."

"A tiny scratch? It's almost three inches long."

"So? Why are you so obsessed with some dumb old painting anyway?"

Danielle, infuriated, was too angry to respond. She'd tried pointlessly so many times to explain to her sister how much she loved that painting, but she could never understand. She was far too interested in skipping school and fooling around with her friends. The arts and books were something she viewed as boring and akin to schoolwork.

"Come on, let's get out of here," laughed Lucas as he swayed from side to side.

"Yeah, let's go," agreed Cecilia, rolling her eyes at her sister.

Danielle watched as they both walked out the house, laughing all the way out the door.

"Bitch," she muttered under her breath as she turned back to the painting.

As she lightly touched her hand to the scratch on its surface, she felt her heart sink. Her father would be so angry if he noticed. Or rather, when he noticed. But as mad as she was, she knew she would never tell on her sister. They might have disliked each other and argued relentlessly, but they were still sisters.

She stood for a long while staring up at the painting, her eyes moving up to the cherub in the right hand corner. It still looked as beautiful as it had all those years ago when Bill had explained its significance to her, but she still couldn't see the resemblance to herself.

Chapter 10

Bill

August 7th, 2023

The noise of Bill's first night in Belmarsh was deafening. Before his arrival, he'd thought nights in prisons were gloomy, but at least quiet. He was now discovering this was far from the case. As soon as the cells were locked for the night and the lights turned off, it felt as though the building had been torn open like a Pandora's box of anguish.

Whether it was guilt that kept most prisoners awake, claustrophobia, anger or pure homesickness, they suffered through the dark hours howling into the shadows of their cells like caged dogs.

From down the corridor, Bill could hear the incoherent babbling of a prisoner as he banged his fists against his cell door. Further up, someone was crying, their voice echoing towards him through the stone walls. Meanwhile, to his left, another two prisoners were holding a casual, though loud, conversation amongst themselves through the wall.

"Oi, Gerry! You never guess what I got today."

"What?"

"A letter from my missus."

"Aw, mate that's great. What she say?"

"She's coming to visit next month when she's back from Marbella!"

"Marbella? What's she doin' over there?"

Bill huffed and rolled onto his side before grabbing his pillow and pulling it around his head to stifle the noise, but it was pointless.

"It's like a fucking zoo in here," he muttered to himself.

He'd found it impossible to get used to his new surroundings, and couldn't decide what he hated most. The fact the entire building smelled like a mixture of piss, sweat and cabbage, or that his toilet was merely inches from his bed.

"Urgh!"

He rolled over onto his other side and pressed the pillow harder against his ears, but it did nothing to stop the cacophony of voices around him. Clenching his eyes shut, he tried his hardest to sleep, although it was impossible. Thoughts raced through his head.

Where was Sarah now?

Did she miss him?

How much did she understand about what had happened?

Then his thoughts arrived at a more selfish place.

The money he'd offered for his freedom. He was serious about it, but were others serious too? Was there someone out there already working on getting him out?

As he lay shivering in his damp cell with the smell of the toilet stinging his nostrils, he hoped to God that was the case.

***

August 8th, 2023

Morning came and Bill opened his eyes immediately feeling a shooting pain up his spine from being curled up freezing all night. Ripping off his itchy blanket, he sat up and rubbed his eyes just as his cell door was being unlocked and opened. By the time Bill reached the door on stiff limbs, the guard was already halfway down the hall moving at speed.

"Wakey fucking wakey!" he yelled with another turn of the key.

Bill heard the murmur of annoyed men as they awoke in neighbouring cells, but he didn't think about them for long because in the distance he was noticing the pay phone. When he'd arrived he'd been given a pin number that provided him with an account through which he could make calls. The whole concept felt so antiquated to him. He'd have done anything for his IPhone that he'd taken for granted.

He wasted no time in rushing to the phone before anyone else could, and with an angry index finger he punched in Lucien's number which he knew by heart.

"Hello?" came his groggy voice.

"Lucien. Listen up. Get here as soon as you can."

"Bill?"

"Yes, it's bloody Bill. Did you hear me? Get here at once."

"I can't just turn up whenever you feel like it. You'll have to wait until visiting times."

"Fuck. Fine. Just, get here when you can."

Bill slammed the phone back down and huffed. It was only now that he felt eyes on the back of his head. Turning round, he saw people emerging out their cells for breakfast only to pause on the landing to watch him.

"You're Sir Bill, ain't ya?" came a mocking voice. "How was your first night?"

They knew fine well how his night went.

Not knowing what to say, and feeling intimidated by the numerous staring faces, Bill put his head down and said, "It was fine," before descending the stairs and joining the queue for breakfast.

Chapter 11
Fitz

August 9th, 2023

He knew he shouldn't have been there, but who could stop him? It wasn't as if he was going to hurt her, he'd never do that. He wasn't even going to talk to her. All he wanted was to catch a glimpse of his daughter for a fleeting second.

Walking up to the gates of her private prep school, he looked up and saw the CCTV cameras pointing down at the playground from the Victorian red brick mansion that had been converted into St Sellon's School for Girls. It wasn't the kind of school he would have sent Sarah to, a place where she would gain no understanding of the real world, but it was the same school Danielle and her spoiled sister had attended, and a logical choice for Bill.

Morning break time had just rolled around, but unlike other schools, there weren't hordes of children screaming and play fighting in the playground. With a population of only sixty students, and the pupils being encouraged to keep a quiet disposition, the playground was in relative silence with the girls quietly sitting at benches eating their morning snacks of croissants and orange juice.

A stern looking house mistress watched over them wordlessly. She looked like the kind of woman who didn't exist in the twenty-first century, or even the twentieth century. Fitz imagined her as a ghost of the mansion, a remnant from when it was first built when she would thrive with a cane in her hand.

His eyes scanned the playground, resting on each picnic table until he reached the third one and time stood still. There, six-year-old Sarah sat, her hair shining beneath the morning sunlight. In front of her, a chess board lay where she put the pieces in place with a tight lipped look of concentration. In front of her, a red-headed girl with a thick smattering of freckles impatiently bounced up and down in her seat anxious to start the game.

Since when did she start playing chess?

He was both proud and enthralled by the sight of her, and walked further down the length of the playground to get closer. He curled a hand around the fence post and watched her intently.

My God she looks so much like her mother.

The look on her face intensified when she made the first move on the chess board, moving her pawn only one square ahead. Then her friend leaned forward and plotted her next move.

"Can I help you?" came a cold, officious voice.

Fitz looked up to see the house mistress glowering down at him through her circular glasses. To him, she looked like an aggressive though inquisitive owl.

"No," he replied, his eyes moving back to Sarah.

"Am I going to have to phone the police?" she said, making the question sound more like a threat.

"No, sorry. I was just leaving."

He backed away from the playground as her intense gaze bore into him. It felt impossible to drag his eyes away from Sarah, but he knew he had to. With a heavy heart, he turned his back on her and walked away.

I shouldn't have come here. What did I think would happen? That she'd run smiling into my arms?

As difficult as it was, as he walked away, he tried to console himself with the fact she was at least happy and getting a good education. And with Bill's money she'd not want for anything.

He was so lost in this thought that he barely noticed the scream coming from across the road until it pierced his ears for the second time.

"Help!"

His eyes darted up in time to see a heavy set man with his red hoodie pulled up over his head as he wrestled with a young student intent on keeping his hands off her backpack.

"Get away from me!"

"Hey!" Fitz called out, diving across the road.

He didn't think twice as he lunged at the man, knocking him to the ground with a single punch that saw him fall flat on his back. Winded, he let out a sharp gasp then clutched his cheek where Fitz' knuckles had just connected.

"Oh, God thank you so much!" cried the student, taking hold of her backpack. "My laptop's in it and I'm halfway through my dissertation."

"Don't worry about it," said Fitz. "You wanna call the cops?"

The girl looked down at her attacker who was still winded and moaning with a now swollen face.

"Nah," she said. "Think he got his comeuppance. Prick. Thanks, though. If I see you around I owe you a drink."

"Don't worry about it. Better get yourself to uni."

The girl walked away still shaking and looking over her shoulder to make sure the man was still on the ground. Fitz bent down and pulled the hood back from his face to get a better look at him.

"You're a piece of shit. Robbing a girl like that in broad daylight and... Nate?"

The man looked up through his hand that covered half his face and squinted.

"Fitz?"

"What the fuck, Nate! What happened to you?"

"You nearly knocked me out is what happened. Christ, I think you just broke my cheek bone."

"I mean generally what happened to you?" asked Fitz as he took Nate's hand and pulled him to his feet. "The nick of you. You look like shit."

"Yeah, well I feel like shit."

Nate dusted himself down and ran a hand through his hair which Fitz saw was greasy and matted. He also noticed the hollows under his eyes and the way his cheekbones protruded.

"Seriously," he said to Nate. "You look terrible. When was the last time you ate?"

"I'd be eating right now if I got that bird's bag."

"Fuck sake," sighed Fitz. "Come with me. I'll get you some breakfast."

***

"I don't want you thinking I'm in the habit of rewarding arseholes who mug girls in the street," said Fitz as he sipped his coffee and watched Nate shovel a fry-up into his mouth. "Just so you know."

"Yeah, Fitz. You're a good guy. A real good guy," replied Nate, chewing. "I know that. You've always been a solid guy. Kinda surprised to see you. Thought you'd been put away."

"Well, I'm out now."

"I can see that."

"I'd heard the same thing about you, though. Heard you got sent down for armed robbery."

Nate chewed in silence for a second and mopped up his burst egg yolk with a buttery slice of white bread.

"Yeah, was away for a while. Been down on my luck ever since."

"What happened? You were always a bit nuts but you were never a scumbag. Never a -rob a girl in on her way to uni- kind of guy. Last time I saw you was what? A good few years ago now? And you were talking about marrying Sharon. She was pregnant last time I saw her."

Nate's eyes darkened and he looked down at his now empty plate before reaching for his cup of milky tea.

"She lost the baby," he said. "We split up not long after that."

"Aw... I'm sorry."

"Don't be. It's in the past."

Fitz studied him closely and saw how much he'd aged. Saw the deep lines around his eyes and mouth and the scars that dotted his grey complexion. There was no denying he'd had a rough time.

"Look, thanks for breakfast," he said. "I don't deserve it."

"No, you don't. But I can't exactly let an old mate go hungry now, can I? Besides, I really do think you got your comeuppance. That cheek of yours is swollen like an egg."

"I wasn't joking when I said you broke it."

"Think I might have broken my hand too," moaned Fitz, looking down at his swollen knuckles.

The two of them forced a cheerless laugh then looked out the window.

"Where you staying?" asked Fitz, still staring out the window as the rain began to fall.

"You know the bridge at the end of Denham Road?"

"Yeah."

"Under there."

"You're living under a bridge?"

"You make it sound like I'm a troll or something. I've got a nice tent under there."

"Jesus fucking Christ, Nate. Really? I know you said you were down on your luck but I didn't realise you were homeless."

"I have a home. It's just..."

"A tent under a bridge."

"Like I said. I'm down on my luck."

Fitz reached for his wallet, pulled out a twenty pound note and slid it across to him.

"I'm only giving you this so you don't go out and fucking rob someone, alright? This isn't charity."

"Thanks, Fitz," Nate said solemnly.

He pocketed the money without skipping a beat in case Fitz changed his mind.

"So you've got cash to spare," noted Nate.

"I didn't say that."

"You used to be rolling in it. You know, when you were at the top of your game."

"That was a long time ago now."

"Retired?"

Fitz nodded. Although he wasn't sure if retirement was the right phrase. The word conjured up images of living out the last years of your life watching the sunset feeling as though you'd accomplished everything. He felt a million miles away from that.

"I mean it," said Nate. "You were the best in the field until..."

Nate lowered his head.

"You know until the whole thing with Danielle and -"

"I know I was the best," snapped Fitz. "But don't mention her name."

Chapter 12

Danielle

December 10th, 2015

"You know I'm glad you're finally letting your hair down," shouted Cecilia over the music. "It's about time you got your nose out of a book and had some fun."

But Danielle didn't feel like she was having any fun. School had ended six months previously and she'd shifted seamlessly into university life. Although Cecilia had done the opposite and done nothing but party since she graduated with three A-levels.

"Why do I need to study? I've got money," she'd always say.

She just couldn't understand why Danielle was so obsessed with books and why, of all the subjects in the world, she wanted to study art history at Cambridge.

"You're just looking at a bunch of dusty old paintings by dead guys," she'd moaned to Danielle. "Where's the fun in that?"

But to Danielle that was fun. There was nothing she liked more than going through archives looking at old paintings.

"It's Dad's fault you're such a bore," Cecilia had said so many times.

Danielle had to admit she wasn't wrong. The very moment that tiny cherub had been pointed out to her in that Caravaggio painting, was the second she fell in love with art. Even if she didn't fully appreciate it at such a young age.

Now, in the VIP booth of the Lilywhite nightclub, Danielle coyly sipped her champagne as she watched her sister drunkenly flirt with a boy at her side. She vaguely recognised him as someone she'd seen at one of her sister's parties, but she couldn't put a name to his face. Or any of the other so-called friends that crowded around their table like vultures.

It seemed like Cecilia had a never ending supply of friends ready to have a good time at her expense, or rather, their father's expense. All Cecilia had to do was pluck a credit card out her designer purse and every kid in a three mile radius knew they were in for a good time.

It felt to Danielle as though the music was getting louder. And what was it anyway? Techno? House? She had no idea. All she did know was that she hated it.

"Come dance!" shouted Cecilia, rising from her seat as her short skirt rose up her thighs. "Come on!"

"No, I'm okay here."

"Oh, come on. Don't be lame."

"I'm fine here!"

"Urgh, fine. Suit yourself."

Danielle watched as Cecilia took the boy's hand and dragged him through the red velvet rope of the VIP lounge and out into the dance floor. Danielle couldn't think of anything worse than being squashed in between all those sweaty bodies.

Looks like a meat market.

She was so focussed on the movement of all the people writhing together hypnotically that she didn't realise one of Cecilia's male friends had sat beside her until she felt his thigh press up against hers. As she turned to him, she saw a sleazy smirk spread across his face.

"Hey," she saw him mouth over the music.

She felt something creep up her leg like a damp spider, and as she looked down she saw his sweaty hand attach itself to her thigh.

"Hey, get off."

"What's the matter?"

The guy leaned in further and drew his hand up to brush the hair from her face. Somehow the feeling of his fingers against her cheek was worse than when he'd touched her leg. She reeled back, repulsed.

"You know you're a lot prettier than your sister," he said. "Wanna come dance with me?"

She shook her head violently then squeezed herself out the booth to get away from him.

"Hey I was just being nice!" he yelled after her.

Having had enough of the busy club and everyone in it, she slipped her way through the hundreds of dancers, barging her way passed the bouncers out into the smoking area. She sucked in lungfuls of the cold night air even though she hated the smell of tobacco.

Finding a bollard at the side of the road, she took a seat and rocked her aching feet back on her heels.

This was a mistake.

I should never have come out.

"Bad night?" came a soft voice.

She couldn't be bothered with another guy hassling her, so she ignored it and stared down into the pavement, her eyes fixing on a glob of chewing gum.

"Yeah, I don't blame you for hating the place. Not my scene either. Only here because my mates dragged me here."

"My sister dragged *me* here," she replied looking up.

Only now did she see the face behind the voice. The first thing she saw were kind, chocolatey eyes set above high cheekbones. Then she saw the smile. Unlike one she'd seen on many of the cocky faces of the men inside the club, this smile was warm and friendly and asked nothing of her.

"I saw you in there," he said.

"Oh, did you?"

"Well, behind the velvet rope. You looked bored."

"I was bored. Still kinda am. I should be at home studying."

"Student?"

"Cambridge."

"Impressive. What are you studying?"

"History of art."

He raised his eyebrows and took a step towards her, but still managed to keep a respectful distance.

"Smoke?" he asked, flipping open his pack of Marlboro.

"No, thanks."

Although she had the strangest urge to take one. Never in her life had she wanted to smoke, but there was something about the look in his eyes that made her want to join him.

"You know I'm a bit of an art lover myself," he said.

"Really."

"Yeah, really."

He smiled again and she felt herself warm to him a little more, even though she didn't want to.

You didn't come here to meet a guy. Make your excuses and go home to your books.

"You don't believe me, do you?"

"Then name me three expressionists."

"Easy. Klee, Schiele and Kandinsky."

She was stunned into silence for a moment and stared at him, her mouth dropping open ever so slightly. From the main door of the club, a group of young guys spilled out yelling rowdily. She felt as though their noise was assaulting her ears.

"Okay, I believe you," she said. "You're an art lover."

"Wanna talk more about art somewhere a little more private?"

Oh, here we go.

"No, thanks. I need to find my sister and tell her I'm leaving."

"Sorry, I didn't mean to sound like a creep. It's just, I could do with sitting somewhere a bit quieter myself."

His eyes moved over the top of her head to a late night greasy spoon cafe across the road. There appeared to be no one inside except a couple old men eating chips.

"Share a pot of tea with me?" he asked.

"I can't believe I'm about to say this but... Sure. Tea would actually be nice."

"Wonderful."

He threw his cigarette butt onto the pavement and stubbed it out with his shoe.

"What's your name by the way?"

"Danielle. You?"

"Fitz," he smiled, extending a hand towards her. "It's lovely to meet you."

Chapter 13

Bll

August 10th, 2023

The visiting room was filling up with prisoners' families, and Bill couldn't hide his disgust at them all.

"Tramps. The lot of them," he said to Lucien who was sat across from him looking into his briefcase as usual.

"How have you been getting on?" asked Lucien, looking around the room.

"How do you bloody well think?"

"That good, eh?"

"Look, I'm going to put this bluntly," said Bill, leaning forward.

He couldn't take his eyes off everyone in the room and kept looking at each of them in turn as though afraid they'd pounce at any moment.

"I need out of here," he said. "And my offer still stands."

"The half of your assets to whoever can-"

"Yes, yes. I'm sticking by it."

Lucien blinked a few times like a startled pigeon.

"What's that look for?" asked Bill, annoyed.

"I'm just surprised."

"Surprised?"

"By the whole offer."

"Why?"

Lucien didn't know where to start so he slammed his briefcase shut and looked nervously around the room. He wondered how many of these people he'd defended. Or how many he'd put away.

"It's just... madness," he said. "The amount of money you're offering. *What* you're asking for. It's insanity."

"It's potential freedom."

"Ever heard of anyone doing anything like this before?"

Bill smiled wryly to himself and relaxed back in his seat.

"No one's ever existed like me before."

Lucien held his gaze for a second taking in the seriousness of Bill's tone.

"Bill," he said. "What do you want me to do?"

"Hold a press conference. Tell the world the offer still stands and it's serious."

Lucien shook his head and blinked a few more times.

"Just do it," urged Bill. "I'm paying you to do what I say."

Lucien swallowed hard as he thought about the monumental task ahead of him. There would be media outlets to contact, news stations and some journalists he'd rubbed shoulders with over the years. Then there would be the announcement.

Bill's offer was ludicrous. Illegal. Absolute madness.

"I'll do what I can," he said, standing up and grabbing his briefcase. "But I think you're nuts."

***

August 11th, 2023

Bill suffered another sleepless night and felt as though he was ageing a year for every hour he spent in Belmarsh. As he walked down to the canteen for breakfast, he smelled the greasy meat and fat from the kitchen and felt nauseous. He couldn't bear another cheap bacon sandwich and cup of watery, milky instant tea. He also couldn't stand how every time he left his cell he felt the hairs along the back of his neck rise.

He didn't belong in a place like Belmarsh and not only did he know it, so did everyone else. It appeared to him that many of the men around him were seasoned veterans of Her Majesty's Prisons and had friends they could latch onto for safety. Bill had never known a single person in his entire life to be imprisoned except for a distant uncle put away on an assault charge. He knew nothing and nobody, and as he sat choking down to his breakfast, he felt terrified.

Eyes burned the back of his head. He knew people were talking about him, sizing him up.

Just eat your food and leave.

Don't engage with any of them.

"Oi, Bill!"

He refused to turn around.

"I said Bill, you old toff! You deaf?"

Bill took a deep breath, swallowed his food and inched his head around to see who was shouting. He spotted a guy that looked to him to be little more than a child in a blue track suit which hung loosely from his slender frame. A thick, gold chain was slung around his neck which Bill noticed was covered in tattoos.

"Yeah you!" pointed the guy at him.

Shit, this is it. This is the moment you've been waiting for when some twerp decides to start on you. Make a name for himself. That's all he wants to do.

"You're on the tele!" yelled the young guy, pointing into the TV room behind the canteen. "Look!"

It was then that Bill noticed there was no malice on the guy's face, only a look of surprise mixed with something else. *Excitement?* Thought Bill. No, it was a bit more than that. *Mania?*

"Is it true?" asked the guy.

Everyone in the room was now staring at Bill. It felt like they were all part of something he wasn't.

"Don't act like you don't know what he's talking about," moaned an old man at the table beside him. "Your lawyer's all over the news. Don't tell me you ain't seen it."

A smile broke across Bill's face as he rose from his seat and strode into the TV room. Groups of people were gathered in front of it, staring up at it on the wall with their eyes wide and hungry. So enraptured by the sight of Lucien holding a press conference on the steps of his office, they barely noticed the subject of it was standing behind them.

"Look, they're showing it again," someone said. "Turn it up."

The tallest guy in the room walked over to the TV and pressed the volume button until it was so loud it crackled the speakers.

"I am standing here today to speak to you on behalf of my client, Sir Bill Lovecroft."

Bill watched as Lucien spoke nervously. He never was any good in front of the cameras. He didn't have the voice or the face for it and watching him squirm amused Bill.

"Reports have been circulating," continued Lucien. "Of a large sum of money, thirty-eight billion Great British pounds, half of Sir Bill's assets, being offered to one or more persons who are able to secure his safe release."

"Well done, you fox," muttered Bill under his breath. "Keep it sounding vaguely respectable."

"My client is aware of the unusual nature of this offer," said Lucien. "Yet that does not diminish the power of his promise to release funds to those skilled enough to secure his freedom. However, my client does not encourage any illegal activities that result in his release. We thank you in advance."

Bill watched as the crowd of reporters in front of Lucien moved forward en-mass to hurl questions at him, but he was already walking back up the steps to his office, the glass doors swinging shut behind him.

Instantly, the group of men in front of the TV burst into excited chatter.

"Thirty-eight billion! Fuck me!"

"You could go into space with that money!"

"What does he mean by secure his release?"

"You know fine well what that means? Means break him the fuck outta here."

The chatter reached a fever pitch before one by one, each of them noticed Bill standing at the back of the room. They turned to regard him with faces like starstruck teenagers.

"You really mean it?" said the nearest man to Bill. Someone he gauged to be around thirty with a thick abdomen, a barrel chest and bald head that glistened under the light. "You'll really give all that money to someone if they can bust you outta here?"

The silence in the room instantly grew oppressive as everyone waited for his answer. Eventually, with a look of pride, Bill crossed his arms across his chest and leaned back against the wall.

"I mean every word of it. Thirty-eight billion. It's for the taking."

**

August 12th, 2023

Morning rolled around again, but this time it wasn't the usual sound of the key turning in the lock that awoke Bill. It was a blaring alarm that made him feel as though his skull was splitting.

"What the bloody hell?"

He jumped out of bed with his heart hammering in his chest clapping his hands over his ears. Total disorientation flooded him. He was so overcome by the sound he felt close to losing his balance. Rushing to the door, he tried to look out through the miniscule gap to make sense of what was happening. But all he saw through the tiny slit was the rush of guards' dashing in front of him in a blur.

"What's going on?" he yelled, but his voice made no impact against the alarm.

Panicked, and feeling as though his head was bursting, he backed away and lowered himself onto his bed. Grabbing his pillow, he curled it around his head and clenched his eyes shut.

***

He had no idea how long the alarm had rung for. All he knew was that when it finally stopped, he felt like his brain had been left in a vacuum. The relief of the sudden silence was so acute he felt every muscle in his body release. Falling flat on the bed, he stared up at the ceiling and sucked in a long breath. But before he could relax properly, he heard the key turn in his cell door.

There was a shuffle of footsteps as he sat up and watched the three men enter with solemn faces. Two of the guards he recognised, but the man standing in between them he'd never lay eyes on.

"I'm Governor Corour," he announced.

"I've heard of you. Always in the habit of visiting prisoners on an individual basis?"

"Only the ones who create a cash grab so vast a literal JCB was crashed into our east wall this morning."

Corour waited for a response, but it took a moment for the realisation to hit Bill.

"A JCB?"

Corour, looking unimpressed, stepped away from Bill and pointed to his few possessions in the corner of his cell.

"You're giving me a headache," he said. "I used to like you before all this. Now every Tom, Dick and Harry is going to attempt to break into here. Get your things. You're moving."

"Moving?" replied Bill, his ears pricking up with optimism.

"Don't get your hopes up, Old Bill. You're not escaping that easily. Where you're going is maximum security."

"What... does that mean?"

"Don't play dumb. If no one can get in to grab you then you can't get out. It's as simple as that. I don't trust you among the general population."

Corour pointed to his belongings again then turned to the guards.

"See he gets there quickly," he said as he departed. "Whole situation's a clusterfuck."

Chapter 14

Hawkins

August 1th, 2023

Two days had passed since Hawkins last saw Richard. She'd been trying to keep things cool between them. She could sense he wanted more from her, so she pulled away. It was nothing personal. Richard had his uses. But it just wasn't her style to get too close to a man. Any man. She needed her freedom.

But when the sun was barely up and she heard her doorbell ring, she was surprised to find herself happy to see him, if only because he was holding breakfast in his hands.

"Brought bagels," he said. "And some coffee."

"Wow, you're here early."

"I, erm, was just passing on the way to the office. Thought I'd stop in."

He thought she looked radiant as the morning light fell across her pale cheeks. She stood at her front door in her silk pyjamas, her hair still tousled and her face bear. It was most likely a time when she felt her most vulnerable, less like herself. It was a million miles away from the sky scraper heels she usually wore and the power suits. But it was at times like this Richard found her the most beautiful, because she appeared to him more human and less like the devastatingly beautiful, yet robotic, femme fatale she was in court. He loved that side to her too. It was what attracted him to her in the first place. But this early morning softness set off small fireworks around his heart.

"Are you coming in, Dickie? Or are you just going to stand there?"

He chuckled softly and followed her into her kitchen where she pulled out two plates.

"Can't help but think you have an ulterior motive for being here," she smiled as she took a coffee from him.

"Oh, yeah? What would that be?" he grinned back, leaning towards her and squeezing her thigh.

He so badly wanted to kiss her, but before he could, she gently pushed him away laughing.

"Not that," she said. "I gathered you were here about Bill. The whole JCB into the wall thing. Thought it would have you panicking."

"Well, that's *part* of the reason I'm here. It's a shitstorm at Belmarsh. Had Corour on the phone to me yesterday blowing my ear off. As if it's got anything to do with me."

"Not anything to do with me either. It's that weasel faced lawyer, Lucien. Never trusted him. Did you see the press conference?"

"Who hasn't?" moaned Richard, biting into his bagel. "It's a joke, right? It has to be."

"Not to Bill it isn't."

"Thirty-eight billion. Thirty-eight bloody billion. He had to know this kind of thing would happen."

He put down his bagel as though the thought made him lose his appetite and wiped the back of his hand along his mouth.

"Corour was lucky this time," he said. "The gang that decided it would be a sterling idea to ram a JCB into Belmarsh were amateurs."

"Oh, I'm *so* surprised."

Richard leaned back around the table and felt for her leg again, this time not letting go.

"You're so sexy when you're sarcastic," he said, leaning in to kiss her.

He felt a rush of warmth when she kissed him back. Then felt the sensation move south. It always astounded him that he could feel this way for her after all this time. Still so excited, as though it was the first time. He kissed her hard, pushed his tongue into her mouth and moved in closer.

His hands were hungry as they explored her body beneath her pyjamas. He didn't know what was softer, the silk on the back of his hands or her breasts against his fingertips. Sinking himself into her, he relished the feel of her body and felt himself get lost in the moment.

It was his phone that sparked him out of it. He tried to ignore it and carry on kissing her, but it wouldn't stop ringing and vibrating along the kitchen counter.

"Fuck," he moaned, pulling away from her.

Answering angrily, he felt his erection disappear as he heard three words that would ruin his day.

"It's happened again."

He closed his eyes for a second in dismay and listened to the rest of the story. Then he hung up and lowered his face into his hand.

"Dickie? What's up?"

He couldn't believe the words he was about to say.

"A fucking bomb just went off outside E Block in Belmarsh."

She stared at him for a second.

"A... bomb?"

"Composition C to be precise. Detonated at Sir Bill's old block."

"The one he was in before he got moved to maximum security?"

Richard stared into space for a second before absent mindedly picking up his bagel and eating it on autopilot.

"Was anyone hurt?" asked Hawkins.

"Luckily no. Not this time."

"But there'll be a next time."

Richard nodded as he chewed.

"For thirty-eight billion, I reckon there'll be more than a few next times."

Chapter 15
Bll

August 12th, 2023

He felt himself close to throwing up as he watched the door slam shut. It felt inconceivable this cell was smaller than the last one, or that the toilet smelled worse. Looking up at the walls, he saw mould snake its way up to the ceiling and felt a draft through the bricks. With a shiver, he edged himself down towards his bed, but he felt too scared to sit on it.

The filthy thing looks infested.

"Hey!" he called out. "There's been a terrible mistake!"

There was no reply, and the silence offended him. He wasn't used to being ignored, so he shouted louder.

"HEY!"

"What?" came a hostile voice. "You've just arrived. What could possibly be wrong already?"

"There's been a mistake."

"So you said."

"Look, can I just... I need out of here."

A reply came in the form of a raucous laugh. Outside his door, he could hear heavy boots pacing up and down.

"Please, listen to me," he said. "There's been a mistake. I shouldn't really be in here as it is. But this cell?"

Bill heard the door open with a clunk and a click. Now, he could see the man behind the heavy footsteps. Standing in front of him, a guard with cropped, chestnut hair and angry eyes stood. To Bill, he looked a little too short to be a prison guard, a little unfit too, but it was his face that showed his hardness; pockmarked and scarred with deep lines.

"There's been no mistake," said the guard. "You're meant to be here, and I'm meant to be guarding you. I'm sorry it's not the Ritz, but it's where you live now."

The guard, already fed up, moved to depart the cell and Bill stepped forward to stop him.

"At least tell me your name," said Bill.

"I don't have to do that."

"No, but if you're going to be charged with spending your working day outside my door, don't you want me to know who you are?"

The guard shrugged. He didn't care either way, but he found himself replying, "If you must know, it's Terry."

"Terry... How long have you been working here?"

"I don't need to tell you that either."

Bill grit his teeth. He hated the guy, and not just because he was the one keeping him under lock and key.

"Okay.... Terry. You don't have to tell me anything but..."

He cut himself off as he decided to try a different tact.

"You don't look very happy, Terry."

Terry glared at him.

"I don't mean to offend you, of course. It's just that... Well, you strike me as someone who's worked this job for many years. It's in your blood now, isn't it?"

Terry hated the way he was being spoken to. He suddenly felt as though he was fourteen again and being chastised by his old headmaster.

"I've been here for almost twenty years," said Terry. "Bet that's longer than anytime you've spent in a job. A real job that is."

"Ah, and now we get to the crux of the matter. You despise me. Think I've not earned my money."

Terry raised his eyebrows and crossed his arms before blowing out a long exhale through his nostrils.

"No billionaires earn their money," he moaned. "You're all born with silver spoons in your bloody mouths. There's no justice in it. Now if you don't mind me, I'm goin' on a tea break."

He stepped back and grabbed the door, but before he could close it, Bill stepped towards him, hands outstretched in a gesture of friendliness.

"I understand," said Bill. "I really do. You work here for decades spending every day holed up with the worst humanity has to offer and you get a measly salary in return. If you're lucky a few hundred pounds gets flung your way as a bonus at Christmas, am I right?"

"You might be."

"And that makes you feel what? Under appreciated?"

Terry grimaced at him in response and refused to answer, but the look in his eye was all Bill needed to see to understand how he felt. To him, Terry looked like a broken and bitter man who hated his job and everyone in it. Bill could use that to his advantage.

"Enjoy your tea break," said Bill as he watched Terry close the door over.

Terry slammed the door and felt a heavy feeling form in the pit of his stomach. In all his years on the job, no one had ever appeared to understand how he felt more than Bill had in just a few words.

"Bloody well right I'm under appreciated," he said to himself as he walked down the hall towards the kettle. "But what the fuck does he care?"

Chapter 16

Fitz

August 14th, 2023

The queue for the checkout was excruciatingly slow, especially as all Fitz got was a pint of milk and some bread. He stood staring into the back of the old woman in front of him. He felt as though he'd been looking at her for so long he knew every inch of her neatly styled brown wig.

Craning his neck, he looked over her head and down the queue to see what the hold up was. It appeared an old man was berating the young checkout girl for a mix up with his lottery tickets.

Fitz sighed and pinched the bridge of his nose. To his right, a baby wailed from inside its pram. Just what he needed. He glanced over to the baby wondering why its parents weren't doing anything to quieten it down. He noticed the mother was standing behind the pram engrossed in the newspaper headlines on the stand behind her.

Picking up one of the tabloid papers, she scanned the headline then turned it open, the front page directed at Fitz. Only now did he see the object of her fascination. Bill's face stared directly at him, an iconic photograph of him that had been used time and time again in publications over the years.

Above it, the headline read - RACE TO 38 BILLION.

Fitz cringed at it while simultaneously feeling rage build up inside him. Everyone was talking about Bill and his money. All that money and it was turning Belmarsh into a circus. There hadn't been a single mention in the media about Danielle let alone Sarah.

He felt his fingers clench around his milk bottle so tight his knuckles turned white.

Where is Sarah in all of this?

"You really think someone will get their hands on all that dosh?" came a voice from behind him.

He looked over his shoulder to see a man in his fifties in a worn out bomber jacket wearing a series of gold hoops in his ears.

"Thirty bloody billion," he said. "Can you imagine that much money?"

"No... I couldn't," replied Fitz, his eyes darting back to the newspaper.

"For that amount of cash I'm tempted to break into Belmarsh myself."

Fitz laughed awkwardly and shook his head.

"The world's gone nuts."

"You saying you wouldn't be tempted by the money?"

Maybe at one point in my life, thought Fitz. *But not now. Money's meaningless if I don't have my daughter.*

"Don't give a toss," he said to the man. "Money doesn't make you happy."

The man chuckled as the queue finally began moving forwards.

"You're the one who's nuts," he said. "Of course money makes you happy."

Chapter 17

Hawkins

August 17th, 2023

"Hello, darling."

"Lizzie!"

Hawkins elegantly snaked her hips around the tables in the cosy Italian restaurant and greeted her old friend, Samantha warmly.

"It's been so long," she said, kissing her cheek and giving her a quick hug. "I've been wanting to catch up with you for so long, but one of us always seems to be busy."

"Tell me about it," said Samantha, picking up the wine list. "Since I got promoted I've barely had time to get my hair done let alone go out for lunch. By the way I was thinking about a red?"

"Really? Surely a white with pasta?"

"You're right. A white it is. Anyway, tell me everything. The whole Sir Bill Lovecroft fiasco is pure insanity!"

"Urgh, please. I can't bear to talk about him for a second longer. It's all anyone gibbers on about now."

"Are you surprised?"

A handsome young waiter with a golden tan and perfectly groomed hair appeared at the table to take their drinks order. Hawkins could immediately see by the way he looked at her and flashed a smile that he liked what he saw.

"A bottle of your best Sauternes," said Hawkins. "St Emilion?"

"Yes, we have that. I'll be right back."

He flashed another smile at Hawkins, completely ignoring Samantha and departed.

"Jesus, he was all over you," said Samantha.

"Oh, was he?"

"Don't act coy. His tongue was almost hanging out. How do you do it?"

"Do what?"

"Look so bloody attractive while being twice that boy's age?"

Hawkins shrugged and smiled as she watched him move behind the bar to get their glasses. But she wasn't thinking about him. She was looking forward to a glass of wine and a long catchup with Samantha. Men, and certainly boys, couldn't be further from her mind.

When he returned, his smile was still stretched wide across his face as he set down the glasses and pulled the cork out the wine bottle.

"Would you like to taste it?" he asked Hawkins.

The innuendo was showing heavily in his eyes.

"No, please. Just leave the bottle."

"Well, if there's anything I can get you please call me over."

"Will do."

He departed once again, looking over his shoulder to catch one last glimpse of her.

She turned her attention to the wine, taking a long sip and savouring the taste.

"Lizzie?"

"Uhuh."

"Is that your phone ringing?"

Her heart sank as she heard it. The thing never managed to stay quiet and all she wanted was a couple hours of peace.

"Wonder who it is," she said, reaching into her purse. "Oh, that's weird. It's my next door neighbour. Not spoken to them in ages ."

She answered mainly out of curiosity and heard the panicked voice of Mrs Rogers.

"I'm so dreadfully sorry to call you," she said. "But there's been an accident."

"What kind of an accident?"

"A pipe burst in my bathroom and it appears to be flooding into your house."

"You're kidding!"

"I'm so sorry. There's a plumber dealing with it right now. I really hope everything's okay on your side."

Hawkins felt her good mood dissolve as she instantly forgot about the wine.

"I'll be right there," she said, hanging up annoyed.

Samantha looked to her, worried.

"Sorry," said Hawkins. "I'll pick up the tab on the way out. And the toy boy's all yours."

***

She arrived home to find the plumber waiting for her on the doorstep.

"You must be Miss Hawkins."

"Yes, what's happened?"

"We've stopped the flood for now, but looks like a considerable amount of water got into your place I'm afraid."

She frantically fumbled for her keys and pushed open the front door. Part of her expected to see a cascade of water flowing down her stairs but was pleased to see nothing.

"Where was the burst pipe?" she asked the plumber.

"Third floor."

She rushed up to her own third floor taking two steps at a time.

"Anything?" asked the plumber breathlessly as he followed her.

"Not yet."

As she reached the third floor, she saw a large, dark patch blossoming out from the center of the wall.

"Aw, shit," she said. "This is a nightmare. Plasterwork is buggered. And I'll have to paper the wall again."

"It's not that bad," said the plumber as he emerged at the top of the stairs. "I was expecting worse."

He walked over to inspect the damage and pressed his fingers to the wall.

"A couple days with a good dehumidifier should have it sorted. I've actually got one in my van. If you want it."

Of course he'd say that, she thought. *Anything for a few extra quid.*

"Sure, thanks. I'll take it."

"Nice. I'll go grab it."

He huffed and puffed his way back down the stairs and she turned back to face the wall. She wasn't sure a dehumidifier would do the trick. Tracing her fingers across the wall, she tried to feel for how far the water damage travelled. It didn't take long to realise it was worse than she previously thought.

"Shit!" she exploded as she saw the water didn't only just spread across the wall, but also into the nearby closet fixture. She rushed to open the door.

"Please, no. No, no, no."

She felt roughly in the darkness of the cupboard for water, her fingers feeling for the shoe box she kept on the top shelf. Her body sagged with relief when she felt it was dry, but she grabbed it anyway and ripped off the lid to double check. Nestled in a pile of official documents was sat a single pen drive. It had been years since she'd last held it.

Her stomach lurched as she remembered it all.

Should have got rid of this when I had the chance.

Should have destroyed it all.

But she knew she couldn't. It gave her too much power over Richard.

Placing the box on the floor, she knelt down and pulled out the papers; transcripts from various interviews and assessments conducted over Richard's actions on that night along with the offending officer.

Danielle came into her mind again. Then she thought of Sarah.

How long can I keep all of this?

She picked up the pen drive and flipped it over in the palm of her hand. There was nothing she wanted to do less than watch the video that was on it, but she also felt the urge to.

Some old wounds need to be picked.

Walking into her bedroom, she reached for her laptop and pushed the drive into the side. A moment later, the video player launched and she was faced with a grainy CCTV image showing the back fire escape of The National Gallery.

She pressed play and watched as four riot vans and three police cars screeched into shot. The fire door flew open and three figures of Fitz' team flew down the steps only to be immediately tackled to the ground by waiting officers. Two more figures ran out the fire escape. Despite their faces being covered she knew exactly who they were and her heart hammered when she saw Danielle's figure come into view.

At the bottom of the screen, she saw the rush of the riot squad as they bolted out the vans. She also noticed the one figure that was hanging back from the rest of them. One she knew by name but had never met. One who she had pulled numerous strings for because Richard had said so.

"Dickie, how could you?"

She'd seen the recording so many times, but it never got less shocking or less painful.

The member of the riot squad continued to keep his distance, holding back from his colleagues. With his face covered by his shield, he lowered his hands inside his padded jacket. The weapon was barely visible in the degraded video, but for a split second, there was just enough light to catch a sliver of something metallic; a gun clasped between gloved fingers. It was raised up at the fire escape steps. A second later, a flash of light came from the barrel and Danielle's figure slumped forward.

Panic intensified within the scene as Fitz, in obvious distress, fell onto his lover's body.

Hawkins felt a tightening sensation in her gut as a lump formed in her throat.

Why did I have to watch this?

Outside her bedroom, heavy footsteps sounded followed by the huffing and puffing of the plumber.

"Brought up that dehumidifier!" he called out.

She slammed her laptop shut and raced out her bedroom.

"Thanks," she said. "What do I owe you?"

Chapter 18

Danielle

December 10th, 2015

"You know I've never been in one of these places before," said Danielle as she sipped her tea.

What she also wasn't saying was that she'd never drank tea that was so awful either, but she didn't want to complain. Across the table, Fitz couldn't even taste the tea because all his concentration was focussed on Danielle's face.

He'd known from the moment he'd seen her sitting behind the velvet rope of the VIP suite that she was different from all the other girls in the club, and not just because she was more beautiful than them. She had a look in her eyes that set her apart from everyone else, an expression of intelligence behind her ultra feminine features and blonde hair. He could also see she didn't want to be there.

He'd so badly wanted to climb over that velvet rope and speak to her, but he didn't dare. He saw the way other men looked at her and he didn't want to be like them. But when she'd come out the club and appeared right in front of him, he felt as though he'd been given a chance he couldn't pass up.

"You've never been somewhere like this?" he asked. "What do you mean?"

"You know. A cafe like this."

"Really?"

Now, away from the distant thump of the nightclub and the raucous voices, he could hear her accent more clearly now. It was several upmarket neighbourhoods and tens of thousands of pounds worth of elocution lessons away from his.

"Sorry, it's not that fancy, is it?" he laughed.

"Suits me fine though. It's quiet here. And they're playing It's A Wonderful Life on the TV."

He hadn't noticed until now, but as he glanced behind the counter, he noticed the waitress dabbing her eyes as she sat in front of an ancient, large-backed television watching the black and white film.

"It's one of my favourites," said Danielle. "Even if it makes me cry every time."

He could see how her slight smile dropped to reveal a misty eyed expression.

"It's one of my dad's favourites too," she said. "We watch it at Christmas every year together."

Fitz detected the sadness that now entered her eyes wasn't directed at the film, but rather at her father. He wasn't an expert in psychology, but he'd known enough people over his eventful life to be able to read people well. In his work he needed to be able to know if he could trust someone, and he'd developed a skill of deducing large amounts of information from only a few minutes in someone's company. And the last few minutes with Danielle had taught him two things. She was a sensitive soul and possibly a daddy's girl.

"You get on well with your dad?" he asked.

"Yeah," she nodded. "When he's around."

"Oh, is it complicated? I mean, I don't mean to pry but..."

"No, no. It's not complicated. It's just that he's busy a lot of the time. Travels for work a lot."

"So he's a high flyer?"

She nodded but didn't elaborate.

Fitz' eyes moved down to her soft hands where he noted the absence of the fake nails he so often saw on women, but what he did notice was a small, silver ring with an opal set in the centre. It was as modest as Danielle was, but he could tell it was worth a small fortune. All the experience in his game had taught him how to tell if something was real or not, and how much it was potentially worth at a quick glance.

"Lalique?" he asked.

"Excuse me?"

"Your ring. Is it Lalique?"

Shocked, she blinked a few times and let out a slight gasp.

"How on Earth did you know that?"

"I've handled a few."

Which was an understatement. He'd stolen precisely seventeen Lalique pieces over the course of his career. Some from museums, others from exclusive dealers. Never from someone's home. He may have been a thief, a master of the heist, but he tried to at least hold onto some morals. He robbed from companies that had proved themselves to be unethical bastards, and he never took from an individual. Sure, there were countless people he'd met over the years who had robbed grannies in the street or had busted their way into terrified families' homes to raid their antique collections, but he was a cut above that. At least, that's what he told himself.

"I can't believe you know what this is," said Danielle, clutching her ringed hand to her chest.

My God he's wonderful, she thought. *First the expressionists and now this. Who is this man?*

"I've been wearing this since I was fifteen," she said. "And never has anyone asked me about it let alone told me it was a Lalique."

She was already attracted to him, but with each passing minute, he became more magnetic. She wanted to know everything about him. What other artists he liked and what other antique jewellery he'd handled.

I swear if he impresses me one more time I might do something I regret.

Her eyes moved down to his hands, but she noticed that strangely, for someone with an eye for jewellery, he wasn't wearing anything. His wrist was even bare of a watch. In fact until now she hadn't even noticed his clothes which appeared to be modest to the point of being invisible. Dressed in black, his clothing showed no labels, no personality, nothing at all. He was a blank slate. But where this would have made other men appear boring, it only made him mysterious.

Then there was his face. Handsome and boyish he had the looks to act like an arrogant swine, but his mannerisms hinted that he couldn't be bothered.

"So..." she said, her heartbeat quickening. "You live around here?"

"Yeah, not far from here. You?"

"Kensington," she said.

"Should have guessed."

"What's that supposed to mean?"

"Sorry. I didn't mean to sound so snippy. I just meant..."

"It's okay," she laughed. "I know exactly what you meant."

They shared a smile, then Danielle glanced away as she felt her cheeks burn. She reached for her tea again but tasted it had gone cold.

"Won't your friends wonder where you are," she said.

"Maybe."

She got the impression from how he answered that although he probably had many friends, he didn't need them. He carried himself in a way only a lone wolf could.

"You still haven't told me what you do," she said. "You're an art dealer or-"

Her words were cut off by the sound of the cafe door slamming open, the bell above it ringing as the clatter of high heels entered the room.

"Danielle! Good grief what are you doing in here?"

Cecilia and her friend stood in the middle of the room looking around as though the sight of the place offended their senses. Their eyes moved from the old men still poking their greasy chips into their ketchup then over to Fitz who stared back at them deadpan.

"I've been looking everywhere for you," moaned Cecilia. "Why are you in... here?"

She turned up her nose at the waitress and made a gagging motion that humiliated Danielle.

"Just wait outside," pleaded Danielle. "I'll be out in a minute."

"The car's already here to pick us up. We're leaving now."

As Fitz looked out the window, he wondered where the taxi was, but then he realised it was no taxi arriving for the girls. Instead, a sleek black Maybach was waiting outside the club. He noticed the number plate - LVCR4FT.

For a second, his mind wandered to the author, HP Lovecraft, but then he dismissed the thought.

"Come on!" moaned Cecilia again, grabbing Danielle by her sleeve making her spill cold tea down the front of her dress.

Fitz couldn't understand how two sisters could be so different. Cecilia was everything Danielle wasn't with no manners, harsh eyes and an even harsher, demanding voice. He looked her over, scanning her clothes and saw the countless diamond rings on her fingers, so large they were an obvious statement of her wealth.

"Get off me!" cried Danielle as she rose to her feet. "I'm coming."

"Wait," interrupted Fitz.

But Cecilia was already trying to push Danielle out the door who, after a moment's struggle, managed to pull away and turn back to Fitz.

"Do I get to see you again?" he asked her.

"I hope so. I -"

"Danielle!" screamed Cecilia drunkenly. "Let's go. I'm starving. Daddy had the chef from St Luke's over tonight, remember? He made us both our favourite."

"Yeah, don't want to piss off Daddy when he went to the effort of hiring *the* chef Loudard from St Lukes," chuckled Cecilia's friend. "Gotta keep Sir Bill happy."

Sir Bill? Thought Fitz. His eyes darted back to the registration plate on the Maybach and it clicked into place.

"Sir Bill Lovecroft is your dad?" he asked.

Danielle blushed and gave a shrug. Meanwhile, Cecilia just stared through Fitz as though he was barely human. Danielle knew exactly what she was thinking. Fitz didn't fit her narrow requirements of what made an attractive man.

He wasn't white.

He clearly didn't go to private school.

And he'd taken her little sister into a greasy cafe for cheap tea.

"Come on," ordered Cecilia.

Danielle dug her heels in and shook her head.

"Actually, I'd like to stay."

The look that shot out of Cecilia's eyes froze Danielle to the spot.

"If you don't leave right now I'm telling Daddy you ran away with some boy from a council estate."

"Why have you got to be such a bitch?" muttered Danielle under her breath. "I'm not doing anything wrong. And I'm an adult."

"Only just."

Danielle couldn't understand why her sister couldn't let her have her fun, or why she'd even dragged her to the club in the first place knowing fine well she'd hate it.

"Fine, I'm on my way," she sighed, following Cecilia outside.

She turned and gave Fitz an apologetic look as she departed.

Outside, Cecilia climbed into the car with her friend jumping on top of her. They started kissing immediately leaving Danielle to sit beside them staring at them in disgust.

"You humiliated me in there," she said to Cecilia. "That guy was lovely you know."

"You're kidding," laughed Cecilia as she pushed her friend off her. "He sounded like a total Jeremy Kyle case."

"You're an outrageous snob, you know that?"

"And you're naive. He was probably just after your money. No doubt saw you in the VIP lounge and thought he'd take advantage. I was just looking out for you."

"Why does it not feel that way?"

She couldn't remember the last time Cecilia had her best interests at heart, but as the car pulled out into the late night traffic, Danielle stared out the window and wondered if she was right. Was he really after her for her money? He had noticed the Lalique ring after all.

No, she thought. *He wasn't like that.*

He was genuinely interested in her. She could tell. She'd never had a man talk to her like that before. In a way that made her stomach flip.

Still staring out the window she shivered and absent mindedly reached her hands into her coat pockets for warmth. Something crinkled against the tips of her fingers and she pulled the contents out her pocket to see what it was.

To her confusion, an empty sugar packet sat between her fingers. Scrawled in biro along the torn front read – *Same place, same time next week?*

How did he manage that?

Years of experience as a child had taught Fitz how to enter someone's pocket without them noticing. It was a skill he hadn't used in a long while. It was also the first time he had placed something *inside* someone's pocket. But Danielle had no way of knowing that, so she held the sugar packet in her hand and smiled to herself.

Same time next week. It felt like forever away.

Chapter 19
Bill

August 20th, 2023

"Is it true?" Bill asked Terry. "That guards smuggle things into prison if the pay's worth it?"

Terry sipped his tea and raised a single eyebrow. Over the course of the last few days, he had begun to find his new prisoner more tolerable to the point where he found himself hanging around his cell more often than was expected. He'd even taken his tea break with Bill today. He wouldn't go as far as to say he liked the old man, but there was a feeling of mutual respect growing between them. And Terry found himself being charmed by the many stories Bill had to offer. His life had been full of adventure, splendour and achievement mixed with a touch of celebrity gossip that Terry found entertaining enough to repeat down the pub to his drinking buddies.

"He once had a threesome with these two supermodels back in the seventies," he'd told his mates. "In the Bahamas. The old geezer's done it all."

In return for these titbits of gossip, his friends bestowed on him a sense of esteem and a little ego boost. It was something that kept him coming back into Bill's cell.

"Bill, what you doing talking about smuggling in shit? What could you possibly want? I mean, besides your freedom."

"A phone," lamented Bill. "This payphone fiasco. Can't handle it. I need regular contact with my lawyer and my grand-daughter."

"Well, that's not something I can get you. If I get caught bringing you in a phone. Jesus... I'll get fired."

"Would you really?"

Terry thought about the consequences. There had been dozens of guards over the years who had brought in a vast array of contraband ranging from pornography and drugs to venison sausages. Whatever prisoners missed the most from home. But Terry hadn't been one of those guards; people he thought were corrupt and to be treated with contempt. After all, weren't they supposed to be the ones upholding the law not breaking it?

But I've been serving this prison and obeying the law for almost two decades and where has that got me? Single, piss poor and miserable with nothing but a beer belly.

"I can make it worth your while," said Bill. "I'll give you ten grand."

"Fuck off."

"I'm serious. Ten thousand pounds for an IPhone. That's half your yearly salary probably."

Terry knew he was right. Ten thousand pounds was an exorbitant amount of money and all he would have to do was bring in a phone. He wondered if he could push for a little more.

"Make it fifteen grand and we got a deal."

"Fine," said Bill without hesitation. "Fifteen it is."

***

August 21st, 2023

The next morning, Terry looked over his shoulder, saw the camera across the hall from Bill's cell was directed away from him and proceeded to pull out the box hidden in his over sized jacket.

"You delivered," beamed Bill when he saw it.

"When do I get the money?"

"When I call my lawyer. I'll make sure you get it. Don't you worry. You've been very good to me, Terry. I appreciate it."

He smiled warmly at the guard, the bond between them growing. From down the hall came the sound of a commotion followed by Terry's superior shouting for him.

"Don't tell a soul, Bill," he said as he walked out the cell.

"Don't worry, Terry. Who would I possibly tell?"

Bill waited until the door was once again locked and Terry was long gone before he cracked open the box and began setting up the phone. A long sheet of paper was inside the box, phone credit for the amount of fifty pounds.

"What the bloody hell is this?" he moaned.

He'd never encountered anything so annoying.

It felt to Bill as though it took an age to set up but after it was charged and good to go, he tapped out Lucien's number and waited.

"Lucien speaking."

"It's Bill."

"How are you calling me?"

"Doesn't matter. What matters is that I can speak to you when I want now."

"Oh... That's great, Bill," lied Lucien.

Bill was a handful at the best of times, and him having been in prison had finally given Lucien some breathing space.

"Tell me everything," demanded Bill in a hushed voice.

"Where do I start? I get about a hundred calls an hour from lunatics wondering how they can get their hands on your cash."

"Some of them must be serious."

"Yeah, serious criminals. Guy from Belarus called me this morning. Said he'd negotiate the exchange of a nuclear warhead in exchange for breaking you out."

"And?"

"And what, Bill? What the bloody fucking hell do I do with a nuclear warhead?"

Lucien sighed. From the other end of the line, Bill could hear the constant ringing of phones in the background of his office.

"I've got to ask," said Bill. "Fitz. Has he come forward?"

"You mean... Danielle's..."

"Yes."

"Strangely... No. He hasn't called."

"Are you sure?"

"Positive? I would have remembered."

This sent Bill's mind whirring.

"I'd have thought Fitz would be one of the first people to attempt to make a deal with you," said Lucien.

"Me too."

Bill sat back on his bed, pressing his back against the cold, brick wall and stared up at the ceiling. His mind was still racing. He was the best at always being a step ahead of everyone else, but Fitz wasn't like everyone else. There was always hostility between them, but one thing Bill couldn't hold against Fitz was that he was simple. He was a dark horse who kept his thoughts and intentions guarded. Many men in his position were easily predictable and often the victim of only four vices; sex, power, money and drugs. Or all of them at once. But Fitz wasn't motivated by those things. There was always something else going on in his mind. Something that Bill could never figure out.

As he sat there, his eyes fixed on a single moth that fluttered its wings against the bare light bulb, one thought came to mind.

Of course he hasn't come forward for the money. It's not cash he wants.

"Bill, you there?"

"Yes. Sorry, was just lost in thought there."

"You're thinking about Fitz."

"I despise him. Hate him. Wanted him dead along with Danielle but..."

"He's the best at his job."

Bill, still looking at the moth, nodded to himself.

He was always the best.

"Think he can get you out?"

"I know he can."

"But if he's not interested in the money..."

"Perhaps not the money but..."

He was drifting away in thought again, the gears in his brain crunching away at the options.

"Lucien I want you to go pay him a visit."

"And say what?"

"I'll tell you what to say. Just go as soon as you can. Oh, and one last thing. Send a cheque for me. To a man named Terry Chapman."

Chapter 20
Fitz

August 21st, 2023

He felt the cramp set in as he reached the steps at the bottom of his flat. Looking at his phone, he saw he'd run ten kilometres in just under forty-eight minutes. His best time yet, but he was suffering for it. A rising nausea moved inside him as he felt for his keys and walked up the last few steps to the landing.

As he looked up, the first thing he saw was a tailored Savile Row suit. The second was a face he instantly recognised and disliked.

"Hello, Fitz. I'm-"

"I know who you are. Old Bill's lawyer."

Lucien extended a hand to shake, but Fitz ignored it and pushed the key in his front door.

"Don't know what you're doing here."

"I'd like to have a word with you."

"I don't have anything to say to you."

He walked into his hallway as Lucien stepped in behind him to follow

"Please," he said, his foot already in the door. "Just five minutes."

"No."

"You don't have five minutes to talk about the deal of a lifetime?"

"Any deal you have is one I'm not interested in."

But Lucien wasn't put off by his refusal and strode inside to Fitz' annoyance. He sneered as he looked around at the cheap decor. Reaching the living room, he stood awkwardly in front of the fireplace, his eyes moving over to the framed photograph of Sarah and Danielle.

"A beautiful picture," he said, picking it up.

"Put it back."

"Of course... Look, I'll make this quick. Time is valuable. Especially for Bill."

Fitz grabbed the picture and immediately wiped his shirt sleeve against the glass to erase Julien's fingerprints.

"Bill's time is valuable? You're having a laugh. He's got plenty of it now he's in the slammer."

"He's an old man. Doesn't want to spend his last years in Belmarsh."

Lucien could feel the tension in the air, could almost smell the anger coming off Fitz. He knew he only had precious seconds before he was tossed out the flat onto his arse.

"Bill wants to make you a deal," hit out Lucien.

"Let me guess, some bullshit about thirty-eight billion."

Once again, Lucien looked around the room and thought the place was depressing. He wondered what a man like Fitz would even do with thirty-eight billion pounds.

"Bill needs your help."

Fitz raised a single eyebrow mockingly in Lucien's direction.

"My help?" laughed Fitz. "What the fuck could I do for him?"

"Don't play dumb. You know what you're capable of."

"What's that supposed to mean?"

Lucien walked over to the nearby armchair and gestured down towards it.

"May I?"

"Suppose. If you have to."

He took a seat to show he wasn't planning on leaving anytime soon. Awkwardly, he crossed one leg over the other and looked up at Fitz who was still standing beside the mantel piece as though he was guarding the picture of Danielle and Sarah.

"Look, I'll shoot straight, Fitz. Bill knows what a talented man you were. Still are, I'd imagine."

Fitz said nothing for a moment, and the curling of his top lip couldn't hide the fact he hated the man in front of him.

"I don't need your flattery," he told Lucien. "Just get on with it."

"Fine. Bill wants out of jail."

"I'm aware of that."

"And he *needs* you."

Fitz let out a snort then leaned his head back to laugh mockingly.

"It's no laughing matter," said Lucien. "He really needs you."

"But I don't need him. And I sure as shit don't need his money."

"He knows that. That's why he's wanting to give you something worth more than cash."

Fitz frowned as he watched Lucien's twinkling eyes.

"Sarah," he said, his eyes flicking up to the framed picture behind Fitz. "He'll give you custody of her, no questions asked."

A squeezing sensation gripped hold of Fitz' stomach. Sarah was all he ever wanted, but he was reluctant to jump at the offer. He didn't trust Bill, and he definitely didn't trust Lucien. The offer sounded too good to be true.

"Can't help but see the scepticism in your eyes," noted Lucien.

"Is that really what Bill said? That I'd get my Sarah?"

"It is."

Fitz' mind raced. He had too many questions and there were to many warning bells ringing at the back of his mind.

"How exactly would it work?" he asked Lucien. "I'm just one man. How am I supposed to bust out Bill?"

Lucien smiled smugly and leaned back in his seat.

"But you're not just one man, Fitz."

He paused to prolong Fitz' curiosity then made a dramatic gesture of inspecting his finger nails.

"I have people," said Lucien, lowering his hand. "As you can imagine over the span of my career I've represented a vast array of, how do I put it, talented hoodlums."

Fitz glared at him.

"So what?"

"So, I can provide you with a team."

"A team?"

"That's right. A team of the best."

"What, so you're going to just give me a rag tag group of cons for me to project manage?"

Lucien laughed.

"That's exactly it."

Fitz shook his head. If he thought the offer was stupid before, he thought it was ridiculous now.

"Get the fuck out," he ordered.

Lucien blinked at him, bewildered.

"I mean it. Get out."

Lucien kept blinking at him.

"What about Sarah?"

"You think this is going to work? That I'll get Bill out and not get caught? And I'll do it with a bunch of people I don't even know? If they were represented by you then I sure as shit don't want near them. And you think after it's all over that Bill will just hand over Sarah?"

He clicked his fingers for emphasis.

"You must think I button up the fucking back."

Lucien was still staring at him, surprised. This was more difficult than he had anticipated.

Why wouldn't he jump at the chance to get his daughter back?

But in Fitz' mind, he couldn't see how any of it could go right. And all he could think was that Bill was dangling an impossible to reach carrot in front of him from an infinitely long stick.

"I have to say," said Lucien, rising from his seat. "That I think you're making a mistake."

Fitz showed him out the room, down the hall and opened the door.

"I've made a lot of mistakes, but this isn't one of them. Now go."

Lucien shook his head and walked out into the stairwell.

"You'll be in touch," he said as he walked away. "I know you will."

Fitz slammed the door shut in response and walked back into the living room still shaking his head in disbelief.

***

Fitz was in a deep but restless sleep. He tossed and turned, sweating profusely as he dreamed the same dream. In his mind he saw Danielle in front of him, felt her lifeless body in his arms and saw the blood spill from her body. He heard himself screaming, but then he realised the sound wasn't coming from his dream, but from his own mouth as he awoke and sat upright in bed.

He held a hand over his mouth to stop the noise, then sat for a moment shaking as the sweat cooled on his body. His heart was beating so hard he felt ready to pass out. Scrambling to the bottom of the bed, he leaned over and opened the window to feel the cold night air. Outside, traffic whooshed by like the waves of a calm sea.

But he still couldn't calm down. Climbing out of bed, he tried to move to burn off the adrenaline in his body. Walking into the living room, he paced from one end to the other as he tried to rid the memory of Danielle's death from his mind. Out the corner of his eye, he saw her photograph. Picking it up, he stared into her face, then drew his eyes to Sarah's face.

Tears burned his eyes as they fell onto the glass.

I want you back so much, he thought. *Both of you.*

His mind drifted back to the earlier conversation with Lucien, and he tried to make sense of the ridiculous offer. He couldn't believe for a single second it could work. And even if he did get Bill out of Belmarsh, how could he guarantee he wouldn't get arrested and be put away himself? And how could he say for certain that Bill would really let him have Sarah?

He sniffed and wiped his tears away with the back of his hand. And it was then that a voice entered his head. He wasn't sure if he was going crazy and imagining it, if it was really there, or if it was simply his own mind telling him what he needed to hear. But it was crystal clear.

Surely it's worth the risk to get Sarah. What have you got to lose?

He moved impulsively back into the bedroom where he picked up his phone. The number for Lucien's office was easy to find online, and despite the time of night, he dialled the number impatiently.

He expected to reach voicemail, so was surprised when one of Lucien's assistants answered with a yawn.

"Office of Lucien…"

"Is he there?"

"Erm… No, he's at-"

"Give me his mobile number."

"I can't I have to-"

"He's expecting me."

"Oh..."

The assistant paused for a second nervously, then began reciting Lucien's mobile number.

Fitz hung up in a hurry and dialled it. Lucien answered on the first ring. In the background, Fitz could hear the sound of lounge jazz playing along with soft laughter and the clinking of glasses.

"Knew you'd come around," said Lucien, his voice jovial from his last few hours drinking.

"I'll do it," said Fitz. "For Sarah."

Chapter 21
Billie Brandt

August 23rd, 2023

"Hello, hello, Billie Brigade! Thanks for tuning into my live stream. Today we have possibly one of my most daring challenges as requested by follower Unicorn-eighty-nine. So thank you. Your wish is my command."

Twenty-one year old Billie pushed her way through the crowd outside the town hall used for the latest Labour Party Conference. Not only was she years younger than most the people around her but she appeared even younger. In her pigtails and duffel coat, she could have been mistaken for a child and she played up on her appearance, making sure to not wear any make-up and to giggle and look demure when everyone looked her way.

In her hand, her phone was held out as though she was taking pictures of the event, when in reality she was recording herself for the one million followers she had amassed on YouTube.

When she'd first started her channel during the first year of her journalism degree, she saw it as nothing but a bit of fun. She had been a well-behaved child and attended a private girls' school that taught her to put her head down and study. And her parents had ruled over her with an iron fist. Especially her father, a history professor who had drilled into her mind that life revolved around academia.

But she'd wanted more than that, and although she excelled in her schoolwork, she always had a sense that there was more out there for her. And so her channel, Billie's Adventures was born. At first her videos were nothing more than short clips of her breaking into abandoned buildings around London. But as her followers grew so did her confidence and soon she found herself taking on greater challenges and realised her skill of blagging and breaking her way into forbidden territory could have a positive effect.

She'd protested on behalf of PETA at the BAFTAs the year previously. Lying her way onto the red carpet under the pretence of being a young, up and coming actress. Once the first reporter had lunged her way with a microphone, she pulled out a bottle of fake blood from her purse and poured it over her head in front of the cameras.

"Fur is murder!" she screamed as the security dragged her away.

She gained fifty thousand followers that night. And even though many of them didn't agree with her sentiment or supported PETA, they admired her confidence and chaotic energy.

Her next stunt involved her following a local Conservative councillor as he walked down a high street in an attempt to meet members of his constituency like a man of the people. Billie took the opportunity to follow him step for step with a saxophone she had no idea how to play. Each time he opened his mouth to speak, she would blast the loudest bum note her breath could manage until he gave up and left, escorted away in his blacked out Mercedes. That day, almost a hundred thousand people would find themselves clicking the subscribe button on her channel.

Today, she stood outside the town hall ready to begin the greatest challenge of her online career. She should have been nervous, but she wasn't. Instead she was excited and supported by her followers. As she looked into the corner of her screen, watching the view count rise with each second, she felt a rush of joy.

"I'm standing here outside Holystone Halls," she began. "At the Labour Party conference many of you have spoken about."

Despite her stunts, she didn't care much for politics. If anything, she held a nihilistic view where she despised all politicians no matter what party they belonged to. She was an agent of anarchy, and wanted to do nothing more than create a huge sense of disarray while being the centre of attention.

She beamed as she moved backwards through the crowd towards the entrance to the building, filming as she walked. Around her neck, a crudely faked press pass had been created for her by one of her followers. She looked down at it and wondered if it would fool the security at the door.

"Okay, I'm just making my way in," she told her fans. "Well, hopefully anyway. What do you guys think? Is the fake pass going to cut it?"

Immediately, a flurry of comments fell down the side of her screen.

Hurry up and get in there!

The pass looks great!

That meathead on the door would fall for a Mars Bar wrapper. Don't stress.

She took a deep breath, lowered her phone slightly to not look so conspicuous, then walked up to the security. As she lifted her press pass, her heart hammered and her mouth turned dry with excitement.

There's no way he'll fall for this.

To her surprise, he barely even looked and simply nodded her through with a dismissive gesture of his hand.

Her mouth opened into a wide O as she took the opportunity to dash into the main hall then through to the venue that was already packing out with reporters and photographers. A television crew were mere inches from the stage where tables were set up with extended microphones.

Billie lifted up her phone to show the view behind her as she grinned to her viewers that were multiplying by the second.

"I'm in!" she declared.

She looked around her for signs she was being noticed, but everyone appeared too occupied in their own endeavours. Poking out her bony elbows she jostled her way to the front of the audience, always looking over her shoulder to see if security had clocked who she was.

This is too easy.

She kept moving, aware she was getting on people's nerves as she pushed through the crowd. As she took her seat in front of the stage, her stomach finally churned with nerves. She was sure that at any moment someone would come along and tell her to move, or that she was in their seat. But as she looked around, she felt as though the entire room was in chaos with each reporter for themselves.

Looking to her left, she noticed several members of parliament she recognised from the news and winked to her followers.

"Look who's behind me," she said, pointing her thumb behind her making sure to get a view of both her face and the older gentleman in the tweed suit a few seats away.

"Anyone remember when he was caught by The Daily Mirror for having an affair with his nanny?" she said softly, making sure no one beside her could hear.

Her followers responded with a barrage of emojis and insults directed at him.

The energy in the room changed as people started walking out on stage, and as she looked to the back of the room, she saw the security were now closing in behind the crowd. She eyed each of them up in turn. All of them were men at least ten years older than her and four times her size.

Shit, one of them could take me out with his pinky finger.

But she held her resolve. She was here now, hundreds of thousands of people were watching her and she'd never given up on anything in her entire life.

Silence descended over the room as Labour MPs took their seats on the stage and the reporters leaned in with anticipation. Meanwhile, Billie held her phone as discretely as possible at an angle so her audience could see both her face and part of the stage. She didn't want to admit it, not even to herself, but there was a rumbling feeling in her gut that told her she was out of her depth.

Ahead of her, her main target walked onto the stage, but instead of taking a seat at the line of tables with his peers, he walked up to the podium with a sense of entitlement pulling up his nose.

"Alan Strasburg," she whispered into her phone as she kept one eye on him and the other on her phone screen. "That's our man."

Her followers' comments immediately caught fire down the side of her screen.

Crooked bastard.

You know he embezzled funds that were meant to go to children's lunch funds.

He shagged his nanny too I'm sure.

Do your thing Billie!

Billie wasn't sure what her *thing* would be until she arrived. She had a vague plan to cause chaos, to scream and shout and storm the stage. She'd even had a plan at one point to cover Strasburg in a bucket of slime, but the logistics of that were too complicated. All she had managed to bring with her was a can of whipped cream which she now held in the inside pocket of her coat. She felt it press against her breast and thought it was pathetic.

I need to do something better.

Something the followers will really go nuts for.

And then it struck her.

An idea she never thought she would stoop so low to have, but it clicked in her head and her mind was set.

As Strasburg opened his mouth and grinned like a wolf out over the audience, she took one glance behind her at the security and knew she only had a few seconds to act. Her stomach churned more and she began to sweat.

It's now or never.

Looking into her phone, she winked to her followers and gave them a thumbs up.

"Here it goes," she said.

Her hands worked quicker than her brain as her fingers moved to first unzip her coat, then her shirt. She suddenly jumped up like she'd been electrocuted and ran at the stage. Strasburg's eyes caught hers as she ran at speed, lifting her shirt up over her head and throwing it to the ground.

The security immediately fell into a panic and rushed forwards, but they weren't quick enough, and by the time they reached the bottom of the stage steps, she was already unclipping the back of her bra and swinging it around her head. An aghast rabble of outrage rippled around the room as she flashed her bare breasts at Strasburg. His face moved through a series of emotions from shock, to disgust to something akin to desire.

"That's that brat of YouTube!" someone from the audience yelled.

The cameras closed in on her, almost blocking the security guards as they ran at her. One of them pulled off his jacket and threw it at her, wrapping it around her shoulders as he lifted her like a ragdoll.

"Strasburg stole food out of children's mouths!" she screamed as the room erupted into pandemonium. "Bastard!"

***

The excitement had worn off and now Billie was sat in a cold, airless interview room with the security guard's jacket still draped around her.

"Hello again, Billie," came a voice as the door opened.

She looked up to see Lucien arrive with his briefcase and his usual smug smirk.

"Hey, Luce."

"Must you always call me that?"

She didn't reply and stared into the centre of the table. There were two overriding thoughts eclipsing her mind.

My parents are going to kill me.

And

I wonder how many new followers I've got.

Lucien sat down and opened his briefcase with ceremony.

"Getting your tits out," he sighed, shaking his head. "At least you've got a nice pair."

Her cheeks reddened as she stared at him.

"Don't look at me like that. Everyone's seen them by now. Daddy's not going to be so chuffed, is he?"

"He'll probably never speak to me again," she said to herself.

Lucien watched her sorry face and tapped his fingers on the table.

"Was it worth it?" he asked her.

"I don't know."

"The last few raps I've got you out of were nothing but scrapes, but this? Well, it's not good, is it?"

"No."

"Regret it?"

"A little."

He smiled as he watched the misery spread across her features. He knew there was a way to exploit it.

"Look, it's okay," he said, trying his hardest to put on a reassuring, fatherly voice. "I'll get you out of this. Or at least make sure you get nothing more than a few hours community service at the most."

"You really think you can do that?"

"Absolutely," he said, shooting her a slimy smile. "But you'll have to do something for me first."

Panic spread through her.

"Oh, no. You sleazy weirdo, don't tell me you want me to fuck you and-"

"Calm down, Billie. I'm not asking you to do that. You're not my type. No offence."

"None taken," she sighed with relief. "So what have I got to do?"

"I can tell you later. Just know that it could make you very rich. And your YouTube channel? Let's just say it's going to explode."

Chapter 22

Bll

August 24th, 2023

Bill felt a sharp pain pierce his head as the siren woke him.

"Aaaaargh!"

He pulled his pillow around his head and curled up into a ball.

He couldn't hear it, but he could sense panic in the building, could almost smell it. There were vibrations rumbling through the walls as he felt dozens of pairs of feet running down the corridors.

He curled himself up even tighter. As he clenched his eyes closed, the siren eventually stopped and he found himself lying with silence ringing in his ears.

***

He didn't know how long he had slept for, only that when he awoke for the second time that morning, the sun was shining through his window. It made the sensation of being trapped in his cell all the more painful. As he rose and walked to the window, he looked out towards the yard and saw sunshine on the sparse patches of grass. He longed to be outside more than ever.

In an attempt to not think about it, he pulled out his phone and began reading the news. It was something that normally soothed him and made him feel connected to the world, but as he saw the headlines, all he could do was laugh.

Trust fund kids attempt Belmarsh break in - one headline screamed.

Private school alumni attempt daring raid of Belmarsh dressed as laundry workers – read another.

"Bloody hell," chuckled Bill.

He was so engrossed in the news he didn't hear Terry open his door until he felt the draft from the corridor. He turned round to see Terry's haggard expression as though he hadn't slept in days.

"You look like shit," said Bill.

"Yeah, you would too if you were dealing with the shitstorm that just took place. *Your* shitstorm, may I add."

He saw Bill's screen and noticed the news article.

"So you know what happened."

"Was it really like that?"

"Yeah, buncha rich brats thought it would be really fucking fantastic to dress up as laundry staff and blag their way in here. They did as well. Only got caught when they reached the staircase at the end of this corridor."

"Where were they schooled?" asked Bill.

"Why does that matter?"

"Just tell me."

"Harrow, I heard. Don't know why they bothered. It's not like they need the money."

"Anyone can desire the money I'm offering," grinned Bill.

Terry let out a yawn and walked over to the window.

"Nice day, ain't it?"

"Don't remind me."

"Ah, it'll be alright. In the late afternoon the sun comes in this way and you'll get a nice little sunbeam on your bed."

"Woop de doo. I could be in Casablanca by dinner time if those kids got a few feet further."

Terry shot him a glacial look over his shoulder.

"It's the sunbeam or nothing."

"Yes... Sorry," said Bill, trying to stay in Terry's favour.

Terry looked into his eyes and saw a genuine look of melancholy.

"I've been thinking," said Terry. "I'm aware you don't have a lot to do in here."

"Understatement of the bloody century."

"Yeah, well, anyway, I've been thinking. There's been a flurry of funding in here. Some new art class has been set up for some of the worst of you lot."

"You think I'm one of the worst?"

"I didn't say that. I'm just saying, perhaps you might benefit from something a little more entertaining than your phone and the window. I'll put a word in for you. Especially as you've been under your best behaviour. And of course you've been kind to me Bill. Really kind."

Bill thought of the prospect of an art class and felt his spirit lift a little.

"That would be really nice, Terry. I'd appreciate that."

Chapter 23

Richard

August 24th, 2023

"Richard? Richard!"

The commissioner entered his house and leaned against the bannister at the foot of the staircase. He looked up wearily towards the shrieking voice of his wife.

A moment later came her thundering footsteps across the landing. She appeared at the top of the stairs in mismatching pyjamas with her arms crossed over her chest. There were dark half-moons beneath her eyes and her previously blonde shimmering hair now had the consistency of straw.

"Where have you been?" she demanded to know.

"In the office."

"Really, Richard? It's almost one in the morning!"

"Yes, I've been working late."

He moved to take off his coat and hang it on the stand beside the front door. He felt her eyes burn into the back of his head as he walked.

"Don't give me your shit," she spat down the stairs. "You must think I'm an idiot. I know what you're up to."

"I wasn't up to anything. I was in the office."

And perhaps for possibly the first time, that was true. He'd been lumbered with a mountain of paperwork and had to issue a bollocking to the officers tasked with keeping an eye on the Labour conference that afternoon. He'd watched the TV in his office in amusement as a young student in pigtails rushed a gawping Alan Strasburg with her breasts swinging.

"Richard, I don't believe you for a fucking second," said Sandra.

The anger had dissolved from her voice but it had been replaced with a tired sadness.

"Sandra... Please, I'm exhausted. I've had a long day. Whatever's in your head, we can talk about it tomorrow."

"But I want to talk about it now," she said, her bottom lip quivering.

Richard hated to see her like this, even though he knew it was his own fault. He yearned to hold her and made an attempt to climb the first step, but she reached out a pointed finger at him and narrowed her eyes.

"Don't," she said. "Don't come a step closer. I can't bear to... to smell her on you again."

"How many times have I got to tell you? I've been in the office."

She searched his eyes for the truth and realised that she saw it. But she hadn't on other nights, she was sure of that.

"Richard, I know there's someone else," she said.

"But-"

"Don't try to deny it."

He lowered his head.

"I just know," she continued. "It's obvious."

Once again, he tried to climb the stairs, but her icy gaze froze him to the third step.

"You're not staying here tonight," she said. "I can't bear to have you near me."

***

Richard stood outside Hawkin's front door and looked at his watch. It was nearing two in the morning and the rain was falling sideways. He shivered and looked up at her bedroom window where he noticed a light still shone.

With a nervous hand, he reached up towards the doorbell and wondered if he should press it. But as the rain picked up and he felt a cold blast of wind, he felt it was better than going back to the office. He heard the bell ring from inside the house followed by the creak of the stairs. A few moments later, the door opened.

Hawkins appeared in front of him, calm and beautiful as always, her hair backlit by the glow of the hallway light.

"Hello, Lizzie."

"Dickie. What on... What on earth are you doing here? Look at the state of you. You're soaking."

She studied the look on his face for a moment then realised.

"She's finally done it, hasn't she?"

He bowed his head.

"Kicked you out, has she?"

"Not quite."

"I'm not letting you in," she said, pulling her lips into an apologetic though cold line. "Not exactly wooed by the idea of being your second choice."

"You've never been my second choice," he said, and as the words came out, he realised they were words he had always wanted to say.

The words, *I love you*, started to form in the back of his mind, but he wasn't brave enough to say them. He remained standing in front of her, the rain seeping into his clothes.

Even Hawkins wasn't so unfeeling as not to feel a little sorry for him.

"I guess you should come in," she said, taking a step back. "Don't want to be responsible for you getting pneumonia."

He gratefully entered her hallway and sighed with relief as he felt the warmth of the nearby radiator.

"Here, let me help you," she said.

Goosebumps rose up his spine as he felt her soft fingers remove his clothes. He felt as though he could melt against her. Bundling up his wet clothes, she left him standing in the hallway in his boxer shorts as she walked into the kitchen. When she returned, she was carrying a large, clean towel she'd taken from the hallway cupboard. Draping it over him with a maternal smile, she kissed his cheek and took his hand.

"What will I do with you, eh?"

"Take me up to bed?"

"Maybe... But don't think you're getting lucky."

But the pleasures of her body weren't all he desired. He just wanted to be next to her, to feel the warmth of her body and if fortune dictated, the smoothness of her lips. He followed her up to the bedroom, saw the bed with the covers pulled back and felt the urge to dive beneath them. But before he could, his foot bumped against something on the floor. He looked down and saw a shoebox, the contents having spilled as he kicked it.

Documents spread across the carpet. On top of them lay a thumb drive. For a long moment, he stared at it in disbelief, then glanced up at Hawkins who had dropped her hand from his. There was obvious fear in her eyes and the colour had drained from her cheeks.

"You... You said you'd got rid of this."

She took a deep breath and composed herself.

"Dickie... You and me both know I'm no fool. You really thought I wouldn't keep some proof?"

She raised an eyebrow mockingly at him and any fondness he felt for her vanished in an instant and turned to anger.

"For fuck sake! You've been holding onto this the whole time!"

"Like I said, I'm no fool."

She smiled at him, and his desire for her returned. He grew angry at himself. The effect she had on him was instant and powerful and he couldn't believe how weak he was.

"So are you coming to bed or not?" she asked him, climbing beneath the covers. "You have a right to be angry. And I've got a right to protect myself. A smart man like you should understand."

He looked behind towards the door then back at Hawkins who was now lying down and running a hand through her hair. He knew what he had to do. Bundle up the contents of the shoe box and disappear out the door, but he found himself sinking into the bed beside her instead.

You weak idiot.

Chapter 24

Fitz

December 17th, 2015

"I thought you wouldn't come back," said Fitz with sparkling eyes as Danielle entered the cafe and sat across from him.

"And miss this tea?" she laughed, wrapping her fingers around the cheap teapot.

In her pocket, the sugar packet from the week before was worn away to almost nothing from the countless times she had unfolded and read it.

"You're a difficult girl to get out my head," he said as he watched her.

He cringed at his own words.

You sound so cheesy.

But it had been the truth. He hadn't been able to stop thinking about her, but he had it fixed firmly in his mind that there was no chance she would come back to see him.

She's too good for me. What's she doing here?

"I'll admit it," she said, sipping the terrible tea. "You've been worming your way around my head too."

"I'd see a doctor about that."

They both laughed and relaxed back in their seats. A feeling of comfort came over them both as though they'd known each other forever.

"Your sister around?" he asked her.

She shook her head and laughed.

"Not this time. She's at a party. One I wouldn't want to be invited to."

He looked over every micro movement of her face. He couldn't take her eyes off her, not just because she was beautiful, but because he saw how genuine she was.

"I have an idea," he said. "How about we get out of here? Go somewhere more fun?"

"Like a party?"

"My mates are having a small get together in Hackney. If you wanna come... I mean you probably don't want to and-"

"I'd love to!"

A wide smile spread across her face and he had the strongest urge to jump over the table and kiss her. But instead, he just slid his hand towards hers and wrapped it around her fingers.

"Cool," he said. "They'll love you."

***

Fitz was right. All his friends did love her, and as he arrived at the party, he felt like he'd arrived with a celebrity. No one could take their eyes off her, even if she didn't notice. He could see everyone wanted to be close to her, but knowing she had come with him, they kept a respectable distance.

He watched her from across the living room of his friend, Harry's house as she sat on the couch between two of his other friends, John and Rick. They appeared to be enthralled by one of her stories of a holiday to Marrakesh where she lived with a family to learn about their pottery crafting methods.

Only she could make something like that sound so exciting and glamorous.

"How the fuck did you get her?" came Harry's voice from behind him as he appeared with a can of lager.

"Not quite sure myself."

"That's Sir Bill Lovecroft's daughter. I mean, Jesus. It's a bit down market here for her. Although she likes it by the looks of things."

"Yeah, I think she likes you guys. Although I'm not sure why. You buncha hooligans."

He playfully elbowed Harry in the ribs and cracked open his beer.

"Harry?"

"Yeah."

"I think I'm going nuts."

"What makes you say that?"

"I feel like I'm really falling for her."

"Really? Thought you just met."

"Yeah, we have but... You ever just... *know* something?"

Harry stared at him like he had two heads.

"What are you talking about, Fitz? Since when did you get so soft?"

"I'm just saying, I really like her."

As he sipped his beer, Danielle felt his gaze on her and looked over at him. He felt as though his insides had caught fire, and she smiled back feeling the same.

Chapter 25

Cecilia

August 25th, 2023

The bubbles lapped around her fake breasts as she luxuriated in the warm water. She took a long sip of champagne and lay her head back.

This is what I needed, she thought. *After all the stress I've been through.*

But no sooner did she feel her muscles soften when her phone buzzed from the shelf above her head. She didn't want to answer it, but she had also never ignored her phone. She was addicted to it.

"Hello?" she asked, annoyed.

"Cecilia, honey. It's me."

"Papa?"

"Oh, it's so great to hear your voice. How are you?"

"Well, I was having the time of my life at Champney's Spa trying to forget about you but... Oh, never mind. How are you phoning me from a mobile?"

"Don't worry about that. I just need to know you're okay."

"I'm fine, Papa. Actually that's a lie. I'm in a terrible state thanks to you."

"I'm sorry. It must be so difficult for you to see your old man in prison and-"

"It's not just that. It's the money, Papa. You're offering half of my inheritance to any criminal scally. That's partly mine, Papa. Mine!"

Bill took a deep breath and pinched the bridge of his nose as frustration set in. It wasn't that he regretted calling his daughter, but he did wish she was a little more bearable.

Trust her to be angry about the money and not about missing her father.

"I understand why you're angry," he told her, taking a deep breath. "But you've got to understand that..."

He knew that what he was about to say next was going to enrage her.

"Sweetheart, what's my favourite Rolling Stones song?"

"What? Oh, I don't know... That silly one. The annoying one. What's it called?"

Cecilia waved her hand around dramatically as she tried to find the words, bubbles scattering from her manicured hand.

"Oh!" she remembered. "It's called, You can't always get what you want."

"Exactly..."

There was an awkward silence between the two as Bill waited for the penny to drop. When it did, Cecilia shrieked, "Papa! What do you mean?"

"It means..."

He took another deep breath.

"It means I think I've been very good to you. You've never wanted for anything, have you?"

"Why are you talking like this?"

"And I think I gave you so much more than you needed as you were growing up. Especially after Danielle and..."

"Papa what are you saying?"

"And... I think I've given you too much maybe."

"What!"

He licked his lips and noticed his mouth had become dry. He realised, as he stared at the wall of his cell, that this was the first time he'd stood up to Cecilia. She had bullied his way into his bank account for so long, and he had convinced himself he was being a good father, but now, as he listened to her, he was fast coming to the conclusion he had raised a spoiled monster.

"Cecilia listen. I'm your father and I know what's best for you. You need to learn to stand on your own two feet."

Terror filled Cecilia's body and she started to feel the champagne burn the pit of her stomach.

"My own two feet?" she said, swallowing hard.

"What I mean is. You've never had to work for money in your life."

"I don't need to."

"And I feel like you're not really getting the most out of life."

Dread was making her cold despite the heat of the bathwater.

"You're so intelligent, Cecilia. You did so well at school and what are you doing with that big brain of yours?"

She bit her lower lip and scowled at the bubbles.

"Nothing," continued Bill. "Diddly squat."

"And? What do you expect me to do? Get a job?"

"I'm expecting you to use your talents."

"Erm... In what way?"

Now was the moment Bill was dreading more than ever.

"Help me, Cecilia. A brain like yours could get me out of here and you know what? If you do, I'll give you everything. Thirty-eight billion will seem like pocket change compared to what I can give you in assets and equity. All the houses, they're yours. The stocks, yours."

"No way," raged Cecilia. "I can't believe you'd use your own daughter to help break you out of jail. How could you?"

But as the words fell out her mouth, her brain started ticking. She thought about all the money and the property Bill owned. She thought of his whole empire and imagined what it would feel like if it was all hers.

My inheritance was just the cash... but the properties too. There's hundreds of them. And the stocks...

"You'd love to see your Papa get his freedom, wouldn't you?" asked Bill.

"Of course!"

"I knew you would. Danielle would have too. God... My Danielle. If she was here-"

"I wondered how long it would take before you mentioned her."

Bill paused as he heard the anger in Cecilia's voice.

"Can I not be reminded of how much she was your golden girl for five seconds?"

Tears came to Cecilia's eyes. But they weren't just born of anger, but from knowing that Danielle would have rushed to her father's side in a heartbeat. That if she was there now she would have made it all so much more bearable with just one of her smiles. Cecilia's mind was in two. Half jealous of how much her father still loved Danielle, the other half still grieving hard for the loss of her. What she would do to just have Danielle back for a day. Even if they did spend it arguing.

She couldn't fit all her thoughts into words, so she just started screaming, "I'm fed up of hearing about her!" and hung up before launching her phone across the room.

It hit the wall, the screen cracking instantly, but Cecilia didn't notice as she dipped her head below the bubbles. Her tears mingling with the hot water.

Chapter 26
Amelia

August 25th, 2023

"Where have you been all day? I thought you were going to be home for dinner."

"I said I *might* be home for dinner," replied Amelia as she unzipped her coat in the hallway.

To her right, she could see into the cramped kitchen of her parents' high rise flat. The smell of jerk chicken and home-made roti reached her, making her stomach growl. It was one of the many things she had missed about living with her parents, but getting nagged at was not.

"Amelia you definitely said you'd be home for dinner," her mother moaned, slamming down one of the serving plates. "You can't just come and go as you please."

"I'm an adult, Mum. I'm twenty-fucking-seven."

"Language!" exploded her father, slapping the dinner table. "You might be twenty-seven but you're living back home with your parents now so you live by *our* rules."

Amelia cringed and lowered her head as she hung up her coat. She sat down at the table wordlessly as her mother dished out a juicy chicken thigh onto her plate. She felt like a teenager again ready to get a telling off for staying out past her curfew.

As she stabbed her fork into her chicken, she caught her mother giving her a disapproving glance.

"Don't look at me like that."

"Don't take that tone with me, girl," replied her mother as she dropped into her chair. "I'm putting a roof over your head. Putting food in your stomach."

"I know. You keep reminding me."

"Then show some gratitude."

Amelia lost her appetite and placed her fork back down.

"Mum, I do appreciate everything-"

"You damn well should. Especially after what you did."

"I didn't *do* anything."

"That's what you keep saying," said her father as he chewed on a chicken bone. "The paper's say otherwise."

"Why would you believe the papers over me?" gasped Amelia. "How would they really know what happened?"

Her father shrugged and dropped the chicken bone on the edge of his plate.

"All I'm saying is *MET officer found robbing safety deposit vault at scene of crime* wasn't the headline I wanted to read about my daughter."

"You know that's not what happened. My squad fucking left me there! It was them that had an informant tell them where to get the cash. They took it all and bailed leaving me there and-"

"Enough!" yelled her mother, raising the palm of her hand to Amelia's face. "Let's just eat."

"I can't," said Amelia, pushing her plate away. "I don't get why you don't believe me."

"Why would the MET police lie?" asked her father. "You're telling me they're corrupt? That *they* were the robbers?"

"Yes!"

He shook his head in disbelief.

"I want to believe you."

"You should. You know just how corrupt the MET are. Dad you've lived in London since you came here from Trinidad. You're not stupid. You know what the police can be like."

He said nothing, just picked up another chicken leg and dipped it into his hot sauce.

"And you know that fucking prosecutor, Hawkins had it in for me," continued Amelia.

"Language!" yelled her father.

"Why have I got to mind my language when the MET get to wipe the fucking floor with me because of who I am?"

She rose angrily from her seat, her chair scraping hard against the kitchen floor.

"Why have I got to be treated like a child after what they've done to me?"

"Amelia sit down."

"No. You know why they made me a scapegoat, don't you?"

She searched the faces of her parents for a hint of understanding, but all she saw was denial.

"I was the only black officer in the squad that night. You know that, don't you? The only woman too. Never a better person to blame for almost a million quid going missing, eh?"

She kept staring into her parents' faces looking for a shred of sympathy, but there was nothing. She wanted to cry, but swallowed down her feelings and looked her father straight in the eye.

"I don't fucking get it," she said. "You should know better. What you went through when you first got here. What you campaigned for. All the riots you were in. But you won't believe your own daughter when the very thing you campaigned against happens to her."

She waited for him to say something. Anything to calm her down, but all he did was start chewing on another chicken bone with his gaze still boring into hers. It felt pointless. He'd never believe her.

Backing away from the table, she reached for her coat in the hallway and blinked away the tears.

"Where are you going?" her mother demanded to know.

"I need to walk."

"Wait!"

But she was already slamming the front door shut and jogging down the stairs towards the main door that opened onto the high street. She wiped away tears with the heel of her hand as she walked at speed, pushing her way through groups of people ready for a good night out in the various pubs.

There was no idea in her mind of where she was going. Only that she had to walk. A corner shop caught her attention out the side of her eye and she stopped in the middle of the pavement. It had been six years since she'd last smoked a cigarette, but now she felt as though she craved one more than ever.

Don't do it, said half her mind.

Fuck it. You deserve it, said the other half.

She walked in and asked for twenty Lambert and Butler then shuddered when she heard the price.

"Jesus. Gone up a bit, hasn't it?" she asked the old lady behind the till who responded with a stony silence.

She left and stepped out the wind into a nearby doorway where she struggled to unwrap the pack of cigarettes. She pulled one out and regarded it for a second. She hadn't realised just how much she had missed them. Reaching for her lighter, she raised the flame to the end and placed the butt in her mouth. The moment the flame met the edge of the paper, she saw it. A dark, blacked out Mercedes parked up in front of her.

The back window glided down and out popped a pale face.

"Fucking hell," she said. "Never wanted to see you again."

"Charming. You're smoking?"

"And?"

"And you look like you're having a bad night."

"You been watching me?"

"Might have been. Why don't you come in and we'll go for a drink. I'd like to talk to you."

"Lucien... There is absolutely nothing I would like to do less than talk to you, but I do need a drink."

She breathed in the acrid taste of tobacco and felt it hit her brain and lungs simultaneously.

"There's a decent boozer round the corner," she said, approaching the car. "Not really your kind of place, though."

***

The Fox and Weasel had been a dangerous hangout of gangsters and hardened alcoholics until the hipsters moved in. Now, although it kept some of its old charm, the usual punters were either dying or being edged out by the ever growing prices of a pint. A few of the remaining old boys clung to the back corner underneath the television, and it was here that Amelia sat with Lucien.

He kept looking over his shoulder at every raised voice and laugh while Amelia sipped her pint of Stella Artois. She hadn't realised until her first sip just how much she needed it. But despite the effects of the alcohol, she wasn't entirely comfortable. She watched Lucien stare at the pint he'd bought to fit in but clearly didn't want, and thought he looked like a rat.

"So you were following me," she said. "If you hadn't been the one to keep me out of jail I might have swung for you."

"You make me sound like a creep."

She stared at him with a tight lipped grimace and said, "What is it you want? Never thought I'd see you again after the court case."

Lucien awkwardly picked up his pint with his slender fingers and took a sip before wrinkling up his nose.

"Tastes like piss."

He put his pint down and sat back in the old, battered leather chair that was turning threadbare at the arms. He wasn't sure what was more depressing, this place or Fitz' flat.

"Look, I'm sorry about... You know, the whole thing with you."

"What are you sorry about? You got me off the hook, didn't ya? Even though I'd done fuck all."

"Yeah but you still lost your job."

She stared miserably into the centre of the table. Her mind wandered back to the recent argument with her parents. It was less than an hour ago but it felt so much longer than that.

"It was terrible the way the MET treated you," said Lucien. "I mean that."

Amelia nodded solemnly.

"There's nothing I can do about it now, is there?"

"You found a new job yet?"

"No. Been applying for security jobs but... Well, my name was in the papers. No one will hire me."

"Well..." said Lucien, leaning forward and lowering his voice. "I could have a job for you."

She raised an eyebrow.

There was something about Lucien she never fully trusted, something she couldn't put her finger on, but she found herself interested, if only because she couldn't bear living with her parents any longer.

"I'm listening."

"You know about Sir Bill's offer, don't you?"

She felt her heartbeat quicken slightly as she slid forward in her seat.

"The thirty-eight billion?"

Lucien nodded.

"I need a team, and every team needs someone with insider knowledge. And what's better than that special someone hating the MET, eh?"

He smiled to himself and tried his beer again, pulling a disgusted face.

"What could be a better way than sticking two fingers up to the establishment that cocked your life up than breaking out old Bill and becoming stinking rich in the process?"

Only two things moved through Amelia's mind.

I've got nothing to lose and fuck the MET.

"I'm in," she said.

"You are? Don't you want to know more details?"

"You can fill me in over my next pint."

Chapter 27

Hawkins

August 26th, 2023

Hawkins sipped her white wine and ate a forkful of salmon as she tried to remember what event she was at. Since her early retirement, she attended at least three charity dinners a week, often being paid to speak at them for a princely sum of money she didn't need.

She looked around the room and saw the usual faces in tuxedos then looked towards the stage where a cello player was serenading the room. Casting her eye up to the banner above him, her memory was jolted.

Ah, yes. Literacy. That's today's cause.

A slight pang of guilt hit her as she realised her negligence, then she took one last bite of salmon and left the table. She was halfway to the ladies room when she became aware of eyes on the back of her head, but as she turned around, no one stood caught her attention. Still, there was the prickle of hairs running up the back of her neck.

She entered the ladies room and looked in the mirror as she pulled out her favourite red lipstick. As she focussed on the curve of her top lip, she noticed the door behind her swing open and a well dressed blonde woman enter. She looked vaguely familiar, but Hawkins couldn't quite place where she'd seen her face.

Clicking the lid closed on her lipstick, she noticed the woman wasn't moving into any of the toilet cubicles. Instead, she was staring at Hawkins' reflection.

Why is she looking at me like that?

The woman bit down on her lower lip as though she was trying to stop it wobbling. It was then the realisation hit and Hawkins took a shocked step back.

"Sandra?"

"It's true, isn't it? You've been fucking my husband."

"Aw, Jesus."

Hawkins slumped against the edge of the sink and crossed her arms.

"Look, Sandra I'm not going to deny it. I'm also not going to get caught up in some drama like high school girls scrapping in the toilets."

"That's it? You don't have the decency to even deny it, you slut!"

Hawkins didn't blink as the insult was hurled at her. She just looked Sandra dead in the face and said, "I can understand why you hate me. But if it means anything I don't love Richard. If anything he drives me a little nuts."

Hawkins kept staring into Sandra's face and could see just how much pain she had caused.

This poor idiot loves him.

"Okay," relented Hawkins. "I'm sorry."

Sandra shook her head, unable to accept the apology.

"How long has it been going on?"

Hawkins couldn't bring herself to say how many years she'd entertained Richard in her bed, so she lowered her gaze and said, "A few months."

"That's it?"

"Yes."

"You don't love him?"

"No... I don't. But I can see you do."

Sandra blinked as tears came to her eyes before burying her face in her hands. Hawkins' stomach clenched itself into a knot. She may not have wanted to become embroiled in some romantic drama, but she also didn't enjoy seeing Sandra fall apart in front of her.

She took a tentative step forward and pressed her hand to Sandra's shoulder in an attempt at comforting her.

"I didn't set out to hurt anyone," she said, honestly. "I'll stay away from him."

"You're fucking right you'll stay away from him," seethed Sandra, thrusting her hand into her purse. "Because if you don't, I'll leak this to everyone who needs to fucking know."

Hawkins looked down in shock as Sandra pulled out a small thumb drive from her purse and shoved it in her face.

"I watched what's on it. I'll show everyone."

Hawkins instantly grew dizzy.

It looks just like the one at... But it can't be...

She began backing away from Sandra who was still holding the thumb drive up triumphantly.

"I mean it!" she yelled as Hawkins backed out the bathroom. "I'll show everyone what you've been hiding."

***

Hawkins burst through her front door, dropped her purse in the hallway and bounded up the stairs two at a time. As she arrived in her bedroom, she fell to her knees with a thump and started ransacking the shoebox.

"Please. Oh, fuck. Please be here."

She scattered the contents across the carpet, the papers sliding across the floor, but there was no sign of the thumb drive.

"Fuck. Fuck. Fuck!"

She started searching the floor frantically with her hands, and when she still couldn't find it, she stood up feeling like she was being strangled.

"No... No..."

She dashed from the room running back down the stairs to find her purse. Pulling out her phone, she slammed her finger against Richard's number. It rang for what felt like an eternity.

"Lizzie?" eventually came Richard's voice. "Well, isn't it nice to hear from you at this-"

"You took it, you little shit."

He was silent for the longest moment as Hawkins' mind whirred itself into a panic.

"Lizzie..." said Richard with a calm flatness to his voice. "You didn't think I would just let you have that footage now, did you? I may be a slave to that delicious pussy of yours, but I'm not an idiot."

"Yes, you are an idiot. Your wife has it now!"

Chapter 28

Fitz

August 26th, 2023

Fitz felt the beginning of a runners' high tingle at the back of his head as he reached Richmond Park. The air felt clear and crisp, there were only a few people in the park so early in the morning and the sun was shining on the frosty ground. With his earbuds in, he focussed on the rhythm of the music and the beat of his feet as he took one step after another.

Just one more step. Just one more mile. Keep going. Always going. Always moving forward.

He was so lost in the feel and beat of his body that he wasn't paying attention to the running blonde woman until she was right in front of him. The first thing he saw were the eyes.

He stopped dead and yanked out his earbuds.

"Shit! I thought you were... Cecilia... Your eyes..."

"Are the only thing Danielle and I shared. She was the one who got the looks."

"Yeah, you'll brook no argument from me there. What are you doing here?"

"Trying to find you. Been yelling your name like a mad woman for ages. You made me run after you. And in these heels."

Fitz couldn't stop looking into her eyes. They made him feel haunted. As though he was staring into his past.

"Did you say you were looking for me?" he asked.

"Yeah, Lucien said you jog here every morning."

"You've been talking to that twat?"

"He's pretty much family," she said, rolling her eyes. "You know, like a creepy, weird uncle."

"What do you want?"

She shifted her gaze left then right to make sure no one was listening then delved into her Prada purse for her Vogue cigarettes. To Fitz's surprise, before she lit her own, she offered him one. It was quite possibly the first sign of manners he'd ever seen from her, and it made him suspicious.

"No, thanks," he said. "I've quit."

"Good on you. I can never get rid of these babies."

He watched as she held up her engraved Zippo and sparked a flame. From each of her elongated mannerisms, he could tell she was taking her time. Time he didn't want to spend with her.

"What is it you want?"

"I want in."

The words hung in the air for a second with Fitz' confusion growing.

"You want in... on what?"

"Don't play dumb, Fitz. You might be a dirty crimmy but you're not stupid."

"Hey, did you just come and find me to insult me or-"

"Okay, okay. I'm sorry. I shouldn't have said that."

She breathed in a lungful of smoke and inhaled it slowly into the breeze.

"But I do want in," she said. "In your team. Lucien told me everything."

"He did? God, why?"

"Because Papa wants me to help you guys."

"Oh, for fuck's sake."

Cecilia reeled back offended and blew out smoke through her glossy lips.

"I didn't expect you to exactly jump for joy," she said. "But I at least expected some enthusiasm."

"Enthusiasm to work with you?" laughed Fitz. "You're 'avin a laugh."

"I thought you would want all the help you could get."

"Not from you. What are you going to do? Moan Bill's way out of Belmarsh?"

With one last shake of his head, Fitz stepped away from her and began jogging the rest of the way down the path. Cecilia watched him for a second in disbelief. She wasn't used to being ignored.

"Hey, Fitz!"

She teetered after him in her heels, smoking as she ran.

"Fitz come back!"

He stopped and looked over his shoulder, amused at the sight of her struggling to keep up.

"You're serious, ain't ya?" he laughed.

"I am."

"Why?"

He turned to face her and screwed up his face, confused.

"You don't need the money."

"It's not just the money. It's the rest of Papa's assets and…"

"And what?"

"Nothing…"

Fitz studied her face. There was a look in her eye he couldn't quite identify. Then it dawned on him.

"Wait… I know why you're doing this."

"Same reason everyone else is. The money, right?"

"Wrong. I reckon you're just after Daddy's love."

She flinched as she heard this but didn't protest.

"I'm right, aren't I?"

"No."

"Shut up. Of course I am."

Her eyes darkened as she blew out her last mouthful of smoke, threw her cigarette butt on the ground and watched it dissolve in a puddle.

"Danielle was always his favourite," she admitted, staring at the ground with her eyes glossed over. "Feels like she still is."

Chapter 29

Jacques

August 27th, 2023

Jacques Beaumont had to work at looking like a hippy. It wasn't that he didn't agree with the sentiment of being one, but rather his background just couldn't be washed out of his appearance. Even unwashed he looked clean.

He stood on the stage at Hyde Park and looked out at his sea of followers. There were thousands of them; mainly first year students who were mad at the world and were hell bent on changing it. Jacques had been like that once. When he'd first left home at eighteen to attend Cambridge University and began joining the various clubs and societies the place had to offer. His eyes had been opened to issues his parents never talked about.

Pollution? It had just been a buzzword in the news until he'd learned about the Kenyan dye mines. So was climate change, slave labour and a myriad of other terms that had meant nothing to him in childhood, but now held the meaning of his life.

He was in the third year of his PhD when he decided to start a small blog called Power to the Planet where guest writers could update his small following on the various injustices they were campaigning against. He had no idea it would grow to the proportions it had, or that social media would make it explode.

When he decided to get a few t-shirts printed he thought he would only sell a couple to his friends. He had no idea they would sell out. Or that the next run of them would be sold out before they were even printed. Then there were the stickers and the posters, the tote bags, the IPhone cases and the baseball caps. Now it was no longer a little blog out to create change, it was an international business with thousands of followers that came to think of Jacques as a leader.

He was an introvert at heart, but he couldn't help enjoy the attention he got, especially from girls. He'd been a shy awkward child with the mannerisms and charm of a baby bird. He didn't even kiss a girl until he was seventeen and was still a virgin when he started university. But now there were dozens, if not hundreds of girls messaging him daily desperate to work for his cause, for free. They turned up in their droves in their dungarees and self-cut hair with starry eyes and he could never say no.

As he now looked out across the sea of faces, he couldn't help but notice there were significantly more females than males. His eyes focussed in on a blonde girl three rows from the front, the sun glinting off her septum piercing. She was staring up at him as though he was God and for a second, he felt he was.

He was so caught up in the moment, he forgot his speech which he had scrawled roughly in his sketchbook he held in his hands. He forgot everything. All he thought was, *I'm getting her into bed later.*

"Oi, Jacques?" came a voice beside him.

He turned to see his best friend, Freddy staring at him like he was an idiot.

"Are you going to talk or what?"

"Oh… yeah…"

He looked down at his sketchbook then back out over the crowd. His palms started to sweat as he realised just how many people he was talking to. More than had previously turned up to his rallies. Then this delicious, golden feeling came over him that made him feel Godly, and he opened his mouth.

"Yaasssss everyone!" he yelled, raising his hand to address the crowd. "Look at you all, you beautiful bastards!"

They all roared back in response and he felt like he was shining from within. He loved the feeling so much he didn't even care what he was planning to talk about any more; how nuclear waste was set to be transported on the public railway through the outskirts of London. All he cared about were all the eyes on him, and that pretty blonde girl who was still staring at him.

***

The crowd were still roaring as he stepped off the stage to be replaced by the punk band he'd brought in to liven things up. People crowded around him as he jostled his way backstage to a small tent that had been set up with a table of snacks and beer.

People kept slapping him on the back and telling him how great he was, how he was using his privilege to really make a change, but all he kept thinking was, *Where's that blonde girl?*

As he took a can of beer and cracked it open, he felt a shiver as though someone was staring at him. Looking up, he saw the one thing he never expected to see at one of his events, a man in a suit.

"Lucien?"

"Hello, Jacques. That was quite a speech."

Lucien moved to shake his hand and Jacques did so reluctantly. He'd always hoped he'd never have to see his lawyer again. Sure, he was fantastic at getting him off his charges. Breaking into the detention centre that housed refugees had been the last charge Lucien fought in court for him, getting him nothing but a few hours community service.

"He's the best," his angry, though rich, parents kept telling him. "The next time you're in trouble call Lucien before anyone else."

Although Jacques knew this was the sensible thing to do, he couldn't ever bring himself to like the guy. There was just something about him that set him on edge, something he couldn't trust.

"What... are you doing here?" he asked him. "Didn't think you gave a shit about nuclear waste."

"I don't."

Lucien looked around like he was on the cusp of being mugged at any moment.

"Look, I don't want to hang about," he said. "I need to talk to you."

"Well, talk."

"Not here. Somewhere a bit more quiet and less smelly."

Jacques laughed and took a long sip of his beer.

"That way," nodded Jacques behind him. "There's a coffee shop. Probably a little more to your liking."

Lucien sighed with relief and followed Jacques out the tent, shuddering as he passed a group of male students smoking weed. They laughed at him as he passed, and he vowed to never come to one of these rallies again.

Scrubbers, he thought as he followed Jacques. *Fucking do gooders.*

***

The coffee shop was busy, but quiet with people at each table working on their laptops. It wasn't where Jacques wanted to be. He wanted to be back at the rally at the centre of attention with his arms around that pretty blonde, but there was something about the commanding tone in Lucien's voice that made him stay put.

"Did my parents send you?"

"Oh, God no. Actually, if you speak to them, tell them you never saw me."

"Oh?"

Jacques' interest was now piqued.

"You here off the job then?"

"I'm here for a job of sorts," said Lucien. "Listen, I'll hit you with it straight. You've heard about Sir Bill Lovecroft-"

"And his offer of thirty-eight billion? Yeah, fuck, everyone's heard of that."

"Exactly."

They both stared into each other's eyes for an extended moment.

"I'm putting together a team…" began Lucien, tangling his fingers together on the table. "To, erm, help Bill."

"Help Bill?"

"Yes… To aid him find his freedom."

"You mean to break him out of Belmarsh!"

"Shh! Keep your fucking voice down."

Lucien looked around nervously, but was pleased to see no one was looking up from their laptops.

"Yes," he said, keeping his voice low as he sipped his espresso. "I need a team of the best. That means I need you."

"Me? Why me?"

"Do I need to spell it out? Did you see how many people were out there hanging on your every word? You've got a literal vegan army of tree fuckers who'll do anything you say."

"And?"

"And what would they love more than to have Sir Bill out free?"

"Why would they want that? He's a billionaire. Do you think my followers sympathise with billionaires?"

"I thought you'd be a little more enthusiastic given how much he donated to your organisation."

"Yeah, he donated thousands. Do you know how much that is to someone like Lovecroft? Pocket fluff. Nothing more. He throws a few crumbs to the good folk every now and again for some good press."

"But what about the hydrogen car? You can't call the money he threw into that pocket fluff?"

Jacques thought for a second and stirred his latte.

"No, I suppose not."

"Besides, the money. Your share of thirty-eight billion could really benefit your causes couldn't it? You could get a ship like Greenpeace. I mean, Christ, you could get a whole fleet of fighter jets with that money."

A light went off inside Jacques head.

Fighter jets.

How fucking rad would that be?

How many girls could I fit in a fighter jet?

And a ship.

Yeah, a cruise ship full of birds.

"I can see you like the idea," noted Lucien.

"I might…" replied Jacques, trying to play it cool, but his face was shining red with enthusiasm. "I mean, I could do a lot of good with that money. You know, save a lot of the environment and that."

Lucien smiled and sipped the last of his espresso.

"Shall I assume you're on board?"

Jacques' opened his mouth, but his attention was pulled away from Lucien and out the window. Standing across the road waiting at the lights was the blonde girl and she was staring right at him.

"Yeah, yeah," said Jacques, rising from his seat. "I'm on board."

Chapter 30

Bil

August 28th, 2023

"Morning!" came Terry's chipper voice as the door opened with a clang.

Bill had already been awake for three hours. Since before the sun had risen. He'd been plotting and talking to Lucien on the phone, thinking until his head hurt. He stood at the window now with his back to Terry. He couldn't take his eyes off the sun or the way it glistened off the wet grass at the edge of the yard.

"Oi," said Terry.

Bill turned to face him with a tired sigh.

"Jesus, Bill. You look like shit."

"Thanks very much."

"Look like you've not slept."

"Could you sleep in here?"

Bill shrugged.

"S'pose not."

Terry dithered by the door for a moment studying Bill's face. It looked like he'd aged ten years in as many days.

"Any news on the art class?" asked Bill.

"I'm working on it. Until then you can have the library for an hour a day."

"Well! I suppose that's something."

"I can take you there now, if you want. I mean, after breakfast."

"I'll skip breakfast," shuddered Bill.

He still couldn't get to grips with the low culinary standards of the place.

"Well, come on then," urged Terry.

He led Bill out into the hallway, slamming the door closed behind them both before leading him down the staircase. The smell of breakfast from the canteen worsened the further they walked, and Bill found his stomach churning.

"You alright, Bill?" asked Terry.

"Just keep walking."

Bill waited until there was no one in ear shot before leaning in towards Terry.

"I need you to get me something," he said.

"Sure, Bill. Anything."

"Good. I need you to go to Fortnum and Masons and get me some decent food."

"Fortnum and Masons? Yeah, like I'm going to fit in there, ha!"

"Please, just... I can't stand the food here any longer."

Terry laughed and nodded.

"Sure, mate. Just give me a list."

"You're a good guy, Terry. I'll pay you whatever."

Terry smiled and couldn't believe how much he'd lucked out. Having Bill under his watch felt like having his own personal cash machine.

"Nearly there," said Terry as they turned into the corridor housing the library. "Bet a man like you is bored out his mind without books."

"That would be an understatement. I've read that shitty magazine you left with me three times already. Couldn't you at least bring me The Financial Times?"

Terry rolled his eyes in jest.

They were fifty feet from the entrance to the library when a sharp siren sounded making them both flinch.

"Oh, bloody hell!" moaned Bill, clapping his hands over his ears.

A wall of guards pushed past them aiming for the door to the library. It was now, as Bill squinted through the noise that he saw a trail of blood snaking its way out the library entrance into the hallway. It moved towards him like a crimson tendril seeking him out, viscous and burgundy red.

"What the fuck?" he saw Terry mouth.

"Stabbing!" one of the guards yelled as he strode at speed past the pair. "Place is in lockdown! Get Lovecroft back to his cell."

Bill could feel his heart rate rising, could taste the blood in the air and smell a mix of fear and testosterone. He didn't need to look inside the library to know someone had died. He could sense the death. Could feel its darkness wash down the hall along with the panic.

"Back up. Back up," said Terry, his eyes on the stream of blood.

A gust of air blew over them as a team of medics rushed into the scene with a stretcher. Bill felt himself shake, but he couldn't step away. He was fixated on the blood. Fixated on the idea that he could be next.

***

Darkness fell and Bill was sat on the edge of his bed chewing on his fingernails, something he hadn't done since childhood. He couldn't get the sight of blood out his head, and he was sure, as he sipped on a glass of water, that he could still smell it.

Thank fuck I didn't see the body.

There came the usual clunk-click sound of the door as it was unlocked, and he looked up to see Terry wander in.

"That's me away, Bill. You got that shopping list?"

"No... I... forgot..."

Terry saw a haunted look in Bill's eyes and gave him a sympathetic look.

"If it's any consolation the guy was a nonce. He died pretty quick too. Bled out instantly."

"Oh..."

"That's what happens to paedophiles in prison. Sooner or later anyway."

Bill started to feel even more nauseous.

Paedophiles being murdered mere feet away from him. What had his life come to?

"You're pretty shaken up, aren't ya?" asked Terry.

"Just a bit."

"It'll be okay."

"Will it?"

Terry didn't know how to answer.

"Try not to concern yourself with the drama that takes place in here," he said. "Just focus on yourself. You're in your own little world in here. Just think about that."

But that just made it all the more depressing for Bill. His only solace from the murderous crowds beyond his door was the squalor of his cell.

I need out.

"So, that shopping list," said Terry. "You better write it out properly for me 'cos if I have to go in and ask for some fancy shit in French…"

"I'll write it out for you," said Bill, grabbing his leather bound notebook from the nearby table.

Pulling out a page, he began scrawling the names of items he so desperately craved.

Foie Gras

Dark chocolate and ginger biscuits

Somerset Brie

Sourdough Bloomer

Gravlax Salmon

"I'll need a fridge," he thought out loud as he wrote.

Terry burst out laughing.

"I can bring you just about anything but don't think I can smuggle in a Smeg fridge freezer. I'm not that talented."

Bill sighed.

"No salmon then."

Terry looked around the room and laughed again.

"You'll be alright without salmon," he told Bill mockingly.

But Bill wasn't so sure. He stood up and walked over to the small mirror above his sink and inspected his skin.

"I'm not getting enough omega 3 fatty acids," he moaned.

Terry rolled his eyes and shook his head.

***

August 29th, 2023

Morning came again and Bill had spent another sleepless night plotting his escape and staring at the ceiling. Once again came the clunk-click of the door and the arrival of Terry. He felt as though the routine of the place was killing him. Everything was repetitive; the smells, the noises, his bowel movements.

As he looked to Terry, he thought for a moment he had put on a significant amount of weight. It wasn't until Terry entered his room and started pushing items out the bottom of his sweater that he realised he had been hiding his shopping. A wheel of Brie rolled onto the bed followed by a tin of foie gras.

"The sourdough bloomer's still in my backpack," said Terry. "I'll bring it later."

"Terry, my boy. I could kiss you."

"Please don't."

Bill held up the Brie as though it was a priceless artefact and took a slow sniff.

"It smells wonderful."

"If you say so. Smelled like rotten socks all the way in on the bus."

"You got the bus in?" gasped Bill.

"Yeah… my Bentley broke down."

They both laughed and once again Bill showed his gratitude, standing up and shaking Terry's hand vigorously.

"You're a top bloke," he told him. "Thank you."

Terry felt himself blush and looked away embarrassed. He couldn't remember the last time he'd been given a compliment.

"So!" he declared, changing the subject. "I've got some news."

"Good news I hope," said Bill.

"Well, it depends on how you look at it. Amnesty International have been talking about you in the press."

Bill frowned. He wasn't interested in Amnesty International, only the whereabouts of his sourdough bloomer he so badly needed to have with his foie gras.

"What the hell do they want?" he sneered at Terry.

"They're worried about your human rights."

Bill laughed so hard he snorted.

"*My* human rights?"

"They've given a statement to the press saying you're cooped up in solitary for your own protection."

"Isn't that what they should want?"

"They say you're stuck in a cell without access to the outdoors."

"And?"

"And they're likening you to a caged chicken, Bill. Apparently they'd like you to be a bit more free range."

Bill laughed again and shook his head.

"Anyway," continued Terry. "The guv'nor's under pressure from them."

"You're kidding me."

"Nope. He's been taking what they say pretty seriously. Seriously enough that I had to have a meeting with him this morning."

Bill frowned at Terry, confused.

"And?"

"And the Guv says you need to go outside. See the sun or something."

Bill felt a little swell of happiness inside him.

"He did?"

"Yep! You've got one hour in the yard."

"That's fantastic."

"With all the others."

"What?"

The happiness that had quickly grown in Bill subsided in an instant.

"With the... others..."

His mind instantly returned to the stream of blood and to the sounds and smells of the other inmates. He thought of the way they all looked at him in the canteen. He wanted to be sick.

Murderous vermin, he thought to himself. *They'll kill me if I go out into the yard.*

"Bill, you alright? You've gone a bit grey."

"No I'm not bloody well alright. I can't go out into the yard! I thought I was meant to be kept away from all those animals."

"Actually," replied Terry, leaning against the doorway. "You were meant to be kept in protection from people trying to break you *out* of prison. You'll be well protected in the yard. There'll be eyes and ears everywhere and I'll be watching too. You'll be fine."

Bill couldn't feel anything further from fine.

"No... No..."

"Whatsa matter, Bill? You've been moaning about wanting to see the sun for days."

"But..."

"Get your shoes on, eh? I'll take you out now."

"Now?"

Bill stood up and received a sudden attack of vertigo.

"I can't!"

***

Despite his protests, Bill now found himself on the edge of the yard with one foot searching behind him for the safety of indoors. He felt a breeze against his cheeks for the first time since his arrival and shivered.

He felt eyes on him. Dozens of them. But he couldn't bring himself to raise his gaze to any of them.

They'll eat you alive.

"Well, go on, Bill. You daft sod," came Terry's affectionate voice from behind him along with a nudge in his spine. "You'll be okay."

Bill took one last glance over his shoulder at Terry and scowled, then he straightened his back and turned back to the yard. He knew any sign of weakness would put him in danger. He had to look as though he belonged.

They're just men, he tried to tell himself.

But another voice at the back of his mind intervened.

You've met thousands of men, but none of them murderers. How many men in this yard have killed a man? Which one of them killed the paedophile?

He took a deep breath, and knew his fate came down to how he behaved in the next few seconds. With this in mind, he pressed his shoulders back, grit his teeth and stepped out into the yard. The heat of everyone's eyes intensified, but he refused to drop his gaze or lower his head.

"See, you're okay," said Terry as he walked away. "Think of it as your first day at school."

Bill kept his eyes straight ahead focussed on the chain fence at the bottom of the yard. Beyond it was a concrete wall but behind that he could only imagine. The outside world felt too far away.

Gradually, he started to feel the energy around him change as though it was reaching boiling point. He heard whispers from all directions that turned into a low grumble. There was the shuffle of footsteps behind him, but he didn't dare turn to see who they belonged to.

"Oi, mate. You can sit here," came a voice from below his gaze.

He looked down and saw a man about his age, bald and built like a barrel. DIY tattoos climbed their way up his limbs and a long scar trailed its way across his forehead.

"Well, you gonna sit here or what?" he asked Bill, who had just realised he was holding his breath.

"Yeah... Sure," he eventually said, lowering himself down across from the human barrel.

"Weird seein' you 'ere," he said to Bill. "I mean, in prison. The tracksuit ain't like your usual Savile Row suit."

Bill had been so caught up thinking about his mortality that he'd forgotten momentarily about how uncomfortable his tracksuit was. Now it itched him in sweaty places and he found himself shifting in his seat.

"I'm Reg," said the barrel. "Nice to finally meet you."

He outstretched a chubby hand towards Bill who shook it cautiously.

"Bill. Nice to meet you."

It felt strange to Bill to be having such a polite encounter in what felt to him like a zoo.

"You can stop looking so petrified," laughed Reg. "You're sittin' wiv me now. You'll have no 'assle."

"You sure?"

"Fucking positive."

Bill looked over his shoulder at everyone. They were all still staring at him, still sizing him up, but the menace appeared to have shrunk in their eyes. The air felt lighter around him, like the threat to his life had been removed. Turning back to Reg, he looked up and down his tattoos and his scars. Took in his mannerisms and body language. He was sat on the bench like he didn't have a care in the world, his head tilted slightly back like a king surveying his kingdom.

"You looked as though you were gonna shit yourself there," he laughed at Bill. "But you got nothing to worry about, have ya? Nah... Nah... You'll be fine. We all love you in here, Bill. You're a national treasure. I feel the need to say it's a real honour to be doing my time alongside ya."

Bill, surprised, cocked his head to the side and regarded Reg with slight amusement.

"You really think so?"

"Of course I bloody well do."

Reg grabbed his hand again and shook it violently as he flashed a smile to reveal four gold teeth in the centre of his mouth. Suddenly, Bill felt eyes on the back of his head again. It was a superpower he'd developed since he'd arrived at Belmarsh, the primitive skill of knowing who was watching him. As he turned his head he saw Terry at the back of the yard watching him closely. Reg noticed him too and leaned in closer.

"So how you liking solitary?"

"I hate it."

"Obviously. But that Terry. He's alright, so he is. He's been here as long as I have."

"How long is that?"

"Twenty odd years."

"Jesus, how long were you sentenced for?"

"Life."

Bill turned to look into Reg's eyes.

"Life... As in."

"Life," confirmed Reg. "As in life means fucking life. I'm one of the few prisoners in the whole of the United fucking Kingdom that was given a life sentence that actually means life. I'll die in these walls, Bill. But they're my walls now. No one knows them like I do. No one knows the people inside them like I do either."

Bill felt a cold chill tingling at the top of his spine.

He knew there weren't many true lifers in Britain that were sentenced to spend their dying days behind bars. A few dozen at the most. And they were the worst of the worst. There was a burning urge inside him to ask Reg what he'd done that was so bad he'd been given such a sentence, but part of him was too afraid to ask. Words flashed up in his mind;

Paedophile

Child killer

Rapist

Reg had been one of the few friendly faces he'd met since he'd arrived in Belmarsh, and he couldn't bear to put one of those labels on him.

"Wanna game of cards?" Reg suddenly asked.

When Bill looked down at the table, he saw that Reg was already dealing him a hand from a pack of cards that seemingly materialised out of nowhere.

"Okay... What are we playing?"

"Fumble."

"I've not heard of it."

"Made it up myself."

"Oh..."

"Don't worry. I'll tell you the rules as we go along. Pick up your hand."

Bill did as he was told and tried to relax.

It's just a game of cards with a new friend.

But everyone around him was watching, whispering, waiting to see what was going to happen next.

"Relax, mate," said Reg. "Don't worry about all the gossipers. They'll get bored and piss off eventually."

And to Bill's surprise that was exactly what happened. Gradually, as the game began and Bill became engrossed in the many rules of Fumble, the people around him started to mind their own business. But the sense of being watched never quite left Bill's mind. He still felt the urge to look over his shoulder every few minutes, but the terror that had filled his guts when he first stepped into the yard had become manageable.

Time moved quickly, and soon people started finishing up their exercise routines and making for the building's entrance.

"Gah," declared Reg. "Time's up."

"Already? There's no way that was an hour."

"It's Fumble, I tell ya. Most entertainin' game ever. Even if I did kick your arse at it."

"Obviously you did. You made the rules up."

They both laughed and Reg grabbed Bill's hand for another violent handshake before squirrelling his cards away back inside his tracksuit bottoms.

"It was real nice gettin' to teach you the game," he said. "A real honour."

"It was nice to learn the ropes," replied Bill, and he meant it.

It was finally good to have his mental skills challenged with something new and strategic, like a prison crafted card game. And as he now looked at Reg, he no longer saw his tattoos or his scar, but noticed a friendly smile and twinkling eyes. He saw a friend.

"I guess I'll be seeing you tomorrow," said Reg as he walked away. "I mean, if they let you back out into the yard."

"Yes, they will. I'll see you tomorrow."

As he watched Reg return indoors, Bill now realised he was the last prisoner in the yard. Once again, he felt Terry's intense gaze on him.

"What the hell are you up to?" asked Terry as he walked up to Bill as though he was retrieving an unruly child. "Reggie Stables. You're kidding me."

"Reggie Stables…" he repeated. "Should I know him?"

"Know him? Everybody knows him. He's one of the most dangerous bank robbers this country's ever seen. Killed two guards doing a bank job in Hackney. Killed just as many inside."

"Inside..." Bill chewed over the word. "You mean he killed two people inside here?"

"What did you think I mean? Jesus, Bill. I thought it would be good for you to get some fresh air. Didn't realise you'd go around fraternising with the worst. Reg is king in here. What he says goes. He's linked to everything and everyone and..."

Terry lowered his voice, gripped Bill's arm and pulled him closer.

"When he orders something it gets done, know what I mean?"

Bill's face blanched. He didn't need it spelled out.

"Wouldn't be surprised if that poor sod in the library was done in under his orders," said Terry, guiding Bill back indoors. "Jesus, Bill. If there was one person I'd tell you to stay away from it's him."

Bill felt his stomach clench as he returned indoors and smelled the stale air.

Killer, he thought to himself as he returned to his cell. *I'm friends with a killer.*

Chapter 31

Danielle

January 25th, 2016

Danielle let herself into the hall and felt her heart drop.

"What the fuck?"

She wasn't prone to swearing, and her use of a curse word had caught the attention of the housekeeper who was nearby dusting a bannister.

"Danielle? You've gone pale."

"The painting. Where's the painting?"

She ran to the spot on the wall where it usually hung and gawped at the empty space. In all her life she couldn't remember the space on the wall being so bare.

"Don't worry. It's in the wine cellar," explained the housekeeper. "Your father is having it moved. At least that's what I heard because…"

Danielle didn't hear the rest of her sentence because she was already dashing through the house, running down one corridor after another before she reached the kitchen. At the back of the room lay the door that led down to the wine cellar which she now noticed was ajar. As she approached, she heard voices coming from beneath; her father's and a northern accent she didn't recognise.

"It's okay, Bill," said the voice. "It'll be safe where it's going."

"Where's it going!" yelled Danielle as she pushed through the door and stood at the top of the staircase.

As she looked down, she saw her father leaning against one of the hundreds of shelves stacked with vintage wine. He had a cigar in one hand, and what appeared to be an invoice in the other. Beside him stood a stranger in blue overalls. In front of them both lay the covered shape of the Caravaggio painting, its canvas shrouded in linen.

"Dad?" she asked.

He stared up at her, his eyes widening in surprise.

"Where's it going?"

His eyes shifted nervously to the man beside him then back to Danielle.

"I wasn't expecting you back from uni today," he said. "I thought you were spending the weekend with your friends and-"

"Where's it going?" she asked again, her voice flat but tinged with anger.

Bill once again looked over at the man in overalls who took the hint and bowed his head.

"I'll, erm, give you a moment," he said, making for the stairs. "Left me phone in the van anyway."

He kept his head down as he brushed past Danielle and moved through the kitchen and out to the patio. Danielle waited until she heard the van doors open until she exploded.

"Dad what are you doing! Where's the painting going? Are you selling it!"

Bill had never heard his daughter raise her voice before, and the shock froze his mouth open.

"Dad, answer me."

"Sweetheart, I'm not selling it. You know I could never do that. It's just getting a little clean-up. That's all."

"A clean-up? What does that mean?"

"Well, it's old. Needs a bit of conservation."

"Why didn't you tell me?"

"Because... I knew how much it would upset you having the painting leave the house."

"You're so right it's upsetting me."

Her eyes moved from the painting up to her father's face. There was something in it she didn't quite recognise. A look she didn't quite trust. She couldn't explain why, but she couldn't shake the feeling this was the last time she would ever see the painting.

She descended the stairs and lay her arms across the frame, making sure not to touch the delicate canvas as the linen bunched up beneath her hands.

"It'll be okay," said Bill.

"When will it be back?"

"I don't know."

"You don't know?"

"Well, it can take a long time to do conservation work on something so priceless. It could take years even and-"

"Years!"

"Or maybe just a few months."

"Months?"

It was still a long time, but it felt more palatable than years.

Slowly, she bent down and pulled up the linen to glimpse the canvas, her eyes immediately searching for the cherub her and her father loved so much.

"Dad?"

"Yes, sweetheart?"

"Who is doing the conservation work?"

"Does it matter?"

"I just want to know it'll be in good hands and..."

"And...?"

"And isn't it supposed to be one of Caravaggio's unknown works? I thought it was, you know, under the radar, so to speak."

"It is."

"Then I'm supposing the work being carried out on it will be under the radar too."

Bill placed his hands on her shoulders.

"You don't have to worry yourself about any of this, okay? It's in good hands. I can promise you that. And it'll come back looking better than ever."

"You promise?"

"Of course, sweetheart. Now how about we open one of these bottles, eh? This Bordeaux looks lovely. I've been saving it for a special occasion."

"What's the special occasion?"

"I get to spend the evening with you," he beamed. "I really thought you were far too busy to come home these days. Especially after you met that... boy."

Danielle didn't like the way he spat out the word boy. He'd never met Fitz, and knew nothing about him except what Cecilia had complained about, and she didn't know Fitz either.

"Don't look at me like that," laughed Bill, grabbing the wine bottle and walking up the stairs. "He is a boy, isn't he?"

"Yes, but you didn't have to say it like... Never mind, I'll grab a corkscrew."

***

Danielle was on her second glass of wine and nibbling her third slice of Camembert when she noticed a dark look enter Bill's eyes. They'd been chatting and drinking for the past hour, her telling Bill all about the new, exciting people she was meeting at university and him telling her about his latest business ventures.

But now, as the conversation lulled, a sombre silence fell over the kitchen.

"What's the matter?" asked Danielle.

"Just... thinking about the painting. I'll miss it too."

He stared into his glass of wine and sighed.

"I really love that painting, you know."

"Me too, Dad."

"Yeah but..."

He paused and stared more intently into his wine.

"Your mother really loved it."

Danielle felt her heart sink. They never talked about her. Not even when Danielle had asked about her growing up. Bill would always close down the conversation, would cut off any attempt at discussing the woman he'd loved so dearly and never been able to forget never mind replace.

"Mum..." said Danielle.

She felt her throat tighten as she said the word. It felt weird to say it. Her friends threw the word around when discussing their own mothers as though they didn't quite grasp the importance or the luxury of it.

"Mum..." repeated Danielle. "You never told me she liked the painting too."

"It was her who chose it," remembered Bill.

There was both sadness and joy in his voice.

"We'd gone to view it together when a friend of ours offered us a private viewing in his gallery. It was all very hush hush. So very exciting. Her eyes had glittered when we walked in and she saw it for the first time. She said the cherub looked just like you. Said she had to have it. So I bought it of course. It made my heart light up to see her so happy. Of course it was the same day that..."

He choked on his words and took a big gulp of wine to compose himself.

"It was the same day we got the news."

"The news that…"

"She was dying."

He took another gulp of wine and set his empty glass down.

"We'd just made arrangements to have the painting delivered and had come home deliriously happy. We'd cracked open a bottle of champagne right at this table. She'd sat where you are now. Christ, you look so much like her. She was smiling so much. Then the phone rang."

Bill's gaze dropped away from Danielle's face and settled on a point in the distance at the back of the room.

"The phone rang and it was the consultant we'd met at the hospital the previous day. He had news. Said the results were back from the myriad of tests he'd been doing on her for the past few months. Jesus, there were so many tests."

He paused again. Swallowed hard and looked away from Danielle.

"Dad… You don't have to talk about this if-"

"No, it's okay. No point in pretending it never happened. I did what I always tried to do, threw money at the problem until it went away. But nothing could change the prognosis. He said the results were bad. The cancer had spread to her lymph nodes. That she had six months to live at the most."

Danielle noticed his leg started to bounce beneath the table and slid her hand over to him to rest it reassuringly on his arm.

"Oh, Dad… That must have been so awful."

"It's good you don't remember that period," he said. "You were too young. Of course Cecilia remembers some of it. But she was so young too and…"

He cut his own words off, scared he might burst into tears.

"Dad, you never told me about that day before," said Danielle, reaching for the bottle of wine to top up Bill's glass. "I didn't know Mum had ever even seen the painting."

It was a thought that filled Danielle with conflicting feelings. She was happy to know that although she could barely remember her mother, that they shared this joint love of the painting. But how she wished her mother was still there with her now to enjoy it.

"I just wanted to forget that day," said Bill, reaching for his glass. "It was an awful day. She cried so much. So did I. It was the most terrifying day of my life. Knowing that the person I loved so much was dying and there wasn't a single thing I could do to save her. My money was useless."

He leaned across the table and took both of Danielle's hands in his.

"Sweetheart, you've got to promise me that if there's one thing you learn in life, it's that money can buy you happiness to a point. It can make your life easy, make it comfortable, enjoyable even, but it can only go so far. In the end, all you really have are those you love. And you have to love them hard."

The intensity in his eyes scared her and she pulled away.

"I promise... Dad..." she said, weakly. "I know money doesn't mean everything."

He smiled back at her, his eyes still clouded in sadness.

"Good... Good... Now tell me everything about this boyfriend of yours," he said, suddenly changing the subject.

"Urgh... What has Cecilia told you?"

Chapter 32

Fitz

August 29th 2023

"I don't like how this is going," said Fitz, sipping his coffee.

After much negotiation about the place of the meeting, Lucien had eventually agreed to meet Fitz in the restaurant of a Hilton Hotel where they both sipped coffees and tried to blend in. But the two looked like an unlikely pair of friends and jarred on everything from clothing to body language.

"What don't you like?" asked Lucien.

"Everything. You've just been gallivanting about picking up guys for the team and I know nothing about them."

"Don't you trust me?"

"No," came Fitz' emphatic answer along with a laugh and a shake of his head. "Not in a million years."

Even Lucien let out a slight chuckle.

"You're a lawyer," said Fitz. "It's like trusting a great white shark when you're dripping in blood."

"I'll take that as a compliment."

"Only you would. Look, my point is, I'm not going any further with this until I have a say in who's in the team."

Lucien pursed his lips and drummed his fingers along the table.

"I suppose that's fair," he said, thoughtfully. "And I'm assuming you have your own people you want in the team."

"I might…"

Chapter 33

Marcus

August 29th, 2023

Marcus stood outside the pub looking in the window at his old friends who were crowded around the bar. All of them were laughing ferociously at a most likely vulgar joke, but Marcus' face was stony and still. At his sides, his hands shook. He tried to pull a pack of cigarettes from his jacket pocket but dropped them.

Shit, why did I agree to this?

I can't do it.

But remember what the therapist said. Just give it five minutes and see how it goes. The biggest step is walking in.

But as he turned towards the entrance to the pub, he felt frozen to the spot.

"Hey, Marcus!" came a voice.

At first he thought it was the bouncer talking to him, then he realised the voice was coming from behind him. A head popped out, and he recognised his old school friend, Taj who was waving like a maniac and grinning.

"Marcus, mate! Good to see you!"

Taj ran at him, engulfing him in a bear hug. It was the first time Marcus had been hugged in so long. Too long. He felt so overwhelmed by the moment. By the pub, by the feel of having a friend on the outside. He felt close to tears as he pulled away from Taj, and once again tried to pull out a cigarette. He managed it this time, but only because he took deep breaths as he moved, sweat pooling inside his shirt.

"It's been so long since I've seen you," beamed Taj, slapping him on the back. "Gotta say, was pretty surprised when I got your Facebook message. How long's it been? Ten years? Where've you been?"

Marcus felt himself struggle to breathe. He felt strangled by all the questions. Right in that moment he hated his therapist. It was her idea to send a Facebook message to his old friends with the offer of meeting up for a drink. As though he was a normal person who could do that sort of thing. As though he was perfectly used to being outside in public enjoying himself. As though he hadn't been inside Belmarsh for the last eight years.

Freedom... He thought. *Is this what it is? I'm not used to it. I don't want it.*

His hands trembled as he smoked. He tried his best to answer Taj's questions, lying through each one.

He'd been working as a holiday rep, he said. Had just touched down in England two weeks ago and was getting back in touch with all his old pals.

"Where were you a holiday rep?" laughed Taj. "Finland? Ain't a tan line on you."

"I was in the Swiss Alps."

"Oh, very nice. Didn't know you could ski."

"I, erm, snow-snowboard. Yeah, snowboard."

"Nice one. Well, you comin' in?"

Marcus took another deep breath and threw his cigarette end in the gutter, then he followed Taj into the pub. The second he took a single step inside the building he felt the rush of adrenaline that signalled a panic attack. His breath stopped and he instantly felt dizzy. It felt like his lungs were bound in a rubber band and his legs turned to jelly. Disorientation engulfed him and every cell in his body was telling him to run.

"I, erm, j-j-just realised..." he stuttered. "Meant to call my missus before I came in. Meet you at the bar in a minute?"

"Sure," grinned Taj.

Marcus didn't look back. He fled as though he was running for his life, turning the corner and dashing into a nearby alleyway. The smell of the rubbish strewn across the cobbles mingled with his panic made him projectile vomit against the wall. He could barely stand up or see, couldn't breathe or think straight. It felt like his insides were melting and he was losing control of his thoughts.

"Fuck," he managed to gasp as he wiped his hand across his mouth.

It was then that he felt the presence of someone standing behind him. He couldn't bear to see Taj's eager face and have to answer any more questions. So he was relieved when he looked over his shoulder and gasped, "Fitz?"

***

"Mate, you look rough."

"I feel it."

Fitz had walked a shaky Marcus back to his flat where he was now handing him a strong cup of milky tea laden with sugar. Marcus took it gratefully with still shaking hands.

"How did you find me?" he asked Fitz, his eyes moving over the living room.

For a second, he saw the framed photograph on the mantel piece of Danielle and Sarah. He knew about them of course, and knew better than to pry.

"Gotta be honest," said Fitz, sitting on the couch across from him. "Stalked you on Facebook for a bit. Saw you said you were going for a pint at The Stafford. Hung around outside until..."

"You saw me puke my guts up?"

"Yeah... You okay?"

"Yeah, man. I'm fine."

"You don't look fine."

Marcus sipped his tea and felt the sugar relax him slightly. Or at least it took the taste of vomit out his mouth.

"Agoraphobia," he suddenly burst.

Fitz stared at him.

"My doctor diagnosed me with agoraphobia. And depression. And generalised panic disorder."

"Shit."

"Can't stand busy places, or open places, or being far from my flat. I'd lock myself in my bedroom forever if I could."

"Shit, man. That's not good. How'd you end up like this?"

"You know why."

Fitz nodded. He should have guessed. He'd heard of people struggling the second they stepped out of prison from a long sentence. People who had come to think of places like Belmarsh as their home and felt like freedom was something they couldn't handle.

"Institutionalised," said Marcus, swallowing his tea. "That's what folk say in the forums I read online. Been inside so long I just can't adjust to outside life. Can't... be *normal*."

"Mate, you were only inside eight years. Some guys do twenty and -"

"Eight years was long enough to change me."

There was a long silence between the two men as they stared into their tea.

"I'm sorry," said Fitz. "I had no idea you were having such a bad time. Wouldn't have found you otherwise."

"Why did you find me?"

Fitz glanced up at the photograph of Danielle and Sarah.

"I need you to do some work for me."

"What kinda work?"

"It's, erm, not gonna be easy but-"

"Will it get me sent down?"

"What?"

"If I get caught will I get jail time?"

"Maybe but-"

"I'm in."

"Ay? You don't even know what it is yet?"

"I don't care. I'm in. You need a fall guy? I'll be it. Need a scapegoat? I'm in, alright? I want back in Belmarsh more than anything."

Chapter 34

Bill

August 30th, 2023

"Well, fuck. You absolutely floored me," declared Reg as he lost another round of Fumble. "I only taught you this the other day and now you're better than me."

"Oh…" chuckled Bill modestly. "It was just a fluke. Think I lucked out."

The truth was that Bill had lay awake for the last two nights thinking over the game's rules. Not because he wanted to beat Reg, but because he needed something to occupy his mind when he thought he was going nuts daydreaming about breaking out.

A few of the older inmates noticed Reg grimacing and came over to check if it was true.

"You beat Reg at Fumble!" said a wiry, old guy as he tucked his greasy hair behind his ear. "Bloody hell."

More people came over to see for themselves and soon Bill found himself surrounded, and he grew nervous.

Shit. I shouldn't have beaten him. I wasn't even trying that hard. What if they all turn on me?

But there was no anger on the faces around him, just respect. A little glow of pride started to form in Bill's stomach.

"Guess that makes you one of the team," said a voice behind him.

He looked round and saw a man about his age with a red handlebar moustache and a shaved head. At first, Bill thought his arms had both been dipped in black paint, but then he realised he was blacked out in tattoos. There was barely an inch on him that wasn't black. Even his cheek had what appeared to be a cross inked into his pale skin.

"One of the team," smiled Bill nervously.

"What do you say, Reg?" asked the redhead. "Shall we make him a member?"

The nerves welled up in Bill once again.

"Hold on. I'm not looking to join a gang."

Reg laughed and the others joined in to please him.

"You make us sound like a group of hooligans."

"I don't mean to be rude," smiled Bill. "But aren't you?"

They all laughed again and Bill tried his hardest to look composed.

"Well, I suppose we're not gentlemen," said the redhead. "Even if you are, but I reckon you'll fit in with us. What d'ya say, Reg?"

Reg nodded sagely and gathered up the cards to deal another game.

"I say we'd be honoured to have you in the team," said Reg. "But we're not a gang."

"So what are you?" asked Bill.

Reg thought for a second as he dealt the cards.

"A lovable band of rogues."

"Do you have a name?"

"No... No. We're not like an official gang. Just, you know, a brotherhood."

"Like the Masons?"

Reg laughed so suddenly and violently that it frightened Bill and he jumped.

"Yeah, like the Masons," laughed Reg. "We look out for one another. We do favours. That kinda thing."

Bill's brain started whirring into overdrive.

A brotherhood that do favours.

That would most likely do any favour I ask if I give them money.

"This brotherhood sounds tremendous," he grinned as he picked up his cards. "I'd be honoured to join. But if it's possible, I'd like to make a demand of you all first?"

They all fell silent and leaned in. Tension rose in the air.

This wasn't what usually happened. The men who joined usually simpered and graciously accepted their newfound place. They didn't make demands.

"You're making a demand?" asked Reg with an edge to his voice.

"I'll make it all worthwhile for you all. I promise."

"I'm listening."

"Take an art class with me. All of you."

There was silence for a second, then Reg burst out laughing again.

"What? I'm no fucking Picasso. Can barely hold a pencil."

"You don't have to. You just have to turn up. I'll pay you all for coming. How about five hundred quid a lesson?"

A murmur of excitement rippled throughout the group.

"Five hundred quid?" gasped the redhead. "You serious?"

"I'm serious. You in?"

"Fuck yes. I'm in," said the redhead.

"Me too!" yelled Reg.

Further murmurs of 'me too' erupted throughout the group, and Bill felt the excitement rise inside him.

A brotherhood, he thought. *A brotherhood that can help me get out of here.*

Chapter 35

Fitz

August 30th, 2023

"This is ridiculous. What are we doing here?"

Fitz looked around at the audience and sighed. Beside him, Lucien was staring at the stage expectantly with a lustful look in his eyes.

"Hey," said Fitz, nudging Lucien in the side. "What are we *doing* here? I hate magic shows."

"This is not a magic show."

"The poster outside literally has a review from The Daily Mail saying it's the most risqué magic show ever seen."

"Urgh..."

Lucien, annoyed, turned away from the stage and addressed Fitz like he was a stupid child.

"It's so much more than just plucking a rabbit from a hat. This is... This is... Well you'll just have to see."

Fitz huffed and crossed his arms across his chest. He looked across the audience again and saw the excitement on everyone's faces.

They all look way too old to be into this crap.

He stared at the stage and saw the glittering, red curtain. Behind it was a mystery, but Fitz could sense movement along with a growing excitement in the air.

"How long is this thing gonna be anyway?" moaned Fitz.

"Shhh! It's starting."

Lucien pointed at the curtain which began to draw itself to the side. Immediately, Fitz' eyes were assaulted by a strobing light as upbeat music that sounded better suited to a fairground entered his ears. He hated it and more than ever wanted to make a dash for the exit. Sensing his mood, Lucien, clapped a hand on his shoulder and grinned.

"Wait," he mouthed over the music. "You have to see her."

Fitz rolled his eyes and sat back against his seat feeling like a kid forced to sit through an excruciating school play. The music grew louder, reaching a crescendo and he felt his patience become paper thin.

Then she appeared.

A figure so willowy and dainty it looked like a fairy had appeared on stage through a haze of fog. Wild, red hair waved itself throughout the mist as she twisted and turned, dancing and weaving across the stage as a large tank of water was wheeled out behind her. He had to admit the dancing figure on stage was mesmerising, and she hadn't even started her magic act yet.

"The great Phenomena!" declared a voice over the sound system, and the crowd erupted into applause.

She danced closer to the edge of the stage as though playing hide and seek with the tank of water. She was close enough that Fitz could see her heavily painted features clearly. An elfin nose rested above plump, doll-like lips as her green eyes scanned the room. For a second, he was sure they met his with something close to desire, but as soon as the moment came it left, and she was back dancing across the stage again. She leapt towards the tank of water as though it was a lover, wrapping her limbs around it as the music lowered itself to a bassy rhythm.

Gradually, the music faded away leaving nothing but a loud heartbeat playing across the venue. Fitz could feel it in his chest. So could everyone around him as the entire audience leaned forward in their seats, watching as Phenomena climbed the water tank like a sprite. She lingered on the top as one of her muscular male assistants lifted off the lid. Another assistant of equal strength and size rushed to her side with a length of chain in his hands.

He took her wrists roughly in his fingers and began shackling her hands behind her back as she pouted.

"This is a bit raunchy ain't it?" said Fitz to Lucien.

Lucien didn't answer. He was too entranced by the spectacle of Phenomena as her male assistants tangled up her lithe limbs in chains before holding her above the water tank.

From the speakers overhead, the heartbeat grew faster, and faster becoming in time with Fitz' own. Then, without warning, the assistants dropped a wriggling Phenomena into the water tank.

The crowd let out a collective gasp as they all reached the edge of their seats, and the lights were slammed off. For an extended, terrifying moment, the audience was left in complete darkness and silence. The energy across everyone sizzled. It was dynamic. Contagious. It made Fitz feel as though he was on the cusp of panicking.

Then again, without warning, the lights slammed back on to show an empty water tank. From the corner of the stage, with great ceremony, arrived Phenomena dancing and winding her way seductively across the stage. The audience exploded into a cacophony of applause, but Fitz wasn't impressed.

"That was shit," he moaned. "She just climbed out the tank when the lights were off. Total con."

"Then why is Phenomena's hair dry?" asked Lucien with sparkling, awe-filled eyes. "Eh?"

"Oh yeah," mumbled Fitz, still unimpressed. "I guess that's something."

***

"What an utter sausagefest this is," complained Fitz as they entered the backstage lounge and saw a crowd of suited men trying to get Phenomena's attention.

Now out her stage outfit, she was dressed in a silk, emerald green dress that flowed down her wispy body. Despite being obviously exhausted from her performance, she smiled and talked to everyone, taking her time to make each man who shook her hand feel special. There wasn't a single one of them who said goodbye who didn't think there was a chance she was in love with him.

Fitz watched as she worked her magic. Not the magic she'd performed on stage, but the real magic that came from her charm and wit. That came from making every single person adore her. She had the kind of magnetism only the luckiest of people encounter perhaps only a handful of times in their life, and Fitz could recognise her talents.

She'll come in handy, he thought. *She could probably just smile her way into Belmarsh.*

The pair walked to the table at the back of the room, picked up a glass of champagne and waited their turn at the back of the room.

"She's wonderful, isn't she?" said Lucien.

"She's... talented."

"Yes, very, erm, talented."

Fitz couldn't take his eyes off her. Not because of her beauty, but because she appeared to hypnotise every man who came within six feet of her.

He watched as a man in his late forties, suave and immaculately dressed with salt and pepper hair, a deep tan and dazzling, white teeth, approached her. He took her hand, kissing the top as she giggled. Then he stepped in closer as though he was pulled by an unseen force.

A flash of something pale caught Fitz' attention and he noticed as Phenomena's hand snaked its way down the man's arm. He waited for her to take his hand, but instead she slipped it into his pocket and pulled out his wallet which she expertly flicked out of sight.

Fitz, aghast, looked around to see if anyone else had noticed, but there wasn't a single person in the room that wasn't caught up in her smile.

"Jesus," he said to Lucien. "She could probably rob a bank and the guards would help pack her bags."

"She's something, isn't she?"

***

Fitz looked at the clock and saw it was almost three in the morning. Only now, almost three hours after Phenomena's show ended, did the group of men around her start to dissipate.

"I'm starting to wish we hadn't agreed to wait for her," he yawned." I need my kip."

Exhausted, Fitz flopped down on the couch at the back of the room. Only one man hung around Phenomena now, and as she shook his hand and said goodbye, her eyes flicked over to Fitz. Her gaze lingered on him for a moment, then she swayed towards him, her smile never falling as she approached.

"Can't believe I have to come over and say hello myself," she said, her light voice dripping in sarcasm. "Were you ever going to come over?"

Before Fitz could rise from the couch or speak, Phenomena lowered herself down beside him, so close her thigh pressed against his. Fitz froze as he saw her up close and caught the scent of her perfume. The last woman he had been this close to was Danielle, and he didn't know how to act.

She's so beautiful.

But she's not Danielle...

"So you're the quiet type," she purred, leaning in closer to him.

He felt the rise of goosebumps up his spine.

"Why is that?" continued Phenomena. "A man that looks like you. You'd think-"

"Oh, glad to see you've finally met!" burst in Lucien, zipping up his fly drunkenly as he stepped out the bathroom.

After hours of waiting for the droves of fans to leave, he was finally relieved to see there was only the three of them in the room.

"Lucien..." she said, looking up from Fitz, obviously annoyed at his intrusion. "I was sure I saw you lurking around. I hope you're not here on business."

He shared a conspiratorial look with Fitz and smirked.

"As a matter of fact I am but... I think it'll be of interest to you."

Walking over to the table where the refreshments were turning stale, he picked up a glass of champagne and handed it to her.

"I'll fill you in," said Lucien. "I think you'll be very interested."

Chapter 36

John

August 30th, 2023

The only light that shone on the building that held the safety deposit box vault came from a dying street light. It flickered ominously against the concrete walls making John imagine the beginning of a zombie film.

He sat in the passenger seat, his balaclava already pulled down over his meaty face. Beside him, his getaway driver sat sweating nervously. In the back, was the only other member of the team, Darren. A young boy fresh out of a juvenile detention centre John had managed to bring on board at the last minute.

His spirits sank as he looked around the car. This wasn't the team he wanted. He should have been able to procure people of a much higher calibre, but everyone he asked kept turning him down.

"If Fitz ain't on board then neither am I?" was the most popular response.

Fucking Fitz... he thought as he watched the flickering light. *He thinks he's too good for this.*

He remembered back to that night he'd met him in the pub and still couldn't believe the change in him. He wasn't drinking. Wasn't smoking either. Who did he think he was, Jesus?

"Right fellas, ready?" he asked the car.

The only response came in the sound of the getaway driver's nervous wheezing. John watched as he fumbled in his pocket and pulled out his blue asthma inhaler which he sucked on hungrily.

"Jesus Christ," moaned John. "Don't fucking die on me."

"Sorry it's just... I've never done anything like this before."

Once again, John felt his nerve crumble.

A loud, nagging voice at the back of his head kept telling him to call the whole thing off. To go back home, make a cup of tea and watch TV like any sensible person would do. But as much as he knew that was the right thing to do, he couldn't stop thinking about the contents of the safety deposit boxes.

He had a meeting at the Job Centre the following morning. Another demoralising and utterly humiliating experience he couldn't bear to have again. Each time he met his work coach, Cheryl, a stout woman who always stared over the top of her glasses at him as though he was shit, he felt less than human. He was always getting badgered into applying for jobs that he'd rather kill himself than do. Jobs that he'd have to work for decades in to make a fraction of what lay in those safety deposit boxes.

I'm not stacking shelves in Tesco. Cheryl can go fuck herself.

"Right, let's go, Darren," he announced to the boy in the back seat.

He was met with a blank, terrified stare.

"Darren?"

"Yeah, yeah... I'm ready."

"So why are you just sitting there?"

Darren moved towards the door, but the second his hand reached the handle the anxiety hit him and he vomited hard against the window.

"Aw, for the love of God," moaned John, slapping his hand against his face. "You alright, Darren?"

Darren's response was to vomit again, but this time managed to open the door first. When he'd finished, he sat shaking in the back seat with his head in his hands.

"Fuck sake, you're useless to me," said John.

"I'm sorry, mate. I can do this. I can."

"No... Just... Sit here. Both of you."

"You're not gonna do it alone, are you?" gasped Darren, reaching for a bottle of water. "You can't. Wasn't the plan I'd knock out the guards?"

"You can't even knock your stomach into shape let alone the guards. Just fucking stay put."

Now propelled by anger, John jumped out the car. He pushed his hand down the front of his jeans as he swaggered across the road, the flickering light making him disorientated.

His fingers gripped hold of the handgun he'd bought from a friend. And as he pulled it out, he felt a surge of confidence.

I can do anything with this, he thought, swaggering right up to the front door of the building.

But as the entrance came into view, along with the two guards at the door, he realised just how badly planned out his scheme was. Or rather, there was no plan at all.

There was so much adrenaline in his body he felt sick with it, felt close to passing out. But he couldn't back out now. He took one step closer to the entrance, both security guards noticing him at the same time. They knew instantly something was wrong.

"Can I help you?" asked the taller of the two, but as the words came out his eyes fell on the gun in John's hand.

Instantly, both guards reached for their walkie talkies, their voices crackling. If John wasn't panicking enough already, his nerves were now reaching boiling point. He looked down at his gun, the only thing that could give him power in that moment.

"Let me inside and no one will get hurt!" he yelled, raising the gun to the taller guard's head.

John expected a look of fear to cross his eyes, but what he got instead was a calm response.

"The police are already on their way said the other guard."

John's heartbeat rose so fast he grew dizzy.

Their on their way already...

But I'm not leaving here empty handed!

He knew the sensible thing was to run and dispose of the gun quickly. But all he could think of was how he couldn't bear to see Cheryl at the Job Centre and how he needed cash. It was a need that, merged with his panic, made him do something he didn't even know he was capable of.

"Let me inside and I won't kill you," he said, forcing his voice to stay steady.

The two guards shared a look between them as though they thought they were dealing with an idiot. Sensing this, John grew angry, pointed his gun at the nearest guard and fired.

Until then, John had never fired a gun before. He'd brandished one a number of times in a show of bravado, but had never before found the inner strength needed to pull the trigger.

The deafening noise of the bullet exiting the barrel and lodging itself into the guard's kneecap terrified him. He stood dazed for a second, knowing he had crossed a line.

He looked to the other guard who's face had blanched at the sight of his colleague's blood running down the pavement.

"I'll do whatever you say," he told John. "Just don't shoot."

A sense of power swelled inside John's and he gripped the gun tighter.

"Just take me to the boxes," he ordered.

In fear of his life, the guard nodded and opened the door to lead John inside.

"You arsehole!" yelled the other guard who was now lying on the ground screaming through gritted teeth. "Call me a fucking ambulance!"

"Ignore him," ordered John, prodding his gun into the guard's back. "Just walk."

He could visibly see the guard shake with fear as he led him through the labyrinthine walls of the building until they were standing in front of a steel door. The guard punched in the code then watched with his face dripping with sweat as the door swung open.

John's excitement grew then tumbled when he found himself staring at another door. The guard tapped in a different code until this one swung open, then finally, when John thought it would never happen, he found himself staring at a long, narrow room filled floor to ceiling with safety deposit boxes.

Bingo.

He could feel his fingers itch with the need to grab them, but the second he took a step forward, he heard sirens in the distance.

"Fuck!"

He reached into his back pocket, pulling out series of folded bin liners he'd placed their earlier. He peeled one free and threw it to the guard.

"Start filling this."

Before the guard could move, the sound of screeching tires grew from the street and John knew his time was up. He didn't have enough time to fill one let alone a series of bin liners, and as he jolted towards the wall of boxes, ripping one free, he realised the thing was so heavy it tore right through the bin liner.

"Shit!"

Nothing was going to plan and everything was falling apart. He knew he only now had seconds, and he'd have to flee with what was in his hands; one miserable safety deposit box he grabbed at random.

He heard the sirens grow louder, and knew they'd be reaching the front of the building any second.

"Is there a back exit?" he asked the guard.

"There's a fire escape."

"Take me there. Now."

The guard walked at speed out the room with John breathing down his neck, a solitary safety deposit box gripped in his sweaty hands.

"This way," said the guard as they reached the end of the corridor.

He paused for a second, looking over his shoulder.

"Well, fucking open the door!" raged John.

He didn't need to raise his gun again, the guard knew what he was capable of. Pushing against the metal bar, he swung the door open to reveal a metal staircase that wound its way down into the alley below. It was slick with rain as John launched himself down it. In the distance, red and blue lights danced off the wet pavement. He ran in the opposite direction, his lungs burning with the effort.

Behind him, he heard a car's engine roar to life. Fearing the police, he ran faster, but felt relief wash over him when he heard the familiar voice of his getaway driver.

"Get in!"

The car drew to a halt for a brief second, just long enough to fling the passenger door open and jump in.

"Jesus, you've actually made yourself useful," gasped John, shaking uncontrollably as the car sped away.

"I hit the gas the second I saw the flashing lights," grinned the driver.

John felt his shaking eventually subside as they left the scene. Looking down at his lap, he saw the one safety deposit box he'd managed to escape with.

I just hope it was worth it.

***

Back in his flat, John sat alone on his couch. He kept glancing out the window for the police, certain they would roll up to his flat at any moment. On the coffee table in front of him surrounded by cigarette ends and empty beer cans sat the safety deposit box.

He was simultaneously excited and too scared to open it in fear of what he would find. Half of him wanted to find thousands of pounds in cash or diamonds.

But what if there's nothing in it?

In his hand, he held an old hammer and chisel from his toolbox. For a few more moments, he just kept staring at the box. When his curiosity felt like it was close to killing him, he jammed the sharp end of the chisel against the lock and hammered as hard as he could. On the third strike of his hammer, he heard the lock shatter as the lid jumped open.

Holding his breath, he pulled it back to peer inside. At first, he thought he was staring at nothing but an empty box, then he saw it. The small thumb drive nestled against the corner.

John felt his heard sink.

I shot a guy for this…

He picked up the thumb drive and stared at it in dismay.

His mind started to race.

What's on this that's so important it had to be locked away?

He jumped off the couch and ran into his bedroom where he jammed the thumb drive into the side of his laptop.

"Come on. Come on. Hurry up."

He waited for the file on the drive to load, and when he did, he clicked the play button so hard he almost crashed his finger through his laptop.

"What the fuck we got here?" he asked himself as he watched grainy CCTV footage come into view.

He saw a set of fire escape stairs similar to those he had just run down. He saw bodies dashing down them and riot vans rush to their side. Then he saw the flash of gunfire. Saw a body at the top of the stairs hit the metal steps, obviously dead.

"Jesus…" he thought out loud.

He watched it again. Then again. Then one more time.

The more he watched it, the more the realisation came to him. What he had in his possession was potentially worth more than money. He wasn't sure what he could do with it, not yet anyway. But what he did know was that the video he'd just watched was not meant to be seen by the public, and someone somewhere would pay to keep it hidden.

Chapter 37

Fitz

August 31st, 2023

Daylight was starting to shine across the skyline by the time Fitz stepped out onto the street with Lucien and Phenomena by his side. He yawned and rubbed his tired eyes, but he noticed Phenomena didn't share his exhaustion. If anything, she looked refreshed. As Lucien had told her of the details of their plan, her eyes had grown wider and wider with interest until she was almost leaping out her seat.

"I'll be in touch," Lucien told her, a look of desire rising in his eyes. "I do assume that-"

"I'm on board?" asked Phenomena. "Of course I am."

But as Fitz watched her talk, he could guess there was more to her saying yes than just the money. It was a chance for her to flex her brain and make use of her talents somewhere offstage.

"I'll call an Uber," yawned Lucien. "Assuming you'll share?"

Phenomena took a step back from Lucien towards Fitz and said, "Actually, I was wondering if Fitz would like to come back to mine for a coffee?"

Lucien raised an eyebrow, a look of jealousy flashing in his eyes.

"Thanks for the offer," said Fitz. "But I've got to head home."

"Oh, don't be like that," smiled Phenomena, placing a hand on his arm. "It's just a coffee."

"Just a coffee…"

"Of course."

A passing cab with its light on approached and Phenomena stuck out her hand. The driver, noticing her, came to a fast halt and she jumped in the back seat, pulling in Fitz after her.

"No, really," he protested. "I should really be going home."

But she was already leaning over him and pulling the door closed as the driver pulled out into the road. Fitz looked through the back window at the sight of a surly Lucien glowering after him.

"Jesus, you're smooth," he laughed, looking at Phenomena.

He wondered if anyone had ever said no to her.

"Where we heading?" asked the driver.

"Dolphin Square," replied Phenomena.

Only now did she show her exhaustion, yawning wide like a kitten before leaning her head against Fitz' shoulder. He felt the urge to wrap an arm around her and draw her closer to him, but didn't dare. Instead, he sat bolt upright, awkwardly feeling the heat of her body against his.

***

When they stumbled sleepily out the cab twenty minutes later, Phenomena was still glued to his side. Leading him up the stairs silently, she fished in her purse with her long, elegant fingers for her keys.

"I'm just on the second floor," she said, taking his hand.

He was torn between wanting to grip her hand tighter and wanting to push her away. Somehow, being close to her felt wrong, but there was the tingle of a thrill too.

As they reached her flat, she let go of his hand and unlocked the door. As she opened it, Fitz was hit by the feminine scent of candles and expensive perfume, and as they stepped into her flat, he couldn't help but take notice of the fine furnishings and expensive art on the walls. He wasn't surprised at her having good taste. He was, however, surprised at how easily she felt comfortable in front of him. The first thing she kicked off were her shoes. The second was her dress which she slipped off her shoulders and dropped to her ankles. She stood in front of him in nothing but a g-string.

"Please, can you put that back on?" he asked.

"Seriously?"

He couldn't help but hear a hint of hurt in her voice.

"If you don't mind."

"Oh... Okay."

She hurried to pull her dress back on, now embarrassed as her cheeks turned scarlet.

"You're... You're strange," she said to Fitz.

"I'm not trying to be strange, just respectful."

She furtively turned her back on him and walked through to the kitchen.

"I'll, erm, make that coffee," she said, still blushing.

He followed her while keeping his distance.

"You never told me your real name," he said, changing the subject and looking around the room.

The surfaces were scattered with brand new appliances, but it looked as though none of them had been touched, and she didn't strike him as the sort of person who spent her weekends baking.

"It's Felicity," she said, her back still turned to him. "Not quite as glamorous as Phenomena, is it?"

"I actually prefer it."

She turned to face him with a smile.

"Really?"

Behind her, the coffee machine spurted into life.

"Yeah, it suits you."

"I always hated it. I was named after my grandmother. She was a bitch."

They both laughed and the tension lifted in the air.

"Wanna take a seat in the lounge?" she suggested. "I'll be through with the coffees."

"There better be biscuits too," joked Fitz as he walked down the hall.

He entered the living room and sat on the couch, studying the bookshelves that lay on either side of the fireplace. Phenomena's literary tastes appeared to be split in two, with romance novels stacked up on the left and non-fiction on the right. His eyes were drawn mostly to the right, to the second shelf that housed a long line of books based on magic and illusion.

From behind the couch came the sound of cups teetering on a metal tray as Phenomena entered.

"I've only got ginger nuts, that okay?" she asked.

"I can see you're a fan of Ace Malburn," said Fitz, ignoring her question. "You've got all his books. Is he the inspiration for your show?"

"My inspiration and my mentor. He trained me."

"Wow. I remember his show, Aces High from when I was a kid. Used to watch it every Saturday night with a Chinese takeaway. How did you end up working for him?"

"Lucien introduced us."

"Get outta here."

"It's true."

Fitz noticed she was still blushing as she set the tray down on the coffee table. Her eyes met his for a split second then darted away.

"About earlier," she began.

"It's okay."

"I'm sorry."

"Let's pretend it never happened."

"I'm just so used to guys..."

"I can imagine. Forget about it."

"I feel like an idiot."

"Don't say that. And let's not dwell on it, okay? I'm more interested in Ace. I'm assuming he taught you how to divert a crowd's attention."

"Splitting focus? Absolutely! He was the best at it."

"Tell me about that," said Fitz, reaching for his coffee. "And by the way, yeah. Ginger nuts are fine."

Chapter 38
Danielle

June 20th, 2016

She stood in the hall staring up at the space on the wall where the painting was supposed to be. It felt like part of the family was missing.

"It's been six months," she said to Bill behind her. "Why haven't we got it back yet?"

He placed his hands on her shoulders to comfort her and gave a slight squeeze.

"I know you miss it, Sweetheart, but it will be back soon."

"You've been saying that for weeks."

"Urgh, you're not still gibbering on about that painting are you?" moaned Cecilia as she walked down the stairs and saw them both. "If it's not that painting you're talking about it's that bloody boyfriend of yours."

Danielle stared daggers at Cecilia as she flounced down the stairs past them, across the hall and out the front door leaving a trail of Chanel No5 after her.

"So…" said Bill. "What time is Fitz picking you up tonight?"

Danielle spun round and shot him a panicked look.

"How did you know that-"

"I overheard you on the phone earlier."

"Oh."

"So is this finally the night I get to meet him?"

She blushed and stepped away from Bill. She hadn't been keeping Fitz from her father on purpose, but wasn't in a hurry to introduce the two of them. Bill had only heard good things about Fitz from Danielle, but she was worried her father would judge him in the same way Cecilia was so keen to do.

"Well?" asked Bill. "You've been seeing him for how long now?"

"A whole seven months."

"Then invite him in. If he managed to turn your head he must be a keeper."

***

Eight o'clock rolled around and Danielle checked her appearance in the mirror for the third time. She couldn't shake her jitters as she touched up her eyeliner while constantly glancing at her phone.

"How can he still make me feel this way?" she asked her reflection.

Despite being on dozens of dates with Fitz, she always got butterflies like she was meeting him for the first time. But the second he flashed his warm smile at her, she'd relax and fall into his arms. Her favourite place in the world.

Her phone beeped and she looked to see his message flash on the screen.

Parked outside :)

Her stomach flipped as she grinned to herself. Then she quickly typed out a reply.

Come inside. My dad wants to say hi.

A moment later, she heard the sound of his car door opening and closing and the sound of his footsteps crunching up their long driveway. Rushing down to the front door, she watched on the intercom screen as he approached and pressed the button to open the gates.

"Dad!" she called out. "He's here!"

Bill appeared in the hall like he'd materialised out of thin air, and Danielle felt her stomach clench with nerves.

A firm knock sounded on the front door, and Danielle moved to open it. As she drew the door back, she saw Fitz dressed in pressed, black trousers and a black polo neck, the neckline accentuated by a thick, silver chain. She felt her body respond to him immediately and fought the urge to throw herself at him in front of Bill.

"Good evening," said Bill, striding towards him to shake his hand. "I've heard so much about you."

Fitz, as polite as ever, shook his hand and gave a curt nod.

"I've heard a lot about you too," he said. "It's a real pleasure to meet you."

Danielle noticed an insincere smile fixed on her father's face.

What is he thinking?

But she knew what was on his mind? He was judging him the same way Cecilia was. Hearing nothing but his broad, working class voice. Fitz could have been the smartest, richest man in the world and still all Bill would hear was his cockney accent.

"So, where are you taking my daughter tonight?" asked Bill.

"We're going to see a movie."

"What kind of movie?"

"A horror movie. It's called The Reckoning."

Bill's smile fell.

"Then what?"

"My God, Dad," interrupted Danielle. "Enough of the inquisition."

Bill looked down at her with a stern gaze and said, "I've just remembered I've got something in the kitchen for you. Fitz, if you could just give us a minute?"

"Of course."

Fitz, sensing Bill's instant dislike of him, looked down at the floor as they both walked away down the long hall and into the kitchen. Once there, Bill took Danielle's hand and said, "Are you sure about him?"

"What are you talking about, Dad?"

"It's just that…"

"That what?"

"I don't trust him."

"Dad! Why would you say that?"

"Look, Sweetheart. Listen." He took a seat at the breakfast table and sighed. "I've been around the block a few times. I'm a good judge of character."

"Then you should know that Fitz is nothing but lovely."

He pursed his lips and gave her a condescending look.

"Sweetheart, where was he schooled?"

"Why should that matter?"

"Just tell me."

"His local comprehensive."

"Oh, Danielle. Really? You can do so much better than that."

"Dad! I can't believe you're being like this. How can you judge someone on what school they went to?"

"I'm just trying to look out for you."

"You're being just like Cecilia," she raged, walking away from him. "I love Fitz regardless of where he came from."

"Wait, Danielle-"

But she was already storming out the kitchen and into Fitz' arms.

Chapter 39

Bill

September 3rd, 2023

The art teacher, Miss Higgins walked into the room in a flurry of handmade, patchwork clothing and curly, ginger hair. As she saw her class stare at her, she felt her stomach close to bottoming out. When her sociology supervisor for her post-graduate course told her about the work placement she jumped at the chance to apply. But she never thought she'd actually get the job, and now she wished she hadn't.

Art had always been a hobby of hers, and she had passed a module on her course about art therapy, something she thought would equip her to teach this course at Belmarsh. But as she stood in front of everyone, she felt she knew nothing. University didn't teach you how to talk to murderers, rapists and bank robbers.

She felt her mouth turn dry as she tried to speak.

"He-he-hello everyone."

"Speak up!" shouted someone from the back.

"I'm Gwen!" she said, forcing a smile. "I... I didn't realise the class would be so busy."

She was expecting half a dozen people at the most, not the thirty that were squashed into the stiflingly hot room in front of her.

"Hi, Gwen!" a few of the inmates chorused back to her mockingly.

From the back of the room someone whistled as someone else muttered dirty comments under their breath.

"Enough!" yelled Bill. "Looking around the room. Let the young lady talk."

The room fell silent. Not because they were in fear of Bill, but because he was the one holding the purse strings and everyone was still hoping to get paid five hundred pounds.

"Please," he said, turning to Gwen. "Continue."

She felt a surge of relief as the room came under Bill's control, and she decided to ignore anyone else but him. He had the calm demeanour of her grandfather, albeit with a greater sense of confidence.

"Thank you," she said. "I'll start again. My name is Gwen and I'm so pleased so many of you are interested in this class. Art can have so many therapeutic benefits that I'm sure you all can enjoy."

"I can't draw for shit," blurted out Reg from beside Bill. "All I can do are stick figures."

"That's great!" beamed back Gwen. "There's no right or wrong here."

Pulling out sheets of paper from her satchel, she started walking up and down the aisles placing one on each desk along with an HB pencil.

"Today, we're going to learn to draw our feelings," she said. "And like I said, there's no right or wrong."

"Do other people have to see these?" asked Reg.

"No, you can keep them to yourself or you can show them off if you like. No pressure."

Gwen's kindly presence started to have an effect on the room, and gradually, they all started to relax.

"Okay, shall we begin?" she asked. "We'll start off easy. I want you all to draw a shape that you think corresponds with a feeling you are having right now."

"What does correspond mean?" came a voice from a young inmate who was fidgeting nervously with his sleeve.

"I mean draw a shape you think looks like your feelings."

He stared back at her perplexed, but nodded anyway.

"Shall I put some music on?" she asked, her eyes moving to Bill.

"Bang on some gangster rap!" someone yelled.

"How about some classical?" suggested Bill.

Gwen nodded and pulled out her phone to find a playlist. She set it down on her desk just as the first few notes of a Philip Glass song tinkled out across the room. Taking a seat at her desk, she noticed she had been shaking, but as she looked out across everyone with their heads down and their pencils moving across the paper, she realised she had nothing to be afraid of.

Her eyes fell on Bill. Only now did she realise who he was, that she was sitting in front of THE Sir Bill Lovecroft. She had been so caught up in her own nerves that she hadn't registered who he was until now.

She'd seen him on TV plenty of times. Watching him ooze charm and charisma on talk shows. And she could see his presence fill the room now, even though he was silent. She watched his face as he stared at his page. He appeared to be intently drawing something with his pencil scurrying across the paper.

"How's everyone getting on?" she asked the room.

"No idea what I'm doing," said Reg.

"Me neither," someone else chimed in.

"I think I've drawn my feelings," said someone else. "Maybe."

"That's all great. You don't have to know what you're doing. Every drawing is valid."

Standing up, she began walking down the aisles.

"Very good!" she said, looking down at everyone's work.

She paused in front of Reg and saw he was hiding his page with his hand.

"You don't *have* to show me," she said. "But I'd like to see what you've drawn."

Gingerly, he pulled back his hand to reveal a crude drawing of a dagger.

"Oh?" she said. "That's not really a shape, is it?"

"A knife is a shape," replied Reg.

"And this is what you're feeling?"

He nodded.

The nerves returned to her stomach as she backed away from him.

"And what have you done, Bill?"

"Oh, it's nothing. Just a doodle."

"Can I see?"

He leaned back so she could bend down and look.

"Wow!"

"Really, it's nothing."

But Gwen was astounded and spent a long moment staring at the image on the page. Staring back at her wasn't a shape, but a face.

"Goodness, Bill. This is beautiful. Who is she?"

He eyes lowered sadly to the page as he replied, "My daughter."

Chapter 40

Richard

September 4th, 2023

Six in the morning came and Richard flopped out of bed. As he rose, he realised Sandra wasn't beside him, and he frowned. As he pulled on his dressing gown he realised he could hear her raised voice from downstairs.

It grew louder as he descended the stairs. As he walked into the kitchen, he saw her sucking on a cigarette as she talked on the phone, her cup of coffee steaming in front of her.

"You keep saying gone!" she screamed. "But when are you getting it back? What do you mean you don't know? You *have* to know!"

Reg, assaulted by her loud voice so early, walked over to the coffee machine and poured himself a cup before sitting across the table from her just as she hung up. She slammed her phone down on the table and buried her face in her hands.

"Oh, God," she cried.

"What's going on?"

"That was a PC Tamworth," she said. "Letting me know my safety deposit box has just been stolen."

"I... didn't know you had one."

An awkward silence fell between the couple.

"Sandra? You never told me you had one. What was it for? Your jewellery?"

She nodded, but there was a strange look in her eyes and he knew she was holding something back.

"Sandra... What was in the box?"

"Like you said, my jewellery."

"Anything else?"

"No."

"You're lying."

She lowered her hands from her face and met his gaze.

"What was in the box, Sandra?"

Her hands began to shake as she moved to light another cigarette.

"Sandra?"

"I kept the..."

Before she could finish her sentence, the sound of Richard's phone ringing filled the room. He answered it on the second ring, rising from the table.

"You're kidding me," he said. "When? What do you mean dead? No... no. Fuck, this is a nightmare. I'm coming in."

He hung up and took a large gulp of coffee before slamming down his cup and jumping up.

"What was that?" asked Sandra.

"There's been another attempt at Belmarsh," he said, pulling off his dressing gown. "Some lone wolf tried to shoot his way inside and got bloody killed in the process."

"No way..."

"Yeah, shot through the head apparently."

Sandra felt guilty at feeling relief. She was just glad, as she watched Richard dash out the room, that she hadn't been able to tell him the thumb drive with the footage of Danielle's death was now in a criminal's hands.

Chapter 41
Fitz

September 4th, 2023

Fitz arrived outside the bar where Lucien agreed to meet him, pulling up in his second hand Ford Focus. Lucien took one look at it from where he stood on the pavement and turned up his nose.

"Get in," ordered Fitz as he slid down his window.

Lucien glanced up and down the street like he was making sure no one saw him get into such an unglamorous car.

"I could have made my way to the safe house myself," he moaned, climbing into the passenger seat. "But no, you had to insist on picking me up."

"Don't want you turning up in a fancy car. You can't look conspicuous."

"Fair enough."

They drove in silence for a few minutes with Lucien constantly checking the time on his Rolex.

"You never told me where we're going," he said, looking out the window at the setting sun.

"Catford."

"Why are we going to Catford?"

"I've set up a meeting," explained Fitz. "The whole team will be there."

"Why am I just finding out about this? Did you not think to tell me you were setting up a meeting? Especially with so many of the team being my clients after all."

"Chill," said Fitz. "I wasn't being shady. I was just trying to keep things under wraps until the last minute. The last thing I want is for word to get out we're all meeting up."

Lucien looked at him out the corner of his eye. He didn't like how he'd not been kept in the loop, but he also couldn't fault Fitz' logic.

"So... What's in Catford?"

"Our safe house," announced Fitz proudly. "Sorted it with an old mate of mine who owes me a favour."

"And it is actually safe?"

"It is."

"You can trust this friend?"

"With my life. We were in Wandsworth together. He has my back."

Lucien didn't feel convinced. The word of someone he didn't know who'd served time in prison wasn't enough for him, but he kept his mouth shut.

"Here," said Fitz, pointing through the windscreen. "We're here."

At first, Lucien couldn't understand what he was looking at. When Fitz told him they were driving to a safe house, that's what he had a imagined, a house. But now he found himself down the bottom of an industrial estate staring at what looked like an abandoned warehouse. As darkness fell over it, he could just about make out the faint glow of electric light seeping out through the rusted shutters.

"Don't look so disgusted," laughed Fitz. "You'd think I'd just presented you with a giant turd."

Lucien shot him a telling look as he reached to open his door.

"Looks like the scene of a horror movie. Pretty sure I'm going to walk in to find some psycho waiting with a dentist's chair to pull out my teeth with pliers."

"Christ, you're so dramatic, Lucien."

Fitz laughed again and led the still nervous Lucien towards the building. As he approached, he could hear everyone's voices talking over one another. Billie's was the loudest followed by Jacques'. They seemed to be in a heated debate over a new tax hike that had recently been announced in the news. Gradually, their voices softened as the sound of Fitz rolling up the shutters echoed out across the warehouse.

He was revealed to them in the haze of the outside street lamps, the silhouette of his figure towering over Lucien beside him. Silence filled the warehouse as they all regarded him.

The team were sat around a fold up table in the centre of the room, each of them looking out of place in their own way.

"I see you've got to know each other," Fitz said, looking at Billie and Jacques.

He felt a soft hand land on his arm and glanced down to see Phenomena looking up at him with her wide, admiring green eyes.

"Right then," said Fitz. "Let's get down to business."

He pulled up a folding chair and took his place at the top of the table with a shiver. He could smell the damp in the building, could feel a cold draft slide up his back. It wasn't the most luxurious of settings, but it suited him perfectly. They were out of sight here, and thanks to his friend, the building was kitted out with CCTV that was linked to his phone. If anyone came near, he'd be notified.

Behind him, Lucien lurked in the shadows.

"Aren't you joining us?" asked Fitz over his shoulder. "It was you that brought us all together."

As Fitz spoke, his eyes fell on Phenomena once again. He'd known Lucien had represented most of these people over the years, getting them the best deal on various charges, but what was Phenomena in trouble for?

You're a dark horse.

Turning back to the team, he saw all their expectant faces stare back at him. Billie was the first to address him.

"Thirty-eight billion quid, right? You promise we'll get our hands on all of that?"

Her enthusiasm was so aggressive Fitz felt assaulted by it.

"All I can promise is that if we stick to the plan properly, all do our part, and nothing goes wrong, we are in with a chance."

It wasn't the answer Billie wanted, but before she could complain Phenomena interrupted.

"What *is* the plan, Fitz?"

He looked back at Lucien and gave a slight nod. Now was the time to spur things into action.

"The plan..." began Fitz.

It had been keeping him awake for days, had been tormenting him. It had been the main source of conversation between him and Lucien. It had been eating him from the inside out.

"The plan has to be seamless," he began. "Now everyone listen up."

Chapter 42

Hawkins

September 4th, 2023

It was raining so heavily it sounded like gravel was being hurled at the windows. In the kitchen, Hawkins smiled inwardly under the assurance that she had a quiet day to herself. There were no charity engagements today or consulting jobs. Just her own company in the warmth of her own home.

Sitting at the kitchen table, she looked through the day's papers while savouring her coffee. It were moments like this she wondered if she should get a cat. Dogs were too much effort, too much like children, but a cat would suit her. It would certainly share her aloof personality and independence.

As she reached the end of her coffee, she thought she'd indulge herself with a bar of dark chocolate, one she kept for special occasions in her bottom drawer. As she plucked it out, she felt her craving for it grow. Sitting back down, she snapped off a square and placed it on her tongue.

Hmmm better than sex.

She closed her eyes for a second, listening to the rain batter the windows as she revelled in the warmth of her kitchen and the taste of the chocolate. The rain was so loud, she didn't hear the doorbell until it rang for a third time. But she was in no mood to answer it. It wasn't until it rang once more, this time with a sense of urgency that she sighed, placed the chocolate down on the table and acknowledged her personal time was over.

The sound of the rain grew louder as she walked down the hall. As she looked through the frosted glass of the front door, she could already tell who her visitor was.

"Dickie," she said with contempt, opening the door. "I suppose you're back with that thumb drive."

"Fuck that. For now…"

They stared at each other for an extended moment, any sense of passion between them long gone.

"Are you going to let me in?" he asked through wet lips as the rain lashed his face.

"Not unless you've got the drive."

"I'm not here about that. I need you."

"You need me? Seriously, if you think you're going to get lucky then-"

"Not like that. Listen, there was another break in attempt at Belmarsh this morning. The poor sod got fucking shot in the process. The press are going wild, as you can imagine. It's created a shitstorm for me."

"And what's that got to do with me?"

"I need your help to put a stop to this whole Bill Lovecroft nightmare."

"Pffftt… That's your problem, not mine."

"But you were the best…"

She stared into his eyes and saw a look of desperation.

"I mean it," he continued. "You were the best at your job."

"I was a good prosecutor. I'll admit that. But my time doing that is over."

She moved to close the door over but he leaned in to block it.

"I'll set you up with a task force," he said. "You'll get the best people, and I'll make sure you're paid the best-"

"I'm not interested. I don't need the stress and I definitely don't need the money."

"I know you don't need the money. But don't you want one more chance at taking down the bad guys. One last blaze of glory?"

"You're talking like we're in an old western," she said, rolling her eyes. "I'm done with this. I just want a quiet life."

She moved once again to close the door, this time, he didn't try to stop her.

"Just think about it!" he said as the door closed on him. "I really need you."

She stormed back down the hall into the kitchen, needing the chocolate more than ever. As she snapped off a square, she realised it wasn't enough and she needed a glass of wine. Rummaging in the top drawer for the corkscrew, she raged inwardly at the audacity of Richard.

Prick. Steals that USB and now he's crawling back saying he needs me.

She poured a glass of red Bordeaux and took a liberal gulp.

As she set her glass down, she cursed herself for ever getting involved with him.

"Fuck him," she said, taking another gulf of wine. "And his wife."

***

She was still angry as she settled into bed. The rain was still lashing the windows, drowning her bedroom in the sound of white noise. As she lay her head down, and stared at the ceiling, she felt more wide awake than ever, and the wine had done nothing to soothe her anger.

Forget about him, she told herself, rolling over and pulling the covers up over her shoulders. She closed her eyes and tried to fall asleep, but all she kept seeing was the image of Richard standing at her front door with the rain dripping down his face.

She was relieved when the sound of her phone distracted her from his image.

Who the hell is it at this time? she thought, leaning towards the bedside cabinet for her phone.

She didn't recognise the number, and felt the urge to ignore it, but curiosity got the better of her and she tapped the green button.

"Hello?"

"Lizzieeee!"

"Who is this?"

"For Christ's sake, Lizzie. It's me, India!"

"Oh... OH!"

She sat up in bed. In the background, behind India's voice, she could hear a Motown classic blaring.

"So!" yelled India. "Some of the old uni girls are having a little get together tonight. I sent you an email invite."

"Sorry. I've been a bit distracted. Must have missed it."

"I can't belieeeve you're not here!" squealed India. "I was so looking forward to seeing you."

"Maybe we can catch up soon."

"Why not come down now? We're in The Luxe Club."

"Oh... No. I can't."

"Why? Don't tell me you've had a better offer."

Hawkins looked across her empty bed and sighed.

"No, it's just that-"

"Just get down here!"

Hawkins once more looked across her empty bed and knew she faced nothing but a sleepless night stuck with her own thoughts.

"I'll call a cab," she smiled down the phone. "I'll be there in an hour."

***

When Hawkins arrived at The Luxe Club she noticed the admiring gazes of a group of men sat at the bar. Ignoring them, she moved through the crowds of people until she found the booth at the back of the room from where she could hear India's shrill laugh.

"Lizzie!"

India teetered over in her heels and threw her arms around her.

"You made it."

She looked across the booth and was delighted to see the faces of old friends she'd promised to catch up with, but hadn't managed to in so long. They all beamed with smiled as they said their hellos. And as she hugged them all and squashed herself down into the booth beside them, reaching for a glass of wine, she felt like they'd never been apart.

But as she relaxed back in her seat and soaked up the atmosphere, she felt the heat of someone's gaze on her. She turned her head to look at the table beside her and recognised the long blonde hair immediately. It was groomed to perfection in the same way it had always been, flowing down over sharp features and around cold, pale blue eyes.

She felt herself stiffen as India topped up her glass.

"What's up?" she asked, sensing Hawkins' discomfort.

"You never told me *Lucille* was going to be here."

India looked over her shoulder at the icy blonde and gave Hawkins an apologetic smile.

"Sorry," she said. "I couldn't leave her out."

"Yes, you could have."

Hawkins leaned in closer towards India's ear.

"Nobody here likes her."

"I'm aware of that," laughed India. "But how long have we all known each other? Thirty years? And how long have we decided that as women we should all stick together after uni, especially in this business. She might be a bitch, but we're all sisters in this."

Hawkins laughed so hard she snorted.

"You're kidding me. That bitch has never seen herself as a sister to me. A rival, yes. An enemy, definitely. But never a sister."

"Please, don't take her being here so personally. I know you two never got along, especially after that last little mishap."

"Little mishap? She literally swooped in and stole my client from under my nose, the hawk-faced harpy."

India chuckled at the insult, then quickly let her smile fade.

"I'll pretend I didn't hear that. Anyway, you should take it as flattery."

"Flattery?" asked Hawkins, raising an eyebrow.

"Yeah, flattery. She knew you were the best and she wanted to beat you, wanted to be up there with you and she didn't have the talent so she turned to underhanded tactics."

"That's one way to look at it."

They both detected movement from behind them and turned just in time to see the flash of blonde hair and the hawk-eyed face approach.

"Lizzie Hawkins," came a sharp voice. "I thought I heard your voice. How about a drink?"

"Got one. Thanks."

"Aw, come on. Don't be like that. You're not still sore, are you?"

"Sore? About what exactly?"

"About that little client of yours."

Hawkins said nothing. She didn't want to engage in any conversation, didn't want to even think that Lucille even existed. She simply wanted her to disappear. But instead, Lucille lowered herself down into the seat beside Hawkins and reached for the champagne that lay in the ice bucket on the table. India, sensing instant tension between them, slid off her seat and pretended to notice someone at the bottom of the bar.

What the Hell, India? Don't leave me.

Silence lay thick across Lucille and Hawkins. Hawkins wanted to remain her usual cool self, but she also didn't trust herself to not shoot a barbed insult at Lucille if the opportunity presented itself. She took another sip of her wine and thought, *I should have stayed at home.*

"So, early retirement..." said Lucille, her voice heavy with meaning. "You always did like to get off early."

Hawkins said nothing, and instead focussed her gaze on a handsome older gentleman standing at the bar. He looked like what Richard wished he looked like; tall, bronzed and sporting a slick salt and pepper haircut.

"So, tell me," continued Lucille, not getting the hint to leave. "What do you do to fill your days?"

"I'm extremely busy. Have a lot of speaking engagements. Charity events. Consulting work."

Hawkins turned to see a knowing look in Lucille's eyes that made her fight the urge to slap her. It was the same look she'd given her when she'd stolen her client.

"Sounds like you've got your hands full," she smirked. "I guess you're too busy to join the task force."

Hawkins froze and felt her stomach flip.

"What... did you just say?"

"The MET's new task force, of course," smirked Lucille. "I was visited by the commissioner himself today. Said you'd turned him down. That has to be a first. You, turning down Richard. I've got to say I'm pretty surprised. Especially as it was you who put old Bill in jail in the first place. Wouldn't you be intent on keeping him there?"

Hawkins felt her jaw clench so tight it sent a shooting pain into her temples.

"As you know," said Lucille. "I'm never one to settle for second best, but when he asked me to join, I did say I'd have to think about it. The money after all, who could turn that down? And imagine getting to put that on your CV. Leader of the Belmarsh breakout task force. That's not the kind of experience you get in court rooms. This is real life. This is the stuff movies are made about."

Hawkins' heart pounded. She hated Richard and wanted nothing to do with the task force, but she hated Lucille more.

"I bet you jumped at the chance to bag that job," said Hawkins.

"Actually," laughed Lucille. "I said I'd give it twenty-four hours to mull it over. You can never be too keen with these things, can you? Make them wait and their rates go up. Isn't that always the way?"

Hawkins found her body rising from her seat before she realised. India noticed her walking at speed past her and tried to grab her attention, but her gaze was laser focussed ahead. Her phone was out her purse and in her hand by the time she reached the entrance to the club. As she stepped out onto the pavement, she tapped Richard's number.

"Lizzie?" he answered with a yawn.

"I'll do it. Set up a team and my own office. I'll be there at six tomorrow morning."

She hung up before he could reply. Then she looked down at the time on her phone. She had five hours before she began.

Chapter 43

Fitz

September 4th, 2023

"Right," began Fitz, walking up and down in front of the team. "Everyone listen up."

They all watched him in awe as he stepped slowly with controlled steps, his mind whirring into action as he moved. Phenomena, especially, couldn't take her eyes off his physique, and as she turned to Amelia, she saw a look of desire also rise in her eyes.

Don't you dare, she thought. *He's mine.*

Although as her arousal for him grew, her mind travelled back to that moment in her flat when he'd made her put her dress back on. An incident that only made her want him more.

He's both a gentleman and a thug. I just hope he's a thug in the bedroom.

Beside her, Billie was fidgeting in her seat like an aggravated toddler, bored of waiting to hear the plan.

"I think I should be the face of the team," she announced. "I have the most YouTube subscribers."

"No, you don't," said Jacques. "I do. And I have more *real* followers. You know, ones that actually turn up to see me. You're just a tiny face in a tiny screen and-"

"Right, shut the fuck up!" yelled Fitz, his voice cutting through the room making everyone jump. "This is how it's going to go. I'm going to speak and you're all going to listen. Got it?"

They all nodded back at him in silence.

"So, Billie," he said, walking up to her. "Since you're so keen on the idea of being famous, I've decided you *will* be the face of the team in the form of a distraction. You can use your big following and your even bigger mouth to cause a diversion. Sound alright to you?"

She nodded.

"And Jacques your massive following are going to come in helpful to us. I've seen the videos of you speaking to the crowds in Hyde Park. You're like some vegan fucking green juicing Jesus to those braided hippy birds. They'll do anything for you."

Jacques leaned back and smiled to himself knowing just how true that was, and remembering how especially true it was with the girl he took home the night before. She'd done anything he asked without question. The beginnings of an erection stirred in his boxers as he remembered this, and he quickly turned his attention back to Fitz' stern face to make it go away.

"So..." continued Fitz. "Your job is to mobilise those followers of yours. You've literally got an army at your disposal. Get them working underground. Ever heard of the Maginot Line?"

"What? Is that some kind of kids' show?"

"Jesus," moaned Fitz. "I thought you were supposed to be smart. The Maginot Line! Google that shit. Right, moving on, Marcus and Amelia."

Until now, the two had remained silent at the back of the room with Marcus nervously watching the evening unfold. On the other hand, Amelia was the opposite of nervous, but had decided to keep a calm and quiet exterior as she watched Billie and Jacques squabble like brats.

"You two," said Fitz, pointing at each of them in turn. "Are the muscle."

"Muscle?" laughed Jacques. "Amelia's a girl."

"Hey!" burst Amelia. "I'm twice the size of you, you little private school twat. I could crush your windpipe with my thighs."

"Quiet!" shouted Fitz. "What did I fucking say?"

"You talk, we listen," murmured Amelia, still seething at Jacques.

Yeah I'm a girl all right. One who'll never join your army.

She looked over at Marcus and saw his arm shaking. There was something about him she liked immediately but couldn't quite identify. A sense of vulnerability, a need to be nurtured. She felt the strongest urge to lean over and hug him. Something he looked like he desperately needed.

That man's been through a lot. I can see it in his eyes.

"Okay, now Cecilia," continued Fitz.

Everyone turned to her thinking the same thing. *What is she doing here?*

She remained on the periphery of proceedings, with her chair a few feet back from everyone else like she didn't want to be too close to the common people. Amelia had disliked her on sight. She was the kind of girl she'd encountered when patrolling the streets on the weekends. The kind of rich, spoiled girl she'd catch drink driving but never got prosecuted because of her status as someone's daughter.

Bill's daughter, she thought. *The spoiled bitch.*

"Cecilia," said Fitz, pulling up a seat to face her. "You're going to use your connections. You've got enough of them."

Cecilia nodded then reached into her purse for her cigarettes.

"Ew, don't light that thing around me," said Phenomena. "Can't you go outside?"

"Outside!" cried Cecilia, as though she'd been asked to enter a sewer.

She lit her cigarette anyway, despite Phenomena's protests and exhaled the smoke cockily.

"Connections," she said to Fitz. "What do you mean?"

"Your old school friends. You have the benefit of having classmates in high places, friends who frequent all the most exclusive clubs. Use them."

Cecilia nodded as she breathed in more smoke.

"I can do that. They'll be so excited to be part of this."

"No!" exploded Fitz. "You don't tell them shit. No one in this room tells anyone anything. I thought that would have been obvious."

He was growing weary of talking to his team already.

They're like a bunch of badly behaved cats.

"Promise me, everyone," he said, looking into each of their faces. "That what you hear in this room never leaves your heads. Got it?"

"Got it," they all answered.

"Okay, now Phenomena," he said.

Her eyes twinkled as his attention turned to her. She hated how she was so attracted to him, and how her body reacted like he was the first man she'd ever seen.

"Your job," he said to her. "Is perhaps the most crude. You're an attractive woman. You know that. You're a charmer and an illusionist. It's a killer combo."

She felt a flurry of excitement as she absorbed his compliments.

"The guards are trained to keep prisoners under control and the prison impenetrable, but they'll be putty in those magic hands of those."

She smiled, but across from her, Cecilia bristled with jealousy.

I'm hot too, she seethed to herself. *I can charm the guards as well.*

The night was wearing on, and the team, though excited, was growing tired. Meanwhile, Fitz didn't want to bombard them all with too much information on their first meeting. He wanted to get a feel for all their personalities, wanted to see how they would all behave around one another. And he was starting to see tension and potential cracks. There wasn't a single sideways glance or comment he missed. He could plainly see how Cecilia glared at Phenomena, could see how Phenomena stared lustily at him. He could feel the hatred between Billie and Jacques. And he could feel something else stirring between Amelia and Marcus. He stared down to the back of the room where they sat and noticed them exchange a glance. It lasted less than a second, but he knew what it meant.

Oh, God. They've only just met and they're into each other.

The last thing he needed was added romantic drama, and he definitely didn't need jealousy and hatred stirring between the other members.

"Okay, that's enough for tonight," he said. "I want you all back here at the same time tomorrow. I've got something planned."

"We're going to finally start the break-in?" asked Billie.

"Eh, no. You're not ready yet. Before that I need to know you can all work as a unit. That you all trust each other. One broken link in this chain and the whole operation is going to turn to shit, got it?"

Billie nodded and the others all stared at one another.

"You're all going to be doing some team building exercises tomorrow."

A collective groan emanated from the group.

"Team building exercises," moaned Jacques. "Really? Like some corporate training day. Christ."

"You're doing it, okay?" said Fitz. "I need you all to prove you're in this together. That you've all got each other's backs. I don't want any of your egos getting in the way. You're a team."

"Sounds like communism to me," said Cecilia, tossing her cigarette end on the ground and snuffing it out with her Louboutin heel.

"What it sounds like," said Fitz. "Is that you all need to learn that none of you are above anyone else. You're a team. You're going to be a well oiled machine by the time I'm done with you all. Now go home, think over everything and come back tomorrow."

Everyone rose from their seats and aimed for the door. Everyone but Phenomena, who was still in her seat staring at Fitz.

Chapter 44
Danielle

July 2nd, 2016

Danielle had never seen her father's face so red before. He was almost frothing at the mouth, pacing back and forth in front of her and Fitz who were pressed up against each other on the couch. Behind him Cecilia was staring at her with the look only a big sister could give. A look that said - *I'm his favourite now.*

Danielle felt her face burn with a mixture of fear, embarrassment and sadness. Arguments between her and her father were rare, if ever, but they had escalated since she'd first brought Fitz home the month before. Just one month. And it felt as though everything in her world had changed.

"I don't believe this!" yelled Bill, still pacing.

He was smoking a Cuban cigar as he clenched his jaw. His fingers flexing as he waved his hand to emphasise his angry words.

"How could you have been so bloody stupid!" he yelled, his eyes moving in between Danielle and Fitz.

He stopped pacing, walked up close to Fitz and leaned down to speak into his face.

"You did this on purpose you little scally," he seethed. "Knocked her up so you'd be in the family. So you'd get your hands on some cash."

"No!" cried out Danielle. "Dad, no. It was an accident. It wasn't Fitz' fault."

She began sobbing. In her hand lay the positive pregnancy test she had taken three days previously which she had thought she'd hidden well. She'd been in a state of constant panic since the moment she'd taken it, deciding to wait until the right time came when she could break the news to her father on her terms. But her plan had fallen apart when

Cecilia had been rootling about her room in search of clothes to borrow and found it in a drawer.

Danielle still felt the anger surge in her, felt the betrayal at having her sister break the news to their father when she had begged her to say silent. She looked up at Cecilia now and wanted to strangle her.

How could you do this to me? she said with her eyes. *You're supposed to be on my side.*

Cecilia read the look on Danielle's face and glanced away.

"Dad, please... Can you calm down?"

"Calm down!"

"Please!"

"How am I supposed to be calm when I've just discovered my little girl is pregnant for Christ's sake."

"Dad... I'm not a little girl. I'm an adult."

"Barely."

"But I am."

But Bill couldn't see her that way. She would always be his little girl. Would always be the little innocent cherub from the painting. The painting that had still failed to materialise back in the hallway. He looked down at her now sobbing and his heart ached. Despite his anger, he dropped to his knees, stubbed out his cigar in the nearby ashtray and took her in her arms.

"Danielle, sweetheart. We'll fix this. He cupped her face in his hands and kissed her forehead. We can make this all go away and you can carry on with your studies."

She pulled away and looked into his eyes.

"What do you mean... go away?"

She glanced nervously to Fitz who was fiddling with the sleeve of his jumper. He'd been biting his tongue for the past half hour. Wanting to yell back in Bill's face and stand up for Danielle. But out of respect he'd remained silent. He knew the situation was bad. Knew that the last thing he wanted to do was anger Bill even more.

"Go away," repeated Bill. "You know what that means."

The realisation hit Danielle and she flinched in her seat before jumping up off the couch.

"No, Dad. I'm not getting rid of the baby!"

"Oh, sweetheart, it's hardly a baby at the moment. Get an abortion now and it won't be a bother. I can have the best obstetrician here today. And by tomorrow we can forget this whole thing ever happened."

He tried to grab Danielle to hold her but she stepped back.

"Dad, no! I'm keeping this baby. I love Fitz. And I'll love our child."

"You don't know what you're talking about. Love? You love this man?"

"I do," she said with no hesitation. "I love him and I want to have a family with him."

Bill felt a knot form in his chest at hearing the word family. He glowered at Fitz and thought she had lost her mind. When she'd first brought him home he was horrified. What could such a gentle, intelligent person like his daughter see in a thug like Fitz? He tried to tell himself it was just a fleeting infatuation. That she'd tire of his bad boy image and find someone more suitable, like one of the many young men she went to university with that came from affluent families.

He'd waited for this to happen, but could only watch with growing horror as her obsession with Fitz grew. And now she was talking of starting a family with him. The thought made him want to vomit.

Fitz met his gaze with an unwavering strength that unnerved him. He might have been silent, but he'd been emanating a quiet and strong sense of dignity. Amongst all the chaos and anger in the room, Fitz had remained calm and composed, at least on the outside.

Bill stared into his face, feeling as though he wanted to punch it.

"You've ruined my daughter's life," he said. "She could have been anything she wanted, and now she wants to be a mother to your child. *Your* child..."

Fitz could feel the hatred wash over him like a wave of energy. He knew in another setting, if perhaps Bill wasn't so much of a gentleman, that fists would be flying. He ignored the way Bill looked at him and slowly rose off the couch to approach Danielle. He took her tenderly in his arms and kissed the top of her head, his eyes never leaving Bill's face.

"Bill..." he said, holding Danielle closer. "You and me both want the same thing."

"I doubt that."

"We do. We both want Danielle to be happy. I'll make it work."

"What does that mean?"

"It means I'll do whatever it takes to make sure both she and our child have the best life. She can stay at university, I'd never take her education from her. You can hate me all you want, Bill. I respect that. I'd hate me too. But who we both love is Danielle. Can we at least agree on that?"

Bill nodded slowly.

He looked at Danielle and saw the way she eased herself so happily into Fitz' arms. Saw the way she looked up at him. It was the same way she used to look at him when she was a little girl with a look of pure adoration.

She really isn't my little girl any more, he thought to himself.

"I love Danielle," said Fitz. "More than anything. And I will love our child."

Bill, despite the anger still simmering at the base of his gut, felt himself relent ever so slightly, if only for Danielle's sake.

"Sweetheart," he said, resting a hand on her shoulder. "This is really what you want? You can't change your mind?"

"This is what I want."

He nodded again, a lump forming in his throat.

"Okay..." he said. "I can only hope that you reconsider, but if this is what you choose I'm here for you."

Chapter 45

Bill

September 4th, 2023

It was dark, and the temperature had dropped significantly in Bill's cell. He sat in bed, the cold and damp from the wall beside him chilling his bones. He couldn't sleep. Could never sleep in this place he refused to think of as his new home. But nobody could sleep.

It always got noisier as the evening progressed. As the cell doors were locked and night fell, the prisoners all around him would be consumed by their thoughts, their regrets and their memories. He could hear someone crying from down the hall on one side of his cell. From the other came the sound of a constant thudding. Someone punching at their door perhaps or was it something more sinister?

He clenched his eyes closed and shivered, pulling up his thin blanket around his shoulders.

It was no use trying to relax. Wrapping the blanket around him, he stood up and walked to the small desk beneath the even smaller barred window. Sitting in the centre was a framed photograph of Sarah he'd asked Lucien to bring during one of his last visits.

Her mother's double.

So much like that cherub.

He thought of her now alone without both him and Danielle and felt his throat tighten.

As he looked at her smiling face, his mind flashed back to a moment he was now ashamed of. A moment in which he had urged Danielle not to have her.

His heart sank at the thought.

Behind him, he heard the familiar clunk click of the door opening and spun round.

"Alright, Bill, it's just me."

He saw Terry enter the cell and close the door behind him.

"Bit late for you, isn't it?"

"Had to stay behind for training," moaned Terry. "Extra training on account of all the people trying to get *you* out."

He couldn't hide the bitterness in his voice.

"I suppose you know all about the latest attempt."

"Yes," said Bill, lowering his voice. "The chap died."

"In the hope of getting his hands on your cash."

"Cash that you're getting your hands on too," Bill reminded him.

Terry didn't reply. Just walked over to the desk and looked down at the picture in Bill's hands.

"Lovely girl."

"My grand-daughter."

"How old is she?"

"Five."

"Same age as my daughter."

"Oh... I didn't know you had children."

Terry stayed silent for a moment as he decided whether to talk about his daughter or not.

"I did," he said eventually. "But... Leukaemia..."

"Oh..."

"She passed away almost fifteen years ago."

"Oh, Terry. I am sorry."

The two stood in silence for a moment, bonded by their grief. Bill suddenly felt as though his new friend maybe understood his situation more than he had first realised.

"Anyway," said Terry, eager to change the subject. "I just came to tell you something before I leave. I've been hearing things through the grapevine. A task force has been set up at the MET."

"For what?"

"What do you think? For you. Apparently the chief has his eyes on that hard arse prosecutor, Hawkins to lead the team. That's the gossip anyway. Jesus, think half the inmates in here are banged up because of her."

"A task force..."

"Yeah, if you thought it was difficult getting out of here before, it'll be impossible now. The chief at the MET is sinking all resources into making sure you stay within these four walls. But you didn't hear it from me."

Terry backed away and opened the door again.

"Thanks," said Bill as he left. "For letting me know."

"Like I said, you didn't hear it from me."

Terry gave him a friendly nod in departure then closed the door back over with a bang. Bill was left staring at it with his mind whirring into action.

A task force... Led by Hawkins herself. Damn she's good.

Chapter 46

Hawkins

September 5th, 2023

Dawn hadn't yet broken, but she was already striding into the newly put together incident room with an extra large Americano in her manicured hand. The sound of her heels clacking on the lino floor brought everyone's attention to her. The first person to notice was Richard. There was a confused look in his eye; a mix of lust and anger.

She did her best to ignore him and stood at the top of the room looking out over the tired faces of her newly put together team. Despite it just reaching six in the morning, the task force that comprised of a mix of six seasoned detectives, four officers and three analysts had turned up early and eager to start work. Hawkins could see the enthusiasm in all their eyes, especially in the red-headed Detective Kane who was sat closest to her.

Perched on the edge of a desk with a cup of tea, he looked as though he'd been up all night like a kid on Christmas Eve. His face shining beneath the harsh office fluorescent lights.

"Hello, everyone," began Hawkins, looking out over the room. "I appreciate you all being here so early."

She could feel Richard's eyes on her as she spoke and tried to ignore him.

"As you'll all appreciate," she continued. "The situation at Belmarsh regarding Sir Lovecroft is critical. Especially after the latest attempt to free him resulted in a fatality."

Everyone nodded solemnly in agreement.

As she spoke, Detective Kane analysed everything about her from the calmness in her voice, to her gentle, though confident, mannerisms. He'd interviewed enough people over the course of his long career to be a good judge of character. And he was always good at spotting a weakness in someone's personality, a little gap in which he could slip in and get out any information he wanted. As he watched Hawkins speak, he tried to find that weakness, and grew annoyed when he couldn't find anything.

She's got the confidence of an ox, he thought. *She looks unshakable, but there's got to be a gap in that well-groomed armour somewhere.*

It was then, as this thought crossed his mind that he noticed her eyes move to the back of the room. He followed her gaze towards Richard and noticed the two of them exchange a look.

What was that? He wondered.

Then the realisation hit him.

The old chief's got the hots for her. Or is it more than just that? The way they just looked at each other... Like old lovers.

He turned back to Hawkins just as she began writing on the white board behind her.

"Okay," she said, drawing a line down the middle of the board. "I want to separate the team into two distinct groups moving towards the same goal, keep Sir Lovecroft in jail."

"You," she said, pointing her marker pen to the group of younger officers, "You'll be my boots on the ground. You'll be doing the leg work. And you," she said, pointing her pen at the other half of the room at the detectives, "You'll be on surveillance. The analysts will be your eyes and ears. I don't want a single word said to Lovecroft without you knowing about it."

Her marker pen was still facing the detectives, its inky tip directed at Detective Kane's nose. He was staring at her so intensely it made a chill run up the back of her neck. There was something about him she didn't trust, but she couldn't quite identify what it was.

"What's your name?" she asked him.

"Kane."

"Kane... Fill me in on what we know."

"Well..." he began. "We have one informant in the same wing as Lovecroft."

"Good. What's he said?"

"That Bill's a real charmer. Makes friends with everyone. Especially a firm of old boys."

"A firm?"

"A gang, Miss. A group of the old hard boys. Most of them bank robbers. They're run by a career criminal Reggie Constable."

"Constable. I've heard of him."

"Surprised it wasn't you that put him away," smirked Kane.

Once again came that intense look on Kane's face that she didn't like.

"So Lovecroft and Constable..." she said. "They're close?"

"Play cards every day in the yard."

"I don't like the sound of that," she grimaced, staring at the floor. "I think we need to hone in on this firm. They sound organised."

"They are," chimed in a young female officer from across the room. "They're well known as the daddies of that wing. They rule everything."

Hawkins frowned and put down her pen.

"And the governor at Belmarsh knows about this?"

"Everyone knows about this," replied the officer. "They've been around for years."

"We'll need to break them up somehow," said Hawkins.

"It's not that simple," chuckled Kane. "Prison politics aren't a force to be reckoned with."

"Of course they are. It's the law that runs the prison, not the prisoners."

Kane laughed again.

That's her weakness. Naivety. She actually thinks people respect the law.

"Okay," said Hawkins, taking a sip of her coffee. "I think I know where we need to start. With this firm, especially keeping an eye on this Reggie Constable. Team, all of you, I want you to dredge up anything you can on everyone in this firm and have it to me by this time tomorrow."

They all nodded. Everyone but Kane who was still smirking. He cast his gaze to the back of the room at Richard and saw he was staring at Hawkins intently.

They're definitely fucking each other.

This is getting interesting.

"Right," declared Hawkins. "Let's get to it."

The team began to disperse as they set about getting to work, but Kane remained perched on the edge of his desk looking at Hawkins. She felt a chill again as he watched her.

"Yes?" she said to him, wondering why he wasn't moving.

"Just wanted to say thanks for inviting me on the team," he replied.

"It was the commissioner who placed you on the team. You come highly recommended."

Kane's smug smile broadened.

"You and the chief work closely?" he asked her, his voice dripping with intonation.

She didn't like the way he spoke to her. He had the uncanny ability to make her uncomfortable without explicitly saying anything offensive. Ignoring his question, she picked up her coffee and moved away from him.

"Tomorrow morning," she said, pointing at him. "If you're as good as you're supposed to be you'll get me everything I need to know on this Constable character."

"Anything you say," he grinned.

Chapter 47

Deective Kane

September 4th, 2023

As lunch time arrived, he looked over his shoulder as he exited the building and crossed the road. He urgently swiped through his phone's contacts looking for the name that always excited him. When he found it, he tapped it hard.

"Detective?" answered an alluring voice.

"Aw, you know how much I like hearing you call me that."

A response came in the form of a giggle.

"Where are you, Melissa?"

"Where you told me to wait for you. In the Ram's Head Inn."

"I'm on my way."

Kane sped walked the rest of the journey down the road and round the corner, always looking over his shoulder to make sure none of his colleagues had noticed where he was going. His face was red with excitement as he entered the inn, his hungry eyes scanning the bar for blonde hair. He caught sight of Melissa sitting at the end of the bar, a glass of white wine in her hand. She smiled as he approached, then slid seductively off the stool to greet him. She kissed him lightly on the cheek then moved away playfully before he could kiss her back.

"You tease," he smiled as she sat down.

Ordering a pint of Guinness, he pulled a stool up in front of her and sat between her slightly parted legs.

His hand instinctively found its way to her thigh and gave it a squeeze.

"Are you here for business or pleasure, Detective?"

"Does it matter?"

She smiled again and his stomach flipped.

"Business," he eventually decided on, despite the stirring inside his boxers. "The lawyer."

"Lucien."

"You're still seeing him?"

"He has paid for my time on several occasions," she said. "If that's what you mean."

"And?"

"And what?"

"And what's the situation with Lovecroft? What has he told you?"

"He doesn't tell me much. Only that he has some big plan."

"What plan?"

"Like I said, he doesn't tell me much. Only that he seems quite sure he'll get Sir Lovecroft out. Keeps talking about the thirty-eight billion."

"What else?"

"I don't know what else to tell you."

He started to grow impatient and moved in closer to her. Cupping her face gently, he kissed her softly, but she could feel the strength in his hand like a silent threat.

"I need you to work your magic on him some more," he said. "I need you to get him talking. Find out more about this plan."

She nodded, licking her lips and kissing him back.

"I can do that."

"I know you can. You can do anything with that beautiful body of yours."

Chapter 48
Danielle

September 16th, 2016

She looked at the clock on the wall behind the ultrasound technician's head, down at her stomach, then back to the clock.

"Shall we begin?" asked the technician.

"Just five more minutes. He'll be here soon."

The technician looked doubtful and glanced up at the clock.

"I guess we can wait another couple minutes," she said, grabbing the tube of KY jelly for Danielle's stomach.

"He'll just be caught up at work," said Danielle. "He said he'll be here."

Again, the technician looked unsure. She'd done enough scans in her ten years on the job to have seen dozens, if not hundreds of partners fail to turn up.

"Where does he work?" she asked Danielle.

"He's an art dealer."

"Oh? Where?"

Danielle stared blankly at her.

"Erm, all over the place," she replied.

She'd asked Fitz about his job so many times, and had always been given vague answers. He was always working in one gallery or another, had many clients that he procured art pieces for, but as she looked into the technician's eyes, she came to the realisation she didn't have a concrete answer.

Once again, they both looked at the clock, and the technician gave an apologetic smile.

"I think we should begin," she said.

Danielle's heart sank as she raised her t-shirt to expose her abdomen and the technician tucked in a paper covering around the lowered waistband of her leggings.

Where is he?

He promised he'd be here!

In the months she'd been dating Fitz, he'd never been late for anything, so why now? Her mind worked its way through a myriad of catastrophic situations.

What if he was in an accident on his way here.

What if he was attacked.

What if he's ill.

But she snapped out her panic when she felt the cold sensation of the jelly being rubbed over her stomach, an image appearing on the screen to her side.

"Very good," said the technician. "Looks like you're about ten weeks along."

Danielle stared at the screen, but could only see what looked like a blizzard of grey and white. The technician, seeing the confusion on her face, pointed to the screen.

"That's your baby," she smiled. "That little thing right here."

"Oh!"

Danielle felt tears spring to her eyes immediately.

"Oh my God. This is wonderful."

It was moments like this that made the technician feel rewarded by her job.

"You're glowing," she told Danielle. "I'll get this printed off."

***

Twenty minutes later, Danielle was standing out the front of the hospital holding the printed scan in her hands. She couldn't stop looking at it. She was so busy staring at the tiny blob in the image that was her child that she barely noticed Fitz' black BMW pull up in front of her.

"Danielle," came his voice as he lowered the window. "I'm so sorry!"

She saw the genuine look of regret in his eyes.

"You missed it," she cried.

"I got held up."

"Doing what?"

"I got stuck at work. I'm sorry. I really am."

It was now that she noticed the scratch that snaked its way across his jaw and how his usually immaculate hair looked tousled.

"Fitz... What's going on?"

"Nothing. Come on, get in the car."

"You look as though you've been in a fight," she said, staying rooted to the spot.

"A fight?" laughed Fitz. "Why would you say that? Now tell me everything about the scan. How did it go?"

"You tell me everything first."

"There's nothing to tell."

"Tell me where you've been."

"At work. You know that."

"*Where*, though?"

He stared at her for an extended moment, a slight look of fear entering his eyes.

"Come on, get in the car."

She lowered herself into the passenger seat, and Fitz' eyes fell on the printed scan in her hand.

"Oh, Danielle," he said, taking it from her. "Oh, my God."

"Isn't it wonderful?"

"It's beautiful."

"You're holding it upside down."

They both laughed, the tension previously between them now evaporating. Fitz held the scan tenderly, his gaze moving in between the picture and Danielle.

"I've never been happier," he said. "This is really happening."

"It's really happening."

"I've been thinking about names."

"You have?"

"If it's a girl I'd like to call her Sarah."

"I like it."

"It's Hebrew for princess."

"Oh... What about if it's a boy?"

Fitz thought for a second, his eyes still focussing hard on the scan.

"I just hope it's a girl."

"Really?"

"Yeah, because she'll be your double."

Danielle felt herself melt into his side, but as she moved to kiss him, she felt a sudden jolt of nausea rise within her.

"You okay?" asked Fitz, noticing her face drop.

"Morning sickness. It's terrible. Do you have any mints?"

Before he could answer, she moved to open the glove box.

"No, wait!" Fitz suddenly burst. "Don't open that."

But it was too late. She was already feeling her way inside, her fingers brushing up against something cold and metallic.

"What the hell is this?" she asked, her hand wrapping itself around the object.

"Danielle, don't."

"Is this... a gun!"

She pulled it out and stared at it in her hand, her mouth dropping wide open. Then she threw it back into the glove box, terrified.

"Fitz, what the hell?"

"I told you not to open it."

"Why have you got a gun!"

He tried to lean over to hold her, but she was already scrambling to get out the car in a panic.

"Danielle wait."

He managed to close the door back over and hold her in her seat, but she kept resisting his touch, pushing him off her.

"Why do you have that thing?"

"I... I can't tell you."

"You have to," she insisted, tears coming to her eyes. "We're having a baby together and..."

She started to sob, her eyes moving back to the glove box and what it contained.

"Who *are* you?" she asked. "Where were you today?"

Fitz lowered his eyes to her stomach, guilt gripping him hard.

"Fitz? Answer me."

He lowered his eyes even further then slid his gaze down towards his feet. He thought of what he was going to have to admit, and how much it would hurt Danielle. He thought of his child inside her body, and how much he knew he couldn't keep living the way he did.

"Okay..." he said. "I'll tell you everything. But not here. I'll take you home."

Chapter 49

Fitz

September 5th, 2023

"So I hope you're all ready for your team building exercise," declared Fitz as he entered the cold, draughty warehouse.

There was a collective grumble throughout the group who were once again sat around the fold-out table. An assortments of coffees in front of them.

"Do we have to?" moaned Jacques.

"Yes," replied Fitz firmly. "If you want to be a part of the team, you have to learn to all bond with each other."

Jacques looked to Billie and shuddered at the thought. Cecilia looked to Phenomena and did the same.

"Jesus," said Fitz, looking at all the unresponsive faces around him. "Can't at least one of you look happy about this? I'm asking you to bond with each other for the chance to bag billions of pounds. Not go to your mothers' bloody funerals."

At hearing the mention of money, the mood lightened significantly.

"So this is what you're going to do," began Fitz, pulling up a chair and facing his team.

He took a moment to look at them each in the eye, then leaned forward on his knees, hands clasped beneath his chin.

"We're going to play a game. We'll go around the room and each of you has to tell the group one truth and one lie, and we have to guess which is which."

"Really?" moaned Jacques again. "Is this a sleepover?"

Fitz shot him a look and he closed his mouth.

"If you don't like it you can walk," said Fitz.

"No, no. I don't want to do that."

"Then tell us a truth and a lie."

Jacques thought for a second, his mind returning to the thought of money once again.

"Okay, fine," he sighed. "I once kissed Jennifer Lopez on a night out. And... I'm a black belt in karate."

"Aw come on!" laughed Amelia from the back of the room. "Clearly they're both a lie."

"Nope," laughed Jacques.

"There's no way either of those are true," said Billie with an exaggerated eye roll.

"One of them definitely is," said Jacques with a smug smile.

"The Jennifer Lopez one," said Fitz, looking up and down Jacques' thin body. "That's got to be the truth. No way you did karate."

Jacques' smug smile grew as he leaned back in his seat with with pride.

"Correct," he beamed.

A burst of protests erupted from the group.

"No way!" laughed Phenomena.

"Yes way."

"No!" screamed Cecilia. "Jennifer Lopez kissed *you*?"

Everyone shook their head in disbelief.

"Okay, you next," said Fitz, pointing at Billie. "A truth and a lie."

She thought for a second, her gaze turning inwards, then she looked out across the room.

"Okay, one year I went on this camping trip to Yosemite National Park and I saw Bigfoot. And I can do a hundred push-ups in under two minutes."

Marcus sniggered and turned to her.

"Well, there's an easy way to figure this one out," he said. "Get on the floor. Let's see your push-ups."

"Aw, no," said Billie. "I'm not up for a demonstration."

"No, come on," insisted Jacques, enjoying the prospect of seeing her struggle. "Let's see your push-ups."

Billie tried to stay in her seat, but when the burn of everyone's eyes grew too much, she shuffled onto the floor.

She moved into the plank position, already feeling her arms start to shake. With a deep breath, she made a valiant effort of attempting a single push-up, but her weak arms buckled beneath her and she fell flat onto her face. Laughter rippled around the room that soon turned to silence.

"Wait," said Jacques. "If you're lying about this then… You saw Bigfoot?"

"I did," said Billie, rolling breathlessly onto her back. "I was lying in my tent one night. Heard a rustling sound and poked my head out. He was as close to me as you are now. Had these big, green eyes. Was at least eight foot tall and he was just… staring at me. Looking at me the way I look at tiny dogs. Like he thought I was cute. He smelled so bad too. Like rotten fish."

"Aw, come off it," laughed Marcus, slapping his thigh. "You expect us to believe that?"

"I swear it's the truth."

The group continued to laugh as she dragged herself onto her chair.

"Fine, don't believe me," she sulked as she crossed her arms. "But I know what I saw."

"Yeah, alright," chuckled Fitz. "Marcus, you next."

With everyone's eyes falling on him, Marcus felt his anxiety rise and the sweat start to form beneath his shirt.

"Erm…" he began, his mind going blank. "I dunno."

"It's okay," said Fitz. "Take your time."

Marcus fidgeted with the sleeve of his jumper, pulling a thread loose and twirling it around his finger nervously. He felt as though the silence was growing thick around him. As though everyone's expectant gaze was pushing him down into his seat.

"Any day now," said Jacques. "While we're still young."

"Shut up!" burst Marcus. "I'm thinking."

He snapped the thread between his fingers as his palms grew sweaty.

"Okay," he breathed. "I did time for armed robbery. Sawn of shotgun. Pointed it at this old missus in the bookies and she went nuts. Screamed her head off and hit the panic button. Cops came before I even saw the money. Got a kicking in the back of the van as well for mouthing off. And… I once went streaking through Margate town centre."

There was an awkward silence as everyone let the words sink in. All of them watching as Marcus stared at the floor growing increasingly sweaty.

"Er…" began Phenomena. "The Margate one… That's the truth?"

Marcus raised his head to her slowly, blinked nervously then sighed.

"I wish it was."

There were another few seconds of silence before Billie piped up.

"Wait, you're an armed robber?"

"I ain't proud of it," said Marcus. "But it's who I am and there's not much I can do about it. The past is the past."

Everyone kept looking at him, wondering how the quietest man in the room now appeared to be the most dangerous.

"Right!" said Fitz, interrupting the silence. "Who's next?"

Chapter 50

Bill

September 5th, 2023

Bill was half asleep when he heard his phone ring from under his pillow. He squinted at the screen as he slid his finger to answer the call.

"Hello, it's getting late. I've been waiting for you."

The voice at the other end of the line spoke quickly, almost too quickly for Bill's sleepy mind to catch up with.

"What?" Bill gasped. "No more contraband snacks? You're kidding.... Alright... Alright... I understand."

He nodded to himself as he listened to the instructions that were being dictated to him, despite him being unhappy at hearing them.

"You're kidding," he said. "That low? I'll have wasted away to nothing. Uhuh... Okay... If you're sure. I trust you."

He was just about to hang up when one more instruction was fired at him. Bill listened intently, picking at his fingernails as he nodded.

"Okay," he said. "I can do that. Yes, yes. Goodnight."

As he hung up the phone and slid it back under his pillow, he felt a surge of excitement. He knew the next few weeks were going to be hard. But he also knew it was starting to come together.

Chapter 51

Hawkins

September 6th, 2023

PC Busby walked at speed through the incident room towards Hawkins' office where she was sat begrudgingly filtering her way through a pile of paperwork.

She looked up as he entered and saw the urgent expression on his face.

"Everything okay, Busby?"

"We've got info."

Hawkins raised an eyebrow.

"On what?"

"Bill's lawyer, Lucien. He's been seen speaking to Bill's son-in-law. Or rather, ex-son-in-law."

Busby placed the file he was holding on Hawkins' desk, opening it up to reveal a crystal clear image of Fitz sitting in the driver's seat of his car. Bending down to speak to him through the window was Lucien, his face holding the same condescending expression as always.

"Hmmm…" said Hawkins, taking a closer look. "That's interesting. Place this up on the whiteboard in there, will you?"

"Will do," said Busby. "Think it means anything?"

"Possibly."

Hawkins rose from her desk, ready to brief her team after lunch. She was pleased to see almost everyone had already arrived looking alert. But there was a conspicuous face missing.

"Where's Detective Kane?" she asked.

Everyone shrugged in response.

"Probably with that bird," someone sniggered from the back of the room.

"What was that?" asked Hawkins, searching for the voice.

"Nothing," came a timid reply from a young officer. "I mean, he's probably stuck in traffic. Loads of the roads are closed 'cos they started building stuff for the climate conference."

"Already? That's not until next month."

"I know," said PC Busby. "But a lot of important people are set to be here for it. World leaders and that. Half of London city centre's going to probably shut down."

"Urgh," grumbled Hawkins. "And I bet there'll be loads of protesters too."

She narrowed her eyes and put both Kane and the climate conference out her mind. Walking up to the whiteboard, she tapped the picture that PC Busby had just taped in place.

"Fitz," said Hawkins. "I want a tail on him. Something's going on here."

And the more she looked up at the photograph, the more she believed this. There was an intensity in the eyes of both Lucien and Fitz, a sense that there were serious words being spoken between them. Hawkins knew Lucien. Not well, but well enough through her long career to know what motivated him. It was what motivated most lawyers, money.

It has to be, she thought. *What else would bring these two together?*

Chapter 52
Danielle

September 16th, 2016

"You're... a gangster..." she said, her words falling flat across the table.

Fitz knew she needed to be in a comfortable place when she heard the news. He couldn't bear the thought of her being stressed out in public as she carried their baby. So he'd brought her back to her home and sat her down in the kitchen with a cup of sweet tea.

She sipped on it now, barely tasting it, her eyes constantly moving from Fitz' face then down to her stomach. Fitz was at least grateful that neither Bill nor Cecilia were home.

"Gangster..." he said, reaching across the table and taking her hand. "I don't like that word."

"But it's what you are."

"People tend to refer to me as more of a gentlemanly thief. It's not like I'm out robbing grannies. I steal paintings made by guys that died hundreds of years ago and jewellery that's been gathering dust for years. It's victimless."

"Then why do you have a gun?"

Danielle shot him a vicious look.

"Because sometimes words aren't the only way to persuade someone. But it's not like I use it. Not really."

"What does that mean?"

"It means..."

"Have you ever killed someone?"

"No. Never."

"Ever shot anyone?"

"Yeah but-"

"Yeah but what!"

"But it was in self-defence. They shot at me first."

"Ever really injured anyone?"

Fitz lowered his head in shame.

"Not because I wanted to, but because I had to. I'm not proud of it."

She took another sip of her tea and tried to swallow down her tears, but it was pointless and they fell anyway.

What have I done? Was all she could think. *How could I have believed Fitz was so perfect?*

"What are you thinking?" he asked her, squeezing her fingers, but he could already tell by the look on her face what she'd say.

"I can't do this," she said. "I can't bring a baby into the world with a criminal."

"You're not saying you're getting an abortion are-"

"Of course not. I'm saying I can't be with you."

"You don't mean that... Do you?"

She nodded.

"Please, Danielle. Give me a chance to show you I'm not a bad guy."

"You turned up late to our baby's scan with a gun in your car," she said, staring him dead in the eye.

There was no arguing with that. What he'd done was wrong, unforgivable, but he still couldn't just let her walk away.

"I love you," he told her, his voice cracking. "I can make this work."

"No," said Danielle, shaking her head. "You can't. You're a criminal. A gangster. I don't want my child to have any part of that."

He was about to answer when they both heard the bang of the front door followed by the sound of high heels clicking down the hallway. A moment later, Cecilia appeared in the kitchen doorway. Sensing the tension in the room, she raised her eyebrows.

"Interrupting something, am I?" she asked, hoping for gossip.

"Fitz was just leaving," said Danielle, scraping back her chair and standing up. "Weren't you?"

He had so many thoughts running through his head. So many things he wanted to say, but he didn't want to cause Danielle any more stress, or give Cecilia the satisfaction of witnessing an argument.

Keep your head, keep it classy and give her some space, he thought to himself as he walked away. *Give her some time. You can win her back yet.*

Chapter 53

Bill

September 8th, 2023

"Not hungry?" asked Terry as he came in to retrieve Bill's lunch tray. He was used to the food he brought Bill being mostly ignored, but he usually attempted to eat a little, even if it was just to insult it. But today, the cutlery on the tray hadn't even been touched, and neither, noticed Terry, had the newest box of biscuits he'd brought him.

"No, I'm not hungry," said Bill with a sigh. "Not been feeling too great."

"Yeah, you don't look so great."

"Thanks."

"I just mean you look a bit unwell."

Terry noticed it the moment he'd stepped into the cell. Bill was usually so clean-cut with a glowing complexion that betrayed his years. But today he looked grey, and white stubble had started to pepper his chin.

"I'll just take this away, shall I?" asked Terry, nodding down to the tray.

"Please."

"Catch you later."

Bill waited until Terry left before he walked over to the mirror. It had only been three days since he'd heard his instructions down the phone, but he was pleased that he was starting to see results.

Lifting up his sweater, he saw his already thin body start to shrink. It wouldn't take long until he was completely emaciated. A few weeks at most. Despite how weak his body felt, his mind was razor sharp with optimism, and he grew excited at the changes in his body. He lowered his sweater and looked at his face.

"Wow, you're starting to look like crap," he marvelled to himself.

He looked deep into his own eyes and could see the exhaustion, but beyond that there was hope. He ran his fingertips over the dark, papery skin beneath his eyes and smiled.

Chapter 54

Danielle

September 20th, 2016

"Danielle Lovecroft?" came a stuffy voice from across the foyer of The National Gallery.

She looked up to see a short man with the mannerisms of a ferret scurry towards her in a tweed waistcoat.

"Mr Barker?" she asked, swallowing down morning sickness.

"Yes, we spoke on the phone," he said, shaking her hand enthusiastically. "It's really such an honour to have you here."

"No, really. The honour's all mine. When I first applied for the internship I knew it would be competitive."

"Competitive?" smirked Barker. "Well, I suppose, but you were definitely in good stead for the position."

"I was?"

"Of course. Sir Lovecroft is one of our most generous benefactors."

"Oh..."

Danielle's spirits sank. When she saw the internship advertised at Cambridge, she'd jumped at the chance to apply, hoping her excellent grades and enthusiasm for conservation would place her with a chance. But now she felt like her grades didn't matter if all Mr Barker was looking at was her surname.

"Anyway, shall we?" he said, leading the way back across the foyer. "You must be excited to get started."

"I am!"

"Excellent. You'll be learning all there is to know about the conservation of the classics and all the restorative processes involved."

She had to half-jog to catch up with him as he reached the end of the foyer, punched a code into a large mahogany door and led her down a sprawling corridor. She marvelled at the flooring, the walls, the cornicing. This was the side to the museum the tourists could never see.

They turned one corner after the other, all the while Danielle's heart was beating faster and faster. She couldn't wait to get up close to the work of the masters. Couldn't wait to learn all there was to know about them, and how proud that would make her father.

"Here we are," announced Mr Barker. "Pushing open the last door at the end of the corridor. "You're in luck today because we have a special visitor who you'll be working alongside."

As he pushed open the door, Danielle found herself faced with a tall, handsome woman in a red dress with piercing eyes. She oozed confidence and intelligence, and regarded Danielle with an officious gaze.

"Miss Lovecroft," said Mr Barker, introducing the two. "This is Elizabeth Hawkins."

Chapter 55

Fitz

September 8th, 2023

He drove at his usual modest speed through central London attracting as little attention as possible, so why did he feel as though he was being watched? Pulling up at a set of red lights, he felt the hairs along the back of his neck stand on end.

It was an unfamiliar feeling. He felt the need to look in the rear-view mirror into the cars behind him, but he recognised none of the drivers. Then he scanned his eyes up and down the street paying attention to the doorways of the pubs, bookies and takeaways. No one stood out, but still he couldn't shake the thought.

I'm being watched.

He was so lost in this thought that he didn't notice the light turn green until the driver behind him honked his horn. With an apologetic hand signal, Fitz released the handbrake and continued on his journey.

As he arrived in Catford, he kept thinking the sensation of being watched was intensifying. Pulling up outside the warehouse, he waited in the car for a moment, looking up and down the street multiple times to ensure there was no one around. When he was satisfied there wasn't, he climbed out the car. Once again, he felt the need to scan the street, paying attention to the crumbling walls of the nearby dilapidated buildings for CCTV cameras. To his relief, he saw none.

I'm getting paranoid.

He tried to force the thought out his mind as he opened the door to the warehouse and saw his team was already waiting for him. This time, in contrast to before, they looked like they were getting on favourably with each other, talking over one another excitedly.

I must be losing it, thought Fitz. *Even Billie and Jacques are talking to each other.*

"Well, this is nice," he said as he arrived, stepping into the group. "Cosy. And you're all early too."

The only person who wasn't chatting was Lucien who was, as usual, lurking on the sidelines. He looked up to Fitz, signalling him with his eyes to move away from the group. Fitz frowned but gave a nod and walked into the dark back corner of the room.

"Be with you all in a minute," he told the room as Lucien followed him. "What's up? You're looking even shiftier than usual."

Lucien's eyes darted over to the group to make sure they were all out of ear shot and preoccupied with their own conversations.

"There was a car," he said. "This morning, outside my house. A blacked out Ford Mondeo. Someone was watching me."

"How can you be sure?" asked Fitz, trying to sound calm, but he realised he wasn't the only one being paranoid.

"I'm sure because they were sat outside my living room window for twenty minutes and when I left, they followed me."

"Followed you? Where? Here?"

"No, not here. Just around the block then they were gone."

"Are you positive?"

"Absolutely."

"Who do you think it was?"

Lucien shrugged and looked down at his shoes with a furrowed brow.

"I can only assume it was police."

"Could be journalists."

"True... but... This car had an aerial."

"Don't they all?" asked Fitz, his eyes darting over to the group who were still chatting. For the briefest of seconds, his eyes met Phenomena's before she glanced away with a smile.

"Yes, all cars have aerials," said Lucien. "But this one had two. Like a cop car."

"Or a taxi."

"Taxis don't have blacked out windows."

The uneasiness in Fitz' stomach was growing by the second.

"I don't like the sound of this."

He thrust his hands into his pockets and shivered.

"Anyway," continued Lucien. "I spoke to Bill. Everything's going to plan."

"Good. That's one thing."

"He looks like shit apparently, and he's starving. Dropping loads of weight already."

"Good.... Good... The closer he looks to death's door the better."

"What did you say?" called out Cecilia from the group, craning her neck over the top of Phenomena's head.

"Nothing," replied Fitz, annoyed.

"You were talking about my Dad!"

"How did you even hear that? You must have ears like a bat."

He tried to ignore her, but she was still staring at him.

"What were you saying about death's door?" she asked, her eyes creasing with concern.

"Nothing!" chorused Fitz and Lucien together.

Walking out the shadows and back to the group, Fitz pulled up a seat and looked directly at Jacques, who he noticed had a new love bite blossoming across his neck.

"Jacques, what do you know about the upcoming climate conference?"

"Everything obviously."

"Glad to hear it. It's time to get things rolling, and it starts with you."

Chapter 56

Bill

September 20th, 2023

"Bloody hell, Bill. You look rotten," said Reg as he watched him enter the art class.

As Bill lowered his shrinking frame into his seat, he could feel the harshness of his bones pressing against the wood. He knew Reg was right, he looked rotten, and felt it too.

"Hey, you ill?" asked Reg, sitting down beside him.

"Yeah..." sighed Bill. "Been feeling rough recently."

"Your clothes are hanging off you."

To illustrate, Reg leaned in and grabbed the waistband of Bill's jogging bottoms and shook them.

"You barely touch the sides of these things."

Bill looked down and saw how they balanced gently against his hipbones, ready to drop if it weren't for the tightened drawstring. Fifteen days had passed since the plan was set into action, and he felt worse every day. But each time he felt the urge to reach for a biscuit or complain, he remembered what he was suffering for.

"I think you need to see a doctor," said Reg. "I'm amazed they haven't sent for one already."

"Oh, Terry tried to get me to see one. But I said I was fine."

"But you're obviously not."

Behind Bill, as the rest of the prisoners began taking their seats and readying themselves for the class, a curious silence fell over the room. Everyone was stunned by Bill's appearance. As he tried to focus on Reg's face, he could feel everyone's eyes on him.

Let them look. Everyone needs to know I'm fading away.

"Goodness!" Miss Higgins suddenly declared as she looked up from her desk.

She'd been busy shuffling drawing exercise sheets, but now stared wide-eyed at Bill. Rising from her seat, she approached him, dropping the exercise sheets on everyone's desks as she passed. As she placed a sheet down on Bill's desk, she frowned, noticing the pale, grey tint of his cheeks that were usually so bronzed.

"I don't think you should be here," she said. "I'm going to call for a doctor."

"No, really. That's not necessary."

Not yet, anyway... Thought Bill. *When the time's right.*

"I think I just have a cold," he tried to assure her.

"Hmmmm... Are you sure?"

"Yes, absolutely. All I need is some rest later back in my cell. Perhaps you could help me recuperate?"

"I'm not sure what I could do."

"If I could practise my drawing back in my cell, I'm sure it would keep my spirits up."

He smiled weakly at her, trying his best to look like a sweet but sickly grandfather.

"That sounds like a good idea," beamed Miss Higgins. "I could get you some extra sheets of paper if you need some."

"Actually... What about... some paint?"

"Oh... I'm not sure."

"Just one tube please. The smallest one you have. It doesn't even need to be full. Just as long as it's green."

She looked nervously over her shoulder towards the door where a guard stood.

"I'm really not sure if I'm allowed to give you that. I'll have to check with my supervisor."

"Really? Just for a splodge of paint?"

She didn't know if it was the look in his eyes, like that of a dying puppy, or whether she just couldn't imagine any harm coming from the treasured Sir Bill Lovecroft owning some paint, but she found herself saying, "I'm not in the habit of giving away supplies, but I don't see how a little tube can hurt."

"Thank you," smiled Bill, his eyes sparkling with appreciation. "That means a lot."

Chapter 57
Danielle

September 20th, 2016

Danielle just reached the ladies' bathroom as she felt the nausea rise up the back of her throat. Flinging herself to her knees in the nearest cubicle, she vomited abruptly into the toilet as her eyes watered. After, as she caught her breath, she dabbed toilet paper to her eyes.

"You okay in there?" came a stern voice along with a knock on the door.

"I'm fine!"

"You don't sound fine."

Danielle recognised the voice and pushed the door open as she leaned against the thin cubicle wall.

"Tummy bug?" asked Hawkins, who stood in the doorway.

"Morning sickness"

"Oh! I suppose congratulations, then."

But Hawkins could see a sad look behind Danielle's eyes.

"Want to join me in the canteen for some lunch?" asked Hawkins. "Might make you feel better."

"Oh, no. I think I'm going to head back to my office. I'm not really hungry, obviously."

"How about some peppermint tea and a biscuit?" suggested Hawkins, lowering her voice to a more friendly and sisterly tone.

"Actually that would be nice."

*

"So we started on the same day," noted Danielle as she poured tea.

The canteen, though busy, was quiet with nothing but the sound of hushed voices and clinking cutlery.

"I didn't realise prosecutors worked in museums," she continued. "I hope you don't mind me asking, but what exactly is it you do here?"

Hawkins smiled and sipped her tea before taking a large bite out of her biscuit.

"I'm working an art forgery case," she explained.

"Oh?"

"A fake Raphael."

"In here?"

"Yes, it hung in here for years."

"You're kidding!"

"Wish I was. Museums like this all have forgeries on their walls."

"No... Surely not... I mean... This is The National Gallery!"

"A jewel in the crown for any budding forger."

Danielle, shocked, sat back in her seat to process what she'd heard.

"So you're doing research here?" she asked Hawkins.

"Shadowing old Mr Barker around the conservation department for a few weeks. He's teaching me the ropes. How paints cracks, how the nails in the canvas rust. All that stuff."

"Wow. That's so exciting."

"Glad you think so. I've been bored to tears. If I have to stare at another paint chip through a microscope again I'll scream."

Danielle laughed, then suddenly felt the twinge of another bought of nausea pull at her stomach. She took a deep breath and sipped some more peppermint tea.

"Ooh, feeling rough again?"

"A little. I'm okay, though."

"How far are you along?"

Danielle looked down at her stomach and smiled.

"Three months."

"Your partner is very lucky," said Hawkins. "I'm sure your baby will be beautiful."

Danielle's smile dropped and she felt a heaviness sweep over her. Hawkins was just about to ask if she was okay when they both heard the approaching, squeaking footsteps of Mr Barker as he walked across the canteen.

"Danielle? Someone's arrived for you."

"Who?"

Mr Barker pulled nervously at his cardigan sleeve and looked worriedly over his shoulder.

"A man named Fitz," he said. "Says he needs to see you. He, erm. Well, I don't mean to sound rude, but he looks like a bit of a rough sort."

Chapter 58
Fitz

September 20th, 2023

He was jolted awake by a thought, a rumbling at the back of his mind that something was wrong. For a long moment, he lay in the dark with his eyes cast to the ceiling. Was the feeling from a dream? Or something else?

Just a dream, he told himself as he rolled over and closed his eyes.

But sleep wouldn't take hold of him and once again he was rolling onto his back and staring at the ceiling, his waking eyes now adjusting to the darkness. The feeling at the back of his mind now dropped into his body, lying low in his stomach like a heavy sense of unease.

He sat up and checked the time. Seeing it was only a few minutes after three in the morning, he lay back down and tried for a second time to fall asleep, but it was no use. He was wide awake and his mind was racing. And no matter how much he tried to relax, there was that sense of unease, a nagging feeling that something was wrong.

Climbing out of bed, he slipped on his dressing gown, shivered as he turned on the heater in the hallway and entered the kitchen.

A drink would settle me, he thought, then immediately pushed the notion out his head. *No... No... Forget about it.*

He walked into the living room, the uneasiness growing. Instinctively, he moved towards the mantelpiece and picked up the framed photo of Danielle and Sarah. Looking into both their eyes, he felt a tug of sadness in his chest. It never went away no matter how many times he looked at the photo.

Something else was tugging at him too. That feeling that something was wrong. It made him place the photograph back down and walk over to the window. There was an urge inside him to pull back the curtain and look out into the dark street. At first he saw nothing. Then a loud bang startled him.

His first thought was *gunshot*. But then he saw the lid of a metal bin rolling down the pavement, and when he turned his head to the right, he saw a bushy fox's tail sticking out from an upturned bin. When it pulled itself back out, it had a discarded packet of ham in its mouth. He watched as it jauntily ran down the street with its prize, its orange fur gliding past a parked car.

It was then that he noticed the car wasn't empty, and he could vaguely see the silhouette of a face in the driver's seat. A face, he was sure was staring right at him. A trail of goosebumps ran up the length of his spine as he looked closer. He thought he was imagining it at first, the long cylindrical shape beside the head. He rubbed his eyes, hoping it was the residue of sleep that made him see things, but as he blinked he realised the shape of the camera lens was unmistakeable.

His first instinct was to run, still in his dressing gown, down the hall and out the front door. His bare feet slapped against the concrete stairs as he flung himself down to the ground floor. He heard a car engine as he reached the street, and by the time he looked up towards the car, it was already on the move, exhaust fumes billowing out the back into the frigid night air.

"Hey!" he called out, still running, but it was pointless.

The car screeched at the end of the road and took a sharp right turn. For a long moment, Fitz stood staring after it.

Stay calm, he told himself, keeping a controlled rage. *I'll deal with this in the morning when I've got a clear head.*

But as he returned to his flat, he knew he'd be getting no sleep.

Chapter 59

Bill

September 23th, 2023

Three days had passed since he'd been at his last art class, and he was pleased that Miss Higgins had kept her end of the bargain by gifting him a small tube of racing green coloured oil paint.

As the sunshine broke through the small window of his cell, he stood up on shaking legs and felt a sense of extreme light-headedness. Taking a deep breath, he walked from his bed to the sink at the other side of his cell in search of the paint. Each step felt like ten, and his hands trembled as he walked. He thought of the pack of biscuits under his bed that would put a stop to all of this. Thought of how he would only become more and more ill as the next few weeks progressed.

Bending down at the mirror, he clutched his thinning fingers over the sides of the sink to balance himself and took another deep breath.

You can do it. Just breathe. Keep standing.

With his shaking hands it was a struggle to unscrew the cap of the paint tube, but as the paint hit the air and he inhaled its distinctive scent, he felt slightly revived. There was always something about the smell of paint that calmed him. To think some of the most talented artists throughout history had smelled the exact same thing brought him a feeling that he was connected more deeply to the art he always loved.

He placed a square of toilet paper onto the side of the sink to use as a palette, then squeezed a dollop of paint onto it no bigger than the size of a pea. Then he reached down and picked up the bottle of Crème de la Mer moisturiser he'd been wearing for years. He wasn't vain about his appearance, but he didn't slack on his complexion either and saw skincare as being as basic as wearing deodorant. He had, however, over the last couple weeks, skimped on his moisturising routine. The last thing he needed right now was for his skin to look hydrated. It had to look the worst it possibly could.

As he scooped out a twenty pence sized splodge of moisturiser and breathed in its smell, he lamented the fact it was probably too good for the job. He needed the cheap, heavy stuff that went on like emollient. The stuff that left a white cast. But he had to work with what he had.

Dropping the Crème de la Mer on top of the paint, he mixed the two together with his finger and watched as the racing green thinned out and became more pale and sickly coloured. It worked remarkably better than he thought it would.

Smearing the paint onto his cheeks, he looked at his reflection for a second and thought he looked ridiculous. Like some eccentric old man dabbing on war paint. He laughed to himself, mostly out of how amusing he thought his appearance was, but also because he felt he was going delirious with hunger, and laughing brought a welcomed sense of absurdity to the moment.

The laughing tired him out, and he felt himself become dizzy again. Taking another deep breath, he focussed on the task at hand, rubbing the mix of paint and moisturiser onto his face. Paying attention to rub the mixture under his eyes more than anywhere else, he noticed it was having the desired effect. Not only was the paint making his skin appear as though it had a sickening undertone of green, but it also gave the effect of making the veins around his eyes appear more red.

Excellent...

He rubbed the mixture in again, making sure it sank deeper into his skin and appeared more natural. Then he pulled off another sheet of toilet paper and dabbed at his face to remove the excess. When he stepped back to regard his work, he noticed the green paint wasn't too conspicuous, but it had done its job of making him appear ill to the point of collapse. Which was almost what he felt.

Behind him, he heard the familiar sound of the door being unlocked and he moved fast to swipe up the tube of paint and stuff it into his pocket.

"Morning!" declared Terry.

"Hello," Bill replied weakly as he turned around to see Terry in the doorway with his breakfast.

Terry seemed unusually chipper as he set down the breakfast tray. A mood that soon dissipated as he looked at Bill and saw his face.

"Bloody hell!"

"What?"

"Bill... Bill, you look like you're dying."

"Oh, thanks very much."

"No, I mean it. I'm calling for a doctor."

"That won't be necessary."

Not yet. Not until the plan's in place.

"No, I have to. You look... You look bloody horrendous, Bill. You're skin and bone and..."

He stepped closer and inspected Bill's face beneath the light. Bill felt his chest tighten in anticipation. This was the first moment his trick with the paint would have to pass its test.

"And you look so pale, Bill."

He cast his eyes over his face once more and Bill waited, hoping he wouldn't suspect anything despite the smell of oil paint in the air. To Bill's relief, he couldn't even see a flicker of suspicion in Terry's eyes.

"I think it's just a flu bug," Bill assured him. "I'm sure it'll clear up soon."

"Must be a nasty bug."

"I'll be okay in a few days."

"Hmm... If you're sure."

"I am. Thank you."

Terry gave him one last look then exited the room. Bill stood for a full minute waiting until he was sure Terry was far down the hall before he moved. Carrying the tray of breakfast towards the toilet, he dumped the contents in the bowl and flushed it away.

Returning his tray beside his bed, he lay down and picked up a book trying his best to look comfortable. When he heard the door being unlocked again half an hour later, he looked up over the top of his book and saw Terry reappear.

"Well, at least you've got your appetite back," he said, picking up the empty tray. "Maybe you're on the mend."

"Maybe I am," said Bill, forcing a sincere smile. "Here's hoping."

Chapter 60
Fitz

September 24th, 2023

"Why are we here and not in the warehouse?" asked Amelia.

She was standing beside Marcus in the centre of the hotel room in Hammersmith's Holiday Inn. Fitz couldn't help but notice the longer they stood in the room, the closer she got to Marcus, as though she was being pulled towards him by an invisible thread.

"The warehouse is off limits for now," he told them both.

"Why?" asked Marcus.

"It just is."

"Where's everyone else?"

"They don't need to be here right now," explained Fitz. "It's you two I need to concentrate on."

Marcus didn't like the sound of that, and suddenly felt under immense pressure. The blood drained from his face and he found himself looking towards Amelia for reassurance. She gave him a comforting smile in return which Fitz noted.

"Marcus, don't look so nervous," said Fitz.

"I can't help it."

"You'll be fine. This will make things easier. Think of it as a dress rehearsal. Literally."

Marcus' confusion grew.

"How quick can both of you get out of your clothes?" asked Fitz.

Marcus and Amelia shot each other a worried glance then looked at the double bed in the middle of the room.

"What?" asked Amelia.

"I don't mean like that," said Fitz with an eye roll, noticing their panic. "I mean this quite seriously. How quick can you change your outfit?"

As he spoke he wandered over to the cheap pine wardrobe at the back of the room and pulled out two identical black suits.

"These will do for now," he said, handing them over to the pair. "They're actually too small for the both of you, but that's a good thing. They'll be harder to get on which will train you to work quicker."

"Wait," interrupted Amelia. "I have no idea what's going on."

Fitz walked to the front of the room and perched against the small, pine desk before pulling out his phone and swiping for the timer.

"What's going on is that I'm going to hit this, and you're going to get into those suits as fast as possible. Got it?"

"Why?"

"Just... I'll explain in a bit, alright?"

"No, it's not alright," moaned Amelia. "I'm not stripping in a room with you two if I don't know what's going on."

"Yeah, fair enough. Can I just tell you it's crucial to the plan? I'm not trying to see you in your pants for fun."

"We'll be doing this as part of Lovecroft's breakout?"

"Yes."

"Hmmm..."

"I'll explain in detail later. Right now, I just want to see how fast you are."

She hesitated for a second and looked over at Marcus who's facial expression matched her emotions exactly.

"Okay, fine," she relented. "But, Marcus, you have to turn and face the other way."

"Sure thing."

He faced the wall and, in turn, she faced the window away from him. Fitz sat in between them, staring at the floor. He had no interest in seeing either of them undress.

"Ready?" he asked. "Out your clothes and into the suits. Got it?"

"Got it," they both echoed.

"Okay..." he said, hovering his thumb over his phone. "Go!"

Marcus panicked for a moment and fumbled with his belt buckle like he'd never seen it before. Meanwhile, Amelia was just desperate to get the whole ordeal over with and whipped off her hoodie and leggings like her life depended on it. She tore at the suit, forcing her legs into the trousers before yanking the tight shirt sleeves over her muscular arms.

Meanwhile, Marcus was still fumbling, pulling one sock off then another.

"Don't worry about the socks," said Fitz.

"Oh... Okay."

He put the socks back on, wasting precious seconds. As he bent down, he found himself accidentally catching a glimpse of an upside down Amelia between his legs as she buttoned up her shirt. He only saw the slight line of her cleavage for a split second, but it was enough to make his head feel funny, and when he stood up he was dizzy.

"Okay done!" said Amelia.

"Fifty-seven seconds," noted Fitz, looking at his phone. "Not bad but needs to be better."

He looked at Marcus who hadn't even wriggled his way out of his clothes yet, the suit still lying inside the bag on top of the bed.

"Okay, Marcus. Let's try again, yeah?"

Marcus heard what he was saying, but he couldn't process it because his eyes and his brain kept focussing on Amelia. She couldn't help but notice his cheeks flush red. For a brief moment, their eyes met, a spark igniting between them. Amelia blushed too and glanced away.

Oh God, thought Fitz, noticing them turn doe-eyed for each other. *What do I do here?*

Chapter 61
Danielle

September 20th, 2016

"What are you doing here?" she gasped as she entered her office and saw Fitz leaning against her desk. "You can't just turn up here."

"I didn't mean to intrude," he insisted. "I was just…"

His words were cut off when he saw her up close. Her skin glowing, despite her eyes being ablaze with anger. Then his eyes moved down to her stomach. Her bump wasn't showing yet, but he couldn't stop imagining the life inside her.

"You were just what?"

"In the area. I remember you saying you were starting here."

He looked around the room and felt out of place, even though he recognised the prints of all the paintings on the walls. Although he knew so much more about them than Mr Barker could ever believe. He looked into Danielle's eyes and sensed how unwelcome he was.

"I just wanted to see you at work," he said. "I miss you, and I'm proud of you for getting the job here."

"I… miss you too."

"Then why are we apart?"

"You know why."

He nodded solemnly.

"I want to put all that behind me. For us. For the baby."

Danielle didn't say anything. Just looked to the ground and wished he wasn't there. Not because she didn't want to see him, but because just looking at his face was making her fall in love with him all over again.

"You need to leave," she said. "I can't have you here."

"Leave? Can we not talk for a minute?"

"About what?"

"About us."

"There is no *us*."

The words cut through Fitz deeply making his chest ache.

"There... has to be," he said.

"There ceased to be an *us* the second I saw a gun in your car."

"But there was destined to be an *us* the second our child started growing inside you."

She felt the urge to cry and became angry, turning her back to him.

"I don't want to do this, not now," she said, swallowing hard and hardening her face. "You need to go."

"Can't we talk?"

"Not now. Not at my work, Fitz. You can't just turn up here."

He knew she was right, knew that he couldn't just invade her space like this, but at the same time he had been gripped by an urge to see her. Approaching her from behind, he gently placed a hand on her back. She flinched and moved away.

"Danielle."

"Go."

He tried to touch her again, this time squeezing her shoulder and she shook him off. But inside, she had to admit that she had missed the warmth of his touch so much, and there was a need deep inside her to turn around and wrap her arms around him.

No, don't do it. Think of the baby. Think of the gun!

She remained frozen to the spot keeping up her stern expression as she forced herself to harden against him.

"Danielle, please. Talk to me."

"No. Get out."

"I'm not going anywhere. You're having my child. I'm not leaving."

Only now did she turn round and see a flash of anger in his eyes. Anger mixed with sadness and lust and regret.

"I'm not leaving," he repeated.

"Is that… a threat?"

"It's an acknowledgement that I'm not walking away from you or the baby. I want to be here for you. I love you. I love you both."

"Then why are you driving around with a gun in your car!"

Her own voice echoed back to her from the high ceilings of the room and she cringed, aware people would be able to hear down the hall.

"You can't expect me to just accept that," she continued, lowering her voice to barely more than a whisper. "To just think I can let a violent man near my baby."

"It's my baby too."

"Not when you're a thug."

"A thug? And what do you mean? That I can't be a father?"

"That's exactly what I mean. You can't be a father when you're driving around playing gangsters."

"I'm not *playing* at anything."

A timid knock came from the door and it opened slightly to reveal Mr Barker looking nervously towards Danielle. Then he glanced at Fitz. Saw the anger on his face and shrunk back.

"Everything okay?" he asked.

"He was just leaving," said Danielle.

"No, I wasn't," insisted Fitz. "I'm not going anywhere."

Panic rose on Barker's face and he stared down the hall.

"Security!" he yelled. "I need security!"

"Security? You're treating me like a criminal."

"You are a criminal," said Danielle.

Footsteps were heard rushing down the hall and a second later two of the museum's security guards blustered into the room. Seeing they were twice his age and half his size, Fitz laughed at them both. Unamused, they closed in on him.

"Right, time to leave," said the closest one.

"I'm not budging."

"Come on. Don't let this get nasty."

The guard moved closer and grabbed Fitz by the bicep. Fitz' reaction was instant and involuntary, his fist lashing out and striking the guard hard in the centre of his face. Danielle heard the crack of his nose as it broke. Saw the blood burst out from his face and drip onto the perfectly polished floorboards.

"Get out!" she screamed.

"Shit, I'm sorry," said Fitz, realising what he had done as though he'd come out of a daze. "He touched me first!"

"Just get out!"

Fitz' heart broke. He'd come to prove himself. To show that he loved her, but all he had proven was that he was the violent thug she thought he was.

In the corner of the room, Barker was clutching his phone as his face paled.

"I've called the police," he warned Fitz as the other security guard moved closer to him. "They're on their way!"

Chapter 62

Hawkins

September 25th, 2023

Every time Hawkins saw Detective Kane's face she felt a weird sensation in her gut that made her want to slap him. She couldn't explain why she felt that way, and it wasn't a feeling she could remember having with anyone else, but it was always there the moment she caught sight of his red hair and smug expression.

Why does he always look like he loves the smell of his own farts?

She was sat in her car now around the corner from the office watching him through the window of the wine bar she'd followed him to. She wasn't in the habit of following her colleagues, but she couldn't trust him. He was always disappearing, always looking at her like he was privy to a secret everyone knew but her.

What's he up to?

She watched as he sat down at a table. To her surprise, an attractive blonde with statuesque bone structure welcomed him with a kiss.

That can't be his wife. She's too beautiful.

She narrowed her eyes at the blonde. Something felt wrong. It wasn't just that she was too beautiful, it was everything else about her too. Her obvious designer clothes, the way she carried herself. Hawkins found herself recognising her Jimmy Choo shoes and her Prada clutch. Found herself almost envious at the way her hair was so immaculately blow dried. The overriding impression she got was, *What would she see in a guy like Kane? A guy who's monthly salary would barely cover her highlights.*

She kept watching as Kane slid a hand up her thigh and kissed her again, this time with a tongue that flicked over her lower lip.

Urgh...

She was both nauseated and fascinated by the sight of them, and so engrossed in what she was seeing that she didn't notice the figure moving up to the passenger side of her car until she heard the rap of knuckles against the glass. She jumped as she heard a knock and turned to see a familiar face peering through the passenger window.

"Richard?"

"I thought I saw you lurking here," he said, opening the door and sitting down beside her.

"Just make yourself comfortable, why don't you?"

"I've been wanting to have a word with you."

"About what? The USB you stole? Or how you still keep staring at my arse?"

He sheepishly look down at his lap as he closed the door over. Hawkins' gaze was still fixed through the window of the wine bar, and he followed it, squinting as he noticed Detective Kane.

"Who's that?" he asked. "The blonde."

"Wish I knew."

"Are you spying on Kane?"

"Not spying exactly just… There's something about him I don't trust."

Richard nodded to himself, his eyes now widening as he watched Kane's hand slide up Melissa's leg.

"I've missed you," he suddenly blurted out.

Hawkins looked at him out the corner of her eye.

"Is that why you're here?"

He said nothing, just looked back down at his lap.

"You stole from me," said Hawkins.

"Only stole what you shouldn't have had in the first place."

"Don't pretend what you did was moral."

"And what you did was? Why were you holding onto that? For leverage?"

Hawkins bristled in her seat for a second, her anger growing the more she looked into Richard's eyes. Then she leaned over him, clicking open the door.

"Out," she said.

"Just a minute."

"Out!"

"Wait."

"No."

"I *have* missed you."

He leaned down and closed the door back over.

"I know everything between us has been a mess," he said. "But I wish it wasn't."

"And I wish you weren't here."

Hawkins leaned back over to open the door, but Richard blocked her.

"Please," he said. "Give me two minutes."

"No."

"I meant what I said. I've missed you."

"Don't. Just... I don't want to hear it."

Hawkins hoped the tone of her voice would make him get the hint and leave, but he only kept looking at her with his puppy dog eyes. She felt her discomfort rise as he raised a hand and placed it on her cheek tenderly, the discomfort turning to revulsion as he moved in closer, his lips lightly touching hers.

"Oi oi!" came a voice from outside the car.

They both jumped in their seats and looked out at the pavement. Detective Kane stood with his face red and shiny, his eyes dancing in the delight of catching them together.

"What are you two up to, then?"

He laughed at them both, and Hawkins shoved Richard in his side.

"Get out," she told him.

Kane, seeing the tension in the car and the horror in Hawkins' eyes, laughed harder.

"Get out," Hawkins repeated through clenched teeth, pushing Richard once more.

He shot her one last sheepish glance and climbed out the car, pushing himself wordlessly past Kane. For what felt to Hawkins like an excruciatingly long moment, Kane stared at her, his grin widening.

"I knew it," he said to her. "Don't worry. Your secret's safe with me."

Hawkins met his gaze, and nodded her head towards the wine bar window where she'd just seen him with Melissa.

"And yours is safe with me."

For now...

Chapter 63

Bill

October 1st, 2023

Bill was acutely aware of everyone staring at him in the prison yard. He shuffled forwards on weak legs towards the picnic benches feeling the heat of everyone's gaze. Reg was the one staring the most, his eyes constantly moving over Bill's skeletal body.

"Game of cards?" he asked him.

"Erm..." hesitated Bill.

His thinking was cloudy. The walk down from his cell had been exhausting, but he needed to be out in the yard. Needed to have everyone see how much his body had changed.

"Bill?" asked Reg, pulling the cards out his pocket. "You alright?"

"Yeah... Yeah..."

He sat down across from Reg, the bones in his bottom painfully protruding into the seat beneath him. He felt the sensation of light-headedness intensify as he watched Reg's hands move at lightning speed, dishing out the cards. He felt dizzy watching him and glanced away.

"Jesus, Bill. You don't look good."

"I'm okay. Just a little tired."

Reg knew he was lying, but didn't ask any more questions. Instead, he looked around the yard to see where the guards' attention was. He could see Terry in the distance watching them intently. Looking towards one of his team, a younger inmate who was still earning his place in the firm, he gave him a silent nod. The young man knew immediately it was an order and knew what to do. He returned the nod to Reg, then walked down the yard.

An older inmate was sitting on a nearby bench reading a book in the sunlight minding his own business. A perfect target for the young inmate wanting to prove himself to Reg. He wasted no time and didn't hesitate. Walking at speed up to the reading prisoner, he grabbed his book and flung it onto the ground.

"Hey! What the Hell?"

The young man grinned as everyone's attention was diverted towards him, including that of Terry and the other guards on the perimeter of the yard.

"I should fucking knock you out!" yelled the older prisoner, bending down to pick up his book.

"I'd like to see you try," said the young man.

"Is that a challenge?"

"Sure is."

The older prisoner lunged at him, aiming his fist at his jaw, but his efforts were no match for the young inmate who simply laughed, stepped out the way then swung his own punch dead into the older man's right cheek.

The guards sprung into action, Terry being the first on the scene as he placed himself between the two prisoners.

"Enough!" he yelled.

With the diversion successfully performed, Reg took his chance and moved his hands beneath the picnic table.

"I got you that thing you asked for," he said, tapping Bill on the knee.

Bill placed his hands beneath the table and felt for the object Reg was handing him before squireling it away in the pocket of his jogging bottoms. Behind him, the sounds of scuffling and shouting grew louder. He glanced over his shoulder just in time to see Terry and another guard dragging the young inmate inside as he kicked and yelled

"Thank you," he said to Reg.

"Yeah, no bother. I know Higgins was being awkward after giving you the paint. She's been real paranoid after that."

"I know. She said she couldn't do me any more favours because the guards were watching her."

"Well, I certainly can. Swiped that out the art room no bother."

Bill gave him an appreciative smile, but as he did, he felt his dizziness intensify.

"You okay?" asked Reg. "I've been saying this for a while now, but you really are looking rough."

"I'm fine. I just need to walk for a little bit."

Bill rose slowly from his seat on trembling legs and took a deep breath, but it only made him dizzier. He tried to take a step forwards, but as he did he wondered why the ground was moving so fast, rushing up to his face. He only realised he was falling when he felt the weightlessness of his body as he sank to the ground face first.

"Aw Jesus. What now?" asked one of the guards, running up to Bill.

Another guard rushed onto the scene, and the two of them knelt down at his side.

"Shit, he's out cold," one of them said. "He's a weird colour too."

He pressed his fingers to Bill's neck and felt for his pulse.

"Better send for a doctor."

"Wait, what's that?" asked the other guard.

"What?"

"There. Looks like something fell out his pocket."

Both guards leaned in closer to see the small metallic tube lying at Bill's side.

"Linseed oil?" asked the guard, picking it up and placing it into his own pocket. "What's he doing with that?"

Chapter 64

Fitz

October 1st, 2023

He recognised the car instantly as the one he'd seen outside his flat. Even the shape of the figure inside it, though dark and silhouetted, looked familiar.

"But what's it doing here?" he asked himself, staring out the windscreen as he tapped his fingers along the top of the steering wheel.

His unease grew to anger. He wanted to jump out the car and approach the figure, but instead he took a deep breath for now.

Out the corner of his eye, he noticed movement out on the street. He turned his head just as the familiar baggy, patchwork trousers and hemp jumper came into view. Winding down the window, he waved a hand out into the cold air.

"Hey," he whispered. "Jacques?"

Jacques froze as though Fitz' voice had come from the skies.

"Over here," whispered Fitz, clicking his fingers.

Only now did Jacques notice him and sauntered over with a guilty look in his eye.

"Why are you whispering?" he asked Fitz.

"Why are you down here at the warehouse? We're not meeting here any more."

"Why are *you* here down at the warehouse if we're not meeting here any more?"

"Touché."

They both stared at each other for an awkward moment before Fitz turned his attention to the car parked in front of the warehouse, the darkened figure in the driver's seat facing away from them.

"Who's that?" asked Jacques, noticing what Fitz was staring at.

Fitz shrugged.

"You didn't answer me," he said to Jacques. "What are you doing here?"

As Jacques opened his mouth, footsteps sounded from down the street and a second later a small figure in an oversized red hoody appeared. The face was hidden in the darkness, but Fitz recognised the bounce of the step in an instant.

"Billie?"

He looked to Jacques, confused, who in turn looked to an approaching Billie then back at Fitz with a guilty grin.

"Hi, Jacques!" she beamed. "Fitz?"

The three of them stared at each other for an elongated moment.

"I thought you two hated each other?" Fitz eventually said, breaking the silence.

Jacques and Billie exchanged a glance and smiled.

"We've put aside our differences," said Jacques.

God's sake... thought Fitz. *First Amelia and Marcus and now these two. Who's next? Cecilia and Lucien?*

Chapter 65

Lucien

October 1st, 2023

He lay on the bed, his eyes to the ceiling as he listened to Melissa in the bathroom. He tried to figure out what she was doing from the sounds she was making. He was sure he could hear her speaking, or was he imagining it? Was sure he could hear her muttering quietly as though having a hushed conversation on the phone. But as he strained his ears her voice seemed to quieten into silence. Now, the taps were running. They had been for some time now.

What is she doing?

He looked up at the modern clock on the wall. He'd agreed to pay her by the hour and twenty minutes had already passed with her in the bathroom. He grew impatient, the bulge in his boxer shorts growing bigger the longer he waited.

"Melissa?" he called out.

The taps stopped running. There was the sound of her heels tapping on the tiles of the bathroom floor, then came the click of the door as it opened. She revealed herself to him in black lace lingerie, her stockings accentuating how thin and toned her thighs were. His eyes darted over her body as he tried to take all of her in.

"Jesus," he said.

She had been worth the wait.

But as he saw her face, he noticed a strained expression.

"You okay?" he asked.

She nodded and smiled insincerely then sauntered in her heels to the foot of the bed where she sat down between his legs and reached for his foot.

"Yes, of course," she said, averting her gaze. "I'm okay."

She stroked his ankle, feeling the cashmere of his socks, then ran her fingers down his shoe, her long nails brushing against his laces. She untied them carefully like they were spun from gold, then looked up at him, biting her lower lip. It was a look that always got to Lucien and he grinned back. But he could still detect a slight look of worry in her eyes. She was a good actress, able to turn on her charm at will, but there was still some emotional residue lurking on her face. She couldn't hide everything.

"Are you sure you're okay? You look a little flustered."

"You're not paying to worry about me, are you?"

She forced a nervous laugh and pulled off his shoe which she delicately placed on the floor.

"This may come as a surprise to you," he said, sitting up and placing a hand on the side of her face. "But just because I pay you doesn't mean I don't care about you."

She flinched as he touched her, not because she didn't like it, but because she was surprised at the tenderness in his fingers. She truly did believe he cared about her, something she'd never experienced from other men. Not even Kane.

Lucien stroked the side of her face. Turning her head away from him, she set her attention to his other shoe, drawing out the seconds as she untied his laces.

"Thank you," she said to him, not looking him in the face. "It's nice to know you care about me. That makes me happy."

"I'm glad that makes you happy. So if there's anything bothering you, I'd like to know. Anything at all."

"Oh, no. You don't pay to listen to my problems."

"I pay for your company. And I think we've been seeing each other long enough that our... encounters... are more than just a business transaction."

"Yes, yes. They're more than that."

"So, if you'd like to talk. I'm all ears."

"Like a therapist?" she laughed.

"Like a friend. Or perhaps more than that."

She thought for a second, working her long nails up the back of Lucien's calves.

"I don't want to talk about my problems," she said.

"So you do have problems?"

"Don't we all?"

"Well, yes but..."

"I'd rather talk about you."

Lucien smiled and watched as she cocked her head to the side, her nails now feeling at the back of his knee reaching a sensitive, ticklish spot.

"Talk about me? Why would you want to do that?"

"Because your life is so glamorous."

"Oh, really. It's not."

"It is! You're a big shot lawyer. You meet so many exciting people."

"I meet a lot of crooks," he chuckled.

"That's exciting. And some of them are famous."

"Some of them."

"Like Sir Bill Lovecroft."

"Ah, yes. Like Sir Bill."

"What's he like? Is he as lovely as he looks on TV?"

She worked her nails up even higher so they lightly pinched at his thighs. Lucien felt a swell of excitement reach his stomach. Felt the delicious heat within his boxers rise.

"He is quite a character, yes."

"Is it all true?"

"Is what all true?"

"All the things I read about him in the papers and online?"

"And what things would that be?"

"That he is plotting some sort of genius escape plan?"

"All of that's in the papers?"

"There are rumours. Aren't the police trying to stop people helping him escape? Especially if he's offering so much money?"

"Oh, I assume they're monitoring things."

They stared at each other, both their heads filled with the knowledge the other wanted.

"So, tell me," smiled Melissa, as she climbed up the bed between his legs, "Let's just say the rumours are true. Let's just say he really is going to give someone billions to break him out of jail. How do you think he'd do it?"

She lowered herself onto her stomach, her mouth only inches from the zip of his trousers.

"How would I know?" he asked, smiling wryly.

"You're a clever man, Lucien. I bet you know everything about Sir Bill. In fact, you're so clever I bet you'd even help mastermind his plan for him."

She moved her fingers onto his zipper.

"I suppose Bill does trust me," he said.

He knew this was the point where he should stop talking, but her eyes were so wide and inquisitive, her face full of adoration as she stared up at him. She was interested in him. Something most women weren't. She was making him feel things he'd not felt in years, possibly even decades. She was making his stomach flip and his mind loosen like he was forgetting how to think logically.

"Does Bill trust you with any secrets?" asked Melissa.

"Oh, yes. Plenty."

Shut up, you idiot.

But it was too late, and the longer he looked into her eyes the more his mouth moved like he'd lost control of it. He continued to speak even though he knew he shouldn't. Words leaving his lips that he regretted as soon as they reached Melissa's ears.

"The rumours are true," he heard himself say. "He has a team, and *I* helped put it together."

"I knew it! I knew you were a clever man."

He felt his ego swell along with the contents of his underwear.

"And who is in this team?"

"Oh, I couldn't tell you that."

"Maybe tell me a little?"

She lowered her head closer to his body until he could feel her breath on him. Her eyes still looking up into his full of wonder.

"Okay... Just a little," he said. "But you can't tell a soul."

Chapter 66
Danielle

November 20th, 2016

Danielle yawned and sipped on her peppermint tea. She'd hardly slept the night before. Her back had started to ache terribly as her pregnancy progressed and she always felt tired. She yawned again and looked down at her work, then over to Mr Barker who was sat at the opposite end of the room, his eyes laser focused on a PDF of a Renoir he'd been studying. She could see the strain on his face, and the way his eyes darted over each zoomed in paint stroke.

"You've been staring at that a long time," she noted.

Only now did he glance away from his screen for the first time in the last hour. He looked down at his watch and did a double take.

"Goodness," he said. "You're right. I didn't even realise it was lunch time. Are you coming to the cafeteria?"

"Not just now, no."

"Not hungry?"

"Not really, no."

"Still suffering from nausea? My wife was the same when she was pregnant with the twins. Her toilet was her best friend."

"I'm starting to feel the same way."

"It gets better," he said, rising from his seat onto stiff legs. "Or so I'm told anyway."

As he walked by her, he gave her a long, protective look. He couldn't help it. He didn't want to intrude himself into her personal life, but he'd never forgotten the way Fitz had turned up and the subsequent fight with the security guards. He'd been worried about

Danielle ever since, and there wasn't a day that passed when he hadn't expected Fitz to return.

"You sure I can't get you anything from the cafeteria?" he asked. "A little bakewell tart maybe."

"No, really. That's kind of you, but I'm okay. Honestly."

He kept staring at her, not moving. Danielle wondered why he wasn't leaving.

"Why are you looking at me like that?" she laughed nervously.

"Like what?"

"Like I'm going to spontaneously combust."

He laughed nervously too, thrusting his hands into his pockets and rocking back on his heels.

"I'm just a little concerned about you, that's all. You do tremendous work here, but I can't help but notice you look a little stressed."

"It's just the pregnancy. I'm fine, really."

He wanted to bite his lip, but being a father himself, he couldn't stop worrying about her. He thought about what it would feel like if one of his daughters was being pursued by Fitz.

"And... the father?" he said.

"Fitz?"

"Yes... Fitz..." he said bitterly. "I hope he's not been giving you any more trouble."

"No, I've not seen him."

"I'm happy to hear that. I mean..."

He looked down at his shoes.

"I'm sorry, it's really none of my business. It's just that you do great work here and... Well, I just didn't like seeing you in that position. You know, when he turned up. It was quite a drama. A young lady like you shouldn't be involved in something like that."

"I appreciate you being concerned, but really, you don't need to be."

She gave him a slight smile and once again yawned, reaching for her tea. As she took a sip, she caught a glimpse of herself in the reflection of the framed picture across from her desk. Though her image wasn't clear, she could still see how tired she looked.

"Actually, a bakewell tart would be lovely," she said. "If you don't mind."

Barker smiled, happy to oblige her and turned on his heel.

"Of course. I'll be back in a jiffy."

As he walked away, a knock sounded from the door before he got a chance to open it. Then came the sound of high heels on the wooden floorboards, and the scent of expensive perfume that both Barker and Danielle had come to recognise.

"Hawkins," declared Barker as she entered the room. "Good to see you. I got your email earlier."

She shook his hand firmly, towering over him.

"Good to see you too. And you, of course, Danielle."

She shot her a warm smile across the room.

"If you don't mind I came to collect those files on the Renoir case."

"Oh, Barker will be pleased to hear that," said Danielle. "He's been working on them all morning."

Barker, instantly forgetting about the cafeteria and the bakewell tart, scurried back to his desk and started gathering the documents he had put together for Hawkins.

But Hawkins wasn't looking at Barker because her eyes were on Danielle. Searching her face, noticing something pulling down the corners of her eyes. She approached Danielle gingerly, softening her features as she approached.

"Oh!" declared Barker from across the room. "I've just realised I've left something in the filing room down the hall. I won't be a moment."

Hawkins barely acknowledged him as he flitted behind her and out the door. She welcomed the chance to speak to Danielle alone.

"You okay?" she asked her. "It's been a while since we had a catch up."

"Yeah, I'm all good. How are you?"

"You look a little..."

Hawkins fished inside her brain for the right word.

"Pre-occupied."

"Oh, just the baby and stuff."

"Everything okay?"

"With the baby? Yes! Just great. Not a single problem at all."

"Oh, that's wonderful news. But if there's not a single problem then why do you look so sad? Don't tell me Barker's working you too hard."

Danielle, surprised by the abruptness of the question, paused and looked down at her desk. Her hand felt for the handle of the top drawer where she pulled out a burgundy red card. Hawkins eyes scanned over it rapidly, taking in the golden writing that spelled out the words *Happy Birthday, Mum*.

"Oh, it's your mum's birthday?"

Danielle nodded sadly.

"It was my mum's birthday recently too," noted Hawkins. "They must be the same star sign. Not that I'm into that kinda thing."

"Did you do anything special?" asked Danielle.

Hawkins huffed and looked down at her shoes.

"Christ, no. Not spoken to the old bat since I was sixteen."

Danielle didn't know what to say. Half of her was overcome with inquisitiveness, the other half filled with the polite urge not to pry.

"Ah, it's okay," said Hawkins, as though she was trying to convince herself. "I'm better off without her. She wasn't, erm... How do I put this? She wasn't much of a mother."

"Sorry to hear that."

"Urgh, it's fine. She did me a favour when she met a waiter on holiday in Kavos and ran away with him. Just upped and left me and my dad like that."

She clicked her fingers for emphasis.

"It hit Dad hard. I, as cold as it sounds, kinda welcomed her departure. At least there were no more fights. Just me and Dad. It was peaceful after she left."

Danielle now noticed Hawkins was staring off into space with nostalgia misting up her eyes.

"Anyway!" said Hawkins, snapping out her daze. "I doubt you want to hear all about my sad childhood."

"No, it's okay. I'm happy to-"

"What about today? Are you doing anything special?"

Hawkins tapped the card with her long, pointed fingernail.

"My mum's dead," sighed Danielle.

A look of realisation came across Hawkins' face as her mouth dropped open.

"Oh! Oh... Of course, you're Sir Lovecroft's daughter and..... Yes, I remember reading about your mother's passing in the news. Cancer, wasn't it? Really sad. I'm sorry."

"It's okay. I was really young when she passed away but..."

"That doesn't mean it's easy for you."

"No."

"And you must miss her."

"I do. It's why I keep writing her these cards. Putting them on her grave. She can't read them obviously. I don't know why I do it. It's silly but-"

"It's not silly. It's a very lovely thing to do."

"You think?"

"Absolutely."

The two shared a look of affection and Hawkins found herself warming to Danielle.

"What are you doing tonight?" asked Hawkins.

"Oh... Just an early night and some Horlicks for me."

"That won't do. How about you and me head out for dinner? A nice girls' night out. Since neither of us can take our mother's out, we could entertain each other."

"That sounds great!" beamed Danielle. "I'd really like that."

The sound of Barker's squeaky loafers entering the room diverted their attention as he approached carrying a large, brown folder he pointed at Hawkins.

"Sorry to keep you waiting. Took me an eternity to find this."

He waved a hand around the air, exasperated.

"Anyway, here it is now."

Danielle now noticed in his other hand, a smaller, slimmer file hung open, its contents revealed to her through a transparent, plastic sleeve. Beyond the plastic was an image. One she recognised immediately and knew every inch of.

"What's that!" she cried, pointing at it.

Barker looked down and nodded eagerly.

"Oh, this! I was going to tell you later. Quite a big piece of news I was saving for the right moment, but I suppose there's no harm in telling you now."

He pulled the printed image out from under the plastic and placed it down on Danielle's desk.

"Isn't it beautiful?" he said. "I can't decide what I find most exquisite. The colour palette or the softness in which the complexions are drawn. The cherubs are just beautiful."

He pointed at the top right hand corner of the painting at a cherub's rosy cheek.

"Have you seen anything so beautiful before?"

"Yes," replied Danielle, her face tensing. "Where did you get this?"

"Incredible story," grinned Barker. "It's been on my radar for months now. Private collector arrived to tell us he's discovered this piece in his collection. But of course, no one believed he had a real Caravaggio. And an unknown one at that. What are the chances? But we've been doing tests for months and it's the real deal alright. Just been acquired and it'll be exhibiting in the next few months."

"You mean it's here!" gasped Danielle.

"Yes, it's already here," Barker smiled back, mistaking her outrage for excitement. "Would you like to come see it?"

I've already seen it, she thought, anger tightening her chest. *It's mine.*

Chapter 67

Bill

October 1st, 2023

There was no such thing as a hospital wing in Belmarsh. There was, however, a cramped sickly coloured room with four beds. An inpatient facility, Bill had been told. As he looked around the room, he thought it looked better suited to the sick bay on the battlefields of the Crimean War rather than the twenty-first century.

He had only been unconscious for a brief amount of time, less than two minutes, but he was exhausted and could barely keep his eyes open.

"Have you been eating?" came a voice from the bottom of the bed.

He barely registered it. It sounded like it came through a long tunnel filled with jelly.

"Bill? Can you hear me?"

His eyes flickered open and shut a few times.

"Get this man some fluids, and some glucose," he heard the voice say.

When he next opened his eyes, he realised he must have passed out again, or fallen asleep. He was alert this time, and he also felt a sharp pain in his left arm. When he looked down, he saw a drip attached an inch above the fold of his arm. He noticed how thin it was, like a twig.

"Oh, you're awake," came the voice again from the bottom of the bed.

Now Bill could clearly see the face it was coming from.

"I'm awake," replied Bill, groggily.

"You were really out of it for some time there. Looks like the glucose has brought you round. But that stuff would make a hummingbird buzz. Good stuff. Anyway, how are you feeling?"

Bill watched as the voice came out the thin lips of a doctor who now perched himself on the foot of his bed. He was struck immediately by how smart and respectable he looked in contrast to all the inmates he'd been in the company of.

"I'm feeling... Okay."

"Glad to hear it. My name's Dr Waller."

"Hello, Dr Waller."

"Do you know what happened?"

Bill cast his mind back. The last thing he remembered was talking to Reg and then... It was all blurry after that. Then a thought struck him.

The linseed oil!

He thrust his free hand into the pocket of his jogging bottoms and felt it was no longer there.

Shit!

"Okay?" asked Dr Waller, seeing the panic on Bill's face.

"Yes... yes."

"Can you remember what happened?"

"I, erm... No."

"You fainted. Quite dramatically."

Dr Waller held a clipboard in his arm that held Bill's chart. He kept darting his eyes between it and Bill's gaunt face.

"I'm assuming you haven't been eating," he said.

"I have."

Dr Waller shot him a sceptical look.

"I'd like to believe that but..."

"I have. You can ask Terry Chapman."

"The guard?"

"Yes."

Dr Waller thought for a second and frowned.

"Nurse!" he eventually called out across the room. "Will you send Chapman in please?"

"He's here?" asked Bill.

"He's been waiting outside this room since you arrived an hour ago. You *are* in his custody."

Dr Waller, feeling that something wasn't right with Bill, kept his eyes on his face as the door behind him opened with the nurse leading Terry inside.

"Jesus, Bill," said Terry as he approached the bed. "You looked bloody dead when you got here. Like a sack of spuds."

Bill could see a genuine look of concern on Terry's face and glanced away, almost embarrassed.

"I'm alright now."

"Well, at least you've got some colour back in your cheeks."

"I brought you in," interrupted Dr Waller. "To ask about Bill's eating habits."

"Well, he moans about the food a lot."

Dr Waller chuckled.

"So, he doesn't like the food in here. Who does? Does he eat it, though?"

"Oh... Yeah."

"Are you sure about that?"

"I bring him all his meals in the day. I bring the tray in and it's empty when I pick it back up. Been doing that since he got separated from the general population."

"Are you sure about that?"

"What, you calling me a liar?" asked Terry, defensively.

"No, I'm just trying to figure out... Never mind. Thank you, Chapman."

Terry rolled his eyes, annoyed at Dr Waller then stepped away from Bill's bed.

"My shift's coming to an end," he said, almost apologetically. "I'll see you tomorrow."

Bill watched as Terry exited the room.

Thank you, he thought. *You said all the right things.*

"So you've been eating," said Dr Waller, now scribbling in Bill's chart. "That's worrying."

"Is it?"

"Of course. You're drastically underweight. We'll need to run some tests."

"What kind of tests?"

"First, we'll see what your antibodies are up to?"

"Are up to? You make it sound like they're secretly messing about or something?"

Dr Waller smiled.

"They might be. We need to see how many you have."

Now was the time for Bill to say the magic words he'd been practising in his head for days. The ones that would start the ball rolling.

"You know..." he said. "This all started when..."

"When what?"

"Well, I don't want to say anything."

Dr Waller lowered the chart and stared into Bill's eyes.

"You don't want to say anything?"

"No, I mean... I know what happens to grasses in places like this. You keep things to yourself in prison, don't you?"

"Bill, if something happened you need to tell us."

Bill did his best to look scared. Even going as far as to scrunch his eyes closed for a few seconds in dramatic effect as he balled his hands into fists.

"No, I can't say. I'm not exactly the hardest person in this place. Don't want to make myself a target like... That poor fellow in the library."

Dr Waller understood. He'd heard the same thing repeatedly over the years. Had almost lost count of the amount of people he'd seen come into the inpatient room needing stitches from injuries the patients refused to speak about.

"I can't force you to talk, obviously," he said to Bill. "But I'd like to think you could confide in me if anything happened."

Bill opened his eyes and faked a tremble in his hand.

"Whatever you say," continued Dr Waller, "Will not go further than these four walls."

He looked over his shoulder at where the nurse was stood. She understood the look on his face immediately, gave him a curt nod and departed the room to give the two men their privacy.

"So if you'd like to tell me what happened."

Bill swallowed hard, looked into Dr Waller's eyes and said, "It happened when I first got here."

He paused for a second, faking a nervous breath.

"What happened?"

"It wasn't an attack... exactly."

"You were hurt?"

"In a way. Not badly. It was just a scratch."

"Where was this?"

"In the yard. I had just been playing cards."

"With Reg?"

Bill raised an eyebrow.

"Word gets around," he said.

"Everyone knows everything in this place," said Dr Waller.

"Then how do I know what I'm about to say won't spread like wildfire?"

"Because I don't gossip, and I am genuinely trying to help you. If something happened and you need help, then I'm here to deliver that help. It's my job."

But Bill could detect something in the doctor's eyes; a starstruck sparkle.

"Okay," sighed Bill. "I had just finished playing cards and we were all filing back inside. Reg went in before me and I found myself at the back amongst a group of people I'd not spoken to before. I don't know what I did to offend anyone. But I must have done something."

"Sometimes, in this place, all you have to do is glance in someone's direction to start a war."

"Yes, I've noticed. Perhaps I was in the wrong place at the wrong time. But as I was about to step inside, I felt a scratch. I looked down at my hand and..."

Bill looked down at the back of his hand now and gave it a sad rub.

"And I noticed what looked like a cat scratch. It's healed up now, obviously. It was nothing."

"What was it from?"

"Here's the thing that worries me. I looked to see where it came from and noticed one of the other prisoners staring at me."

"Do you know who it was?"

"I'd not seen him before."

"What did he look like?"

Dr Waller started to scribble urgently on Bill's chart.

"He was big, stocky. Had dark hair and stubble."

Dr Waller grimaced.

That described most of Belmarsh.

"Any tattoos?"

"I don't remember."

"Did he say anything?"

"He laughed at me. Then he said, 'Celebrity scum. Think you own the place 'cause you've got cash'."

Dr Waller frowned.

"Celebrity scum? That's what he said? Seems peculiar."

"Guess he just hates me because I'm wealthy. Some people are like that. But it's not what he said that worried me. It was what he scratched me with."

"What was it?"

Bill faked fear once again, made his hand shake and started chewing his lip.

"I noticed he had a needle in his hand."

"What kind of needle?" panicked Dr Waller, standing up and springing into action.

"The kind you do heroin with I suppose. I've only seen them in the movies."

"He scratched you with a needle? You're sure?"

"Yes, he was brandishing it at me."

"And you didn't tell anyone?"

"No. Like I said. You don't grass in here. I was afraid of him."

Dr Waller strode across the room in search of the nurse.

"You'll need to get an HIV test, pronto."

Dr Waller disappeared without another word leaving Bill staring at the dull walls as he thought over his plan.

Stay calm and do as you were told.

The minutes ticked by. The nerves were gripping him now, especially as the strength came back into his body via the glucose. It was easy to stay calm when he was hungry. He was simply too weak to worry, but now his brain was starting to work again.

After a fifteen minute stretch that felt to Bill like an hour, the nurse returned to the room without the doctor, pulling on gloves as she walked. On the tray in front of her, was a plastic wrapped HIV test.

"I'm going to need a blood sample," she said.

"Of course. How long will this take?"

"Dr Waller is insisting you get the rapid test. You'll know in thirty minutes."

"Oh... Wow. The marvels of modern medicine."

He forced a smile and tried to stay chipper, but the nurse remained stern and set to work pricking his finger with a needle.

"Just place your finger on here," she said, making sure the blood dropped onto the small window in the test.

"Thirty minutes?" asked Bill, just to make sure.

"Thirty minutes."

She smiled politely then placed the test back on the tray. They both stared at it for a second as the window flooded with blood.

"As you can see," explained the nurse, pointing a gloved finger at the test. "The first line is already emerging. That's normal. If the test identifies the right antibodies, and you do have the..." she lowered her voice for a moment. "HIV virus. Then another line will present itself here."

Bill nodded.

He knew this already, of course. It had all been explained to him. Lying back down on the pillow, he looked up at the ceiling, touching a hand woefully to his forehead.

"I'm feeling a little light headed again," he said.

"Perhaps you need another glucose sachet."

"No, no. That seems a bit much. Maybe just a glass of fruit juice would do. Is that possible?"

The nurse began peeling off her gloves and moved towards the bin.

"Of course. I can get you a glass of orange juice," she said. "Not freshly squeezed, though."

After dropping her gloves in the bin, she walked out the room leaving Bill alone with the test for a few minutes. He took the time to lean down and inspect it carefully and go over the plan in his head one more time.

It's simple. It'll take just a second. Just as long as no one's watching.

When he heard the door open again, he lay back down and waited for the nurse to approach with a plastic cup of orange juice. He took it gratefully and gulped down a mouthful, letting out a satisfied sigh.

"Oh, I feel a lot better now," he said.

"I'm glad. Can I get you anything else?"

"Actually, would it be too much trouble to ask for a biscuit? I'm sorry. That's dreadfully rude of me. You're not a waitress. It's just that-"

"I can, of course, get you a biscuit, Mr Lovecroft. I mean, Sir."

She exited the room once again leaving Bill once more alone with the HIV test. He moved fast, knowing he only had precious seconds. Dipping his index finger into the orange juice, he hovered it over the window of the test where his blood had just dropped and watched as it filled with orange liquid. The moment he leaned back in place, the nurse returned with a small plate covered in chocolate digestives.

"Asda's own brand, I'm afraid," she said as she set them down.

"Perfect."

He took a biscuit and nibbled around the edges. It had been so long since he'd eaten, it tasted glorious.

The nurse looked down at her watch.

"Twenty-seven minutes to go," she said. "Time moves slowly when you're waiting. Maybe you'd like to take a nap while we wait for your result to show up."

"I don't think I could sleep. I'm far too nervous."

"I understand, but lie back and try to take it easy. Dr Waller and myself will be back shortly."

Again, she left the room leaving him alone with the test. He stared at it, waiting, hoping his plan would work. As the seconds ticked by, he felt his nerves increase and tried to take a breath to relax, but it didn't work. After a few moments, he lay back, pulled the sheets up around him with his only mobile hand and closed his eyes.

He breathed in the sterile scent of the room and listened to the muffled sounds of Dr Waller's voice through the door. It sounded like he was on the phone.

What I tell him stays within these walls my arse, he thought. *I bet everyone in this bloody place knows my needle story by now.*

Not that it mattered.

Not that it was even true.

All he needed was for the HIV test to be in front of him.

Through the door, he heard Dr Waller's voice grow momentarily louder, then settle to a hushed tone. A few seconds later, there was silence.

It became so quiet in the room that Bill's ears started to pick up the distant sounds from around the prison. Of doors slamming and guards shouting.

He closed his eyes and tried to pass the time by thinking of what a positive HIV test would bring him.

I'll get out of here.

To a hospital.

To freedom...

Despite his nerves, the exhaustion in his body caught up with him and he found himself drifting off to sleep. It only felt like a few seconds, but when he next opened his eyes, both Dr Waller and the nurse were standing by his side with anxious faces.

"You're awake," said Dr Waller. "I'm sorry but..."

He glanced down at the test on the tray beside the bed.

Bill sat up and looked down, his eyes immediately noticing the two lines forming across the test.

"Bill there's no easy way to say this, but your HIV test has proven positive for antibodies."

"Does that mean that..."

Dr Waller nodded sagely.

"I'm sorry."

Bill had to fight hard to suppress the shock and happiness inside himself.

I don't believe that worked!

"Oh... dear," was all he managed to say, lowering his head to hide his face.

"You'll have to be hospitalised for treatment," said Dr Waller. "But there are plenty of reasons to be optimistic. It's not the death sentence it once was. There are options now."

Bill tried his hardest to look upset, but inside he was laughing. The magic word rang in his head. Hospitalised.

Chapter 68
Fitz

October 2nd, 2023

"You're kidding. It worked?"

"It worked," replied Lucien as he stood on Fitz' doorstep.

"Bloody orange juice?"

"Yep."

"How does that make an HIV test positive?"

"What am I, a scientist? Something about its high acidity levels bonding with the components of the test. Learned it from a former client."

Fitz nodded approvingly.

"He'll be moved tomorrow," said Lucien.

"Shit. That soon?"

"It's what we wanted."

"Sure is. You got everything in place?"

Fitz nodded again, this time vigorously.

"I'll get everyone together tonight. The ball's rolling."

The usual shark-like gaze in Lucien's eyes intensified. He could almost smell the money, feel it in his hands. He could taste the opportunities and joy it could bring him. An image popped into his head of himself on the beach in the Bahamas with Melissa by his side. Without the need to do a single day's work again.

Fitz felt his own excitement, but he wasn't thinking of sun drenched beaches or beautiful women. He was thinking of the plan and nothing else.

He was ecstatic at how fast it was now moving, how seamlessly Bill had executed his part so far. But as he watched Lucien on his doorstep, the uneasiness that had been creeping over him for the last few weeks intensified.

"You shouldn't be here," he said. "We know they're watching."

"I would have phoned but... Well, I wanted to give you this."

Lucien reached into the briefcase at his side, fumbled for a moment then pulled out a brown envelope.

"I was sorting through Bill's things earlier in his office and I found this. Thought you'd want it."

Curious, Fitz opened the flap of the envelope and slid out its contents into the palm of his hand. The shiny paper caught the light of the hallway, beaming up an image that set his heart ablaze with warmth.

"Sarah," smiled Fitz, his eyes growing watery at the sight of his daughter.

"It's her most recent school photograph by the looks of it. Pretty little lady."

Just like her mother.

"Anyway," said Lucien, taking a step back. "I'll call you when I know the exact time of Bill's departure."

"I'll be waiting."

It was all happening now. All those weeks of planning and it all came down to how the next twenty-four hours would pan out. It was all or nothing.

He looked down at his watch and became acutely aware that at this time tomorrow, it would all be over one way or another. It was death or glory, all or nothing. He'd have Sarah back or he'd have nothing but the prospect of being flung back in jail.

He closed the front door over and walked down the hall to his living room. The images of the plan in his head running through his mind at what felt like a hundred miles an hour. To calm his nerves, he looked back down to the photograph of Sarah and felt his heart swell.

This is all for you.

"Looks like whoever visited brought you good news," came a voice from his couch.

Fitz flinched, forgetting he had company. He looked up from the photograph to see Phenomena sitting with her legs elegantly crossed, a cup of tea in her hand and her eyes wide with curiosity.

"Tomorrow," he said, mysteriously.

"What about tomorrow?"

Phenomena stared at him for a second until the penny dropped. Then she almost dropped her tea in shock.

"Tomorrow! That was Lucien at the door? You mean the test worked?"

"Who would have believed it?"

Phenomena knew she should have been happy, excited even, but instead she was overcome with panic. She almost threw her tea cup down on the coffee table and jumped up. Pacing the room, she felt her breath quicken .

"I... I don't know if I can do it," she gasped.

"What! You don't know if you can do it? Of course you can. That's why you're on the team."

Her mind started to race as the nerves set in. She ran through what she had to do in her head. It sounded so straight forward when Fitz had first told her, but now, with the cold realisation that there were only mere hours separating her between now and the biggest stunt of her life, it felt like an impossible task.

"Fitz... I don't know."

"What you have to do is easy."

"If I was on stage it would be easy. But this is going to be out in the real world with some very real consequences."

"And some very real money," Fitz reminded her.

The thought of that motivated her, but only for a second and then the anxiety returned.

"And a very real prison sentence if we're caught."

She paced faster.

"You're gonna tear up my carpet," he moaned. "Can practically see smoke coming off your feet."

"I can't help it. I'm sorry."

Fitz walked up to her, blocking her from walking any further and clapped his hands onto her shoulders.

"Listen, please."

He could feel her tremble beneath his hands.

"You can do this. I wouldn't have you on the team if I didn't think you were the best person for the job. It'll take just a few seconds. That's all. And it'll be over."

"Are you sure?"

"I'm as positive as Bill's HIV test."

The nerves still swirled around her gut, but as she looked into Fitz' eyes, she could see how much he believed in her. She relaxed ever so slightly.

"If you think I can do it..." she said. "Then I *can*."

Chapter 69

Danielle

November 20th, 2016

Hawkins pulled her Mercedes up to the bottom of Lovecroft's driveway. Her stomach was full from a sumptuous dinner, and the bottle of wine she'd left on the kitchen counter was calling to her along with a hot bath.

"That was fun," she said to Danielle who was pulling the seatbelt off her growing belly. "We should do that again."

"Definitely. Thanks so much. Today's always a bit, you know, wobbly for me. It was nice to spend the day with…"

Danielle searched for the right word in her head. She wanted to say mother figure, but thought it sounded too intense. Instead, she smiled and said, "A friend. It was nice to hang out with you. And wasn't dinner amazing?"

"Absolutely. You've converted me into a sushi lover."

Danielle wanted to reach over into the driver's seat and give Hawkins a hug, but she didn't think she was the hugging type.

"How about coffee next week?" asked Hawkins.

"I'd love that."

"Me too."

Danielle stepped out into the night, but just before she could say goodbye, Hawkins leaned over the gearstick and said, "Hey, I don't mean to pry but… Sorry. It's nothing really, but I've been thinking. Earlier, the painting Barker showed you in his file. The Caravaggio."

Danielle visibly tensed up.

"You looked angry about it."

That was an understatement. Danielle raged when she saw it, and all night it was constantly on her mind, ravaging her thoughts with endless questions she needed to fire at her father. Hawkins saw the look on her face and knew she'd touched a nerve.

"Sorry, I shouldn't have mentioned it," she said. "Forgive me, I'm just being nosy. Guess I can't turn off my prosecutor's brain."

"No, no. It's fine. It's just that. I've been a Caravaggio lover for a long time, and I didn't know it was being added to the museum's collection. I'd have liked to have known sooner."

Hawkins could sense there was more to the anger in Danielle's eyes.

"Anyway," continued Danielle. "Thanks so much for dinner. See you next week?"

"Yes, of course. I'll text you soon."

Danielle smiled and closed over the door. Then she turned and faced down her driveway. She could see the light on in her father's study.

Chapter 70

Cecilia

October 2nd, 2023

Tomorrow...

When Lucien arrived at her house with the news, she felt an overwhelming sense of excitement.

Tomorrow I might see my Dad!

But tonight I have to see HIM...

She stood on the doorstep of the Marylebone town house with a bottle of Bordeaux in her hand, the one she remembered as his favourite, and felt a peculiar mix of repulsion and excitement. The racing green door in front of her opened inch by inch to reveal the familiar figure. She was surprised to see he was wearing the same loafers he'd worn the last time she'd seen him almost a year ago. But the hair was different. Freshly cut and coiffed to perfection, he looked and smelled like he'd walked out the barbers moments before her arrival.

"Cecilia!"

"Harold!" she sang back, trying to match his enthusiasm.

"Come in!"

She followed him into his hallway and he immediately wrapped both his arms around her in a bear hug, kissing each of her cheeks.

"Ooh, Bordeaux," he grinned, taking the bottle from her hand. "You remembered."

"Of course. It's your favourite. We always drank it together."

His cheeks shone red beneath the light of the overhead chandelier. She looked up and remembered being in the house one summer when it was being cleaned, and Harold had been yelling and screaming at the poor woman who had been sent to polish each of the crystals. Like everything else in the house, it had been passed down through the generations, its monetary value surpassed by its sentimental. Even the house had been in Harold's family since the early eighteen hundreds.

Cecilia looked up and down the walls of the hallway at all the framed nautical illustrations. At the far end towards the kitchen lay one of the many glass cabinets filled with Naval medals. A couple belonging to Harold himself while the others came from the many men in his family who had lived eventful lives on the high seas.

"Please, take a seat," he said, leading her into the living room.

Cecilia was used to living in a house that looked more like a show home than a private residence. She was used to high standards and pristine living conditions, but the cleanliness of Harold's home had always disturbed her. It was clean to the point of feeling like an operating theatre.

She watched as he popped the cork off the bottle of wine and poured a glass for her. As she took the glass from his hand with a smile, she momentarily panicked that she'd spill a drop on the white carpet.

"So," he said, sitting down close to her. "I've got to say I was quite surprised when I got your message earlier. It's been how long since we last saw each other?"

"A long time."

He searched her face for answers. Answers he'd wished she'd given him almost a year previously.

"Sorry," she said, pathetically as she took a much needed sip of wine. "Things have been complicated."

"No need to tell me. I've seen your father in the news."

"Oh... Yes. You must have. But that's not why I'm here," she lied. "I guess, it's always been playing on my mind. The way I left things."

"Left things? You mean left *me*. And quite suddenly too. I thought things were great between us. We were in love. Or so I thought and then... What? You just dumped me."

"It wasn't like that, Harold. And dumped? You make me sound like a schoolgirl."

But she knew that's exactly what she'd acted like. The truth was that she had grown easily bored of Harold and his constant need to keep everything ship shape. She wasn't on the hunt for a bad boy like Fitz, but she wanted some excitement, some passion, and Harold was just about the most vanilla man she'd ever met. He was all about rules and early bedtimes. And he spent his evenings reading books about military history when she wanted to go out dancing.

She'd finished with him suddenly, and knew she'd broken his heart. But she couldn't handle the prospect of another night watching him stare at ancient blueprints of a ship while she waited in a party dress for him to take her out.

"Anyway," he said, leaning a little closer. "You're here now. Although, I have to say I really am surprised. Maybe you missed me after all?"

"Maybe a little..."

She cringed as the words came out, not realising he would be so pleased to see her. There was a flash of lust in his eyes and she panicked. It was the same look he always gave her when he was just about to kiss her sloppily.

My God. Remember how bad a kisser he was.

She saw him inch closer, saw as he licked his lips in anticipation.

I've got to stop this.

"So... actually," she gulped, swallowing more wine. "I hope you don't mind, but I have a favour to ask you."

"Oh..."

He visibly stiffened, his face falling with disappointment. A cold look swept over his eyes as he set down his wine glass and crossed his legs defensively.

"I should have known," he said. "You couldn't possibly have wanted to come over to, you know, *see me*. No, you have a favour to ask."

"It's about my dad."

"Of course it is."

The bitterness in his voice set Cecilia on edge.

"But it can benefit you too," she began to explain. "Remember how you always wanted to leave the Navy?"

He narrowed his eyes at her.

"Remember how it was always your dream to captain a luxury yacht. Sail around the Caribbean rather than be sent to war zones all the time. Isn't that what you said you wanted?"

Pursing his lips, he reached back for his wine glass and took a laboured sip.

"I did used to say that."

"And how long have you got left with the Navy? A year?"

"Six months actually, but there's the option to sign up for another two. If I have to. If I have no other options."

"Well... That's great!"

"Is it?"

There was still a hint of bitterness in his voice, but it was joined now with curiosity.

"What are you really here for? What do you want from me?"

"Wouldn't you rather want to know what you could get from *me*?"

The curiosity on his face grew.

"Tell me."

"A new life. Away from the rules of the military. I can give you that."

"And how can you do that exactly?"

"My dad became majority shareholder of Prestige Travel just before he went into Belmarsh."

Harold's eyes widened and Cecilia knew he'd taken the bait.

"Is that so?" he said, trying to sound calm.

"It is. Prestige have the biggest clients. It's where billionaires like my dad get all their staff for their travels. Pilots for their private jets. *Captains* for their super yachts..."

"And..."

"I'll make sure you have the best position with the best pay."

"But what do I have to do?"

"It's simple," smiled Cecilia. "When are you next on base?"

"I'm due back on the HMS King Edward in a few days."

The excitement grew inside Cecilia.

Could the timing be any better?

"King Edward..." she said to herself. "I remember you sailing on that before. Portsmouth, right?"

"That's right."

"Okay... I'll tell you what I need. But first, more wine."

Chapter

71

– Billie – October 2nd, 2023

She wasn't fully awake or dressed when she sat down at her laptop. It glowed at the end of the bed, shining up towards Jacques' sleeping face. Billie glanced at him now and wondered if there was still a part of her that hated him.

Maybe, she thought. *That pompous posh boy routine of his gets on my nerves, but my God is he good in bed.*

But right now, her focus couldn't be on what happened between the sheets. She had a job to do. Opening up all her social media accounts on separate tabs, she set about updating them all.

It was short notice. When she got the news from Fitz about Bill's removal from Belmarsh to a local hospital, she couldn't believe the ball was finally rolling. And it was rolling in her stomach now too.

She couldn't decide what she felt more, fear or excitement.

Tomorrow...

Tomorrow!

She thought of the money. Thought of all the people she would be leading. Thousands and thousands of her followers pulled into one of her latest stunts. When she'd made the post only a few hours previously about the meetup she was planning outside the Scotland Yard office, she was shocked at how quickly the responses came in.

PROTEST WITH ME TOMORROW, she'd typed. *Protest the MET's new inhumane strip search policy. School children are being detained and ordered to...*

They were words she knew would grip her followers. She felt a deep warmth as she saw how much her followers loved her. Loved her to the point they were helping her to become a criminal. Even if they didn't know it.

As she set about replying to comments and private messages, she momentarily felt like a tiny dictator leading innocents astray with her devious plan.

Is this... unethical?

Of course it is, she reasoned with herself. *Anybody who gets ahead in life occasionally straddles the line of what's right and wrong. Besides, it's all for a good cause.*

She looked back at Jacques just as he produced a single snore and smiled. Not at him, but at the thought of all the money.

Billions...

She tried to picture the amount in her head. It felt like so big a number she couldn't quite wrap her head around it.

"Billions..." she whispered to her screen.

"You say something, babe?"

Behind her, Jacques rose with a yawn before scrambling down the bed and wrapping his arms around her shoulders. He watched for a moment as she worked. Her fingers moving at lightning speed as she replied to comment after comment. He was just about to kiss her on the cheek when his phone rang. She stiffened in his arms.

"The girl with the septum piercing?" she asked, bitterly.

"No. No, she's long gone."

"Sure about that?"

"Why? You jealous?"

She laughed and shook him off like a dog shaking off fleas.

"Jealous? Shut up."

All she had on her mind was the money and what she needed to do to get it.

"Where shall we go once it's done?" asked Jacques as he lay back in bed and sparked a rolled up cigarette.

"Huh?"

"After it's done. What you thinking? Bahamas?"

"I was thinking of an animal shelter."

"What?" chuckled Jacques.

"Why are you laughing? I thought your whole deal was saving the planet and animals and all that jazz?"

He blew smoke up to the ceiling and nodded.

"Yeah, of course," he said. "I just never pinned you down as the animal loving type of girl."

"Well, I am. I've been trying to save up for years to build my own dog rescue and rehabilitation centre. There'll be other animals there too, but mainly dogs."

"That's... very sweet, Billie. Hey, maybe you could build one in Mexico. Heard there are loads of strays there."

"Maybe," she said, still typing at speed. "Maybe I will."

Chapter 72 – Hawkins – October 3rd, 2023

5.55 AM

The sun hadn't yet risen when Hawkins arrived at her office, but PC Busby was already standing in her room extending the landline phone out towards her.

"Governor Corour at Belmarsh," he said to her. "He's been calling all morning for you. Said he'd been trying to get you on your mobile."

"Yeah," replied Hawkins, taking a sip of coffee. "I have a policy that I don't answer calls before six am."

She took the phone from Busby.

"Governor?"

"He's leaving today."

"What!"

The coffee in Hawkins' stomach churned.

"What do you mean he's leaving?"

"He's being transferred to hospital. He was diagnosed with HIV last night."

"Bullshit," spat Hawkins.

"It's true. I saw the positive test myself."

"I want to see that test too. In fact, I want Lovecroft to take another one right in front of me. My arse does he have HIV."

The governor chuckled, but there was a solemn quality to his voice.

"You know I can't make him do that," he said. "But the man is clearly ill. I went and saw him myself last night. He needs hospital treatment and Belmarsh just doesn't have the facilities."

"All right... Okay..."

"Don't worry. He'll be cuffed to the bed at all times with two wardens by his side."

"I should assume so. I'm going to go a step further and suggest a squad car accompany the ambulance to the hospital."

"That's what I thought you would say."

"You thought right. I'll arrange that right away. I'll call you back."

She hung up abruptly and stepped out her room to find PC Busby standing by the coffee vending machine in the hall, yawning as he shovelled fifty pence pieces into the slot.

"I've got a job for you and PC Clarkston," she said.

He looked up with a slightly nervous expression.

"Sure. Anything to get out the office."

Chapter 73 – Fitz – October 3rd, 2023

7.05 AM

The wind was so crisp as it blew across Brompton Cemetery, Fitz felt like it was biting his ears. He shivered, zipped his coat up higher and walked faster. Ahead of him, a young couple were walking their sausage dog. He watched in horror as they let it run onto a nearby grave, raise its leg and piss against the marble headstone.

"Oi!" shouted Fitz.

The couple spun round looking annoyed to have been disturbed.

"Have some respect, will ya?"

The boyfriend momentarily thought about responding with something witty, but he could see the genuine anger in Fitz' eyes and thought better of it.

"Sorry," he mumbled, yanking on the dog's lead. "Come on, Hugo."

Fitz stared daggers into the backs of their heads as they walked away. He waited until they were out of sight before he approached the grave on which the dog had relieved itself.

He'd passed it many times, and although he didn't know the person buried beneath it personally, he felt a little connection with them.

Lucy Albright was her name. She had been one of the fatalities from the Lusitania. A fact only made clear to Fitz because it was engraved on her headstone. He'd found it fascinating, although morbid..

"All right, Lucy," he said, walking past her grave.

His sights were now set on the one grave he did come to see, the one he had visited so many times it felt like a home to him, a place he could release his thoughts to the one person who would understand him.

"Danielle," he said, softly, approaching her headstone.

As usual, her grave was immaculately kept. Orchids had been planted around her headstone splashing the area in cream and deep purple tones.

Fitz squatted down and picked up some fallen petals before sweeping loose pieces of grass away. In front of him, the marble headstone shimmered beneath the morning sunlight. Clearly, Bill had made sure someone was maintaining the grave site even though he was incarcerated.

"Danielle, it's happening today," he said. "Finally, it's happening. And if it all goes right. I mean it *will* go right. It *has* to go right or I won't get my Sarah back. *Our* Sarah."

He sniffed as he felt his throat close up.

"I'm going to get her back."

His chest ached as he looked at where Danielle lay.

Glancing at his watch, he saw he didn't have long until it all started rolling. His phone had been ringing from inside his pocket, but he needed to be left alone for these few precious moments. Because although he had talked about how everything had to go right, he was aware there was a chance everything could go wrong. And if did, who knew when he would be back here. Who knew if his future held visions of freedom and family life, or the damp walls of a cell.

He placed a hand on the headstone, and felt a slight warmth emanating from where the sun had fallen. An optimistic part of his mind made him believe, if only for a second, that it was warmth coming from Danielle herself.

"I still love you," he choked.

He felt like a fool, kneeling there with tears closing up his throat, but he'd been holding them in for so long. And the release of tears falling down his cheeks made him feel like he'd sucked in a fresh lungful of air after being trapped underwater. It made him feel motivated.

His vision was blurry as he looked down at the ground. At his feet lay the small, marble cherub that had been placed there by Bill years before. Just like the headstone, it had also been polished to perfection. Fitz had always liked it, but he found himself now looking at it properly for the first time. Truly studying the features of the face and the way the tiny rosebud lips were parted into an angelic smile. He was wondering why Bill had chosen it when he heard the crackle of feet on leaves behind him.

He spun round, the hairs along the back of his neck rising to attention immediately. At first he saw nothing. Then noticed the edge of a pair of jeans poking out from behind a gravestone three rows down from him. He stood up and wiped his eyes.

That's when he saw the crouched figure, a hood pulled low over a face hidden in shadow. But it was what was clutched inside the figure's hands that made Fitz' adrenaline pump. The camera with the long lens was pointing right at him like the barrel of a shotgun.

"Hey!"

The figure flinched, stood up and ran so fast they tripped on the edge of a grave before regaining their balance and sprinting down the path.

"Oi!"

Fitz ran, and gained distance fast, catching up with the figure who was no match for Fitz's fitness. His hands reached for the figure's hood, yanking it down hard. The figure let out a yelp as their hoodie tightened around their throat, then they dropped to their knees, the camera tumbling from their hands onto the ground. Fitz tightened his grip on the hood, twisting it to bring the figure closer to him. He could now see the face of a young male. It was almost childlike with smooth skin and bright eyes.

"Who the fuck are you?" he said.

He felt like he was clutching onto a mischievous, runaway teen. But as the man fumbled inside his pocket, breathing hard as he pulled out a Metropolitan Police ID, he realised this was no kid.

"PC Clarkston," gasped the figure. "Let me go, or it's assault on an officer."

Chapter 74 – Bill – October 3

rd

, 2023

7.45 AM

There was no sunlight in the room, but Bill knew what the time was from the way he could hear the distant cell doors clanging open. From the smell of the greasy breakfasts wafting up from the cafeteria and the faraway, animated voices of the prisoners. After his diagnosis the day before, he had been moved into an even smaller room that he suspected had previously been a cupboard. He sat in it now staring at the featureless walls thinking, plotting, fantasising.

Now there were only hours left to wait. Not years or months or days. *Hours...*

He couldn't sit still. Despite his hunger he was full of energy and almost vibrating with excitement.

"Morning, Bill," came Dr Waller's voice as the door opened.

Behind him, the nurse entered pushing a tray of instruments and a jug of water.

Bill couldn't stop shaking. It was like he had a hummingbird lodged in his chest. He kept looking at the faces of Dr Waller and the nurse to see if they were onto him.

"Are you okay?" asked the nurse.

She looked down at his trembling hands.

"I've got a terrible migraine," lied Bill, closing his hands into tight, anxious fists to mimic being in pain.

"I can get you some paracetamol."

He watched as the nurse bent down into a nearby small cabinet, pulling out a box of paracetamol. It was then that he saw what lay at the back of the cabinet. A small tub with its signature blue lid.

Petroleum jelly...

It wasn't going to work as well as the linseed oil he had originally planned to use, but it would do. His eyes were still fixed on it when she brought him the paracetamol and poured him a glass of water. He couldn't help but notice she'd absent mindedly left the cabinet door open.

Meanwhile, Dr Waller was studying Bill's charts.

"I think you're going to respond well to treatment," he said, chewing on his pen as he flipped the page. "How are you feeling this morning? Besides the headache."

"Just anxious to begin treatment."

"I bet you are."

Bill swallowed down the paracetamol, handing the now empty glass to the nurse. She took it with a smile and said, "I'm just going to check your temperature."

She reached for the thermometer and held it to his forehead.

"Little high," she noted to herself. "Blood pressure next."

She fastened the cuff around his arm, winding it several times around his twig-like bicep.

"A little low," she noted as she released the pump. "Okay, that's it for now," she said, taking the chart from Dr Waller's hands and writing down her findings. "It won't be long until you're moved."

She left the room leaving Dr Waller standing at the bottom of the bed. Bill couldn't stop staring at him with an icy gaze.

Get out of here.

Just leave!

But he kept standing there. Kept watching Bill as though there was something on his mind but he was biting his tongue. He stared deep into Bill's face with a look that said, *I'm on to you. I don't know what you're planning, but you are planning something. I just know...* Bill, forced a slight smile and said, "Anything else I need to know, Doc?"

Dr Waller held his gaze for a moment, then glanced away.

"No... No. I'll be back shortly to let you know when the ambulance arrives."

He took a few steps away from the bed, then paused as he reached the doorway. Looking over his shoulder, he stared back with what Bill could only interpret as an accusatory gaze. Bill raised his eyebrows at Dr Waller inquisitively, and he walked away through the door. Bill waited a full ten seconds, just to be sure he was gone, then he leapt into action. On weak legs he staggered towards the open cabinet, snatched the petroleum jelly, closed over the cabinet door and climbed back into bed.

He had only just placed the tub of petroleum jelly beneath the covers when he heard footsteps return and not a second later, the door opened again. Dr Waller returned and pointed towards Bill's chart.

"Forgot this," he said. "I'll need to hand it over."

He grabbed the chart and moved to leave the room again, but something caught his eye and he froze. Bill followed his gaze towards the now closed door of the cabinet.

He knows...

Dr Waller moved to speak, but as he did, the nurse returned and buoyantly said, "The ambulance has just arrived. Bill, you're on the move."

Chapter 75 – Fitz – October 3rd, 2023

7.06AM

Fitz was still gripping PC Clarkston's hood.

"I'll let you go if you tell me everything."

A voice at the back of Fitz' mind was screaming.

What are you doing?

This is the day.

THE day.

You can't mess it up now.

Assault on an officer?

You'll blow the whole plan apart!

But he just couldn't let him go.

"I'm not telling you shit," said Clarkston.

"Then I'm not letting you go."

"Is that a threat?"

Clarkston's hand twitched, and Fitz realised he was moving towards his radio, no doubt for backup.

Shit...

If Fitz got arrested now it would all be over.

Images flashed in his mind of Sarah and he glanced back at Danielle's grave. A sense of guilt came over him. How could he let this shameful scene unfold only feet from where she lay?

He thought fast. He had to save himself.

"PC Clarkston..." he said, chewing on the name "You're not one of those MET officers who was caught up in that Whatsapp scandal, are you? You know, the one where all those officers were caught sharing porn. A couple of the videos showed underage girls, am I right?"

"No," scowled Clarkston. "I wasn't in *that* group."

But there was a look in his eye that Fitz latched onto. A look of guilt, even if it wasn't for what he'd accused him of.

"But you are part of another group chat, right?" asked Fitz, hopefully.

Clarkston's mouth said, "No," but his eyes said yes.

"You are, aren't you? Loads of you officers are. Why is that? The job give you a morbid sense of humour? I don't blame you. I bet you see all sorts of stuff that would mess you up, keep you up at night. Guess you just need a way to share the darkness in your head."

The look on Clarkston's face softened. He felt understood.

"Bet if I looked through your phone I'd see all sorts of stuff," continued Fitz. "I mean, I'm not accusing you of anything, I'm just thinking out loud."

"What are you trying to do here? You can't access my phone."

"I don't want to. I don't care what you've been sharing."

Clarkston attempted to wriggle out of Fitz' grasp, and when he couldn't, he started to claw overhead at his hand.

"Let me go right now," he ordered.

But Fitz just stared at him.

"Let you go and what? Have you radio for backup?"

Clarkston looked into his eyes for a moment and felt the anger rise inside him. He may have had a badge, but in the presence of someone like Fitz who held no respect for it, it was meaningless. Beyond that, all he had to brandish at Fitz was his physical strength, but as he struggled against Fitz' grip, he realised he didn't have enough of it. He started to panic, and with his increasing nerves came a surge of adrenaline.

He lunged forwards, headbutting Fitz square in the stomach. They both fell to the ground, pain shooting through Fitz' torso until he felt close to vomiting. But the pain did nothing to disable him, it only made him angrier.

"Urgh... Bastard," he grunted, throwing out his fist.

He caught Clarkston in the temple sending a shock wave of sharp pain through his skull. Clarkston, enraged, lunged at Fitz.

The two of them struggled, their limbs tangled in a knot as they thrashed against the ground scraping knees and elbows, grunting through clenched jaws. But no matter how much Clarkston fought, Fitz managed to always land on top of him. Pinning Clarkston's shoulders to the ground, he held him in place. Clarkston tried to reach out to hit him, but his arms were powerless. Fear swept through him. If he couldn't move, he couldn't radio for backup. He'd been watching Fitz for weeks, had become so familiar with his appearance he almost took it for granted. And now, as he felt the weight of him against his struggling limbs, he realised just how big he was.

Fitz moved suddenly, his movements more like jerk reactions. It happened before Clarkston could register what was happening. All he could do was watch, frozen as Fitz reached inside his pocket and yanked out his phone.

"Hey!" cried out Clarkston as he saw the screen glimmer in the sunlight.

"Give me your hand," demanded Fitz.

But he didn't wait for Clarkston to respond. He grabbed his thumb and pressed it against the home screen button, unlocking the phone. Clarkston struggled even harder, but Fitz just dug his knees deeper into his sides. Clarkston felt shame burn in his cheeks. He was supposed to be tough. Supposed to keep the streets safe from thugs, but here he was feeling like nothing more than a squashed bug.

"Don't," he said to Fitz.

But Fitz was already fluttering his thumb across the screen and opening his camera roll.

"Don't worry. I'm not going to read your messages."

"Then what are you doing?"

Fitz continued to move through the camera roll. He was amazed at just how boring the photos were. Endless pictures of plates of food and sunsets. Then an image stuck out. A beautiful woman with chocolatey eyes and an olive complexion stared out from behind the table at an upmarket restaurant.

"This your missus?" asked Fitz, turning the phone around.

Clarkston nodded.

"How did a weed like you get someone like her?"

"We've been together since school."

"Childhood sweethearts. Ain't that cute. Married?"

Clarkston shook his head.

"Not yet. We're waiting until after the baby comes."

"There's a baby?"

"She's six months pregnant."

Something clicked in Fitz' head.

"Is that why you've been tailing me? Putting in overtime for extra cash for the baby?"

Clarkston nodded.

"What if I told you that you didn't need to work overtime again?"

Clarkston squinted.

"I can make sure you and your missus never work again. I can make sure your baby has everything."

Clarkston frowned. He knew he should shut Fitz down right now, but curiosity got the better of him and he found himself saying, "What are you talking about?"

At last, the tension between them dissolved enough for Fitz to loosen his grip on Clarkston.

"You got any recording devices on you?" asked Fitz. "You have to tell me if you do."

"No. I don't."

"Then listen. You ever heard of Phenomena?"

Chapter 71

Billie

October 2nd, 2023

He watched as the guard searched through the pockets of his hooded sweatshirt. The search only produced a pouch of tobacco and a lighter.

"You can't go in with this," the guard said, waving the lighter.

"Sure. Just take it, then."

There was something else he wasn't allowed into the visitor's room of Belmarsh with, and it was safely tucked inside his cheek pressing against his teeth. He was sure the guard could hear it as he spoke.

His heart nervously fluttered like it was glitching in and out of existence. He felt the sweat start to pour down his spine. Any second now he was sure the guard was going to pull him aside and demand a full body search. John was already imagining him taking out a pair of latex gloves and ordering him to drop his underwear.

He waited. Then he waited some more. The guard looked deep into his face. They both stared at each other, then the guard gave a sudden flick of his head towards the visitors' room and said, "In you go, mate."

Relief sagged at John's shoulders as he walked into the visitors' room. The USB stick was so tightly jammed against his gums he was starting to taste the blood running between his teeth.

He spotted his friend sitting alone at a table beside the window.

"Alright, Chas?" he said, approaching the table, his mouth filling with spit.

"Why have you got that lisp?"

"Why d'ya think?" said John, sitting down.

He looked over at the guards then up towards the cameras.

"Hang on," he said. "Need to tie my shoe lace."

Bending his head beneath the table, he started to fidget with his shoelaces with one hand. Meanwhile, with the other, he fingered inside his mouth quickly for the USB stick. Removing it fast and tucking it into his sleeve.

When he sat up straight, he placed his arm on the table and said, "Hold my hand, Chas."

"What?"

"Just do it."

The two interlinked fingers for the briefest of moments, long enough for the USB to be slipped out from John's wrist and into the palm of Chas' hand.

"You actually brought it," said Chas. "It's really got what you said on it?"

"Everything I said."

"And what am I meant to do with this? You think I got my own Macbook in here or something?"

Chas laughed bittersweetly and glanced nervously at the guards.

"You can help me," said John. "I know you can. That writer you're working with, the one who's helping you with your biography."

"Nathan? What about him?"

"He's a journo, ain't he?"

"Does his day shift at The Sunday Times, yeah. Although he's trying to make a name for himself as a bit of a hardman covering gangsters' stories. Guess that's why he was so happy to ghostwrite my biography for me."

"Yeah, well. I need you to give that thumb drive to him. Tell him to make its contents public."

Chas nodded, his eyes moving all over the room. He could never relax at the best of times, but especially not now when he held the equivalent of an information dirty bomb in his hand.

"I'll give it to him, yeah. Soon as I can."

Chapter 72

Hawkins

October 3rd, 2023

5.55 AM

The sun hadn't yet risen when Hawkins arrived at her office, but PC Busby was already standing in her room extending the landline phone out towards her.

"Governor Corour at Belmarsh," he said to her. "He's been calling all morning for you. Said he'd been trying to get you on your mobile."

"Yeah," replied Hawkins, taking a sip of coffee. "I have a policy that I don't answer calls before six am."

She took the phone from Busby.

"Governor?"

"He's leaving today."

"What!"

The coffee in Hawkins' stomach churned.

"What do you mean he's leaving?"

"He's being transferred to hospital. He was diagnosed with HIV last night."

"Bullshit," spat Hawkins.

"It's true. I saw the positive test myself."

"I want to see that test too. In fact, I want Lovecroft to take another one right in front of me. My arse does he have HIV."

The governor chuckled, but there was a solemn quality to his voice.

"You know I can't make him do that," he said. "But the man is clearly ill. I went and saw him myself last night. He needs hospital treatment and Belmarsh just doesn't have the facilities."

"All right... Okay..."

"Don't worry. He'll be cuffed to the bed at all times with two wardens by his side."

"I should assume so. I'm going to go a step further and suggest a squad car accompany the ambulance to the hospital."

"That's what I thought you would say."

"You thought right. I'll arrange that right away. I'll call you back."

She hung up abruptly and stepped out her room to find PC Busby standing by the coffee vending machine in the hall, yawning as he shovelled fifty pence pieces into the slot.

"I've got a job for you and PC Clarkston," she said.

He looked up with a slightly nervous expression.

"Sure. Anything to get out the office."

Chapter 73

Fitz

October 3rd, 2023

7.05 AM

The wind was so crisp as it blew across Brompton Cemetery, Fitz felt like it was biting his ears. He shivered, zipped his coat up higher and walked faster. Ahead of him, a young couple were walking their sausage dog. He watched in horror as they let it run onto a nearby grave, raise its leg and piss against the marble headstone.

"Oi!" shouted Fitz.

The couple spun round looking annoyed to have been disturbed.

"Have some respect, will ya?"

The boyfriend momentarily thought about responding with something witty, but he could see the genuine anger in Fitz' eyes and thought better of it.

"Sorry," he mumbled, yanking on the dog's lead. "Come on, Hugo."

Fitz stared daggers into the backs of their heads as they walked away. He waited until they were out of sight before he approached the grave on which the dog had relieved itself. He'd passed it many times, and although he didn't know the person buried beneath it personally, he felt a little connection with them.

Lucy Albright was her name. She had been one of the fatalities from the Lusitania. A fact only made clear to Fitz because it was engraved on her headstone. He'd found it fascinating, although morbid..

"All right, Lucy," he said, walking past her grave.

His sights were now set on the one grave he did come to see, the one he had visited so many times it felt like a home to him, a place he could release his thoughts to the one person who would understand him.

"Danielle," he said, softly, approaching her headstone.

As usual, her grave was immaculately kept. Orchids had been planted around her headstone splashing the area in cream and deep purple tones.

Fitz squatted down and picked up some fallen petals before sweeping loose pieces of grass away. In front of him, the marble headstone shimmered beneath the morning sunlight. Clearly, Bill had made sure someone was maintaining the grave site even though he was incarcerated.

"Danielle, it's happening today," he said. "Finally, it's happening. And if it all goes right. I mean it *will* go right. It *has* to go right or I won't get my Sarah back. *Our* Sarah."

He sniffed as he felt his throat close up.

"I'm going to get her back."

His chest ached as he looked at where Danielle lay.

Glancing at his watch, he saw he didn't have long until it all started rolling. His phone had been ringing from inside his pocket, but he needed to be left alone for these few precious moments. Because although he had talked about how everything had to go right, he was aware there was a chance everything could go wrong. And if did, who knew when he would be back here. Who knew if his future held visions of freedom and family life, or the damp walls of a cell.

He placed a hand on the headstone, and felt a slight warmth emanating from where the sun had fallen. An optimistic part of his mind made him believe, if only for a second, that it was warmth coming from Danielle herself.

"I still love you," he choked.

He felt like a fool, kneeling there with tears closing up his throat, but he'd been holding them in for so long. And the release of tears falling down his cheeks made him feel like he'd sucked in a fresh lungful of air after being trapped underwater. It made him feel motivated.

His vision was blurry as he looked down at the ground. At his feet lay the small, marble cherub that had been placed there by Bill years before. Just like the headstone, it had also been polished to perfection. Fitz had always liked it, but he found himself now looking at it properly for the first time. Truly studying the features of the face and the way the tiny rosebud lips were parted into an angelic smile. He was wondering why Bill had chosen it when he heard the crackle of feet on leaves behind him.

He spun round, the hairs along the back of his neck rising to attention immediately. At first he saw nothing. Then noticed the edge of a pair of jeans poking out from behind a gravestone three rows down from him. He stood up and wiped his eyes.

That's when he saw the crouched figure, a hood pulled low over a face hidden in shadow. But it was what was clutched inside the figure's hands that made Fitz' adrenaline pump. The camera with the long lens was pointing right at him like the barrel of a shotgun.

"Hey!"

The figure flinched, stood up and ran so fast they tripped on the edge of a grave before regaining their balance and sprinting down the path.

"Oi!"

Fitz ran, and gained distance fast, catching up with the figure who was no match for Fitz's fitness. His hands reached for the figure's hood, yanking it down hard. The figure let out a yelp as their hoodie tightened around their throat, then they dropped to their knees, the camera tumbling from their hands onto the ground. Fitz tightened his grip on the hood, twisting it to bring the figure closer to him. He could now see the face of a young male. It was almost childlike with smooth skin and bright eyes.

"Who the fuck are you?" he said.

He felt like he was clutching onto a mischievous, runaway teen. But as the man fumbled inside his pocket, breathing hard as he pulled out a Metropolitan Police ID, he realised this was no kid.

"PC Clarkston," gasped the figure. "Let me go, or it's assault on an officer."

Chapter 74

Bill

October 3rd, 2023

7.45 AM

There was no sunlight in the room, but Bill knew what the time was from the way he could hear the distant cell doors clanging open. From the smell of the greasy breakfasts wafting up from the cafeteria and the faraway, animated voices of the prisoners. After his diagnosis the day before, he had been moved into an even smaller room that he suspected had previously been a cupboard. He sat in it now staring at the featureless walls thinking, plotting, fantasising.

Now there were only hours left to wait. Not years or months or days. *Hours...*

He couldn't sit still. Despite his hunger he was full of energy and almost vibrating with excitement.

"Morning, Bill," came Dr Waller's voice as the door opened.

Behind him, the nurse entered pushing a tray of instruments and a jug of water.

Bill couldn't stop shaking. It was like he had a hummingbird lodged in his chest. He kept looking at the faces of Dr Waller and the nurse to see if they were onto him.

"Are you okay?" asked the nurse.

She looked down at his trembling hands.

"I've got a terrible migraine," lied Bill, closing his hands into tight, anxious fists to mimic being in pain.

"I can get you some paracetamol."

He watched as the nurse bent down into a nearby small cabinet, pulling out a box of paracetamol. It was then that he saw what lay at the back of the cabinet. A small tub with its signature blue lid.

Petroleum jelly...

It wasn't going to work as well as the linseed oil he had originally planned to use, but it would do. His eyes were still fixed on it when she brought him the paracetamol and poured him a glass of water. He couldn't help but notice she'd absent mindedly left the cabinet door open.

Meanwhile, Dr Waller was studying Bill's charts.

"I think you're going to respond well to treatment," he said, chewing on his pen as he flipped the page. "How are you feeling this morning? Besides the headache."

"Just anxious to begin treatment."

"I bet you are."

Bill swallowed down the paracetamol, handing the now empty glass to the nurse. She took it with a smile and said, "I'm just going to check your temperature."

She reached for the thermometer and held it to his forehead.

"Little high," she noted to herself. "Blood pressure next."

She fastened the cuff around his arm, winding it several times around his twig-like bicep.

"A little low," she noted as she released the pump. "Okay, that's it for now," she said, taking the chart from Dr Waller's hands and writing down her findings. "It won't be long until you're moved."

She left the room leaving Dr Waller standing at the bottom of the bed. Bill couldn't stop staring at him with an icy gaze.

Get out of here.

Just leave!

But he kept standing there. Kept watching Bill as though there was something on his mind but he was biting his tongue. He stared deep into Bill's face with a look that said, *I'm on to you. I don't know what you're planning, but you are planning something. I just know...* Bill, forced a slight smile and said, "Anything else I need to know, Doc?"

Dr Waller held his gaze for a moment, then glanced away.

"No... No. I'll be back shortly to let you know when the ambulance arrives."

He took a few steps away from the bed, then paused as he reached the doorway. Looking over his shoulder, he stared back with what Bill could only interpret as an accusatory gaze. Bill raised his eyebrows at Dr Waller inquisitively, and he walked away through the door. Bill waited a full ten seconds, just to be sure he was gone, then he leapt into action. On weak legs he staggered towards the open cabinet, snatched the petroleum jelly, closed over the cabinet door and climbed back into bed.

He had only just placed the tub of petroleum jelly beneath the covers when he heard footsteps return and not a second later, the door opened again. Dr Waller returned and pointed towards Bill's chart.

"Forgot this," he said. "I'll need to hand it over."

He grabbed the chart and moved to leave the room again, but something caught his eye and he froze. Bill followed his gaze towards the now closed door of the cabinet.

He knows...

Dr Waller moved to speak, but as he did, the nurse returned and buoyantly said, "The ambulance has just arrived. Bill, you're on the move."

Chapter 75

Fitz

October 3rd, 2023

7.06AM

Fitz was still gripping PC Clarkston's hood.

"I'll let you go if you tell me everything."

A voice at the back of Fitz' mind was screaming.

What are you doing?

This is the day.

THE day.

You can't mess it up now.

Assault on an officer?

You'll blow the whole plan apart!

But he just couldn't let him go.

"I'm not telling you shit," said Clarkston.

"Then I'm not letting you go."

"Is that a threat?"

Clarkston's hand twitched, and Fitz realised he was moving towards his radio, no doubt for backup.

Shit...

If Fitz got arrested now it would all be over.

Images flashed in his mind of Sarah and he glanced back at Danielle's grave. A sense of guilt came over him. How could he let this shameful scene unfold only feet from where she lay?

He thought fast. He had to save himself.

"PC Clarkston..." he said, chewing on the name "You're not one of those MET officers who was caught up in that Whatsapp scandal, are you? You know, the one where all those officers were caught sharing porn. A couple of the videos showed underage girls, am I right?"

"No," scowled Clarkston. "I wasn't in *that* group."

But there was a look in his eye that Fitz latched onto. A look of guilt, even if it wasn't for what he'd accused him of.

"But you are part of another group chat, right?" asked Fitz, hopefully.

Clarkston's mouth said, "No," but his eyes said yes.

"You are, aren't you? Loads of you officers are. Why is that? The job give you a morbid sense of humour? I don't blame you. I bet you see all sorts of stuff that would mess you up, keep you up at night. Guess you just need a way to share the darkness in your head."

The look on Clarkston's face softened. He felt understood.

"Bet if I looked through your phone I'd see all sorts of stuff," continued Fitz. "I mean, I'm not accusing you of anything, I'm just thinking out loud."

"What are you trying to do here? You can't access my phone."

"I don't want to. I don't care what you've been sharing."

Clarkston attempted to wriggle out of Fitz' grasp, and when he couldn't, he started to claw overhead at his hand.

"Let me go right now," he ordered.

But Fitz just stared at him.

"Let you go and what? Have you radio for backup?"

Clarkston looked into his eyes for a moment and felt the anger rise inside him. He may have had a badge, but in the presence of someone like Fitz who held no respect for it, it was meaningless. Beyond that, all he had to brandish at Fitz was his physical strength, but as he struggled against Fitz' grip, he realised he didn't have enough of it. He started to panic, and with his increasing nerves came a surge of adrenaline.

He lunged forwards, headbutting Fitz square in the stomach. They both fell to the ground, pain shooting through Fitz' torso until he felt close to vomiting. But the pain did nothing to disable him, it only made him angrier.

"Urgh... Bastard," he grunted, throwing out his fist.

He caught Clarkston in the temple sending a shock wave of sharp pain through his skull. Clarkston, enraged, lunged at Fitz.

The two of them struggled, their limbs tangled in a knot as they thrashed against the ground scraping knees and elbows, grunting through clenched jaws. But no matter how much Clarkston fought, Fitz managed to always land on top of him. Pinning Clarkston's shoulders to the ground, he held him in place. Clarkston tried to reach out to hit him, but his arms were powerless. Fear swept through him. If he couldn't move, he couldn't radio for backup. He'd been watching Fitz for weeks, had become so familiar with his appearance he almost took it for granted. And now, as he felt the weight of him against his struggling limbs, he realised just how big he was.

Fitz moved suddenly, his movements more like jerk reactions. It happened before Clarkston could register what was happening. All he could do was watch, frozen as Fitz reached inside his pocket and yanked out his phone.

"Hey!" cried out Clarkston as he saw the screen glimmer in the sunlight.

"Give me your hand," demanded Fitz.

But he didn't wait for Clarkston to respond. He grabbed his thumb and pressed it against the home screen button, unlocking the phone. Clarkston struggled even harder, but Fitz just dug his knees deeper into his sides. Clarkston felt shame burn in his cheeks. He was supposed to be tough. Supposed to keep the streets safe from thugs, but here he was feeling like nothing more than a squashed bug.

"Don't," he said to Fitz.

But Fitz was already fluttering his thumb across the screen and opening his camera roll.

"Don't worry. I'm not going to read your messages."

"Then what are you doing?"

Fitz continued to move through the camera roll. He was amazed at just how boring the photos were. Endless pictures of plates of food and sunsets. Then an image stuck out. A beautiful woman with chocolatey eyes and an olive complexion stared out from behind the table at an upmarket restaurant.

"This your missus?" asked Fitz, turning the phone around.

Clarkston nodded.

"How did a weed like you get someone like her?"

"We've been together since school."

"Childhood sweethearts. Ain't that cute. Married?"

Clarkston shook his head.

"Not yet. We're waiting until after the baby comes."

"There's a baby?"

"She's six months pregnant."

Something clicked in Fitz' head.

"Is that why you've been tailing me? Putting in overtime for extra cash for the baby?"

Clarkston nodded.

"What if I told you that you didn't need to work overtime again?"

Clarkston squinted.

"I can make sure you and your missus never work again. I can make sure your baby has everything."

Clarkston frowned. He knew he should shut Fitz down right now, but curiosity got the better of him and he found himself saying, "What are you talking about?"

At last, the tension between them dissolved enough for Fitz to loosen his grip on Clarkston.

"You got any recording devices on you?" asked Fitz. "You have to tell me if you do."

"No. I don't."

"Then listen. You ever heard of Phenomena?"

Chapter 76

John

September 29th, 2023

He watched as the guard searched through the pockets of his hooded sweatshirt. The search only produced a pouch of tobacco and a lighter.

"You can't go in with this," the guard said, waving the lighter.

"Sure. Just take it, then."

There was something else he wasn't allowed into the visitor's room of Belmarsh with, and it was safely tucked inside his cheek pressing against his teeth. He was sure the guard could hear it as he spoke.

His heart nervously fluttered like it was glitching in and out of existence. He felt the sweat start to pour down his spine. Any second now he was sure the guard was going to pull him aside and demand a full body search. John was already imagining him taking out a pair of latex gloves and ordering him to drop his underwear.

He waited. Then he waited some more. The guard looked deep into his face. They both stared at each other, then the guard gave a sudden flick of his head towards the visitors' room and said, "In you go, mate."

Relief sagged at John's shoulders as he walked into the visitors' room. The USB stick was so tightly jammed against his gums he was starting to taste the blood running between his teeth.

He spotted his friend sitting alone at a table beside the window.

"Alright, Chas?" he said, approaching the table, his mouth filling with spit.

"Why have you got that lisp?"

"Why d'ya think?" said John, sitting down.

He looked over at the guards then up towards the cameras.

"Hang on," he said. "Need to tie my shoe lace."

Bending his head beneath the table, he started to fidget with his shoelaces with one hand. Meanwhile, with the other, he fingered inside his mouth quickly for the USB stick. Removing it fast and tucking it into his sleeve.

When he sat up straight, he placed his arm on the table and said, "Hold my hand, Chas."

"What?"

"Just do it."

The two interlinked fingers for the briefest of moments, long enough for the USB to be slipped out from John's wrist and into the palm of Chas' hand.

"You actually brought it," said Chas. "It's really got what you said on it?"

"Everything I said."

"And what am I meant to do with this? You think I got my own Macbook in here or something?"

Chas laughed bittersweetly and glanced nervously at the guards.

"You can help me," said John. "I know you can. That writer you're working with, the one who's helping you with your biography."

"Nathan? What about him?"

"He's a journo, ain't he?"

"Does his day shift at The Sunday Times, yeah. Although he's trying to make a name for himself as a bit of a hardman covering gangsters' stories. Guess that's why he was so happy to ghostwrite my biography for me."

"Yeah, well. I need you to give that thumb drive to him. Tell him to make its contents public."

Chas nodded, his eyes moving all over the room. He could never relax at the best of times, but especially not now when he held the equivalent of an information dirty bomb in his hand.

"I'll give it to him, yeah. Soon as I can."

Chapter 77

Danielle

March 8th, 2017

She didn't know she was being watched. If she did, she never would have walked so calmly down Oxford Street. The weight in her womb weighed her down, she was exhausted and her ankles throbbed, but it had been the first day in weeks where the sun had shone and she was eager to do some shopping for Sarah.

"Just order it online!" Cecilia had moaned at her.

But she wanted the fresh air and to feel the energy of the busy street as people bustled by. With a collection of pink onesies in a designer bag, she walked with her body feeling heavy like lead. But her spirits were high. The sun was catching her face as she pressed her hand to the top of her swollen stomach.

"I hope you like yellow," she said to her bump. "Because mummy's going to get you a yellow dress."

From inside the bump came a kick as though in response and Danielle managed to both smile and grimace.

The street was so busy that even if she was paying attention it was unlikely she would have noticed the stealthy figure seamlessly blending into the crowd behind her. They'd been trailing her for the past five minutes, loving eyes boring into the back of her head.

But if she had been paying attention, she would have noticed they weren't the only one looking at her. Her glowing face, designer clothes and dazzling smile had caught the eye of someone else too.

"Hello, darlin'."

She looked up. The first thing she saw was a leather jacket that smelled like stale tobacco. The second thing was broken teeth lined up in a crooked smile. She looked further up and saw bloodshot eyes and greasy hair.

"Can I help you?" she asked the stranger.

"You're one of Sir Lovecroft's daughters, ain't ya?"

"Erm..."

She didn't know what to say. The sun was shining brightly on her face and she was starting to grow more tired. She just wanted to keep moving and get away from the sickening smell of tobacco.

With an apologetic smile, she stepped to the side, wanting to edge around the man, but he matched her movements. She stepped the other way and he did the same, laughing as he blocked her from escaping.

"What do you want?" she asked.

"You are one of Lovecroft's daughters. I've seen you in them magazines."

"Okay... And? Do you want a picture or something?"

"That would be nice, yeah."

Danielle sighed and said, "Okay, then. But I have to be quick."

The man smiled and reached for his phone.

"Not here, though," he said. "The sun's too bright. Let's step into the shade."

Before she realised, his hand was around her wrist and he was pulling her into the doorway of an abandoned shopfront.

She waited for him to raise his phone for a picture, but as she looked into his eyes she saw his demeanour change. Saw his look turn glacial. When she next looked at his hand, there was no phone at all between his fingers. Instead, she found herself looking at a knife he had just pulled out his pocket.

"Hand over your purse, rich bitch."

She panicked. The first thing she thought of was her baby. Protectively, she placed a hand on her stomach and cried, "Don't hurt me! Please, just take whatever you want."

With her free hand, she thrust her purse in his direction, but as he reached out a hand for it, he was suddenly jolted sideways. He yelped out in pain, collapsed against the doorway and clutched his face. There was blood running down from his nose that formed small rivers on the pavement around Danielle's feet.

She was in too much shock to scream, but too scared to move. The knife fell from her attacker's hand and onto the pavement with a clatter.

"I'll take that," came a familiar voice.

Danielle, confused, looked round. At first all she saw was a silhouetted figure against the sun. Behind him, a crowd of shoppers had started to gather. She could hear someone already on the phone to the police.

"Fitz?"

He stepped closer to her, grabbed her by the shoulders and pulled her to him.

"Oh, my God," she gasped, wrapping her arms around him. "Thank God you were here."

She looked up into his face.

"But why *were* you here?"

He didn't answer. Instead, he looked down at the man at their feet. He was still groaning. Still holding his broken nose and grumbling in pain.

It was the closest Fitz had been to Danielle in months. He was instantly struck by two things; how big her stomach was, and how she still smelled like her usual perfume. A smell that sent his mind back to memories of lying in bed and smelling the warmth of her skin. Of holding her close. Of feeling so in love it made him dizzy.

***

"You were following me!"

"Shh... Please... Sit back down."

But she was already grabbing her purse and standing up to walk out the cafe. She would have made a speedier exit if it wasn't for her bump.

"Danielle..."

Fitz leaned across the table and took her wrist gently in his hand. Her skin was soft but hot.

"Please..."

"You're nuts, you know that?" she said, shimmying around the table on swollen ankles.

Her sudden outburst had attracted the attention of the other diners in the upmarket French coffee shop they had settled in. She knew what they were thinking. *That's Sir Lovecroft's daughter.* She was even sure she saw someone raise their phone to take a picture.

She hesitated for a second, hating that she was attracting attention to herself. She looked to Fitz, anger rising in her, then she looked around the room at the rubberneckers.

"Don't come near me again," she said, stepping away from the table.

But as her heavy feet shuffled on the floor, she felt a twinge in her stomach.

"Oh, God," she gasped, holding her bump protectively.

"Shit, what's happening?"

"There was just… a pain. I don't know what it was."

"That's it. I'm taking you to the hospital."

A second twinge of pain hit her and she winced.

"Argh, it hurts."

"It's okay. We're going."

Fitz' caring hands landed on her arms and guided her out the coffee shop. She no longer wanted to push him away. All she could think was, *Please let Sarah be okay.*

***

"So you're really sure there's nothing to worry about?" asked Danielle as she looked wide-eyed at the ultrasound technician.

"As far as I can see, there's nothing to worry about. Look, you see her? She's perfectly healthy. And that's her heartbeat there."

Both Danielle and Fitz let out a long sigh of relief.

"I thought I was losing her," said Danielle, almost crying. "I really did."

"It's normal to worry," said the technician. "And you did the right thing coming here straight away. It's always better to be safe. But I really do recommend you take it easy. Rest as much as you can."

"I will."

The technician smiled and rose from her seat.

"I need to pop out for a second," she said, "But I'll be back in a moment."

She left the room leaving Danielle and Fitz alone. Fitz let out another relieved sigh and threw his arms around Danielle. He was grateful when she didn't shift away.

"I was so worried," he said, giving her a squeeze.

"Thanks for bringing me here,"

"You don't have to thank me."

"I probably do have to thank you for saving me earlier, though. That guy was insane, Fitz. I was terrified."

"Again, you don't have to thank me. I want to look out for you."

"Is that why you were following me?"

He pulled away from her, ran his hands down the length of her arms and held her hands. She felt conflicted. Part of her wanted to pull away, the other wanted him to hold her and never let go. With his eyes meeting hers, he nodded.

"I wasn't trying to be a creep."

"How often have you followed me?"

"Just this time."

"Promise?"

"I promise."

"And what a time to do it."

"I've just been so worried about you. I miss you."

"I miss you too. But Fitz, you know I can't be with you."

Fitz felt a lump form in his throat.

"Do you still love me?" he asked.

"Of course I do."

More than ever, she thought to herself.

"Then why can't we make it work?"

"Because you're a criminal. Do you know how scared I was when I saw that gun? I can't have anything like that around Sarah."

"I'd never have anything like that around Sarah. I can promise you that."

She felt herself cracking. She tried to stay strong, but the more she looked into Fitz' face, the more she missed everything they'd had together.

"You promise?" she asked. "You'll say goodbye to that side of your life?"

"In a heartbeat if it meant I got to sleep next to you again. If it meant I could hold Sarah."

Danielle felt her eyes burn, felt her body leaning towards Fitz as though pulled by a magnet. Before she knew it, her hands were sliding around his waist and she was pulling him close.

"I've missed you so much," she said, sliding her hands up to his face and pulling her to him. "I love you."

"I love you too. I love you both."

Danielle's lips met Fitz' hungrily with a raw emotion that made her feel like she was catching fire. She'd yearned for this moment for so long, but had assumed it would never come.

The door opened suddenly and the sound of the ultrasound technician's feet squeaking on the floor made them pull apart.

"I'll, er, get this scan printed off, shall I?" she said, pausing in the doorway.

They both smiled back at her, beaming.

Chapter 78

Bill

October 3rd, 2023

7.55AM

"Right, in you get. Yep, that's it. Just one more step."

Bill struggled to step into the ambulance on his shaky legs, but motivated by the prospect of finally getting out of Belmarsh, he willed himself to move.

"Well done," said Terry, continuing to encourage him.

Beside him, another guard stood watching Bill with a hawk-like gaze. He was the opposite of Terry in every way. Smooth complexioned, squat, silent and mildly hostile. Inside the ambulance, two medics were waiting patiently, both of them not used to the high profile situation of picking up a prisoner from Belmarsh, and a famous billionaire at that.

They all assumed the stance that Terry was in charge, guiding Bill into place.

"Sorry, gotta do this," said Terry, snapping one end of the handcuffs around Bill's wrist and the other around the stretcher's metal frame.

Bill said nothing, just looked at the handcuffs and hoped his plan would work. He looked up as the two medics stepped out the ambulance and slammed the doors closed leaving him with Terry and the other guard.

This is it...

He placed his head back against the pillow and closed his eyes.

"Yeah, you get some shut-eye," said Terry. "I'll wake you up when we're there."

Bill felt the rumble of the ambulance's engine, then the sensation of movement. Despite his unmoving body and the restful appearance of his face, his brain was working itself into overdrive as he ran through the plan in his head.

Seven minutes. That's what Fitz had said. Seven minutes until the ambulance was due to reach Jacques' blockade. It was a stretch of time that felt simultaneously like forever and the blink of an eye.

Bill began to count the seconds in his head to stay calm. Beside him, Terry and the other guard chatted over the top of him.

"Mate, you watch Millwall last night?" Terry asked the other guard.

"Nah."

"Second goal in the fiftieth minute."

"Didn't watch it."

"And then a penalty in-"

Terry cut off his words when he felt the ambulance judder to a sudden stop.

"What's going on?" he called to the driver.

"Police car has stopped us!"

Terry squinted and listened as he heard two car doors slam shut then voices approach the ambulance. He nodded to the other guard, a signal to stay put and moved to the back doors. He flung them open and saw they had only made it about fifty feet from the front entrance of Belmarsh. In front of them sat a squad car. From out of it stepped two young officers at least half Terry's age who stared cockily at him.

"PC Busby," one of them announced.

"PC Clarkston," said the other.

"What? Are you two some sort of double act? We didn't order any strippers."

Both of them laughed mockingly back at him.

"Very funny," said Busby. "We're under orders to escort Sir Bill to the hospital."

"I didn't know nothin' about that."

"Just let us inside a minute."

Both officers barged passed Terry and stepped into the ambulance. They both took a look at Bill cuffed to the bed, his eyes half open groggily and looked to each other.

"Yeah, I think everything's all right in here," said Clarkston, motioning for Busby to follow him back out the ambulance.

"What did you think was going on?" moaned Terry. "You think there was a party or something?"

The officers ignored him and returned to their squad car. Terry watched as they started their engine then he climbed back in beside Bill.

"Guess they've got to keep close tabs on him?" said the other guard.

Terry squinted in thought as the ambulance began moving once again. Something didn't feel right to him, but he couldn't explain what exactly. It was just a gut feeling. Just a thought that niggled at the back of his mind as he'd looked into the officers' faces. A thought that told him to be on guard, although for what exactly, he wasn't sure.

He felt the urge to look back at Bill's wrist to double check it was still cuffed to the bed. When he saw it was, he relaxed slightly and let the rocking motion of the ambulance swing him back and forth until he felt almost sleepy.

But just as he started to feel calm and sink into the movement of the vehicle, he heard something.

Shouting.

His ears immediately pricked up and he sat upright.

"What's that?"

Even Bill was now sitting up, straining his ears to hear what sounded like voices getting closer and closer.

Was that seven minutes already? Bill asked himself.

Now... he thought. *It's happening right now.*

The shouting grew louder until words started to be heard more clearly.

"Power to the planet!" came the chant.

Terry frowned and shook his head.

"Oh, no..." he said, a look of panic falling across his face as he looked to the other guard. "It's them fruit loops that keep trying to save the planet. Bunch of bloody do gooders."

"They blocked the dual carriageway at my bit the other day. Annoying bastards."

"And now they're blocking us here," said Terry. "Hey!" he called through to the driver. "What's going on?"

"I can't go any further!" the driver called back to him.

As he spoke, the ambulance gradually came to a grinding halt as it became surrounded by the repetitive chant.

"Power to the planet! Power to the planet! Power to the planet!"

Power to me, thought Bill as he lay and listened. *Power to me...*

Chapter 79

Jacques

October 3rd, 2023

8.02AM

He was at the front of the blockade as the loudest of them all.

"Power to the planet!" he screamed as the ambulance came to a stop in front of him.

He noticed the squad car behind it, its lights flashing. The siren came on as it tried to edge its way around the side of the ambulance into the crowd.

"Is that them there?" came Fitz' voice through Jacques' earpiece.

"One blond, one with brown hair, both young officers. Look too young for the job."

"That's Clarkston and Busby. Good. It's going to plan so far."

"So far," replied Jacques. "We're only just beginning."

Fitz could detect a hint of hesitation in Jacques' voice.

"You've done your part perfectly," he said, encouraging him. "Just keep going. You need to keep the crowd where they are."

"Considering six people have already glued themselves to the tarmac, I doubt anyone's budging for now."

Jacques moved forward towards the ambulance, waving at the crowd behind him.

"Power to the planet!" he cheered. "Louder!"

"POWER TO THE PLANET!" they all chorused back.

He felt his ego swell. He couldn't believe how many people had turned up. All en-mass as a blended being to do what he said. If only they knew they weren't there to save the planet.

Craning his neck, he looked over the crowd through the various placards covered in protest phrases for the two faces he desperately needed to see.

"Where are you?" he asked through gritted teeth. "You were meant to be here two minutes ago."

Chapter 80

Amelia

October 3rd, 2023

8.03AM

"It's okay. You can do this."

Marcus wheezed in response. He was doubled over at the side of the road, sweat pouring off his forehead.

Beside him was the car him and Amelia had arrived at Jacques' protest in. It was pulled up to the barrier at the side of the motorway. Amelia looked over her shoulder at the enormous crowd that had formed, then ahead of her at the now empty motorway. Then she turned back to Marcus whose face was turning bright red.

"We need to move."

"I can't!"

"What do you mean you can't? We were meant to be at the ambulance two minutes ago."

"I... I..."

Amelia felt the simultaneous urge to both hug him and throttle him. But she did neither and walked over, grabbed him by both arms and pulled him upright.

"You need to get through this. Panic later."

That brought no reassurance to an anxious Marcus who felt close to collapsing. He grabbed at his chest, pushed Amelia away and felt the contents of his stomach swirl aggressively. For a second, he was sure he was going to vomit, but he managed to stop himself. He took a deep breath and looked over the crowd of Jacques' supporters.

This is really happening.

Oh, God.

OH GOD!

Right in that moment he felt like the entire mission was resting on his tensed up shoulders. He felt the need to vomit again as his thoughts started to race. They weren't even making sense any more.

I can't do this.

Why did Fitz pick me?

Is Fitz crazy?

Or is it me that's crazy?

Amelia shook her head as her concern turned to anger.

"Where the fuck are you?" came Fitz' voice through her earpiece.

"We're coming."

"That's not good enough. You should be there by now."

"We're coming! We've just got... a situation."

Amelia looked to Marcus who was still doubled over, hand clutched to his chest.

"Marcus, we need to move."

"I need a moment."

"Now."

"I... Just give me a moment... please."

Impatient, she stormed up to him, grabbed his face with both hands and forced him to look her in the eye. Then she darted her face towards his, pressed her lips to his mouth and kissed him so hard it almost hurt. The shock yanked Marcus out his thought loop and he stared at her, unblinking and stunned into silence.

"You've got this," she told him. "We can do this together."

Chapter 81
PC Busby

October 3rd, 2023

8.04AM

He looked to PC Clarkston in the passenger seat who looked unusually nervous. Then he looked back out over the crowd in front of him. The chanting of *Power to the Planet* was driving him nuts already.

"Do gooders," he mumbled under his breath. "Who do they think they're saving with all this?"

His eyes fell into the centre of the road in front of him where it appeared half a dozen people in high-vis jackets had glued the palms of their hands to the tarmac.

"Urgh…"

He moved to speak into his radio and it gave a crackle as he pressed the button.

"Immediate backup required approximately fifty yards from the Tadwitch Junction. Mass disturbance."

An urgent response crackled back. But beside Busby, Clarkston wasn't listening. He was busy sweating and picking at his fingernails. On his mind was nothing but the money and what it could do for his family.

Busby moved his face away from the radio and stared out through the windscreen at the thousands of people.

"Should we get out the car?" he asked Clarkston.

"And do what? The two of us fight five thousand stoner students? Let's wait for backup."

"I feel ridiculous just sitting here."

Clarkston kept fidgeting. As Busby watched him pick at his thumbnail, he felt someone staring at him. He looked through the windscreen and saw the crowd start to surround the car, the mouths of the protesters widening with glee at the prospect of ambushing a police car.

But there was one pair of eyes that burned brighter than all the others. He looked through the crowd and saw a pretty face staring straight at him with a determined gaze. He saw flaming red hair pushed beneath a black beanie and a patchwork jacket that looked strangely out of place on the svelte, toned body of the protester who was waving a placard in his direction. For a split second his attention was drawn to the placard where he noticed the erroneous spelling of *Powar to the Planut* daubed in black paint across the cardboard.

Idiot, he thought. *She wants to save the world and she can't even spell.*

He looked back at her face. There was something familiar about it, but he couldn't quite place it, and his attention was soon diverted to a blonde girl with a septum piercing who was screaming obscenities at his side of the car.

"Fuck the cops!" she screamed.

"Right, that's it. I'm getting out."

Busby flung the door open and strode towards her, not paying attention to the fact that the redhead was edging closer. Clarkston watched her move from the comfort of the passenger seat. He wasn't in a hurry to step out the car into the crowd. Not yet anyway.

"Fuck the cops!" yelled the blonde girl again. "Are you all seeing this? He's singling me out!"

"You're right I'm singling you out," replied Busby. "Have some respect."

"Aw no... No," muttered Clarkston to himself as he watched.

It wasn't supposed to happen like this. Who was this blonde girl and why had she appeared to distract Busby like this? He was supposed to be getting distracted by Phenomena.

Clarkston looked at Phenomena now and saw her move in closer behind Busby. For a brief moment, their eyes met, and she gave Clarkston an affirmative nod to signal she had everything covered. But he wasn't so sure.

Chapter 82

Phenomena

October 3rd, 2023

8.05AM

It had been years since she'd remembered the formal training of her youth. Skills she'd learned from her years as an apprentice at the age of seventeen. Her mentor, the great stage magician, Ace Malburn, famed for his show, Aces High, had long been deceased, but everything he'd taught her was now at the front of her mind.

Social cues, she said in her mind. People look where they see everyone else looking. And right now everyone was staring at PC Busby as he yelled in the face of a blonde girl with a nose ring.

"Have some respect?" the girl was mouthing back in his face "Where's the respect for the Earth? For our childrens' futures? For humanity!"

Phenomena looked to PC Clarkston in the passenger seat of the squad car and saw his nervous eyes and the way he was chewing on his thumb. Then she looked back to the blonde girl. She wasn't supposed to be a cog in their engine or part of the team, but her little rant right now was going to make her one.

Phenomena thought fast, thinking of ways to use the girl to her advantage. If everyone was looking at her shouting at Busby, they weren't looking at her. She took her chance and edged closer. Her hands became sweaty as she gripped her placard.

She'd never felt nerves like it. There were times on stage when she was anxious, but not like this. This was the real world with some very real consequences that could either make her one of the richest people on Earth, or one of its most high profile prisoners.

You can do it.

Fitz believes in you.

And as she thought of him she heard his voice crackle in her ear.

"What's going on?" he asked. "This is becoming chaos."

She could hear the anxiety in his voice no matter how much he tried to steady his words.

"I got this," she said back, speaking inconspicuously. "It's okay."

"We're behind schedule."

"It'll work."

She edged even closer. The crowd around her was enormous, bigger than anything that had attended her shows. But as she looked around the people immediately in front of her, people that could potentially notice what she was doing, she saw there were maybe only a couple hundred faces. That calmed her somewhat.

"Where are you?" asked Fitz.

"I'm edging around the squad car."

"Make sure not to stand in front of it. Can't have the dash cam picking you up."

"You think I'd let that happen?"

She felt the need to glance up at the lamp posts along the side of the motorway. It was a stretch of road Fitz had chosen for its lack of CCTV. Half a mile further north and there began a sporadic stretch of traffic cameras. The only cameras now able to pick her up were on the smartphones of the protesters.

They're not looking at you, she reminded herself. *They're looking at Busby and that blonde girl.*

Again, she edged herself closer to Busby. It was time for her to cast her mind back to lesson number two, splitting focus. People can't look at two things at once. On stage, Phenomena used her beauty to distract her audience. If they were noticing her come-to-bed eyes and swaying hips they weren't looking at her hands. That's where the placard above her head came in.

Busby and the blonde girl were still arguing, and as Phenomena approached them, she saw people in the crowd behind them start to notice the sign she held overhead. When she had written *Powar to the Planut* with all its errors she knew it would work.

She noticed a few people look up and frown at the words. Even noticed a few people snigger. Fitz might have been growing more anxious, but Phenomena felt a surge of optimism. It was working. Most people were so focused on Busby and the blonde girl arguing that they didn't see Phenomena, and those that did were so busy looking at her wrongly spelled sign they weren't looking at the most important part of the whole operation; her hands.

For a second, she closed her eyes and sucked in a full breath. Then she looked back to Clarkston who was still biting his nails in the squad car and stepped in towards Busby. She saw the shape of the car keys in the left pocket of his trousers. Just a small hint of a silver keyring poked out, but it was enough for her to latch on to.

Phenomena's hand was spindly, almost childlike as she darted it out and felt for the keyring. Her fingertips grazed it as she reached into his pocket.

Just one more second and it'll be in my hand.

But before she could wrap her fingers around it and snatch it swiftly, she heard a scream. During the argument with the blonde girl, Busby had clapped a hand to her wrist and she began screeching bloody murder.

"Assault!" she yelled. "I'm being assaulted by this police officer!"

People began whipping out their phones in unison to film the commotion, and Phenomena had no option but to pull back.

I was so close as well!

She looked to Clarkston who was chewing so ravenously on his finger he looked like a dog with a bone.

Cheers, she thought. *You're so useful.*

Momentarily, she turned her back on the scene and looked down at the floor, letting her hair fall over her face.

"Fitz?"

"Tell me the keys are in your hand."

"Not yet."

There was a long silence. She could feel the wordless fear from him.

"Can you see Marcus and Amelia?"

"No."

She heard Fitz breathe hard. Then he went silent. For a second, she thought she had lost connection with him.

"Fitz?"

There was no answer.

"Fitz? Are you there?"

Chapter 83

Fitz

October 3rd, 2023

8.10AM

Fitz drummed his fingers against the steering wheel with his mind whirring. Beside him, in the passenger seat, sat Lucien. He couldn't help but notice a film of sweat along his top lip.

Parked in a lay-by two miles from the protest, they felt close to the action through the constant chattering that came through the radio. Lucien looked obviously uncomfortable. Not just because of his nerves, but because he had to sit in the laundry van Fitz had acquired for the occasion. And being as insufferably snobby as ever, felt ashamed to be seen inside it.

Fitz scratched the back of his neck. The fake laundry company's cheaply made uniform itching his skin. He caught the fresh but plastic smell of the vinyl logo on the front of his sweater. It had only been ironed on mere hours ago.

On the dashboard lay the battery pack for the radio system, on top of which sat a makeshift ashtray made from an empty coffee cup. It was half full of Lucien's cigarette ends, the smell of which were making Fitz' already nervous stomach unsettled. Unlike Fitz, Lucien wasn't wearing a uniform and sat in possibly the only casual clothes he owned; a pair of Hugo Boss jeans and a black cashmere jumper.

Fitz' hand gripped the radio so tight his knuckles were white. Phenomena's crackling voice was emanating from it, filling the van with panic.

"Fitz?"

Fitz moved to push down the button to reply, but Lucien suddenly slapped a hand over the radio and stopped him.

"Let's think about this."

Fitz glared into his face.

"What's there to think about?"

"We're behind schedule."

"It's not too late."

"It soon will be."

"But not yet."

Lucien lit another cigarette, felt his stomach cramp and looked out the window.

"I'm not giving up yet," Fitz told him.

And as the words fell from his lips, all he thought of was Sarah. To Lucien and the others this was a job, perhaps the last job they'd ever work. To him, it was the future of the person he loved most in the world. His last tie to Danielle. A reason to keep living.

"What if Phenomena doesn't get the keys?" asked Lucien. "She should have got them by now. And where the fuck are Marcus and Amelia?"

"Having regrets about the team you picked?"

Lucien bristled, irritated.

"No, but-"

"I'm giving them all one more chance."

He looked at the time.

"Sixty seconds."

"What more could go wrong in sixty seconds?"

"Fitz? Hello? Fitz, talk to me!" interrupted Phenomena's voice.

They both ignored it.

"What could go right?" asked Fitz.

"I think we should abort the mission."

Fitz was sure he'd heard wrong. Then he saw the serious look in Lucien's eyes.

"Don't say that."

"It's going to shit already."

His hand was trembling as he smoked. Opening a window, he let the breeze wash over his sweaty face. Fitz watched his expression.

What is he thinking?

"Sixty more seconds," insisted Fitz, reaching once more for the button on the radio. "Phenomena? I'm here."

Chapter 84

Hawkins

October 3rd, 2023

8.10AM

"Any word from Busby and Clarkston?" she asked a young officer who stood in front of her desk with a file in his hand.

"Can't seem to get hold of them."

She regretted her third coffee of the day. A tension headache had begun pulsing around her head like an elastic band had been snapped against her skull.

From outside the building, she thought she heard distant yelling, but she dismissed it, her only thoughts now focussed on Bill's transit from Belmarsh to the hospital. But her thoughts were interrupted as footsteps were heard coming at speed into the room. Looking up, she saw Detective Kane enter, his face pink and shiny.

"Outside!" he blurted out.

"What?"

"Have you seen what's going on outside?"

She rose from her seat and dashed out the room behind Kane who lead her hastily across the floor towards the large plate glass windows. The yelling got louder as she approached and looked down at the street.

"Oh, God. What is this?"

"A protest by some You-Tuber," sighed Kane, crossing his arms.

Everyone in the room joined the pair, all of them standing in a line staring at the growing crowd with a disapproving gaze. Hawkins' eyes fell on the small figure of Billie in a red hoody at the front of the crowd. She held a megaphone in one hand, and her phone in her other outstretched hand to film herself.

"The current Metropolitan Police's strip search policy is barbaric and inhumane!" she yelled out to the crowd.

They all yelled back in agreement. Hawkins watched as more people joined the group of protesters with each passing second. They were spawning in front of her eyes like amoebas.

"Get this stopped right now," Hawkins announced to the room.

"They're not doing anything wrong," said Kane. "They're allowed to protest. Unfortunately..."

Hawkins felt her blood heat up, felt her cheeks turn scarlet and her hands involuntarily ball into fists.

"We don't need this right now. Clear them away."

"Detective Kane's right," said one of the younger officers from behind her. "They have a right to protest, and if we start clearing them away, that'll... Well, it won't be great for our public image. MET officers forcibly arresting kids protesting the MET about the MET's behaviour and-"

"I get it," said Hawkins, waving a hand at him. "They're not doing anything wrong for the moment and-"

"Maybe not yet," said Kane, pointing out the window. "But I sense something's about to happen."

To Hawkins' shock, she watched as Billie handed one of the protesters her phone and sign before pulling off her hoody. With some exaggerated, theatrical mannerisms, she then peeled off her t-shirt and faced the crowd in a thin, mesh bra.

"If the MET wants us to strip, then we'll strip!" she yelled.

A roar echoed back from the crowd. Hawkins watched, cringing, as thousands of people in front of Billie began peeling off their own tops.

"Oh, God."

But her eyes widened even further as she saw Billie pull a lighter out the back pocket of her jeans and place the flame beneath the t-shirt. Dozens of the protesters followed suit, holding their own lighters below their outstretched shirts.

"Stop this now."

But it was too late and soon Hawkins and the team were staring at a group of topless protesters waving their flaming shirts in their direction.

Chapter 85

Phenomena

October 3rd, 2023

8.11AM

"Sixty seconds," came Fitz' voice through the earpiece. "One minute to make it or break it."

Phenomena felt her panic rise, but she nodded to herself with a quiet sense of determination. She looked back over her shoulder just in time to see Busby take a step back from the blonde girl. He raised his hands slightly, enough for the crowd to see he wasn't touching her.

"Sixty seconds," she confirmed. "Got it."

She took her chance and moved in, sucking in quick lungfuls of air as her heart hammered hard in her ribcage.

Concentrate, she told herself. *This isn't the time to be nervous.*

Pressing on, she stood directly behind Busby, keeping her distance, and attempted to look like a casual bystander. Her eyes fell on his pocket once again. This time the keys were poking out a fraction of an inch more than before. It wasn't much, but it was still an advantage.

Time was passing so fast, and still she was a couple feet away from him.

"Fifty seconds," she heard Fitz say.

She moved in closer, desperation setting in. Her teeth bit into her bottom lip as she slipped her left hand down towards her pocket. With her right hand, she once again tried to distract the crowd with her poorly spelled sign. The impact was less than before. People had already seen it.

Her fingers grazed the side of Busby's thigh, and once again she felt her fingertips brush up against the smooth metal of the keyring. No one was looking. Most people's eyes were still distracted by the commotion between Busby and the blonde girl, while a few other people had their concentration focussed on the wider chaos of the scene.

"Forty-five seconds," said Fitz.

Just another half an inch and the keys are mine.

She felt her hand become enveloped by the inside of his pocket now. Felt her fingers close around the keyring.

Then she felt something else.

A hard shove in her back propelled her forward just as she grabbed the keys. It made her face hit Busby's shoulder blade just as her balance faltered and the keys, that were only a second ago so tightly gripped in her hand, now tumbled out her fingers onto the ground. She thought fast, standing on them just as Busby spun round.

"Sorry," came a mumbled apology from behind Phenomena as a group of young protesters barged past.

"Watch where you're bloody going," moaned Busby at them, but they were already out of sight. "You all right?" he asked Phenomena."

"Thirty-five seconds," came Fitz' voice.

"Yes, thank you. I…"

Her mind whirred into action, spinning through the lessons once again.

Social cues, splitting focus… What was the third lesson?

Patter!

"*YeahI'mabsolutelyfinethanksforasking.Areyouokay?Areyouhurt?Sorrysorrysorry!*"

She blurted everything out in one continuous word, the syllables falling over themselves as they tumbled out her mouth.

Patter, she remembered. The art of talking at speed so as to short circuit your mark's brain. Not only did it sound annoying, but it also had a scientific purpose. Talking so fast it was barely understandable produced two desirable effects for the magician. Firstly, as the person listening struggled to process the words they were hearing, the language centre of their brain soon became overloaded. Secondly, the auditory centre of the brain became overwhelmed. The result being the listener's mind would temporarily crash like an old computer with fifteen tabs open.

Busby blinked at her, slightly confused as she raced through her words.

"So anyway, I didn't mean to hurt you. If I did. I'm so sorry. Those guys behind me. So rude. So annoying. Yeah, yeah. Just so annoying. They weren't even looking where they were going, were they? Just really dumb. So dumb. Hey, you know you remind me of someone. You have the bluest eyes. Wow, yeah. The bluest eyes I've ever seen."

When in doubt, add flattery, she thought.

"Twenty-five seconds," she heard in her ear, and she spoke even faster.

"Yeah, the bluest eyes, but I bet you get told that a lot, don't you? Bet you have an easy day on your job. Bet criminals just fall into your cuffs if you look at them the right way, right? Right?"

She giggled nervously, and Busby was so focussed on the speed of her words, and the warm feeling he got from her compliments that he didn't even notice her dragging her foot away from him, the keys scraping the ground underneath her boot.

"Twenty-seconds."

She looked down at her boot. He hadn't noticed the keys were missing from his pocket yet, but he'd notice if she bent down to retrieve them from under her foot.

She was down to her last twenty seconds, and her last tactic, getting an emotional response.

Now with Phenomena in front of him, Busby had long forgotten about the blonde girl behind him. It was easier to focus on the woman making him feel good rather than the one accusing him of assault. Phenomena could see a hint of desire in his eyes as he looked at her.

"You know I think I really hurt my face when I got thrown into you," she said, dramatically holding a hand to her cheek.

She could see the concern immediately crease up his eyes.

"Aw, did you? Let me see."

He moved closer to look and she increased the drama.

"I think my cheekbone might be fractured. It really hurts!"

She winced as she felt her face, then doubled over as though in insufferable pain. Busby moved to soothe her, placing a hand on her back.

"Here, let me look. It doesn't seem bruised, but if it hurts we can get you over to the ambulance."

He was so busy looking at her wincing face and rubbing her back that he didn't notice what her hand was doing as she bent down. That her fingers were scrabbling desperately for the keys which she quickly flicked into the inside of her sleeve.

"Ten seconds..."

She stood upright, made sure Busby hadn't seen and said, "Actually yeah, *could* you walk me over to the ambulance?"

"Of course," he smiled. "Let's get you checked out."

Chapter 86

Marcus

October 3rd, 2023

8.13AM

Amelia's hand slipped into his and he felt a surge of warmth and excitement. He looked to her face, saw the encouragement in her eyes and kept moving. They snaked their way down the side of the motorway, heads down and hearts thumping. Around them, the crowd continued to chant.

"Where are you?" Fitz' asked in Marcus' ear.

"I can see the ambulance. It's about twenty feet away."

"Hurry."

He felt Amelia's hand squeeze his and he squeezed back despite feeling the sweat pool between their palms. The chants from the crowd grew louder as they pressed their way through bodies and placards.

"You got this," said Amelia. "Look, there's Phenomena."

As they pushed through the last group of protesters, emerging in front of the squad car, Marcus caught sight of a wisp of Phenomena's red hair poking out from under her beanie hat. She was holding her face as though injured. Beside her, a concerned looking PC Busby held a hand gently to her back as he guided her to the ambulance. Marcus couldn't help but notice how Busby's eyes kept glancing downwards towards Phenomena's bottom.

"Keep going," urged Amelia, the heat of her hand now on his shoulder.

He took a quick look at her.

I've got this, he thought. *We've got this.*

He took her hand and squeezed it before pulling her around to the side of the ambulance. They ducked out of sight for a second to get their bearings before poking out their faces to see Phenomena.

She was staring ahead at the ambulance with Busby by her side. But her left hand was brushing the side of the police car as she passed it. For a split second, she paused. Marcus kept his eye on her left hand.

Now, he thought. *Do it now.*

As though she'd heard him, she took one look up at Busby's face to make sure he wasn't looking, then rapped her knuckles against the police car's passenger door. Clarkston, in the passenger seat, followed the noise and looked up at her. She turned for a brief moment, her eyes meeting his and they both gave each other an almost imperceptible nod.

Then she was walking away, moving at speed towards the ambulance.

Chapter 87

Busby

October 3rd, 2023

8.14AM

"Going to need a location on that backup," said Busby into his radio, straining his ears to hear over the top of the yelling crowd.

"On their way," hissed a response. "But some units are being diverted to Scotland Yard. There'll be a wait."

"What's happening at Scotland Yard?"

"Another protest with fire hazards."

"But we need units here!"

"Doing our best."

Busby sighed, clicked off his radio and turned back to Phenomena.

"You okay?" he asked.

"I'm sore. Need some ice or something."

Busby looked over his shoulder at Clarkston still sat in the car. For a second back there he thought he heard a knock coming from his door, but now he wasn't so sure. There were so many people and noises coming from everywhere.

Useless idiot, he thought, looking at Clarkston. *Still sitting in there like a dummy.*

He turned his attention back to Phenomena.

"Not sure we'll be able to get you ice," he told her. "But we'll get the paramedics to check you out."

He couldn't help smiling as he said this. There was something about the way she clutched at her injured face that amused him. Like a kid faking an injury for attention.

Like she was seeking out *his* attention. He was used to it, of course. Women playing the damsel in distress so a man in uniform could save them. And with his looks and physique he was used to it more than most officers.

More than Clarkston anyway, he laughed inwardly.

As he guided her to the back doors of the ambulance he wondered how he'd get lucky with her. His eyes scanned her body, tracing her waist and hips. He could imagine what lay beneath the baggy, hippy clothes. His fingertips began to tingle with the promise of sliding his hands beneath them.

With a heavy hand, he banged on the ambulance's back door three times.

"Police! We need assistance."

When there was no answer, he yanked the door open and stepped inside. He saw an emaciated Bill lying on a stretcher. Arms outstretched and cuffed to the rails like he was crucified. Standing on either side of him like devoted disciples were Terry and his colleague. They both glanced at him then Phenomena, confused.

"Paramedics," said Busby.

Terry nodded his head towards the driver's seat.

"In the front," he replied. "Probably panicking."

Busby looked at Bill.

Christ. The old boy looks close to death.

He felt Phenomena step in behind him and soon forgot about Bill.

Then something caught his attention.

A smell.

"Is that... smoke?"

Chapter 88

Clarkston

October 3rd, 2023

8.14AM

"You've been taking your bloody time," moaned Clarkston as he squatted in between Amelia and Marcus.

They were all stood at the side of the ambulance facing the embankment, hidden from the protesters.

"Look, we're here now," said Amelia. "Besides you're taking your bloody time too. I thought you said you could start a fire. A boy scout could do better."

He glared up at her, annoyed, but ignored her and carried on lighting the bits of paper he'd brought as kindling. He thought it would be easier than this, but the dismal drizzle was making everything around him damp. Still, he had a slight flame going, and he didn't need much more. Just enough to cause a distraction.

"Almost there," he breathed, stuffing one more piece of paper into the wheel arch of the ambulance.

When it failed to light immediately, he reached into the thick grass behind him and found some decaying leaves that remained largely dry thanks to the thick foliage covering it. He stuffed them in amongst the paper and held up his lighter. A flame grew rapidly, peeling at the paintwork of the wheel arch.

"Go!" urged Amelia.

Clarkston jumped up, pushing Amelia and Marcus back.

"Get out the way," he grunted. "Don't let him see you."

They shifted away backwards, disappearing into the crowd. Clarkston was out of breath as he arrived at the back doors of the ambulance. He took a deep breath, looked up to the sky as though he felt the urge to pray, then pulled open the doors.

"Busby! Fire!"

Immediate panic burst throughout the inside of the ambulance.

"Where?" asked Busby, freezing.

"Back wheel. Looks like protesters set fire to the ambulance. Everybody get out!"

"Setting fire to an ambulance," gasped Terry, disgusted. "Animals."

"Just get out."

Clarkston grabbed Terry's arm and pulled him out the back doors with his colleague in tow only inches behind. The smell of smoke was now thick in the air intensifying the panic.

"I can't leave Bill," cried Terry.

Smoke filled the air, obscuring Terry's view of the inside of the ambulance. The protesters now noticed the fire, adding to the panic. Terry could hear the sound of the ambulance's front doors opening as the paramedics jumped out. He tried to squint through the smoke to see them, but could barely see two feet in front of him. Spinning round to find his colleague, all he saw was more smoke.

In a matter of a few seconds, he'd lost all sense of direction. He coughed as the smoke entered his lungs and doubled over.

"Bill," he spluttered. "Ah, fuck."

Clarkston couldn't believe the plan had worked. He could hear Terry coughing and, knowing he was struggling, took his chance.

He felt for the back entrance to the ambulance. Heard more coughing, followed the sound and stepped inside. His head bumped into something he soon realised was Busby's shoulder.

"Clarkston?" he heard Busby say. "Why aren't you running?"

Clarkston wasted no more time, leaned back and closed the ambulance doors shutting them inside. Busby stood in front of him, angry. He had tried his hardest to escape the vehicle, but Phenomena had latched herself onto his arm and was holding on for life.

"Clarkston, you closed the doors?"

It was more an exclamation of pure fear rather than a question. Busby looked down over his shoulder and saw Phenomena still holding onto him. He tried to shake her off, but began coughing as a wisp of smoke reached his nose.

Behind him, Bill lay motionless. The only thing that showed his alertness was the look in his eyes; desperate, determined, scared.

Clarkston looked to Busby who was still trying to wrestle Phenomena off his arm and pointed at his belt.

"Clothes off, now."

"What?"

"Strip!"

As he yanked at his own clothes and let them drop to the floor, he looked back at the ambulance doors through the smoke. He could still hear Terry coughing, but what about the other guard?

He looked back to Busby who was staring, dumbstruck and still clothed.

"Clarkston, have you gone mental?"

"Just take your clothes off."

"You have. You've gone nuts."

"I won't tell you again."

Clarkston knew if Busby didn't do what he was told in the next few seconds it would all fall apart.

He bent down, wearing nothing but his tight, white boxer shorts and pulled out his service pistol from the holster of his trousers.

"Clarkston?"

Busby's voice was quivering.

"Don't make me threaten you."

"Mate, I don't know what's got into you but we can get you help. Whatever you're about to do, it's not worth it. Please, put the gun down."

But Clarkston was already raising it to Busby's head.

"Take... your clothes off."

His eyes burned and watered through the smoke, his chest aching. He coughed and felt the urge to double over, but kept the gun pointed at Busby.

Busby couldn't believe what he was seeing. Automatically, he felt his right hand move towards his own weapon. A reflex action from training, but as his fingers brushed his holster, he stopped himself.

If he was to pull out his own pistol, he'd have to be prepared to use it. And he wanted no part in Clarkston's sudden act of madness that could end up in his death.

"Alright, calm down," he said, raising his hands up in a gesture of surrender. "It's alright, mate. I'll strip. But please, put the gun down, okay?"

He began pulling off his jacket, his eyes still boring into Clarkston's.

"Please," he repeated. "I'll do whatever you say. Just put the gun down before something happens, okay?"

Clarkston coughed and swallowed down the fear that sat heavy in his throat. With a slight nod, he lowered the gun just as Busby's trousers hit the floor.

Just as a rattling sound came from the back doors.

Chapter 89

Amelia

October 3rd, 2023

8.16AM

She could barely see through the smoke and her burning tears, but she could feel Marcus' hand and that's what kept her moving. Behind her, he spluttered.

"What if this thing blows up," he panicked.

"Urgh, that only happens in the movies."

"That's not true!"

"Just move. We've only got a few seconds. Remember how Fitz timed us."

As she pulled back the door, she found herself confronted with the sight of Busby and Clarkston in their underwear revealed to her through the swirling smoke. Behind them, Phenomena stood. She had her hand reassuringly on Bill's arm.

"Who are you?" asked Busby.

Neither Amelia or Marcus answered. Instead, they stripped fast and grabbed the officers' uniforms. Slipping into them effortlessly.

Twelve seconds, Amelia noted to herself as she straightened herself up.

Looking to Marcus, she saw him zip up his jacket with a satisfied smirk.

I knew he could do it.

"Hey! What the fuck!" burst Busby. "Who are you?"

He wanted to act. Wanted to lunge at the two intruders, but his mind kept returning to Clarkston's sudden change in character. If he was capable of raising a gun to his own partner's head, what else could he do? He thought of his family back home and felt too scared to find out.

A flame of confidence burned inside Amelia now she was in uniform. And she opened the door wider to allow more smoke into the vehicle. The coughing of all its occupants grew louder.

Gotta stop that Busby getting out, she thought. *Gotta make sure he can't see a thing.*

The problem was she couldn't see anything either. She felt for a hand through the smoke.

"Marcus?"

Her hand brushed skin as she felt fingers. But they didn't belong to Marcus. Long, soft and slender, they enveloped hers through the darkness of the smoke. Something metallic dropped into the palm of her hand and her fingertips instantly moved over its ridged shape.

Keys!

"Phenomena?" she called out.

But the hand slipped back into the smoke.

"Phenomena!"

She felt a sudden heavy hand on her shoulder.

"Amelia, let's go!" cut Marcus' voice through the chaos.

Holding her arm up over her nose and mouth, she coughed and let him lead her out of the ambulance. They both dropped down out the back doors onto the ground. The first thing Amelia saw through the smoke were the bright green uniforms of the paramedics.

"Don't go in there," she told them. "We'll cover this."

"We weren't going to," said one of them. "I'm not jumping into a burning van to save a criminal."

Amelia noticed the look of terror on the paramedics' faces as they continued to move away.

"We'll transfer him to hospital ourselves," shouted Amelia. "In the squad car."

"But he needs to be in the stretcher."

"Don't think that matters any more. We just need him away."

In the distance, sirens wailed as the heat from the fire blew over Amelia in waves. She gasped as she looked up and saw the flame grow and engulf the ambulance's roof just as the back doors swung open and out tumbled a spluttering Phenomena.

When she next looked back up at the paramedics, they had almost disappeared into the crowd.

"Run!" one of them yelled. "The oxygen tanks! They're gonna blow."

Phenomena passed her, brushing her shoulder as she fled. Through the open doors of the ambulance Amelia could just about make out the sight of bare limbs as Busby and Clarkston struggled through the smoke. Busby was the first to fall out, staggering in his underwear into the middle of the motorway where he collapsed clutching his chest. Behind him, Clarkston bent over his knees spitting out soot.

There was only one person left in the ambulance.

Chapter 90

Bill

October 3rd, 2023

8.18AM

The heat burning through the wall of the ambulance was excruciating. In his left hand, Bill tried to grip the small tub of petroleum jelly he had hidden earlier. But his fingers were slick with sweat and his hands were cuffed too far apart to bring them closer than a few inches. He fumbled with the lid, dropping the entire tub onto the bedsheets as it popped off.

No....

His hands strained against his handcuffs as he searched the bed covers for the tub. Through stinging eyes, he tried to see it, but the smoke was growing thicker by the second. It was reaching into every part of him. Scorching his eyes, his nostrils, his mouth. He doubled over, coughing so hard his ribs felt close to cracking.

I'm going to die in here.

He felt his already weak body lose the last of its strength. With one great big hacking cough, he collapsed back against the pillow, spluttering. It hurt to breathe. Hurt to think.

I almost made it.

He clenched his eyes closed against the heat and felt himself fade away.

I must be dying, he thought. *Because I can feel her. I can smell her.*

Through the thick smell of the smoke, another scent came to him. One he'd not experienced in years. Floral and sweet, it was a perfume he used to smell as it floated down the stairs. One that used to cling to his clothes as he felt those big hugs he so wished he could feel again.

"Danielle?"

It was a scent that revived him.

He was wide awake now. So sure that he could feel her beside his bed. But as he sat up, all he could see was smoke, and all he could do was cough.

"Danielle!"

He was so sure he could feel her presence.

It was then that he felt it. The smooth plastic of the petroleum jelly tub nestled in the folds of his bed covers. He moved fast, reaching the desperate fingers of his left hand into the tub. Most of its contents had melted but there was just about enough. He smothered his hand in the jelly as best he could, wriggled and yanked against the cuffs.

He felt a bone give inside the palm of his hand from the effort of pushing his fingers so tightly together. Then he felt a sliding sensation along with a sharp pain scraping at his skin. At last, his left hand was free.

"Come on, come on," he urged himself as he felt his nose clog up with smoke.

His right hand proved more of a struggle. It had swollen with the heat from the fire and ached immeasurably. With each passing second, the handcuffs heated up, burning him the longer he remained stuck inside them.

Scalding tears ran down his cheeks mingling with his sweat. He stopped caring whether it hurt or not and started pulling at his hand so hard it was at risk of breaking.

The heat became unbearable. The smoke so thick he felt it consume him. The fear inside him was so great he thought it would kill him.

Then it came again.

The scent of Danielle.

Hallucination or not, it strengthened him to pull his hand hard enough that he felt it give. There was one last squeeze, one last shock of pain against his burning skin, then he was free.

He didn't waste a second. Tumbling from the bed, he fell on his hands and knees. There was a hint of fresh air in the distance. But as he crawled towards it, he felt a sharp pain in his lungs.

His arms and legs gave way beneath him as he spluttered. With as much breath as he could muster, he tried to drag himself towards the open back doors.

A sudden gust of heat waved above him as a flame rose high over the stretcher. He looked up just in time to see it engulf the pillow and the bedding before licking at the sides of the oxygen tanks. Fear gripped him, but he was too weak to move. With one last cough, his body sagged and he fell in and out of consciousness.

Then he felt hands.

Strong but feminine fingers wrapping around his limbs and pulling him up.

"Danielle?" he asked, delirious.

His feet dragged along the floor of the ambulance as he was pulled to safety. A fresh breeze cut through the smoke and hit his face as he was carried down onto the road.

He could barely see, but through the smoke he made out Terry's concerned features.

"Where are you taking him?" he asked.

"We'll escort him to the hospital unit. We've got him."

"But he -"

"We've got him."

Terry's face disappeared and Bill was still delirious.

"Danielle? Is it really you?"

"Hold on," came Amelia's voice. "I got you."

He felt her grip tighten around him as she picked up the pace. As he looked over her shoulder, he saw the flames swallow up the ambulance. The glowing heat from the wreckage chasing them as they reached the police car.

Marcus had already opened the back door.

"I got him!" called out Amelia as she tumbled Bill into the back seat.

Bill heard the sound of the back door slamming shut and felt the safety of the seat beneath him. Through burning, grit filled eyes, he saw Amelia climb into the passenger seat, soot covering her face.

Then the world through the windows started to move as Marcus hit both the sirens and the accelerator.

"Woo!" screamed Marcus. "We've bloody done i-"

His words were cut off by a sequence of bangs so loud they sounded to Bill like they were exploding inside his head. With the last of his strength, he looked out the back window and saw the ambulance fade into the distance as one final bang echoed. The remaining members of the crowd scattered as the last exploding oxygen tank burst through the ambulance's side window onto the embankment.

Far into the distance, Bill could see the flashing lights of the approaching fire engines.

Chapter 91

Hawkins

October 3rd, 2023

9.05AM

The scenes unfolding on the large television on the wall of the incident room flickered across Hawkins' horrified eyes. Her racing pulse throbbed loudly inside her head. She could barely hear the news presenter's sombre words, nor the hushed muttering of her team behind her.

From outside came the chanting of Billie's protesters along with the smell of their burning shirts. The smell of smoke gave Hawkins the feeling she was standing in the scene displayed on the television in front of her. She could almost feel the heat of the burning ambulance.

"Turn it up," she said to the nearest officer.

He was as stunned as she was, and remained open-mouthed staring at the screen.

"I said turn it up!"

He flinched and rushed for the volume button, the news presenter's voice filling the room.

"Scenes just coming in from the Power to the Planet protest that obstructed the transfer of high profile prisoner, Sir Bill Lovecroft."

There was a short, solemn pause as they held their gaze to the camera, then regained their composure and continued.

"Reports are coming in that the ambulance carrying Sir Lovecroft was set alight by protesters and exploded, killing Sir Lovecroft at the scene. Other occupants of the vehicle survived and there were no other injuries."

Hawkins held a hand to her mouth as the camera zoomed in to show the metallic, blackened carcass of the ambulance. Inside which lay a stretcher, the handcuffs on either side dangling empty from the railings.

Outside, despite the police units moving into arrest Billie's protesters, the chants grew louder, reaching a crescendo as officers began pushing them into waiting vans.

But Hawkins didn't notice the noise any more. Nor did she notice the way Detective Kane backed out the room. Or how he was already pressing his phone to his ear, talking to the one person who knew what was really happening.

Chapter 92
Danielle

October 8th, 2017

Danielle synced her phone up to the television in her old bedroom. She watched, embarrassed as her own screaming face filled the screen.

"Why are you filming this!" she was yelling at Fitz, her face bright red and covered in sweat as she pushed through the contractions.

"Just one more push. You're almost there," came the midwife's voice out of shot. "Come on, push!"

"I'm tryyyyying."

"You're doing great, Danielle," came Fitz' voice from behind the camera.

Danielle let out a deafening scream, her face tensing up looking ready to explode. The camera shook slightly as she slumped back against the bed. Then came the sound of a shrill baby's cry.

Danielle was breathing hard and in shock. In the background came the voices of the midwife talking to the nurses as the crying grew louder.

"Fitz, will you put your phone down and bloody hold your daughter!" raged Danielle.

There was a shuffling motion, then the video ended.

"So, you're back," came Cecilia's voice.

Danielle, turned round and saw her leaning in the doorway with rollers in her hair.

"Watching Sarah's birth again? Was it not painful enough the first time?"

"Yeah, I was so full of gas and air at the time it all happened so fast. It was six months ago already, but it feels like it was just the other day."

"I could never watch myself look that bad," said Cecilia. "All sweaty and screaming like that. Can't believe Fitz insisted on recording the delivery."

"He told me I looked beautiful."

Cecilia snorted a laugh out through her nose.

"Anyway... Going out?" asked Danielle, trying to ignore her bad attitude.

"Club Fiore."

"I've never heard of it."

"Yeah, well. You don't get out much these days. Not with..."

Cecilia nodded her head down to Sarah who lay asleep in the car seat at Danielle's feet.

There was a moment of tension between the two sisters, but it softened the longer Cecilia stared at Sarah. Even her cold heart melted looking at her button nose.

"She looks more like you every time I see her."

Danielle smiled.

Cecilia took a step nearer and bent down to look at Sarah more closely.

"She's so beautiful. A little dumpling."

"She certainly is. Anyway, is Dad about?"

"He's floating about somewhere. Need him for anything urgent?"

"No, no. I just dropped in to get some of my clothes and things I left here. I think he has some of my books I wanted to take back with me."

"Trying to get Fitz into literature?"

The condescending tone had returned to Cecilia's voice.

"He already is," replied Danielle, curtly. "Unlike you."

Cecilia rolled her eyes and walked back to her own room.

It was moments like this when Danielle couldn't bear to be near Cecilia. Weren't sisters supposed to grow closer as they grew up? Cecilia only grew colder.

Danielle yawned and sat on the end of her bed, gently rocking the car seat with her foot as she looked at Sarah's face in a daze. She'd lost track of the times she found herself in a trance just staring at her, just feeling a rush of love that blotted out her surroundings.

"I thought I heard you talking to Cecilia," came Bill's sudden voice from the doorway.

"How long were you there?" jumped Danielle. "You gave me a fright."

"Sorry. You looked lost in thought."

"Isn't she perfect?"

Bill walked over and sat beside Danielle.

"She looks just like you did at that age."

"Really?"

"I used to find your mother doing the same thing. Just looking at you as though under a spell."

There was a comfortable silence between them for a moment until Bill wrapped his arm around Danielle's shoulders.

"How are things living with Fitz?"

"Oh, great."

He looked into her eyes to make sure she was telling the truth. He'd be lying to himself if he thought there wasn't a part of him that hoped she was miserable. If only so she could come back and live with him.

"Good," he said. "I miss you tremendously, though."

"I miss you too. That's why I'm back. Well, that and my book about Otto Dix."

"Otto Dix? He's rather dark for you, Danielle? Don't want to pick up one of your other art books?"

"I need that one for uni."

"Ah. And your studying is going..."

"Really well. Even if I don't sleep some nights."

Bill smiled and kissed her forehead.

"So you're back for your books, huh? There's me thinking you heard the news."

"What news?"

He smiled again and tapped the side of his nose.

"Come, I'll show you."

Picking up Sarah in her car seat, he guided Danielle downstairs.

"I was actually just about to call you when I heard your voice," he said. "Then I supposed Cecilia might have told you."

"Told me what?"

"Just you wait."

"Aw, Dad. I hate surprises. Just tell me what it is."

He remained silent. Her nerves mounting as they descended the stairs. When they reached the main hall, she assumed they were almost there, but Bill squeezed her hand tighter and opened the door down to the cellar. There were more stairs, more nerves.

"Dad, what's going on?"

"It's still down here because it just arrived," he explained. "But I'll be hanging it shortly and-"

"What's just arrived? Dad, tell me I'm-"

She froze as it appeared to her at the bottom of the cellar. Her face lit up, delighted even though she couldn't see it, only its shape beneath a large, silk cloth. But she knew its dimensions. Knew it could only be one thing.

"The painting!"

"It's back, darling."

"The restoration's finished?"

"Only just."

She had waited so long she had started to doubt the moment would ever come. Taking a tentative step forwards, she tugged at the silk sheet until it fell to her feet. A wave of joy washed through her as she was reunited with the painting.

But the joy soon turned sour. Her eyes scanned the painting fast, skipping over the brush strokes that were so familiar to her. She felt like she knew them all personally. But as she gazed at them now, she felt they were unfamiliar. They looked alien, wrong, fake...

Bill walked up beside her and looked into her face.

"Darling, what's wrong?"

How could he think I wouldn't notice?

"Dad... This is..."

She thought about what she was about to accuse him of. Knew that it could potentially tear their relationship apart.

"This is... fantastic," she said, changing her mind and forcing a smile. "I'm so pleased it's home."

***

"What do you mean it's a fake?"

"I mean I was just down in the cellar looking at it and I know it's a fake," she whispered through clenched teeth.

Nervously, she glanced at her bedroom door to make sure it was still closed. From down the hall, she could hear the sound of Cecilia blasting pop music. At Danielle's feet, Sarah started to cry inside her car seat.

"Shhh... It's okay. Mummy's here."

For a moment, she put the phone down on the bed to pick up Sarah. When she returned her phone to her ear, Fitz was rambling.

"I mean I just don't... I just don't get it. Why would your Dad bring you back a fake painting? He wouldn't."

"I don't know. All I can tell you is that I saw the real painting at the museum. Really saw it there with my own eyes. And the one I just saw down in the cellar is not the same one. I know it."

"How can you be so sure?"

"Because I grew up with it," she burst. "I've studied it. Not just at home, but academically."

"I thought it was an undocumented Caravaggio," said Fitz.

"It is, but I studied it in my own time like I did all my other course material."

Fitz fell silent for a second. He listened to the sound of Sarah whimpering in Danielle's arms.

"I think someone needs to come home," said Fitz.

"Yeah, she's hungry and cranky. Just need to pick up a couple more things. I better get going."

"Wait. Answer me one thing. The painting in the museum."

"Uhuh…"

"You're certain it's the Caravaggio that used to hang in your house."

"I've told you this before. One hundred percent."

"So… Does your old man know you've seen it in the museum?"

Danielle stared at the floor in thought while rocking Sarah.

"I don't know…"

When she next looked up, Cecilia was standing in the open doorway.

"I've… I've got to go. I'll be home soon."

She hung up just as Cecilia smirked. The rollers were out of her hair now and she wore a full face of make-up and a short, sequinned dress.

"How long were you standing there?" asked Danielle.

"Long enough to hear everything."

Danielle could see the amusement on her sister's face and wanted her gone. But she took up the whole doorway with no sign of leaving.

"What do you know?" asked Danielle.

"Nothing."

"You're lying."

"Me? Lie?"

"Cecilia, you've got to tell me. What do you know about the painting?"

"I don't know anything about some crusty old painting. That's your thing."

"But you know something."

"Just what I heard there. You think Papa switched the painting for a fake."

"Why do you look so happy about that?"

"I'm not happy. I'm just... I dunno, I just find it a tad dramatic that you think Dad's trying to pass off a fake Caravaggio."

Danielle couldn't read the look on Cecilia's face. She never could.

"What are you thinking?" asked Danielle.

"I'm just thinking that maybe, if you are right and the painting is fake, that Dad's been duped by some master criminal who's hiding the real one somewhere."

"That can't be true. Dad can't be duped by anyone."

"Exactly, which makes me think there's something else going on."

Cecilia looked down at her fingers and inspected her freshly painted nails.

"Maybe Dad knows exactly what's going on and is trying to give *you* a fake."

"He wouldn't do that."

"He might if he knew how much a real undocumented Caravaggio was worth on the black market and wanted to cheat you out of your inheritance."

Danielle's mouth fell open.

"You're a monster. Dad would never do that to me."

"Then what *has* he done?"

Danielle didn't have an answer. And before she could think of one, Cecilia smirked one last time and walked away.

***

December 9th, 2017

They stood in their living room, the sights and sounds of family life all around them. From the kitchen came the smell of a healthy home cooked dinner.

"I can't believe we're doing this," said Danielle. "It feels... wrong."

"No, what's wrong is your father screwing you over."

"I can't believe he would... I still don't understand."

"All you have to understand is that tonight you're going to get your painting back. The real one. The one promised to you. It's your inheritance. *Sarah's* inheritance."

Danielle nodded, but she felt nauseous with worry.

There's still time to back out, she thought. *I'm not like Fitz and the others. I'm not a criminal.*

"I know what you're thinking," said Fitz, taking her face in his hands.

"You do?"

"I think I know you by now."

"Then what am I thinking?"

"That you're a good girl and you're scared of entering my world."

"Pretty much. I can't believe I'm about to do this. I can't believe after... after everything I said about wanting to raise Sarah in a safe home away from your old criminal life that I'm making you go back to..."

"Don't do this. Don't analyse it all. It's okay."

"No, it's not. I'm a raging hypocrite."

"You're just someone who wants what belongs to them."

"But we're doing this in the wrong way."

"What's the right way?" asked Fitz.

Danielle didn't know.

"I'm sorry," was all she could say.

"For what?"

"For making you do this."

He pulled her closer and kissed her forehead.

"One last job," he said. "Remember that's what we said. One last job and a personal one at that. This isn't some quick cash gig. This is for you."

She could sense the genuine passion in his voice, but she couldn't share it. All she could feel was how wrong it all was. How it went against everything she believed in.

"I'm going to commit a crime," she said, swallowing down the word. "A *crime*."

Stroking the sides of her arms, he kissed her again and said, "Crime's complicated. It's not always black and white."

But to her it always had been.

***

Danielle's cheek itched inside the ski mask. She pushed her fingers up beneath it and scratched her skin.

"I'm too hot," she panicked to Fitz as she crouched in the back of the van with the rest of the team. "I... I can't do th-"

"Don't say it."

It was dark in the van, but he could just about make out her silhouette. He didn't need to see her face to know how nervous she looked.

"It's going to work out perfectly. Trust me," he said. "I've done this before."

"But I haven't."

He leaned towards her dark shape and felt for her face before kissing her cheek over the ski mask.

"I love you," he whispered. "I got you."

She relaxed slightly in his arms, but the tremor in her voice remained.

"Just tell me we're doing the right thing."

"We are. I know what I'm doing. It'll all work out."

"Promise me."

"I promise."

"I love you."

Slowly, Fitz slid open the side door and the fabric of Danielle's ski mask was illuminated by the lights from The National Gallery.

Fitz could feel the energy rise amongst his team. That electric feeling that came from the danger and excitement.

"Fitz..." came Danielle's quivering voice.

He turned to face her one last time before they made their move. Taking her face in his hands, he looked deep into her eyes.

"It's going to be okay," he promised her. " Nothing can go wrong."

Chapter 93

Fitz

October 3rd, 2023

8.18AM

Nothing can go wrong...

The words came to him now as he sat beside Lucien. The last words he'd said to her before it all fell apart.

If only I'd never talked her into it.

If only she was still here.

"You okay?" asked Lucien. "You've got a thousand yard stare."

"Yeah I was just-"

"We've done it," came Amelia's voice crackling through the radio. "We're on the move. Two hours at the most to Portsmouth."

"We fucking did it!" exploded Fitz.

He let out a long sigh.

"How's Bill?"

"He's okay. I think... We'll update you in thirty minutes."

With another crackle, Amelia's voice clicked off.

"So... We've done it," said Lucien.

"There's still a chance it could go wrong. Still gotta get Bill to Portsmouth."

There was that word again.

Wrong...

Fitz turned the key in the ignition with Portsmouth on his mind when another crackle came through the radio.

"Fitz? Lucien?"

"Jacques?"

"Fitz... I'm injured."

"Shit. What happened?"

"Cops fucking leathered me. Think my arm's broken."

Lucien, reading Fitz' face said, "I'll sort it out."

"We need to get to Portsmouth."

"You go. I'll go back for Jacques. Sort out the mess."

"Are you sure?"

"Sorting out messes is my job," said Lucien with a weak, resigned smile.

Fitz didn't have the time to complain.

"Okay, go. I'll call."

Chapter 94
Bill

December 9th, 2017

"Do you think she knows?" asked Lucien.

They were both sat in the cellar, the painting to one side of them, a wall of collectors' wine to the other. In between them sat a small, rickety, but valuable, table with an open bottle of Châteaux D'Ycem on top. Bill thought for a long moment.

"She didn't appear to notice anything," he said, narrowing his eyes at the painting. "She shouldn't notice. It's an almost perfect replica."

"But Danielle is an almost perfect art student," Lucien reminded Bill. "If anyone would notice it would be her. Especially if she grew up with the replica."

Bill took a long sip of wine and frowned.

"I feel horrible lying to her."

"Which time?"

"Both times."

"There's no reason to feel horrible. You lied for the right reasons."

Bill knew Lucien was right, but he still felt guilty.

"I just wanted her to have the original now. I thought the time was right."

Lucien nodded and took a gulp of wine before lighting a cigarette.

"But why now?" he asked, flipping his gold Zippo shut. "Why switch the paintings now and finally bring the original home?"

"Because she's ready."

Lucien looked confused.

"She's a mother now," explained Bill. "It's a mother's gift. I want her to have what's rightfully hers. She's grown up now. A mother herself. She deserves to have the original. To have what it's worth. Not just for her, but for the baby. It's Sarah's inheritance too."

Bill looked sadly into his wine.

"It's what her own mother would have wanted."

He stared off into space for a second, the smoke from Lucien's cigarette swirling around him along with his thoughts.

"I'd kept the original safe for so long," he continued. "I always felt that was the right thing to do. To keep it safe, hidden. But now it's back here I feel like... Like I've cheated her somehow."

"Bill, don't overthink it. Maybe she has noticed, maybe she hasn't. But the important thing is that the real one is back home and in her hands. Along with what it's worth. That's what you want, isn't it?"

"Of course."

"Then say no more. Come on. Enjoy your wine and relax."

Bill sat and sipped more wine. In the distance, a buzzing sounded.

"What's that?" asked Lucien.

"Sounds like the intercom."

"Expecting anyone?"

Bill shook his head.

The buzzing continued.

With a roll of his eyes, Bill moved to the cellar door and called up the stairs to the housekeeper.

"Can you get that?" he shouted. "Or mute it or something."

He yawned, feeling the effects of the wine and walked back to the table. Lucien was toying with his Zippo, clicking the lid over and over again annoying Bill.

"Sir Bill?" came the housekeeper's strained voice down the stairs. "The police are here."

"Police? Tell them to come back tomorrow."

The housekeeper arrived in the doorway, her forehead creased with worry.

"They're detectives," she explained. "They say it's urgent."

"What in the bloody hell? Fine. I'm coming."

His cheeks were flushed from the wine as he ascended the stairs, but his sleepiness had instantly worn off. As he reached the main hall, he saw the detectives waiting patiently at the front door. Lips tight, eyes sorry, hands nervously picking at their fingernails.

His annoyance at their intrusion soon turned to worry.

"How can I help, detectives?"

"Please… Could you take a seat somewhere?"

"What is this about?"

"Your daughter Danielle… She…"

As Bill listened he felt as though he was melting in and out of reality. He heard snippets of the detectives' sentences, but he couldn't process them.

"The National Gallery… I'm so sorry… There was nothing the paramedics could do… Her partner… Taken into custody."

"Dad?"

Bill heard Cecilia behind him as she dashed down the stairs.

"Dad! Are you okay?"

He felt his legs collapse. Felt as though the bottom of his stomach, the bottom of his world was falling away. Then he was falling too. His knees hitting the ground.

"Dad!"

***

October 3rd, 2023

9.48AM

When he opened his eyes he could see the world pass by upside down from the back windows of the squad car. Trees turned to buildings that soon turned to warehouses. He coughed as the smell of smoke remained buried in his nostrils.

He blinked a few times to rid himself of his dream, but it wouldn't fade. He could still remember the look on the detectives' faces, the way Cecilia screamed.

"How long was I out?" he asked, his voice croaky.

Amelia turned round and said, "Long enough to reach Portsmouth."

"Already?"

"Jesus, you look terrible."

She leaned back and handed him a bottle of water. When he failed to move, she unscrewed the cap and held it to his dry mouth.

"Hang in there. It's almost over."

Bill gulped down the water and felt it revive him. His eyes met Marcus' stressed gaze in the rear-view mirror. The car was hot and stank of sweat, smoke and nerves.

"Hit the sirens again," said Amelia.

As Bill pulled himself upright, he could see the dockyard through the wind shield.

In the distance he could make out the granite coloured shape of HMS King Edward. It grew closer as the guard at the entrance noticed the sirens and raised the barrier. It felt like the car was flying into the dockyard, the large ship growing in front of Bill's eyes as they approached.

Chapter 95

Cecilia

October 3rd, 2023

9.49AM

"Do you know how much trouble I can get in if you're seen in here?"

"Do you know how rich you'll be if you stay in my good books?"

Harold didn't like the way Cecilia spoke to him. Everything sounded like a threat. He was used to having the power. Have people do what he said, but now he felt as though he was at the beck and call of someone who could ruin his life. Who had ruined his love life before at least.

"This is my ship," he reminded her, towering over the top of her head. "You don't make the rules just because you're playing dress up in a stolen uniform. Even if you do look good in it."

She paused and gave a slight, sardonic smile.

"Actually, we're the ones with the money and the ticket to your freedom. For today, we do make the rules."

Harold felt his hands twitch with anger, but the plan was already rolling into action. He couldn't back out now. From outside the ship he could hear sirens.

Striding across the flag cabin to the circular window, he saw the squad car screech to a halt at the edge of the ship. Beside it, the white laundry van sat waiting.

Harold momentarily lost himself in the vision of the flashing lights on top of the car. He couldn't believe what he was about to do.

"Think of Prestige," came Cecilia's creamy voice from behind him.

He felt her warm, manipulative hand land on his lower back.

After this it's just the easy life for me. No more stinking seamen and being cooped up in this war machine for months at a time. Just sunshine, the Caribbean and lots of money.

He closed his eyes already feeling the imaginary warmth of the Jamaican sun on his face. Thought of replacing the hundreds of sweaty meatheads he'd been forced to live and work beside with sun drenched beauties who brought him cocktails on the bow of a luxurious yacht.

The sound of his phone ringing shattered his daydream.

"You should be here by now," came Amelia's angry voice, the siren doubling into a deafening echo from both outside and down the line.

Chapter 96

Bill

October 3rd, 2023

09.55AM

The unending sound of the siren made him feel as though his head was cracking. Through his headache he looked through the wind shield as Harold approached, dashing and authoritative in full uniform. Despite the urgency of the situation he found himself thinking, *Where did Cecilia go wrong dumping him?*

From the corner of his eye, he could see the dockyard's security appearing to see what was happening. Harold raised a hand to diffuse the situation. Marcus cut the sirens and Bill's ears were filled with ringing for a few seconds that faded just as Harold addressed security.

"There was a fight with some new recruits," he told them. "I'm dealing with it."

Bill tried to crane his neck to see if security were leaving, but Amelia slammed a hand on his shoulder.

"Get down," she hissed.

A moment later, Harold was at the driver's side of the car bending down to Marcus' face.

"The cameras are there, there and there," he pointed. "Pull up behind the van and the view will be blocked. I'll get Bill on the inside."

There was the rumble of the car's engine again and Bill closed his eyes as it was manoeuvred behind the laundry van.

"It's the end of our journey with you," said Amelia.

Bill thought he detected sadness in her voice. Or was it fear?

"The ship's doc will see to you," said Marcus. "You look like Hell."

"I feel like Hell," said Bill, still lying in the back seat. "Thank you. Both of you."

There was a brief second of shared appreciation between the three of them. Then they jumped into action. Through Bill's weakened state he sensed it all happening in a series of jerking and rolling motions.

He felt himself being yanked from the back seat, rolled into the van, rolled once again into fresh sheets that smelled like lemon and disinfectant. Then he was being pushed and rolled some more.

His breath became shallow as the sheets cocooned him. He felt sick as he felt himself being wheeled from the van up a ramp. The noises around him became sharp and metallic. The unmistakeable feeling of being on a ship engulfed him. The motions, the smells, the sound of male voices and constant clattering.

He sucked in air through the fabric feeling close to passing out. An unbearable heat making him sweat and panic.

After all of that's happened I'm going to die in this laundry basket.

But just as he was sure he would lose consciousness, he felt the sheets being unwrapped from around his face like an ancient mummy being revealed.

"You made it…"

He screwed up his eyes against the bright, fluorescent lights. Gradually, the piercing whiteness faded until he could see the face talking to him.

"Fitz…"

"I make a pretty good laundry boy, don't I?"

Fitz bent down and helped Bill out the laundry bin. Bill, dizzy and exhausted, struggled to get his bearings. But as he looked around, he started to relax and take in the cramped cabin Fitz had brought him to. He noticed the modest bed and the small sink. It wasn't too dissimilar to the cell he had just escaped. In the centre stood Fitz in the casual, white uniform of the laundry company. Behind him stood Harold, his face holding the tension of a closed fist.

"You stay in here," said Harold. "As far as the ship's concerned you're part of the cleaning team that came down with shingles not long after departure. You're quarantined."

Bill nodded. For the first time in so long, he felt safe, relieved, so happy he could cry.

"Give us a minute?" Fitz asked Harold.

"You need to get off. We sail in two."

"Just a minute."

Harold huffed and walked out the room.

"Thank you, Fitz" said Bill, slumping against the bed.

"Been quite the journey."

"It just begins."

Fitz sat beside Bill on the bed knowing he only had precious seconds left.

"I know you'll start afresh. Start your life again from scratch. You'll have new things but... I want you to have this. Won't be able to buy one of these."

From inside his jacket, Fitz pulled out a brown envelope. Bill took it with shaking fingers and opened it.

"Are you sure?"

Fitz nodded.

"You've got a long journey ahead of you. You'll need it to remember why you've done it all."

Bill looked down at the photograph in his hands. His eyes taking in the sight of Sarah and Danielle and burning with tears.

"I know I'm doing the right thing," Bill said with a sniff. "You'll be a good father to Sarah. God knows you've proved you're capable of anything."

"I just want my family back."

"So do I," replied Bill, but he knew it was too late.

The creak of the door broke the moment. He looked up expecting to see Harold, but felt his heart lift when he saw Cecilia instead.

"Dad!"

She threw herself at him and squeezed him so tight he saw stars.

"Oh, Dad..."

"Honey."

He peppered her cheek with kisses.

"You've done me proud," he told her. "You saved me. Don't think Danielle wouldn't be proud too."

Cecilia felt her chest tighten at hearing Danielle's name.

"I love you, Dad. When will I see you again?"

"I don't know."

"Soon?"

"Sweetheart, I can't say."

A knock sounded from the door.

"It's time!" called out Harold.

"Dad," said Cecilia, turning back to Bill.

"Promise me you'll be okay."

"I'm always okay."

But she wasn't sure. She'd never seen him look so frail. He felt ready to fall apart in her arms.

"I said it's time!"

"Dad..." continued Cecilia, clinging to Bill. "I love you."

"I love you too, honey. It'll all be okay. It'll all be-"

"You need off the ship," interrupted Harold, slamming the door open. "Now. We're about to depart."

Fitz took Cecilia's arms gently and guided her towards the door. Reaching the doorway, he looked over his shoulder at Bill one last time. Bill gave him a slight nod.

"Thank you," he said. "I won't forget this."

"Out. Now," urged Harold, ushering them out the door.

Chapter 97

Cecilia

October 3rd, 2023

9.59AM

"Stop crying," Fitz told Cecilia, striding fast towards the ship's exit. "Look normal. Don't attract attention to yourself."

Cecilia put her head down and followed Fitz' lead. She looked down at her quickening feet until she felt sunlight overhead and heard the metallic clatter of the ramp beneath her.

"Meet me at the end of the road outside the dockyard," said Fitz, pulling out the keys to the laundry van. "It'll look weird for a woman in uniform to get into a van full of dirty sheets. Wait..."

He stood at the back of the van frowning.

"What?"

"I'm sure I closed the back door. It's open."

"Just a couple inches. Maybe you didn't close it over properly."

He glared at her.

"Really? After all this you think I'd leave a door open by mistake?"

"Well, it doesn't matter now. I'll get you outside in two minutes."

She walked away from him, wiping her eyes. There were so many unsaid words dancing on her tongue. Things she'd wanted to say to Bill for so long but had been too stubborn to. Things she hadn't thought of until today but wished she had sooner. Things she wished she could say to Danielle.

From behind her came creaking and groaning as the ship moved away from the harbour. Ahead, the security gate sat. Her last step at the end of this adventure.

"Look normal," she told herself, standing up straight. "Don't attract attention to yourself."

Chapter 98
Bill

October 3rd, 2023

1 0.00AM

"Thank you," Bill said, his voice fading as his exhaustion reached a crescendo.

Harold didn't say anything. Just stood looking down at him with nothing but the promise of Prestige Travel on his mind. But the way Bill looked right now he wondered if he'd live long enough to even make good on his promise.

"Can I get you anything?" he asked Bill. "Food, water?"

Bill nodded and lay back on the bed.

"I'll call the medic. You need treated for smoke inhalation."

"What will you tell him?"

Harold thought for a second, chewing the inside of his cheek.

"A fire on base before you boarded the ship. In the kitchen."

Bill wasn't sure which part of his body felt the worst. The lack of food over the last few weeks had lowered his energy levels, and the smoke had sucked away any remaining strength.

"I'll be back," said Harold.

Bill closed his eyes for what he thought was a second. When he opened them, the ship was in silence. There was no more clanging or voices. Just the rocking motion of moving on top of the waves.

How long was I asleep?

Looking down at the bedside table, he saw a sandwich and a cup of tea. When he picked up the tea, he felt it was cold. He gulped it down anyway. Savouring the many sugars heaped inside.

As he lay back down, he heard a noise from the bathroom at the end of the bed. A slight squeak like the sole of a shoe on a tiled floor.

"Hello?"

There was no answer. Just silence again.

Bill was too tired to give it any more thought. He lay back down and felt sleep take hold of his body. But as he felt himself drift off, he heard it again. Another squeak, followed by a second. Then a third noise. The padded sound of feet on carpet that grew closer to him.

He tried to sit up to see who it was, but the second he moved he felt a solid thump to his chest and a squeezing of his throat.

"Don't make a fucking sound," came a familiar voice.

He looked up convinced he was dreaming. But the pain from the hand pressing tight around his throat told him he was wide awake. He gasped as his eyes widened.

"Lucien?"

Chapter 99

Chas

October 3rd, 2023

10.15AM

Chas sat in the visitors' room fumbling with the USB drive. He kept glancing towards the door waiting for his ghostwriter, Nathan to arrive.

"You alright?" came a voice with a nudge in the back.

Chas looked over his shoulder to see Reggie sitting at the table behind him.

"Yeah, why?"

"You look edgy."

"Nah, I'm fine. Who are you waiting for, anyway?" asked Chas. "Since when do you get visitors?"

"Since I got a nice lady pen pal."

"Wondered why my throat was burning. How much bloody aftershave are you wearing?"

"Gotta make a good first impression."

"On your pen pal? You'll be lucky if it's a woman at all. Probably some weird pervert."

"Wow, you're full of romance."

Reggie rolled his eyes and turned back round. His foot was bouncing up and down nervously. He couldn't remember the last time he'd been in a woman's company. A woman who wasn't that hippy art teacher anyway.

Up in the corner of the room, the TV was turned on with the sound off. Reggie watched it absent mindedly, half in a daze thinking about his pen pal as the news played.

Chas rolled the USB drive around the palm of his hand, his eyes flicking constantly over at the door. He watched, impatient, as everyone else's visitors' entered the room except his and Reggie's.

"Hey, Reg. Is it true?" asked Chas.

"Is what true?"

"About Bill."

"Lovecroft?"

"Yeah."

Reggie spun round, his eyes narrowing with curiosity.

"What's happened with Bill? What have you heard?"

"Nothing much. Just that he got transferred."

Reggie's face fell. He felt a sudden dropping sensation in his gut.

"Transferred?"

"To the hospital."

"Wh-"

"Someone turn up the tele!" came a voice from the back of the room. "What's going on?"

Reggie and Chas glanced up at the television along with everyone else. Images appeared on the screen of the Power to the Planet protesters.

"Clowns," Reggie laughed. "Look at 'em."

But it wasn't the protesters that had attracted the room's attention. It was the image of the burning ambulance; smoke dramatically towering up over the motorway. Beneath it, rolling text ran along the bottom of the screen.

Sir Bill Lovecroft dies in transit to hospital

There was a moment of stunned silence throughout the room. Jaws dropping open as sharp intakes of breath were heard. Then the noise started.

"Bastard!" screamed Reggie, jumping out his seat.

He began picking up things at random and hurling them around the room. Visitors' cans of juice, water bottles, coats, anything he could touch. Two guards sprinted and rugby tackled him to the ground.

"Bastard!" continued Reggie. "He's only gone and bloody done it."

"Reggie calm down," begged a guard.

"He's gone and done it. And he's bloody left us all here!"

"Reggie!"

"Bastard!"

The two guards used all their strength to pin him to the ground as more guards ran into the room.

Members of Reggie's gang who had been dotted around the room now rose from their seats and approached the restrained and writhing form of Reggie in support.

"Everyone back in your seats," ordered one of the guards.

But the anger amongst the inmates grew as they kept looking up at the TV taking in the news.

"He's fucked us!" screamed Reggie, his voice muffled by one of the guard's biceps.

"Yeah!" shouted one of Reggie's gang. "He used us!"

"Reggie..." said the guard, tightening his grip on him as he waited for help. "Sir Bill is dead. Shut your mouth."

The guard flinched as he heard a crash. A tangle of yelled insults surrounded him, flying over his head towards the television. More guards ran into the room. Reggie fought harder.

There was scuffling as the guards ran into the group of angry inmates like knights into battle. The yelling growing louder.

"Bill fucked us over!"

"He left without us."

"He screwed us!"

The yelling grew even louder as bodies wrestled to the ground and visitors screamed and ran to safety. Then the alarm sounded.

"Lockdown!" one of the guards yelled over the chaos.

Until now, Chas had watched the fighting unfold in front of him in terror. He wasn't a saint. Had known a fight or two. But he was too old for a full blown riot, and knew once you got stuck in one you only came out with broken bones and a disciplinary.

He'd backed himself against the wall, keeping as far away from the flailing limbs as possible. But the fists and shouts were growing closer by the second. He edged his way around a knots of arms and legs and grunting. Sweat pouring down his back.

He was was so busy panicking about what was in front of him, so disorientated by the sound of the alarm, he didn't notice the fight breaking out behind him. And as he froze in fright, he felt a hard shove in his back that knocked the air out his lungs. He tumbled forwards, the USB drive in his hand falling from his fingers.

Landing on his stomach, winded, he gasped and looked up into the centre of the room. It was a war zone.

Through it all he could see the small outline of the USB drive on the floor in amongst the bodies and scuffling feet. Then he watched in horror as a guard's boot knocked it out of sight.

"Shit. No!"

He stood and lurched forwards to try and find it, but another shove from the nearest guard pushed him back down.

"Hey! I wasn't doing anything."

He felt himself fall beneath a sea of bodies. Felt himself become pinned to the ground. When he could next raise his head he saw more guards enter the room, riot shields at the ready.

Chapter 100

Bill

October 3rd, 2023

1 1.20AM

He couldn't breathe. Could barely see. He was surprised by the strength in Lucien's hands. Even more surprised by him appearing in his room.

With desperation, he tried to absorb what was happening. His eyes flicked over Lucien's wild gaze and the tiny bubbles of spit that were forming rabidly in the corners of his mouth. Next, he saw the laundry cleaner's uniform on his slender body in place of his usual Italian suit.

"Think I'd let Fitz get a change of clothes and not get one for myself," grinned Lucien maniacally.

Bill tried to struggle against his grip, but in his weakened state he felt useless.

"Think I was going to put the team together and not get more than just some crumbs you'd throw at me," he continued. "They're *my* team. I get the money."

Bill couldn't believe what he was hearing.

"I..." he began to croak in response. "I trusted y..."

The words were squeezed out his throat by an increasingly angry Lucien.

"You... what? Trusted me? Yeah... You trusted me. That's why I was in charge of the team. In charge of your money. I know everything to get my hands on *all* your assets. It was me who wrote your will remember? And it was me who rewrote it adding my name in place of Cecilia's and Sarah's."

Bill felt a deep anger burn inside him, but with consciousness fading, he was too weak to act.

"The only thing standing in my way is you," spat Lucien. "They all think you're bloody dead anyway. They all think-"

BANG!

The noise was so sudden and loud it left Bill's ears ringing. He felt the grip of Lucien's bony fingers fall away from his throat as air washed into his lungs.

"Bill?" came a voice.

He was so dizzy as he gasped for air he could barely see.

"Bill, listen to me. My name's Detective Kane. You're gonna be okay."

Chapter 101

Kane

October 3rd, 2023

9.35PM

It was so dark the two men could barely see the sea, only white pearls of moonlight dancing on the crests of small waves. They both stared out into the darkness, the cold wind roaring at their ears.

"Who heard it?" asked Kane.

"Doesn't matter. A gunshot and a slamming steel door in this place are the same."

Harold was anxious to the point of sickness. This wasn't what he signed up for. He didn't want to touch what lay at his feet.

With guttural grunts, they both bent down and picked up the body.

"Jesus," moaned Kane. "How is he so heavy?"

There was no respect or ceremony as they rolled Lucien over the railing. Nor were there words of regret. It was as simple as tossing a bag of rubbish overboard.

Harold couldn't see the body hit the water, but he heard the splash. Guilt gnawed at him as he stared into the blackness. He'd killed before when he'd been sent to war. But that was from the safety of firing missiles from behind a desk. This was different. This was dirty. And even though it wasn't him that sent the bullet into the back of Lucien's head, he felt as guilty as though it was.

"Need to clean the blood," came Kane's voice cutting through the wind.

Harold said nothing. Just kept staring over the railing. He imagined Lucien's body being eaten by fish. His bones falling to the sea bed.

Taking a step back from the railing, he shook his head to clear away the thoughts. He tried to think of what lay ahead. The money, the end of his Naval career, Prestige Travel and his new life in paradise.

Behind him, Kane stepped back as though distancing himself from what he'd just done.

"How did you know?" Harold asked him.

Kane didn't reply, he just took a deep breath and said, "I'm going back now."

The two man glanced at each other sharing a look that could only mean one thing. *Never speak a word of this.*

Kane gave a slight nod in departure and walked away down the long deck before turning the corner and reaching the stern. Looking down he saw the black police speedboat that brought him on board bobbing in the water. The high-vis jackets of the two officers of the marine division standing out like cats' eyes.

Despite knowing there was no one around to see him, he still glanced around to ensure he was alone. Satisfied he was, he climbed over the railing and down the ladder into the speedboat. Both officers looked at him expectantly.

"False lead," lied Kane. "Sorry for all the bother."

"No harm done," said one of the officers. "Beats paperwork."

The officer started the speedboat's engine and sailed away from the ship. Kane was in a daze as they travelled back to Portsmouth. The noise of the engine filled his head like white noise. He realised as they approached the twinkling lights of the city that he was in shock.

His phone pinged as they grew nearer to the shoreline and his phone's reception returned. He looked down at the screen and saw a message that broke him from his trance.

What happened? Did you get him?

Got him, he typed back. *Thank you, Melissa. Ever thought of going undercover?*

Chapter 102

Richard

October 4th, 2023

"You finally made it, Chief."

Richard stepped out his black Mercedes, smoothed down his tie and shook Governor Corour's hand.

"Just about. Been in meetings all day. Feel like I'm bloody spinning plates."

"Yes... Sir Lovecroft."

"And the protests."

Corour briskly led Richard towards the entrance to Belmarsh. It wasn't a place Richard enjoyed visiting. The smell sickened him; cheap food, sweat, testosterone and something else he could never quite identify. Not that he wanted to.

"What's the damage?" he asked.

Corour sighed in response.

"That bad?"

"That bad."

He led Richard through six locked doors and down four long, cold corridors before they arrived at the centre of the wing that Bill had briefly called home.

"Jesus... Christ..." breathed Richard, looking around. "The smell in here."

As his eyes burned, his pulled his arm up over his mouth.

"Clean up is an ongoing project," said Corour.

"There's shit up the walls and... How did they pull the cafeteria tables out the floor? They're bolted down."

"You should see what they did to the visitors' room."

"I don't want to."

Not that Richard had a choice. He was already being led down another long corridor. The smell worsening with every step.

"Any casualties?"

"Couple of guards with cuts and bruises. Few prisoners with broken bones."

"Visitors?"

"Thankfully no injuries to them, no."

"No lawsuits then."

Corour gave Richard a wry smile over his shoulder. As they reached the visitors' room, he nodded in greeting to the two cleaners in hazmat suits who were scrubbing the carpet. As Richard entered the room, the stench of bleach clawing at his throat, he noticed they hadn't started cleaning the blood off the walls yet.

His gaze felt drawn to the top corner of the room where the television once sat. He noticed it now on the floor in pieces, the screen scattered in shards across the carpet.

"Gov, I appreciate the nice tour and everything, but why exactly are you showing me this?"

"Because during the clean up we found this. Wanted it out of here and in your hands before anyone else saw it."

Richard's stomach tensed in apprehension as he watched Corour reach into his blazer pocket and pull out a slim, black USB drive. Richard could see the small words penned roughly on the top in Tippex.

MET FOOTAGE

Although he recognised the drive, the scruffy handwriting was alien to him.

He tried to hide his rising nerves as he took it from Corour's fingers and thrust it into his own pocket.

"Did you... watch what was on it?"

Corour didn't answer. Just pointed to the floor where they stood and said, "It was found right here. Don't know if it was a visitor who brought it in or... We'll look over the CCTV."

Richard nodded gratefully.

"Of course one of the wardens saw the word MET and handed it in right away."

Richard looked deep into his eyes.

Do you know what's on it? You do, don't you? We wouldn't be standing here if you didn't.

"I appreciate this," said Richard, nodding again, this time in farewell. "I owe you."

***

Richard had the resting heartbeat of a bumblebee on the drive all the way back to his office. His mind whirring with questions.

What was it doing in Belmarsh?

How did it get it in?

Who the hell had it?

He slammed his office door closed and hurried to open his laptop. Thrusting the USB drive into the side, his tapped his foot up and down.

"Hurry up."

At last, the drive's folder opened. He felt compelled to watch the video again. To remind himself of the severity of what he had in his possession. As though the more he watched it, the more he knew he owned it. As long as he owned it, it was a secret.

His eyes flicked over the screen desperately looking for the video file in the drive's folder. But the more he searched the more he realised he was staring at an empty folder.

"Wait..." he whispered to himself. "No..."

He closed the folder and pulled the drive out before putting it back in.

Just a glitch, he hoped to himself.

But once again, the drive's folder opened up with nothing else in it. He held his breath as he yanked it back out the laptop again and shoved it back in.

Again, nothing.

Gradually, as the confusion fried his mind and he felt as though he couldn't breathe, the reality sank in. The USB drive was empty.

Chapter 103

Sebastian

October 10th, 2023

"Nice to see you again, buddy," said the young reporter, Sebastian as he took a sip of his cappuccino.

He'd only been at the national tabloid for two months, but felt as though he was falling behind. Felt as though he hadn't brought anything to his employer that offered enough of a scandal.

So when his old university friend and flatmate, Simon had called him out the blue with a story, he was on the first train to meet him. Mainly out of intrigue, but also out of desperation.

"Still can't believe you dropped out of uni to become a turnkey at Belmarsh."

"Philosophy wasn't for me," sighed Simon, taking a bite of his muffin. "Existentialism doesn't pay the bills."

"Yeah, but it doesn't get your arm broken either."

Sebastian nodded his head towards Simon's plaster cast.

"Is that part of the story? You didn't give much away on the phone."

"No... Well, kinda. This is."

Licking crumbs off his top lip, Simon reached into his pocket and pulled out what Sebastian initially thought was a lighter. It wasn't until it was placed on the table that he realised he was looking at a USB drive.

"What's this?"

"Found it. During the riot. There's a video on it. A video that'll put the shits up everyone at Scotland Yard."

Sebastian paused for a moment, taking another sip of his coffee.

"If you found it during the riot doesn't that mean someone's looking for it? Shouldn't you have handed it in?"

"I've thought of that, alright? Waited until I went home then called my boss and said I found it wedged inside the top of my boot. You know, like it fell in there during a scuffle. Switched it at the last minute."

"So your boss has a decoy one?"

"Yeah. It's identical. I made sure of it."

Sebastian frowned.

"What's on this that's so bad?"

"You'll see."

"Take it you made a copy."

"What do you think?"

Sebastian didn't recognise the man in front of him. A guy who had only a few years previously shared joints on his couch as they watched art films.

"I gotta go," Simon suddenly blurted out, rising from his seat as he took one last gulp of his coffee. "Let me know if your editor's interested."

"Wait, why are you keen to get this published?"

"Because it's messed up."

"Guess the money wouldn't hurt either."

Simon sheepishly looked away.

"That too... I met a girl."

"Oh?"

"She's pregnant."

"Oh..."

"Anyway... You'll keep me anonymous?"

"Yeah of course, buddy."

Sebastian watched as his old friend walked away, disappearing behind the queue at the counter. He waited long enough until he was gone before pulling his laptop out his satchel and pushing the USB drive into the side.

He had no idea what to expect. His pulse rose as the video player started and the grainy CCTV footage began to play on the screen.

Leaning forwards, he made sure no one around could see. Narrowing his eyes, he gazed at the video. He took it all in while holding his breath. The stairs, the approaching blinking lights and police vehicles. The figures in balaclavas who appeared at the exit and began pounding down the steel steps.

There was a flash at the edge of the screen. Then a body slumped against the stairs. He froze, caught his breath and ran the video back. This time he focussed on the edge of the screen from where the flash emanated. He saw the police sniper take aim at the figures on the steps a split second before the flash came out the barrel.

He watched it again.

Then again.

I'm watching a policeman assassinate someone. Someone unarmed. But why?

Feeling uncomfortable, he slammed down his laptop screen and tried to look normal. But he felt as though he'd been watching a snuff film in broad daylight.

When he had time to process what he'd seen, he reached for his phone and called his editor.

"Sebastian."

"Know how you've been really ramping up the stories about the MET recently? What with the group chats and-"

"What have you got?"

Sebastian smirked. Now the shock was wearing off he began thinking about his career. Perhaps this was what could launch it. What could provide the scandal he'd been looking for.

But although he knew what he had seen was big, really big. He had so many questions.

"I'm not sure what I've got yet. But I'm going to find out."

Chapter 104

Cecilia

October 12th, 2023

It was three in the morning and as she sat in her car, hands shaking against the steering wheel, she felt her whole body tense. She felt sick and opened the window to feel fresh air against her face.

Looking up, she saw Fitz' living room. The light was still on. She wondered what was keeping him up so late. Thoughts of Danielle, she imagined. Thoughts that kept her awake too.

"I can't do this," she said to herself, staring blankly out the window.

She thought about turning the key in the ignition and leaving, but how many times had she sat in this exact spot and backed out like a coward? How many times had she waited out here in the middle of the night? Coming so close to ringing Fitz' bell but never quite being able to bring herself to do it. But she knew tonight that she had to. It was all over now. She was leaving the country the next morning. Starting a new life in Spain with her newly gained money. It was now or never.

My conscience has to heal. I have to do this.

As she opened the door, she stopped for a second and tried to swallow down her nervous nausea. Then she pressed on. She reached Fitz' flat. Her hand shaking as she pressed the buzzer.

"Hello?"

"It's Cecilia."

A buzz signalled the main door had been unlocked.

"Well, this is a surprise," said Fitz as he watched from his front door as Cecilia climbed the stairs. "Didn't think you'd ever stoop so low to enter a common man's flat."

She shot him a sorry look and said, "Just let me inside, please."

He saw a genuine look of sadness in her eyes and stepped aside.

"Yeah, alright. Come in. I'll put the kettle on."

"Anything stronger?"

"No. Only tea."

She walked down the hallway and took a seat in the living room, too anxious to take in her surroundings. A few minutes passed before Fitz entered with two mugs of tea.

"Why are you still awake?" she asked Fitz.

"Big day tomorrow. I'm getting Sarah. I feel like a kid at Christmas."

Shit, she thought. She couldn't have timed this worse. He looked so happy. She knew the sparkle in his eyes was going to disappear before he'd even taken a sip of his tea.

"I've got to tell you something."

"Well, it can't be good," said Fitz, sitting down across from her. "Not at this time of night."

She could see the worry in his eyes. He knew something terrible was coming.

"Is it about Bill?"

"No, it's not about Dad."

"Just tell me what it is about."

"Danielle," she began.

She couldn't look at him and fixed her eyes on her hands. They were trembling. She thought about jumping off the couch and running away, disappearing to Spain and pushing it all out her head forever. But she knew she couldn't, because after everything that had happened, she knew Fitz had loved Danielle so deeply he would risk so much to gain a sliver of his family back. To get Sarah back. The only piece of Danielle left.

"It's my fault," she blurted out.

"What is?"

Fitz stared at Cecilia worried she was going crazy. He wondered if she'd been drinking, but he could see the sober fear in her eyes.

"What are you talking about?"

Slowly, Cecilia raised her eyes to his, tears falling freely from them.

"She's dead because of me, Fitz. I told the police where you were that night at the gallery."

Fitz felt a punch in his heart. He could barely breathe.

"You ratted us out to the cops?"

"It wasn't like that."

"Then what was it fucking like?"

She sobbed loudly and pressed the heels of her hands into her eyes.

"I knew what you were doing because I overheard Danielle on the phone to you. I didn't know much. Just that she was getting the painting back. That stupid, ugly painting."

She sniffed and wiped her cheeks with her sleeve.

"I confronted her, obviously. She told me everything."

Fitz couldn't believe what he was hearing.

"She told you? Why would she do that?"

Fitz wanted to leap off the couch and grab Cecilia, but he felt paralysed by the shock of what he was hearing.

"So you called the police. You wanted us caught. Your own sister in jail."

"No! I wanted them to intercept the whole thing before it started. Wanted to stop her from going ahead with it all."

He looked deep into Cecilia's watery eyes with a steely stare.

"She's dead… Cecilia. Because of you."

"I know that! Fitz… I know that. But how could I know it would end like that? I thought they would raid your flat before you started to do anything. I could never have imagined for a second that…"

Overcome by tears, she slumped her head into her hands and sobbed.

"She was murdered because of you, Cecilia," Fitz said to the top of her head as she cried. "Why?"

Chapter 105

Sebastian

October 13th, 2023

It had taken exactly three sleepless nights, but he had tracked him down. The man in the video that held the gun.

"I'm retired," he told Sebastian from the driver's seat of his worn out Vauxhall. "This is all behind me now, but it always got to me."

"You can get it all out now. Set the record straight."

"I've always wanted to but... It's dangerous."

"For who?"

"For me."

Sebastian watched as the man beside him stared into the distance as though lost in his memories. Gerald Alman was only in his early sixties, but looked much older. The serious drinking had begun as soon as his retirement did, and it had taken a toll on his weight and appearance. Now bald with deep lines around his eyes, he scratched at his dry cheeks and looked down the road into the darkness.

"Sorry we had to meet like this," he told Sebastian who was sat in the passenger seat. "It was too risky during the day."

"Why do you think you're still at risk?"

"Look, if that police commissioner bastard can order someone's murder like that," he clicked his fingers. "Then what makes you think he won't do away with me?"

Sebastian stifled a gasp.

"You're saying it was the MET's commissioner that ordered the death of Danielle Lovecroft?"

Gerald nodded.

"He was a sergeant back then, though. And it wasn't Danielle Lovecroft he wanted dead."

"Who then?"

Gerald bore his eyes into the windscreen as he sparked a cigarette.

"That crook, Fitz."

Sebastian couldn't believe the gold he was hearing. He looked down at his phone, double checking it was recording.

"You're saying the now commissioner of the Metropolitan police, Richard McNally ordered the murder of Fitz?"

He needed to make sure he had all the details in the recording.

"That's exactly what I'm saying," confirmed Gerald.

"But the big question I need to ask is... why?"

"Because Richard and Fitz went way back. Back into the days when Richard was undercover. We both were."

"You worked with Richard?"

"We go back years too. Both in the vice squad. Richard had gone undercover with the druggies, you know. That's when he met Fitz."

"Was Fitz selling drugs?"

"No, but his friends were. He was well connected. Knew everyone. There wasn't a crook that didn't respect him. They all wanted to be him. Can't blame them. I kinda wanted to be him too sometimes."

Gerald chuckled throatily and blew out smoke.

"Did Richard respect him?"

Gerald shrugged.

"He feared him. That's for sure."

"Feared him? Why?"

Gerald shook his head again, frowned and lit another cigarette.

"Look, I've been holding this in a long time, alright? I'm in fear too. Sooner or later they'll know it was me who spilled the beans and-"

"It's okay," soothed Sebastian. "You'll get your money and you can get out of here. There's enough for you to start a new life anywhere."

Gerald nodded and breathed in a long drag of his cigarette.

"Just make sure the money's in my bank before the story's out."

"Don't worry. It will be."

Sebastian was growing impatient. He didn't want to talk about money. He wanted juicy details.

"So... Why was Richard scared of Fitz?"

"Because Fitz knew what he was like."

"What was he like?"

"You know... Sleazy and that."

"What does that mean?"

"It means he was into young girls."

Sebastian froze.

"Richard McNally is a paedophile?"

Gerald sighed. He'd been holding it in for so many years.

"Not in the way you're imagining. There's no big cover up. No big secret VIP paedophile ring. Nothing like that. But there was one occasion. A party."

Gerald threw his finished cigarette out the window and reached into the packet for another. But seeing he'd ran out, he threw the empty packet out the window too and threw his head back against the seat.

"All of the boys were there," he said. "Fitz and his friends, and Richard and me. Loads of folk. There were drugs too. Loads of them, and Richard quite liked the nose candy back then."

"And there were children?"

"There was one. A friend of Fitz' little sister. She was fifteen."

"And Richard liked her?"

"Yeah. Liked her a lot. Couldn't keep his eyes off her all night. Was looking at her like she was a steak and he'd not eaten in a week."

"So, he tried it on with her?"

Gerald shifted awkwardly in his seat.

"I'm not saying I know all the details. All I'm saying is that one minute he was offering her a drink and the next she was unconscious in the back bedroom. People were watching, though. Fitz had noticed."

"He caught them together?"

"He went in and found Richard with his pants down and her barely sober enough to stand. Knocked seven shades of shit out of him. I heard the noise from the bathroom and came out to see it all."

"Jesus."

"That's not the half of it. Richard was half naked, right? Fitz saw the wire."

"Aw… God."

"Exactly," said Gerald, his eyes meeting Sebastian's. "Now Fitz knew two things. Richard was a cop, and he'd just raped an underage girl."

"Fucking hell."

"So Fitz had to go. He'd been holding this over Richard and he knew it would all get out eventually. His days would be numbered."

"Who else saw all this this at the party?" asked Sebastian.

"Just me. I think Fitz wanted to keep the information to himself, you know. He covered the girl up and sent her home in a taxi. Told no one. He was a smart lad. Knew he could sit on that information for an eternity. Keep Richard under control that way."

Sebastian looked at the regret that was written all over Gerald's face.

"So I've got to ask you one thing? Why shoot Danielle and not Fitz?"

"The bullet was meant for Fitz, but I didn't want to kill him. I aimed beside him, away from him to the right. I was aiming for the wall. I didn't know Danielle was going to run out at that exact moment just ahead of him. Couldn't have guessed she would be there and…"

His words trailed off as the words stuck in his throat.

"She was a mother," he choked. "I can't live with that."

Sebastian hit stop on his phone and the recording came to an end. He had everything he needed.

Chapter 106
Hawkins

October 13th, 2023

She sat at her desk staring into space. Ten days after the death of Bill was broadcast around the world, the task force debriefing meetings and paperwork had finally come to an end. Through the glass door she could see officers packing up the incident room. Out of her peripheral vision came the sight of a high-vis jacket.

"PC Clarkston... How can I help you?"

"Just came to say goodbye, I guess."

She watched him warily for a moment and he began to blush. He knew what was coming.

"There'll be an investigation," she said. "You know that. The whole thing was a gargantuan catastrophe."

He nodded.

"It was, yeah."

"There'll be questions."

"I know."

"Namely, how did you and Busby come to be discovered in your pants?"

"Our clothes burned off."

"And yet not a mark on either of you. Hmmm... Interesting."

He didn't know what to say. She was staring into his face like she could see into his brain, right into the truth.

She knew why he was there. Not to say goodbye, but to gauge how much shit he was in.

She resumed staring into space. Clarkston watched her curiously. It was as though she had turned to stone. From inside her handbag on the floor came the sound of her phone ringing. She reached for it on autopilot. Her gaze still miles away as she swiped to answer.

"Hello?"

Clarkston watched as whoever was on the other end of the line made her eyes light up. Her expression changed in a split second. Years dropped from her face as her skin glowed. She waved a hand at him, shooing him away to gain back her privacy.

He looked over his shoulder as he walked out the room, wondering who had the power to make Hawkins smile.

Chapter 107

Fitz

October 13th, 2023

An uncanny feeling settled over Fitz. It felt like it was only days ago he'd sat at the end of Bill's long driveway and waited for Danielle, not years.

His heart was fluttering in the same way it had done all that time ago. And as the little figure emerged at the front door, he felt adrenaline mixed with joy.

He did a double take as she began walking, her hand raised to hold hands with her nanny who was steering her down the drive towards him. She had grown so much in the short time since he'd seen her last. Had become to look even more like her mother, if that was possible. Even her mannerisms were like Danielle's.

Fitz only realised he was smiling when his cheeks began to hurt. He couldn't wait in the car any longer and jumped out to meet her. She froze as he ran at her. Staring up with a slight look of fear. Fitz stopped in his tracks and held back from throwing his arms around her. He wondered why she looked so scared. Then it hit him.

She didn't recognise him.

"Are you going to say hello to your daddy?" her nanny prompted.

A frown creased up Sarah's tiny features. Fitz felt his stomach drop.

"Hello," he said, as softly as he could.

He knelt down in front of her, the look of confusion on her face growing.

"You remember me, don't you?"

Her frown deepened as she looked up to her nanny for reassurance.

"It's okay," said Fitz, forcing a smile. "It's been a little while. But I remember you. I remember everything about you."

He noticed the nanny's hand out the corner of his eyes. Her grip on Sarah's hand tightening. As he followed his daughter's gaze up to her face, he saw tears threatening to spill out her eyes.

"I really appreciate everything you've done for her," he said.

His words were met with a silent and teary nod.

"So... Sarah... Are you ready?"

"Ready for what?"

Her voice was clipped and proper. She sounded so much like Danielle. No... Was it Cecilia she sounded more like?

"Are you ready to come home?"

She frowned again at her nanny.

"But I am home."

This is going to be tough, thought Fitz. As he looked into her questioning eyes, he wondered if he was doing the right thing. But the thought was dismissed from his mind as quickly as it came. *Of course I'm doing the right thing. I'm her father. It's what Danielle would want.*

"How about a little treat on the drive home?" he suggested to Sarah, whose eyes immediately widened.

"A treat? Like ice cream?"

"Sure! How about a Mc Flurry?"

"From Mc Donald's! I'm never allowed to go there!"

Her mouth dropped open in wonder as her nanny looked at Fitz with mild disgust.

"Bill always made sure the chef cooked her-"

"Mc Flurry it is!" he interrupted. "Don't worry. She'll not be having them everyday."

He reached out his hand in the hope that Sarah would take it. She hesitated for a second, looking over her shoulder at the house, then eventually smiled and curled her fingers around his. A wave of warmth and love flooded him.

"I've got so much to show you," he said. "I've just finished doing up your new room. There are so many toys and books."

"Books? With stories? I love stories."

"You do? Well, we can read lots of them."

She smiled again. The look on her face turned Fitz' heart into a marshmallow.

"Are you really my daddy?" she asked him.

"I am."

She started to skip alongside him happily, her grip on his hand tightening. Opening the back door, he lifted her gently to place her in the car seat. Her legs swinging like a doll's. Once strapped into the seat, Fitz double checked she was safe and brushed a strand of hair away from her eyes.

"When is Lucy coming?" she asked.

The nanny...

"Erm... Not for a while."

He didn't know how to break it to her that she wouldn't be coming at all. That after all this time without his daughter he wanted to do everything for her. Didn't want to miss out on a single thing no matter how small.

"Come on. Let's get that ice cream."

He settled into the driver's seat and looked at Sarah in the rear view mirror. As his eyes met hers, a sense of tremendous anxiety came over him. It was the same feeling that came over him sitting with Lucien as Bill's breakout unfolded. The same feeling he got moments before a big heist. But the prize now was bigger than any other, more valuable than money or priceless paintings. This adventure would be the biggest of his life, and the one he'd wanted the most.

Epilogue

Terry – December 21ˢᵗ, 2023

"You can't do this to me. I'm innocent!"

"For God's sake," moaned Terry with a roll of his eyes. "Do you know how many people I've heard say that?"

But the prisoner held a pleading look in his eyes as Terry guided him into his cell.

"Now get in and settle down."

The new inmate looked around at his new surroundings and burst into tears. Terry rolled his eyes again and clanked the cell door closed before locking it.

"That one needs a psych assessment," said one of the other guards who stood behind him.

"Yeah, I'd agree."

"Not that I care. Paedophile. The news said at least fifteen victims. I don't think it's right he gets extra protection in here. I say we put him in the wing with the general population. Let him get torn to shreds like that poor bugger in the library."

Terry sighed, exhausted.

"Bit harder, ain't it?" the other guard said to him.

"What is?"

"Your new inmate. Not like the other fella in that cell before. Sir Bill Whatsit."

Terry sighed again, this time sadly. He shouldn't have, but he missed Bill. He replayed that day on the motorway when the ambulance caught fire over and over his head. He could still smell the smoke.

"Yeah, Bill was easy enough," he said. "Anyway, that's me done for today. This boy's all yours."

"Great..."

Terry was eager to get home. The football was starting at seven and he had a pack of six beers waiting in the fridge he'd been thinking about all afternoon. As he had done every night for years, he arrived home after a bus commute of exactly forty-five minutes which he could never remember. It was always the same faces sitting around him, the same wet windows, faded bus seats and grumpy drivers. He walked up the path to the ground floor flat he'd lived in for decades. Nothing had changed since he'd moved in. Even the plant pots along the window ledge were the same ones from the day he'd moved in.

Everything was as it always had been. But as Terry pushed open his front door, he felt it stick against something on the floor. As he flicked the hallway light on, he saw it was an envelope.

That's different.

There was no printed address on the front. Only his first name handwritten in fountain pen. It had obviously been hand delivered. With his interest sparked, he tore it open. Out slipped two pieces of paper, both folded.

He opened the first one and was faced with handwriting that he instantly recognised from the numerous shopping lists he'd been given.

Terry, you were a good friend.

I have not forgotten you and wish you only the best.

I am sorry I could not have been there to give you this in person. You know why.

Enclosed, is enough to see to your future well-being and comfort so that you can perhaps enjoy your days away from the cells.

I have matched the amount as a donation to the Children's Leukaemia Research Trust. Like you, I am the father of an angel.

Take care,

B

Terry read it again. Then again. He thought he was hallucinating. Then he reached for the other piece of paper, it unfolded in his fingers as his eyes opened wider and wider. He now saw he was holding a cheque from the account of Miss Cecilia R Lovecroft.

He saw the zeros below her name. All seven of them and instantly grew dizzy.

"Ten million pounds," he choked, staggering backwards against the front door. "Bloody hell!"

***

Billie - July 5th, 2024

The Tijuana sun burned the top of Billie's scalp. She rummaged about in her backpack, simultaneously sipping on a Diet Coke, and pulled out her baseball cap. As she placed it on her head, she felt it gave her no relief from the scorching sun. It felt like nothing did.

From behind came the sound of English accents. Surprised, she turned around to see a group of, what she assumed were, gap year students ordering drinks and nursing their sunburn. Just a couple more days with the tourists and she was moving further south.

For the second time that day she reached for her phone and dialled Jacques' number. She didn't expect him to answer. He never did any more.

"Hello, Billie?"

"Christ. No freakin' way."

She almost dropped her phone.

"That's a nice greeting."

"Sorry, it's just that I was about to hang up."

"You've caught me at a good time."

In the background, she could hear the loud chatter and music of a busy bar.

"Where are you?" she asked.

"Algiers."

"Really?"

"You sound surprised."

"Thought you had your mind set on The Bahamas."

The noise in the background seemed to get louder.

"I've missed you," she said. "I mean I've been worried about you."

"No need to worry."

"You just took off without warning."

"Wasn't that the deal? Get the cash and go?"

Billie nodded silently to herself. She didn't know why it hurt to have him disappear. And over the last few months she kept trying to remind herself of all the reasons why she hated him.

"So, I made it to Mexico," she told him, changing the subject. "Work's starting on the dog rehab next month."

"No way, Billie. You really did it."

"Yeah... What I've always wanted."

"Streaming the whole thing as you go I suppose."

"Actually, I deleted my channel."

"You're kidding me."

"Didn't need it any more."

There was an awkward silence between the two for a few seconds. Behind Billie, the gap year kids grew merrier.

"So, you never said what you're doing in Algiers."

Jacques' response was to breathe smoke out over his phone so it sounded to Billie like a snake was hissing into her ear.

"I met a girl," he said. "Or rather *girls*."

His words were nonchalant and relaxed, but they hit Billie as though he'd yelled them.

"Oh..."

If he heard the disappointment in Billie's voice, he didn't acknowledge it.

"Anyway," he said, his voice picking up urgency. "Have you heard from Lucien?"

"No. Why would I?"

In the background, Billie could hear a girl's giggle.

"Be with you in a minute, babe," she heard Jacques' say to the girl, and her stomach twisted into a knot.

"Well, I'll let you go," she said.

"Yeah, good luck with your cats."

"Dogs, Jacques."

But the line was already dead and Billie found herself staring at her phone in her hand. The more she looked at it, the more she wondered why she even had it.

"Screw it," she said, rising from the table.

She left a generous tip and, grabbing her phone, walked towards the nearest bin. Unlocking it one last time, she typed out:

Good luck, Bill. Wherever you are. Can't thank you enough.

The second she hit send, she let the phone tumble out her fingers into the bin. As she walked away, she heard it ringing, but she didn't turn back to see who it was.

***

Jacques - July 5th, 2024

Jacques entered the bathroom of the bar, the sweltering Algerian heat bringing out the ammonia smell of the toilet. He pulled the lid down and sat on top as he listened to the phone ring. Why wasn't she picking up? He felt bad at the way he had left things with her, but what could he do? He'd moved on. They all had. Wasn't that the deal?

Still, every time Billie popped into his head there was a sinking feeling in his stomach. A sense of unfinished business. He hadn't meant to sound like such an obnoxious ass a moment ago, but he was distracted by Carmen in front of him. He was only human.

When Billie didn't answer, he huffed and stared at his phone.

There was someone else who wasn't answering, and that felt so much worse. It didn't bring on a sinking feeling but rather an intense rage. He'd been calling for months, even though he knew after the first few times it was pointless. He'd been screwed over, and he couldn't accept it. He'd track the bastard down for the rest of his life if he had to.

He dialled the number now and waited, holding his breath. Like the dozens of times before, he reached voicemail.

"Lucien, you piece of shit. I'm calling you again and I'll never stop until you give me an explanation. Or better still, give me the money you promised."

He'd been doing the maths in his head ever since the money arrived. The two billion he received from a clueless Bill was far from a small sum. There were times he couldn't comprehend how much it was. He'd even written it down several times by hand just to marvel at all the zeros. But it was less than what Lucien had promised. Him and Lucien were supposed to be a team. A secret team within a team that was going to take it all from under Fitz' and everyone else's noses. But the moment Bill was taken on board the ship Lucien vanished.

"Honey?" came Carmen's creamy voice from outside the bathroom followed by a timid knock.

"I'll be out in a second, babe."

He hung up, splashed his face with warm water from the tap that was supposed to be cold and looked at his reflection. He'd been in the sun ever since he left England and it had made his usual youthful complexion leathery. So had the constant supply of cocaine and alcohol. It looked like he'd aged ten years in as many weeks. But he was having the time of his life, wasn't he?

Unlike Billie, who had a plan of what to do with her money, Jacques didn't have a clue. At first, he'd kidded himself into thinking he'd use it for good. Put hundreds of millions into Power to the Planet and save the environment like he'd promised everyone. There was so much good he could do with his money. How many wind farms could he build? How many solar panels?

But for some reason, he couldn't bring himself to care about any of that any more. He only thought of parties and beautiful women. They flocked to him now as though they could smell his fortune.

"Honey?" repeated Carmen from outside the door. "Are you okay?"

"Yeah, babe. Hang on."

He splashed his face with water once again and stepped out to see his latest girlfriend, Carmen waiting for him, her beautiful curls tumbling around her slender, brown shoulders. The moment he saw her, he forgot about Lucien. For now anyway.

"Hmmm... You look good," he said, squeezing her against his chest. "Let's get you back home."

***

There wasn't a surface inside the luxurious bedroom of Jacques' rented apartment that wasn't covered in white dust. On the bedside table sat two empty glasses of champagne. All across the floor, designer clothes were strewn. The room hadn't been cleaned in weeks and the smell of unwashed clothes and bodies melted into the furniture. On the bed, Jacques grunted.

"Ow!" cried out Carmen. "You're hurting me."

"Shut up."

"No! Stop!"

She slapped him hard and pushed him off. He took in a sharp inhale of breath and held his cheek.

"Bitch."

"You were being too rough," she cried, jumping off the bed and gathering her clothes.

"Hey, I was only playing. Where are you going?"

"Away from you."

He was still holding his flaming hot cheek as he watched her slam the door on the way out.

Oh, well. There'll be others.

He looked at the state of the room, at the cocaine on the table and the empty booze bottles.

Was I too rough?

He didn't know.

Money had done things to him. Contorted his thoughts. Or had it made him more of himself? Had it just exaggerated desires that were already there?

Over the last few months he felt he could do whatever he wanted, and no matter how much of a bastard he was, the girls kept coming and so did the drugs. He didn't need to pretend to be a good guy any more. He got what he wanted the moment people caught a glimpse of his money. He felt like he had super powers.

Pulling on his clothes, he looked in the mirror and saw the red hand print on his cheek. But the alcohol and cocaine had numbed the sting of Carmen's slap.

Wired, drunk and now alone, he decided to get dressed and head outside in search of more cigarettes. As he left his apartment, he tipped the concierge generously on the way out and stepped into the night. He had no idea what time it was, or even what day it was. He was living hour to hour like an animal giving into any bodily urges that came along.

He walked down the street to where he'd bought cigarettes at a kiosk the day before, but as he arrived he noticed it was closed up for the night.

"Looking for something?" came a voice behind him.

He turned to see the source of the perfect English spoken in a thick Algerian accent.

"Cigarettes," said Jacques as he looked down at the figure in front of him dwarfed by a red Adidas tracksuit.

At first, he thought he was looking at a child, then he looked into the man's eyes and saw someone perhaps twice his own age.

"Cigarettes?" said the figure studying Jacques' face. "Or something more."

"Maybe... Something more."

"Come with me."

He gestured for Jacques to follow him down a nearby alleyway. Jacques paused at the entrance and peered into the darkness.

"Don't be scared," said the figure. "I have cigarettes. Marlboro, right? Amongst other things I think you'd like."

If Jacques was sober he'd have made a different decision. Done the sensible thing and hurried back to his apartment. But as his eyes adjusted to the darkness of the alleyway, the only thought that came into his head was, *The guy won't try anything funny. He's only little.*

And that's when he felt it.

The white heat that entered just below his ribs. At first he thought he'd been punched. Then he felt blood running down his side, down his legs and into his shoes. He felt small fingers enter his pockets and fish for his wallet.

"Give me everything," ordered the figure.

Jacques looked up in time to see them rifle through the notes in his wallet before tossing it on the ground.

"Give me the rest."

"That's all I've got on me."

"Hand over your watch and earrings. Hurry up."

Jacques grew too dizzy from blood loss to do as we was told and slumped to his knees.

"Come on. Give me that Rolex, rich boy. Think I haven't been following you. Think I don't know where you live."

"Take what you want just don't kill me."

Jacques was now crying. Tears mixing with his blood.

"Take everything. I don't care."

He could barely see, but as he gazed down, he saw his blood run into the stone gutter and catch the moonlight.

"That's for my sister," said the figure.

"I don't know your sister."

"You dishonoured her."

The figure punched Jacques, and he fell onto his back before his watch and earrings were snatched from his body.

"Sheba," said the figure. "Remember her?"

Jacques' eyes fluttered shut.

The name was familiar. Was it last week he'd had her back at his apartment, or the week before? He couldn't remember what she looked like. Had she left in tears like Carmen had? He had no idea.

The heat in his side subsided until he became cold. He shivered as he heard the figure's footsteps hurry away down the alleyway. He managed to open his eyes one last time and see the moon before his eyelids became too heavy and closed again.

He cursed Lucien as he drifted away, then his mind focussed on one last image of Billie as he faded completely.

***

Amelia & Marcus - August 15th, 2024

Amelia rolled over and lay her hand on the bed beside her. Where she was used to feeling a large, warm body, she now felt empty sheets. As she sat up, she heard a sound from the en-suite bathroom.

Was that sobbing? Retching? She wasn't sure.

"Marcus?"

She pushed open the bathroom door to find him hunched over the sink. She saw his face in the mirror, dripping in sweat and deathly pale.

"Christ. Are you okay?"

He breathed hard as though he was struggling to pull oxygen into his lungs.

"Panic attack?" she asked, pulling him into a tight hug from behind.

He nodded without saying anything, but the look in his eyes screamed, *Help me*.

"It's okay. It's okay," soothed Amelia. "You've been through this a hundred times before. You can get through it again. Just breathe okay. In through your nose, out through your mouth. Okay? Got it?"

He nodded again.

She could feel the tension inside his body dissipate slightly the more she held him. At last, he managed to turn around and hug her back as he regained his voice.

"That was a bad one."

"I thought they'd stopped."

"Me too. Not had one in almost a month."

"It's okay. Maybe this will be your last one. You've been doing so well."

He hugged her tight and kissed the top of her head, still gasping, but feeling more normal with each passing second.

"I had a nightmare," he said.

"About what?"

"There was fire, smoke, screaming. You were trapped somewhere and I was struggling to get you out."

"Just a dream," she said, running her hands through his hair. "It's normal to feel anxious now and again."

"How are you able to do that?"

"Do what?"

"Calm me down like this? I feel fine now. My therapist can't even make me feel like this."

"It's just love, is what it is."

She reached up on tip toes and kissed him hard. When she pulled away he was smiling.

"I think you're in need of some breakfast."

"Aw, I couldn't face it," he said.

"Some tea then."

She was already walking out the door, her feet silent against the cool tiles of the bedroom floor. Marcus peeked around the doorway to see more of her as she walked into the hallway. He couldn't get enough of the way her body moved; strong, feminine, and all his.

His panic attack now felt like it happened years ago. Stepping into the shower, he cleansed away the worries he had when he woke up and walked out feeling like a new person. A person excited to face the day with Amelia by his side.

Slipping on his dressing gown, he moved downstairs towards the kitchen. It still amazed him how long it took. In his old flat he could throw his biscuit wrappers into the kitchen from the couch in the living room and hit the bin every time. Now it took exactly forty-five seconds to reach the kitchen from the bedroom. He'd timed it.

When he arrived, he found Amelia pouring boiling water into a china cup. The sun shone through the floor to ceiling windows illuminating the rich amber of the kitchen's original terracotta features. Marcus wasn't much of a cook, but he'd fallen in love with the room the second he saw it. It made him imagine a future with big family meals around the table and endless hours laughing with friends over card games and drinks.

"You okay?" asked Amelia, pushing the cup across the counter at him. "You're looking a bit dreamy."

"Yeah just... happy."

"You sure?"

"Of course, I'm happy. You're here, ain't ya?"

He laughed and leaned across the counter to kiss her.

"*You* don't look so happy, though," he noted, seeing her frown.

"Urgh, it's nothing. Just noticed I had an email from my Mum."

"Oh."

"Yeah..."

"It's never good news, is it?"

"It's not bad news either. It's just moany."

They both chuckled.

"What's up now?" asked Marcus.

"She wants another sauna built."

"What? Why?"

Amelia shrugged.

"So let me get this straight. Until three months ago she lived in a high rise that could fit inside half of this kitchen and now she wants a second sauna."

"Pretty much."

They both laughed again.

"She can have it," said Amelia. "Whatever she wants."

Marcus grimaced. It wasn't that he didn't like Amelia's mother, but he couldn't shake the feeling she was taking advantage of her daughter. The same day the cash from Bill arrived Amelia was on the hunt for a house for her parents. The more she searched, the more her mother came up with increasingly strict conditions.

"Your dad gets a sore back. He'll need to live somewhere warm."

"My knees hurt. I can't have too many stairs."

"I'm going through the menopause. It can't be anywhere too hot."

Marcus felt like sending her to the moon, but Amelia had settled on the French Riviera instead, in a spectacular coastal mansion ten miles from Cannes. It was close enough to be a short flight to their own home in Tuscany, but far away enough that she wasn't on their doorstep. Somehow though, it was never good enough.

"How does she think you're affording this?" asked Marcus, sipping his tea. "She doesn't still believe that-"

"I got an out of court settlement from the MET? Yeah. What else could I tell her?"

Now it was Marcus' turn to shrug.

"What happened to your usual triple espresso latte?" asked Marcus as he saw her sipping a peppermint tea.

A look came across her eyes he'd never seen before. It worried him, but he wasn't sure what to say. She glanced down at her hands and said, "Just trying to cut down on caffeine."

"Why?"

When she looked back up at him, her expression had deepened.

"Because..."

She put her thumb in her mouth and chewed on her nail.

"I was going to tell you first thing this morning because you were asleep when I did the test last night. But then-"

"What test?"

She looked at him panic stricken for a moment before ignoring him and walking out the room. Marcus watched her stride out the kitchen, dumbfounded.

"What test?" he shouted out the kitchen door.

There was no sound for a full ten seconds until he could hear her feet rushing back down the stairs.

"Close your eyes," she said as she returned.

"Eh?"

"Just close your eyes. Please..."

He did as he was told, his nerves rising.

"Now hold out your hand."

"You're not going to put something gross in it, are you? Like a spider."

"Marcus, why would I be putting spiders in your hands? With your panic attacks as well."

She couldn't help but laugh, and kissed his forehead as she placed something long, light and solid in the palm of his hand.

"What's this? A pen?"

"You can open your eyes now."

The first thing he saw were tears streaming Amelia's cheeks. Then he looked down at his hand and was faced with two lines. It felt as though his eyes were glued to them. As though he couldn't look away even if he was being ordered to at gunpoint. Amelia wondered why he was sitting silently for so long and gently pushed his shoulder.

"Marcus, it's a positive pregnancy test."

"I know what it is," he said, his voice strained tight.

Only now did she realise he was crying.

He kissed her hard and squeezed her against his stomach.

"We're going to have a family," he cried, delighted.

He looked around the kitchen and thought of their future again and the big family dinners. And he thought of the one person who would be so happy for them.

"Fitz," he said, squeezing Amelia tighter. "If it's a boy we have to name him Fitz."

***

Cecilia – August 15th, 2024

She snaked her way through the dining tables in search of the bathroom. Above, the golden hue from the chandelier glowed across her face. It wasn't her first time dining at the almost impossible to get a reservation at, Denia Hotel. It was, however, her first date with Dwight. Her nerves had been raging all night. Every time she looked into his blue eyes butterflies fluttered. But what really made her nervous were all the questions he'd asked her.

"I really am sorry about your father. How have you been coping?"

"Did you make your fortune through investing in tech like he did?"

"How did you cope with him being in Belmarsh?"

"Is it all true about the thirty-eight billion pounds?"

And on it went.

She didn't know how to answer, so she had made an excuse and said she needed the bathroom. It wasn't a total lie. She did feel the urge to check on how much her lipstick had shifted after kissing Dwight. It was just the once. Just a quick peck, but it was something she would never normally do. She always played hard to get, so why did she feel giddy like a schoolgirl tonight?

Once in the bathroom, she was pleased to see her lipstick was intact. She fluffed up her hair, ran her wrists under cold water to refresh herself and took a deep breath.

From inside her purse, she felt her phone vibrate. Unlocking it, she saw she'd received a message from Harold. Without thinking, she opened it and saw he'd sent her a photograph. She didn't recognise him at first. Standing on the deck of a luxury yacht with a beautiful woman on his arm, he was at least ten shades darker than the last time she'd seen him and ten times happier.

Just wanted to say thank you. Everything great at Prestige.

"What a handsome chap," came a voice from over Cecilia's shoulder.

She raised her gaze and saw the face behind her in the mirror. There was no mistaking the red hair, perfect complexion and elfin features.

"Phenomena?"

"I thought I saw you come in here. I should have known you were partial to the oysters at Denia. Aren't they the best?"

How was it possible Phenomena looked even lovelier than before?

"Looks like you've been eating more than oysters. You look like you've been sleeping in a tub of collagen."

"Actually, I'm just back from Ecuador," said Phenomena, breezily. "It's been nothing but rest and relaxation for the last few months. I think we all deserved that."

Phenomena walked a few steps away from Cecilia and touched up her lip gloss in the mirror.

"I have to ask," she said, pouting. "Who is that man you're with? He looks familiar. He must be an actor."

"He's a model. He was in the latest Hugo Boss campaign."

Phenomena raised an eyebrow.

"Didn't take you for a girl who liked her men groomed. Thought you liked them more manly."

"You did?"

"Like those military men."

Cecilia didn't say a word. Just kept staring at Phenomena's face.

"I met him at a charity dinner the night I came back from Spain," she said, pulling her eyes back to her own reflection. "Dwight volunteers for an arts program. He's an amazing guy."

Phenomena frowned and turned round.

"You volunteer there too?"

"Actually I do," replied Cecilia proudly. "I love it. Getting to work with the kids. Teaching them about art. We give drawing lessons, help them express themselves. It's amazing."

For a long second, Phenomena thought Cecilia was joking. When she realised she was being wholly serious, her expression morphed into one of pure happiness.

"That's great!" she beamed. "Honestly. That must feel really good to do."

"It does and... Well, Danielle would have liked me to do it."

They both shared a soft, tender look then returned to their own reflections.

"And what are you doing these days?" asked Cecilia.

"Oh, all sorts of things."

"Don't tell me too much," said Cecilia, sarcastically. "You always were the mysterious one."

"I guess I'm just a private person."

Phenomena placed her lip gloss back in her purse and turned to face Cecilia.

"It was lovely bumping into you," she said. "But I better head back to my own date."

"Wait."

Cecilia reached out and lightly touched Phenomena's shoulder.

"I've always needed to know something."

Phenomena narrowed her eyes.

"About me?"

"About who you are. Everyone in the team had their story. Billie had her YouTube thing, Jacques had Power to the Planet, we know Amelia had a bone to pick with the Met and -"

"Marcus was on the other side of the law."

"Exactly. So... What side were you on?"

Phenomena, for the first time, appeared flustered. The look of anxiety in her eyes did nothing to stop Cecilia pressing further. If anything, it piqued her interest even more.

"Just tell me. How exactly did you know Lucien?"

"He was an old friend."

"An old friend or a boyfriend?"

"Does it matter?"

"If you have to ask that question then clearly it's the latter."

"He was never anything romantic to me."

"But he was more than a friend?"

"Not exactly but-"

"He *wanted* to be more than a friend?"

"What's with all the questions? None of this matters now, does it? It's all over. We all got what we wanted."

"Did we?"

"What does that mean?"

Phenomena was no longer anxious, she was angry, and she started to back away from Cecilia towards the door.

"It means Lucien wanted you all along, didn't he? But you were never interested. I don't blame you. He gave me the creeps. But you enjoyed what he could give you. The position on my dad's team, all the money that offered and-"

"It wasn't like that. I loved Lucien."

"So you *were* together."

"No!"

Cecilia was angry now too. Why did Phenomena have to be so stuck up and secretive? Why could she never be an open book like Billie or Marcus or Amelia?

"Like what, then? You loved him but you weren't *in* love with him."

"Oh my God, Cecilia. I've had enough of this."

Phenomena reached for the door handle.

"What was he?" continued Cecilia. "A sugar daddy?"

"He was the man who saved me!"

The ferocity in Phenomena's voice sent Cecilia reeling back.

"He saved me," said Phenomena. "From a life you'd know nothing about. From misery someone as privileged as you could never believe."

There were tears in Phenomena's eyes that burned their way through her mascara. For the first time, Cecilia felt as though she was staring at the real Phenomena. The actual woman behind all the smoke and mirrors and sequins and illusion. And this woman knew what pain was.

"His name was Dan," said Phenomena. "The worst thing that ever happened to me."

"A boyfriend?"

"And a client of Lucien's. One of his high rollers."

She stared down into the sink as though it was where her memories of him lay. Her top lip turning up in disgust.

"I'll spare you the details," she said, if only to spare herself the pain of remembering. "But he was evil. Think of a crime and he'd committed it."

"Let me guess. Lucien saw a beautiful young thing like you in danger and intervened."

"You say that like it's nothing. I was only seventeen. Dan beat the living daylights out of me every day I lived with him. He made me do things that... Things for money that..."

She swallowed hard, unable to continue. Danielle didn't need to hear the rest. She understood.

Stepping closer to Phenomena, she placed a hand on her arm gently.

"I'm sorry. I had no idea."

"No one does. I was a mouse when Lucien met me. Just a kid. But Lucien got me away from Dan. Got me in touch with Woman's Aid. Helped me get away to live a new life. He even introduced me to the man that would become my mentor. If it wasn't for Lucien I wouldn't have my career."

Danielle wanted so hard to believe that Lucien was the kind-hearted good Samaritan Phenomena was describing, but she couldn't shake the image of the man she knew.

"I know what you're thinking," said Phenomena. "You're asking yourself what Lucien got in return."

Danielle glanced away.

"Sure, I could see the way he looked at me from time to time. But if you must know, he kept his distance. Our relationship was complicated and strange, but I valued it. He's why I came back to London. I'm worried about him."

"If there's one person in the world to never worry about, it's Lucien."

"But he's off the radar completely. That's not like him."

Danielle could see the worry in Phenomena's eyes, but she didn't share her anxiety.

"That man's probably across the other side of the world right now living his life to the fullest with my Dad's fortune. Which is what you should be doing too. Get yourself back to Ecuador."

Phenomena sniffed hard, reached across the counter for a tissue and dabbed her eyes.

"I mean it," said Cecilia. "It's time to enjoy yourself."

She reached over and gave Phenomena a quick but tight squeeze, then left the bathroom. She caught sight of Dwight looking for her across the room and gave him a little wave.

"Everything okay?" he asked as she sat down. "You were in there for an age."

"I bumped into someone."

But she was already pushing Phenomena out of her mind along with Lucien and the rest of the team.

"Anyone I know?"

"No, no."

"You look upset."

"I'm fine," she said, reaching for her drink. "Let's just enjoy ourselves."

Back in the bathroom, Phenomena was still dabbing at her eyes. She wasn't entirely lying when she told Cecilia she was back in London for Lucien. But she wasn't telling the whole truth either. There was one other reason.

With a deep breath she reached for her phone and scrolled through her contacts. Hitting dial, she waited, hoping to hear his voice. But just like before, the call went to voicemail.

"Hello, Fitz? It's me. Again. Just wondering if you're still in town. I've been trying to get hold of you but I guess you've gone underground. Obviously. Just let me know if you get this. I…"

She held her breath for a second. She didn't want to sound desperate, but at the same time, she was past caring.

"Fitz, I miss you," she sighed. "And I want to see you again."

She stopped short of saying something else she'd regret, then hung up and walked back out into the restaurant.

***

Fitz - August 16th, 2024

The news reporter looked solemn as she spoke on the steps outside The Old Bailey Court. Fitz watched the TV over the top of his laptop screen almost as though he was hiding behind it. He knew the words she spoke were meant to bring good news, but he didn't feel happy at hearing them. Only numb and distant. They felt meaningless.

"Former commissioner of the Metropolitan Police, Richard McNally was found guilty today of seven charges of corruption. This comes six months after an anonymous whistleblower made serious allegations against Commissioner McNally in a national tabloid. Back at the studio is David Nivens with the story."

The camera cut away from the reporter and back to the BBC studio where a clean-cut, sharp-jawed Nivens sat behind a glass desk with a detached expression.

"Thanks, Tabitha. Yes there have been many allegations against the now disgraced commissioner. The biggest of which being that he ordered the murder of an infamous member of London's organised crime community, Tony Fitzgerald. According to this whistleblower, this resulted in the shooting and subsequent death of billionaire, Sir Bill Lovecroft's daughter, Danielle Lovecroft. I mean, these are exceptional claims with the mystery deepening considering Fitzgerald was reported as a missing person following the death of Sir Lovecroft. And his location still remains unknown."

From down the hall, Fitz heard the sound of Sarah's happy footsteps running over the floorboards and he hurried for the remote to turn off the TV. She grinned as she entered the room.

"Hello, sweetheart. What are you up to?"

"Just playing."

"That's nice."

She grinned, did a pirouette in the centre of the room then ran back out into the hallway.

"I'll be back! I need to get something."

"Sweetheart, be careful running in the house!" Fitz called after her. "You could slip and fall."

"Okay, Daddy!"

Seeing how happy she was distracted him from the feeling he got seeing Richard's face on the news. Of hearing Danielle's name spoken from the mouths of people who'd never met her. Of hearing his own name mentioned...

He knew he should have felt happy Richard was found guilty. But Danielle wasn't coming back. Sarah was growing up without a mother regardless. And he knew an account given by an anonymous whistleblower wasn't enough to secure murder charges. He wanted to feel happy justice was being served at least for the lesser charges of corruption, but his feelings were complicated and conflicted.

He diverted his attention back to his laptop where he saw an unopened e-mail from Marcus. Clicking it open, he read the few short lines of text, his eyes falling on one word that had been written in all capital letters.

PREGNANT!

He was so taken aback he hadn't noticed Sarah had returned until he heard her shuffling about on the couch beside him.

"Daddy? Why are you smiling so much?"

"Because I got some very good news," he said, closing his laptop and opening his arms for Sarah to lean into. "I'm going to be an uncle."

"You are?"

"In a way. Two very good friends of your daddy's are going to have a baby."

"Will they bring the baby here?"

"I don't think so, sweetheart."

"Awwww...."

The sun streamed through the living room windows onto Sarah's now tanned face. Her hair had grown more blonde over the last couple months to the point it was almost turning white.

"What have you got there?" he asked, now seeing what she was holding.

"A bucket."

"And what's that for?"

"Sea shells!"

"More of them? But you have so many already."

Since they moved to the coast, she had developed an obsession with anything to do with the sea. At first, she'd covered her room in mermaids, then whales and dolphins. Then her affection had grown to encompass all marine life and now, this week, she was thinking about nothing but sea shells.

"Come on. Let's get you some more then, shall we?"

There was nothing Fitz liked more than making his daughter happy, and he had the time now to do whatever she wanted.

"Put your shoes on, sweetheart," he said, standing up and looking out the window at the beach.

Luckily for Sarah, the sea she loved so much was only metres away. Sometimes, when the wind was blowing and the waves were swelling it felt like you could reach out the window and touch it. Today, the water was calm with the choppy waves of the early morning diminishing to nothing but a few frothy crests that lapped the sand. In a matter of seconds, Sarah was beside Fitz ready to go.

They stepped out through the French doors into the warmth of the Jersey sunshine. It was a spot on the island Fitz had given so much thought. When the time came for him to split the fortune and leave London, he had first decided he would move to a distant paradise like Billie or Marcus had. He'd even contemplated settling nowhere and instead travelling the world with Sarah, never resting, just having one adventure after another. But then it came to him one day.

Jersey had the best of both worlds. It was familiar enough to feel as though he still lived at home, but warm enough to have the climate of abroad. More importantly, it was a place Sarah could grow up comfortably.

The house he'd chosen, an expansive modern build with a robust security system, was the only house for miles. You could stand on the edge of the front garden and see a car coming from three miles away. And the land as far as he could see was his. Even the beach belonged to him.

Sarah ran ahead, bucket in hand and her hair blowing behind her.

"Wait, sweetheart. Don't run too far."

He jogged to catch up. Sarah stopped as she reached a rock pool and without hesitation, shoved her hand into the water.

"Look!" she gasped. "A crab!"

"Don't touch it, honey."

"I think he's stuck. He can't be happy."

"It's okay. I'll grab him. Move your fingers or he'll nip ya."

Trust her to worry about the feelings of a crab. She's so much like her mother.

Pulling his sleeves down over his fingers, he picked up the crab and placed it on the sand. They both watched as it scuttled away down the beach.

"I'm hungry," Sarah suddenly blurted out.

He laughed and pushed his hand into his pocket.

"Look what I've got," he said, producing a bar of chocolate.

Over the last six months, fatherhood had turned him into a walking emergency kit. Every pocket holding essential supplies, from plasters and snacks to hair bobbles and of course, sea shells.

Sarah took the chocolate with a smile and sat on the edge of a rock to unwrap it. Fitz sat down beside her and kissed the top of her head. As they both stared out to sea, he remembered the day he had collected her. How he had been so worried, so full of fear that after everything, things might not work out with her.

What if she hates living with me?

What if she loves her nanny more than me?

But he needn't have worried. The first few weeks were tense. She was teary and confused after the move and it took some time for the two to rekindle their bond. But when it returned, it only grew stronger with every day. To Fitz, it felt as though she'd always been with him. As though life with her couldn't be more natural.

"What are you looking at?" Sarah asked, looking up at Fitz with a face covered in melted chocolate.

He bent down to place his face beside her.

"See that beach over there," he said, pointing into the distance.

She squinted into the sun and nodded.

"I went there with your Mummy once. On holiday not long after we first met. We ate lobster and ice cream."

"Will I see Mummy again?"

He didn't know what to say.

As Sarah waited for him to answer, the sound of an engine rumbling came from around the other side of the house. Instantly, Fitz was on his feet with the hairs along his neck standing on end.

"Come inside," he said, taking her hand.

He led her back into the living room, closed the door and sat her on the couch.

"Don't move until I come back."

He left her licking chocolate off her fingers as he made his way through the house to the front door then out onto the driveway. Just beyond the gate he saw a red van snaking its way down the country lane.

He cursed himself for finally feeling relaxed. He was always aware someone from his past could come looking for him.

And who is this?

The red van braked softly at the front gate. He watched, muscles tensed, as the driver jumped down onto the gravel.

"Morning!" he called out to Fitz with a friendly wave. "Delivery!"

Fitz tentatively approached the van.

It was only now that he noticed there was someone in the passenger seat with dark eyes that had seen monstrous things. He gave Fitz a serious nod then climbed out to reveal himself as more of a beast than a man. Fitz wondered how a person so big could look so inconspicuous in the front seat. He watched him move. Recognised his movements instantly as those of a military man. Then it dawned on him.

This is no ordinary delivery.

As the two men swung open the back doors, Fitz couldn't help looking over the van.

"This is bulletproof," he said to himself.

"Certainly is," replied the driver from inside, hearing him.

Fitz looked inside to find there were no other deliveries in the van, only his. And it was enormous.

"Who are you?" he asked.

There was no response.

Fitz grew uneasy. He watched as the two men picked up the delivery in their plate sized hands and carefully manoeuvred it out onto the tarmac.

"Where's it going?" asked the driver.

"What is it?"

Again, there was no response.

"Who sent you?" Fitz demanded to know, now angry.

"Look, I don't know the details. All I know is it came with this note."

The driver handed Fitz a small, white card. On which lay two words in handwriting he immediately recognised.

For Sarah

"Bring it inside," said Fitz.

Despite the size of the package, the two men had no problem carrying it in through the front door and down the long hall. Fitz guided them into the living room where Sarah still sat on the couch with chocolate on her cheeks. She looked up, confused as the two men sat the package down and balanced it against the back wall. It was almost as tall as they were and ten times as wide.

"Have a good day," said the driver. "We'll let ourselves out."

Fitz watched them leave then turned to the delivery covered in seemingly endless layers of protective wrapping.

"What's that?" asked Sarah.

"It's for you."

Fitz left the room momentarily and returned with a Stanley blade taken from his toolbox in the garage. Sarah tilted her head up, eyes wide with curiosity as Fitz carefully pushed the tip of the blade into the wrapping and sliced down. He peeled it back carefully, as though undressing a woman, and let the paper and six inches of bubble wrap fall to his feet.

"A picture!" declared Sarah. "Is it really for me?"

"It's for you, sweetheart."

Fitz picked up Sarah and took a step back so she could see it all clearly.

"What do you think?"

"I love it," she beamed with a vigorous nod. "Look," she said, pointing to the corner. "A baby angel."

***

Bill - August 24th, 2024

It didn't look real. The colours were too vibrant. He felt the need to push his hand down through the turquoise water so the coral could touch his fingertips. He floated above it for a few seconds. Or was it minutes or hours? Time didn't exist under the water. It didn't matter any more. Nothing did.

Something hard brushed against his stomach and he looked down to see a turtle float underneath him, oblivious to how beautiful it was. Everything was beautiful under here. It was like exploring an alien landscape. It seemed like every time Bill put on his snorkel and sank into the calm, warm waters of the Cayman Islands he was seeing it all again for the first time. There was something new every time, he couldn't stop marvelling at all the plants and wildlife.

He looked up through the water towards the sky. It was darkening slightly as the sun set casting a red glow overhead. It gave the already mesmerising sights beneath him even more of an otherworldly feel. But it was time to head home. She'd be waiting for him.

He took his time swimming back to the shore. He felt the air cool him as he stepped out the water onto the beach, but it was by no means cold. It never was. Walking slowly, he pulled off his snorkel and listened to the sound of the waves lapping the rocks and sand. It always calmed him. After months of glorious sunshine, the sea, daily swimming and more food than he'd ever consumed in his life, he'd never felt fitter. His skin was a deep brown, his eyes were always shining and his muscles were so relaxed his limbs felt as loose as wet noodles.

"Evening," sang a friendly voice from his right.

Bill looked over to see his new friend and local fisherman, Sam pulling armfuls of nets off his small, wooden boat.

"Nice night, ain't it, William?" said Sam.

"Just beautiful. Successful day?"

"As always."

Bill couldn't get used to being called William, but it was a necessity now. He thought about giving himself a more exotic name, but decided against it. William, at least, felt almost familiar.

The sun set quickly, the sky turning from red to purple. By the time he reached the long, winding path that connected the rocky beach to his house via a thick patch of woodland, it was almost dark. The house was brightly lit from within.

Why does she always have to leave every light on?

As he pushed open the back door, small droplets of water falling from his shorts onto the tiled floor, he realised he was smiling. He found his way to the downstairs bathroom, grabbed a towel and roughly ran it over his newly toned body. His stomach rumbled as he walked back down the hall towards the kitchen, the towel now fastened around his waist in place of his shorts.

Opening the fridge, he spotted a large steak that made his stomach rumble again. He wanted to immediately slam it into a pan with some shallots and red wine but held back. He'd wait to see what she wanted to eat.

"Honey?" he called out.

There wasn't a sound in the house. All he could hear was the now growing noise of the crickets outside.

"Hello, honey?" he called again, walking into the hall and looking up the stairs. "Perhaps she's in the bathroom," he mumbled to himself.

Walking into the living room, he noticed her silk bath robe draped across the arm of the sofa nearest the TV. No doubt she'd been relaxing all day. She deserved it. As he flicked on the lamp that sat on top of the coffee table, he noticed the light catch the reflection of the picture framed and placed in the centre of the mantelpiece. He couldn't help himself and walked over to pick it up. A ritual he did every day.

When he first placed the photograph of Danielle and Sarah there it had brought him sadness. His heart aching every time he saw it. But now it comforted him. Made him feel as though they were both with him. He looked down at it now, the glass of the frame covered in fingerprints from him constantly holding it. He was so engrossed in the image he didn't hear the soft footsteps behind him.

When he felt the warm hands slide around his waist, he flinched, then realised who it was and relaxed.

"How was it today, darling?"

He put the picture back on the mantelpiece and turned around.

Hawkins stood in front of him, her hair now long and flowing over her tanned shoulders. She was wearing his favourite silk blue nightgown that always made her eyes sparkle.

"It was phenomenal," he said, sliding his fingers into her hair and kissing her softly.

He glanced back over at the picture of Danielle and Sarah.

"You know this is going to sound crazy but sometimes when I'm under the water I feel like Danielle's with me."

"That's not crazy. I'm sure she is."

"Really? I never thought you'd believe that kind of thing."

"I don't usually but I'll make an exception."

Hawkins walked over to the mantelpiece. Bill assumed she was going to lift up the picture of Danielle and Sarah, but instead she reached for the framed photograph beside it. The one of her and Bill at the charity evening they'd first met at all that time ago at the National Gallery when she worked alongside Danielle.

As a generous donor to the establishment, and with his secret Caravaggio being displayed there, he had been invited as a guest speaker. The moment Hawkins was introduced to him, she felt the energy between them. It wasn't a spark, but more of an explosion.

As they shared a drink that night and talked, they both soon realised they had finally met their intellectual equals. They couldn't have been with each other now if it wasn't for the genius they shared; the drive, the motivation, the knowledge they could move mountains to achieve anything they wanted.

"Danielle would be so happy if she could see us," she said, putting the photograph back down. "I'm sure of it."

"I think so too."

Bill pulled Hawkins into a hug and kissed her. Once again that strange feeling came over him. That Danielle was there with him. That he was truly at peace.

Also by Julian Papadia

Hope:

He wanted to give her freedom.

She wanted her daughter back

Also available on Kindle

by Julian Papadia AMAZON *4.1 out of 5 stars*   43 ratingsSee all formats and editions

What is the difference between justice and fairness?

What are the limits you are willing to overcome for the one you love?

When DCI Paul Peterson meets Hope for the first time, he confronts a struggling teenager with her hands and shirt full of blood. It seemed to be the easiest of cases to close seeing as she has confessed to her double murder.
So why does Paul feel his mission must be to prove her innocence rather than close the case? What are the secrets Hope is hiding?

When Helen, Olivia's mother and celebrated neurosurgeon, chooses her dedication to work instead of the long-awaited vacation trip to Paris with her husband and daughter, she doesn't know she is making one of those decisions able to change her life forever. How far can a mother go to keep her hope alive?

Sometimes the culprit is the real victim.

Hope is a gripping and mysterious thriller with twists you won't see coming.

Printed in Great Britain
by Amazon